# THE AMERICAN IMPERIAL GOTHIC

# The Cultural Politics of Media and Popular Culture

Series editor:
C. Richard King, *Washington State University, USA*

Dedicated to a renewed engagement with culture, this series fosters critical, contextual analyses and cross-disciplinary examinations of popular culture as a site of cultural politics. It welcomes theoretically grounded and critically engaged accounts of the politics of contemporary popular culture and the popular dimensions of cultural politics. Without being aligned to a specific theoretical or methodological approach, *The Cultural Politics of Media and Popular Culture* publishes monographs and edited collections that promote dialogues on central subjects, such as representation, identity, power, consumption, citizenship, desire and difference.

Offering approachable and insightful analyses that complicate race, class, gender, sexuality, (dis)ability and nation across various sites of production and consumption, including film, television, music, advertising, sport, fashion, food, youth, subcultures and new media, *The Cultural Politics of Media and Popular Culture* welcomes work that explores the importance of text, context and subtext as these relate to the ways in which popular culture works alongside hegemony.

**Also available in this series:**

*Representations of HIV/AIDS in Contemporary Hispano-American and Caribbean Culture*
*Cuerpos suiSIDAs*
Gustavo Subero
ISBN: 978-1-4724-2595-9

*Media and the Rhetoric of Body Perfection*
*Cosmetic Surgery, Weight Loss and Beauty in Popular Culture*
Deborah Harris-Moore
ISBN: 978-1-4094-6944-5

*Disability, Obesity and Ageing*
*Popular Media Identifications*
Debbie Rodan, Katie Ellis and Pia Lebeck
ISBN: 978-1-4094-4051-2

# The American Imperial Gothic

## Popular Culture, Empire, Violence

JOHAN HÖGLUND
*Linnaeus University, Sweden*

LONDON AND NEW YORK

First published 2014 by Ashgate Publishing

Published 2016 by Routledge
2 Park Square, Milton Park, Abingdon, Oxfordshire OX14 4RN
711 Third Avenue, New York, NY 10017, USA

First issued in paperback 2016

*Routledge is an imprint of the Taylor & Francis Group, an informa business*



**British Library Cataloguing in Publication Data**
A catalogue record for this book is available from the British Library

**The Library of Congress has cataloged the printed edition as follows:**
Höglund, Johan Anders.
The American imperial gothic : popular culture, empire, violence / by Johan Höglund.
pages cm – (The cultural politics of media and popular culture)
Includes bibliographical references and index.
ISBN 978-1-4094-4954-6 (hardback) 1. American literature–History and criticism.
2. Imperialism in literature. 3. War in literature. 4. Gothic fiction (Literary genre) 5. Popular culture. 6. United States–Foreign relations–21st century. I. Title.
PS169.I45H64 2014
810.9'358–dc23

2013034137

ISBN 13: 978-1-138-24910-3 (pbk)
ISBN 13: 978-1-4094-4954-6 (hbk)

# Contents

# Acknowledgements

There are many individuals and institutions that have made this book possible and for whose help I am immensely grateful. First, I want to thank everyone in the Concurrences group who has contributed very useful commentary at different stages during the compilation of this manuscript. In particular, I want to thank Maria Olaussen, Gunlög Fur, Anna Greek, Hans Hägerdal, Margareta Petersson, John Hennessey, Peter Forsgren, Jens Andersson, Emilie Wellfelt, Niklas Hållén, Jenny Siméus and Cecilia Jonsson, who gave crucial feedback during the final stage of preparation. In addition to this, this book benefitted immensely from the most incisive and useful comments from Concurrences visiting scholars Diana Brydon and Wumi Raji. Finally, Karen Swartz not only carefully amended the language of the manuscript, but also improved its content through many useful comments.

I furthermore want to extend my gratitude to The Swedish Research Council for their support of the Concurrences project. Without this funding, this book would not have been written. I also want to thank the Linnaeus University Centre for Concurrences in Colonial and Postcolonial Studies, a centre that grew out of the Concurrences project, and, again, its director Gunlög Fur. This is the research hub that gave me the confidence, the intellectual stimulation and challenge and the means with which to complete this project. In addition to this, some of the material discussed in this book was developed in connection with the research network *Nordic Network for Literary Transculturation Studies* funded by Nordforsk and I want to thank this institution and the hard-working network directors for a number of very stimulating and transnational meetings.

I must also thank the dedicated people at Ashgate Publishing; my editor Neil Jordan in particular but also Tricia Craggs and Rebecca Storr who got my manuscript into shape. Finally, I need to express my gratitude to the remarkable institution of the British Library without which locating and accessing much of the secondary material discussed here would have been impossible.

This is a new study and the individual chapters have not been published before. However, some chapters in this book build on matters that I have previously addressed in various published articles and fragments of these articles may remain. I want to thank *Foundation: The International Review of Science Fiction* which published my paper 'Hollywood and the Imperial Gothic' that forwards some ideas developed in Chapter 9 'Tales of Torture and Invasion'; *The European Journal of American Studies* which published my paper 'Taking up the White Man's Burden? American Empire and the Question of History' that explores some of the same issues as my Introduction; *Game Studies: The International Journal of Computer Game Research* which published my paper 'Electronic Empire: Orientalism Revisited in the Military Shooter' that makes points developed in Chapter 8 'Militarising the Virtual Gothic'; and finally the editors of the conference anthology *Memory Haunting Discourse* which published my paper 'Gothic Haunting Empire' that functioned as a starting point for my discussion in Chapter 7 'Afghanistan, Iraq and the New Frontiers of the Imperial Gothic'.

On a more personal note, I want to thank my parents for their love and support and my wonderful wife Cecilia who kept me sane throughout some of the more difficult periods. I would not have been able to complete this text without your help, patience and love. Thank you also Edith and Hilda for countless smiles and for welcoming me into your family. Finally, thank you David and Agnes for being two radiant suns round which my life obliquely circles.

# Preface

This book is a study of a form of culture I have termed the American imperial gothic. I argue that it manifests in many different genres and media and that it has helped explain, justify and enable the growth of US power since the late eighteenth century. The American imperial gothic is transgressive and it sometimes allows concurrent, discordant and nominally subaltern voices to surface. However, these voices are generally described as dangerous, even monstrous, and the imperial gothic typically insists that the racial, political, cultural and sexual boundaries on which the US empire relies must be violently defended. Failure to do so will result in the collapse of modern society, in the burning of cities, in plagues, pestilence and cannibalism, in an Armageddon that brings only ruin in its wake.

While writing, and rewriting, this study, I have tried, on good advice, to avoid approaching my subject matter from the perspective of a general, Western or even American 'we'. I cannot make any general assumptions about the reader of this text or the society he or she lives in. Also, I have made an effort to avoid becoming too subjective, leaving the pronoun 'I' out of the text as much as possible. Yet, the decision to write this book, to engage with these narratives, was, of course, personal. This preface is an opportunity to elaborate on this and to comment on the way that the American imperial gothic operates on a personal level, across national and ideological borders.

I grew up consuming and often admiring the imperial gothic; the British as well as the American. Although born in Sweden, I made it into my own culture. It was easy. In many ways, it is a form designed for the type of person I was, or rather wanted to become: strong, fearless in the eyes of horrific danger, always on the side of goodness. A point here is that the border between good and evil is often absolute in the American imperial gothic. If you are not with the power of goodness, you are with the terrorists. If you are not the exorcist, you are that which must be exorcised.

I wanted to be the exorcist; the killer of demons whatever that meant. It provided me with a form of purpose and also conveyed a sense of entitlement. For a young, white, male, middle-class heterosexual citizen of a Western nation, the sense of prominence and privilege that these narratives conveyed was seductive. I became vaguely aware that I belonged to a category of people who were born to rule the world, and whose duty it was to selflessly defend this world against the demons, parasites, vampires and other monsters that threatened to invade the global social order from the racial, geographical and ideological periphery. Although far removed, geographically at least, from the US, there was the sense that this was also my birth right and my burden. I want to believe that I never actually thought of myself as belonging to a class of people (or worse, a race) literally born to rule the world. Perhaps I understood, even as a young teenager, that something was wrong with the films and the novels I consumed so voraciously. Even so, a sense of entitlement and privilege was always there, and is sometimes still difficult to shake off completely.

This sense of entitlement is important when trying to understand the way that the American imperial gothic operates. In many ways, this book is an indictment of US exceptionalism and imperialism. My motivation for writing it has been the need to critically place US popular culture alongside the popular culture of the former British empire. I believe that doing so may help dispel the notion that US imperialism is somehow better and more benevolent than previous forms. In the wake of the Invasions of Afghanistan and Iraq, and the global havoc caused by these conflicts, it is arguably crucial to understand US foreign policy as a form of imperialism as ruthless and careless as any other.

Mapping the ways that American popular culture has justified, encouraged, and at times queried, the expansion of the US empire is, I believe, an important part of this project. In democratic nations, imperial and colonial practices are very difficult to effect without the open or tacit compliance of the people. It is important to note that the West comes into contact with US imperialism primarily in its form of economic privilege or as narrative. Few citizens of the West experience the violence with which the US empire asserts its dominion outside Western borders. No drones circle the Texas deserts, or the Swedish mountains, in search of large gatherings that may signal a meeting of insurgents. Also, relatively few participate in the actual violence as soldiers or as agents in the Middle East or in other parts of the world formally or informally colonised by the US. Unburdened by this violence, American citizens, as well as people in the West in general, contribute to the maintenance of the US empire through patterns of consumption and investment, through tacit support at the voting booth, through taxes and through patriotic ritual, or by simply saying nothing.[1]

The point I want to make here is that the American imperial gothic is a form of culture seemingly designed to stimulate this type of quiet acceptance of US imperialism. Not only does it encourage its audience to think about global relations strictly in terms of good and evil, it also provides a sense of entitlement that discourages the protest at this simplification that is perhaps lodged in the audience's throats. As I will argue, an important purpose of the

1 Of course, some people inside the US (under surveillance, in prisons, at airports) do experience the anxieties, even the violence, of empire. In addition to this, many Americans and other people from the West do speak up against empire and this book tries to account for and rely on their research.

American imperial gothic is to furtively align the gothic horror stories that it tells with the politics and practices that sustain the US empire. By doing so it indirectly urges the cultural consumer to also take a political stand that will help support the actual material privileges that many in the West enjoy.

From this perspective, this book is also an attempt at dispelling that sense of entitlement. I know that my whiteness does not give me the right to rule the world. The demons that crawl out of the dark in the American imperial gothic do not emanate from any real colonial periphery. They are manifestations of a general desire to rule that seem to accompany all imperial cultures, and also of the fear that comes with this desire. As Nina Auerbach has observed, the monsters that the gothic presents us with are ourselves.[2] Thus, the demons that face us in the imperial gothic must be exorcised not with a bullet to the head but through a nod of recognition.

2 Nina Auerbach, *Our Vampires, Ourselves* (Chicago: University of Chicago Press, 1995).

# Chapter 1
# Introduction: The American Imperial Gothic

## Introduction

In *Legion* (2010), the archangel Michael totes an M16A4 with attached grenade launcher and a Heckler and Koch MP5K submachine gun, and he fires them double handed into hoard after hoard of possessed humans – white collar workers, ice-cream truck drivers, women, children – the shell casings clicking onto the ground and dispersing in slow motion. God has lost faith in humanity and decreed the destruction of the one human being that may be able to redeem the species: the unborn child that Michael tries to protect with his many firearms. This is the apocalypse, the end of days. Darkness reigns outside the California desert diner where the action takes place. Swarms of flies shut out the sun, and possessed humans grow pointed teeth, scale walls and ceilings, their eyes black and full of inexplicable hatred and malice. The relentless gun violence performed by the tattooed and muscular angel is the only bulwark against this gothic onslaught. Michael's assault rifle lights up the darkness throughout the movie.

*Legion* is one of a multitude of gothic narratives that represent the possibility of the end of the world as we know it, the collapse of society to the forces of darkness. These narratives rely upon a very similar formula. The world has been invaded by the gothic Other in the form of angry ghosts, vampires, zombies, atavistic monsters, serial killers, cyborg hordes let loose from hell, robot machines or extra-terrestrial invasion forces that overrun the planet. To prevent this apocalypse, goodness must arm itself. With the right dedication, and the right hardware, chaos can be out-gunned. In these narratives, the forces of darkness represent the threat of many different political entities: extremist Islam, Chinese economic competition, Russian imperialism, or even the anti-war, and anti-gun, liberal left. However, as this study will argue, the social, political and cultural organisation that these forces seek to overthrow and which the powers of goodness aim to defend, gun in hand, is best described as an increasingly unstable and anxious American empire.

The concept of American empire used to be a controversial notion. In 1955, William Appleman Williams observed that one of the 'central themes of American historiography is that there is no American Empire. Most historians will admit, if pressed, that the United States once had an empire. They then promptly insist that it was given away. But they also speak persistently of America as a World Power.'[1] This paradoxical view of America's political history has persisted throughout the twentieth century. In May 2001, George W. Bush argued that 'America has always been committed to enlarging the circle of human freedom, not reaching for the crown of empire'.[2]

Even a cursory examination of US history shows that since its inception it has grown tremendously in terms of both territory and power. Originally a relatively small strip of land on the North American East Coast, it now stretches from coast to coast, it spends as much money on its military as the world's other top 12 military spenders put together, it operates more than 700 military bases worldwide, and it has a long history of global intervention.[3] In recent years, and especially since the invasions of Afghanistan in 2001 and of Iraq in 2003, historians, sociologists, political scientists, international relations experts and postcolonial scholars have attempted to revise the way that this history and the current US predominance are understood. This still on-going revision is further discussed below but can be summarised here by international relations writer and former US officer Andrew J. Bacevich who argued in 2002 that: 'like it or not, America today is Rome, committed irreversibly to the maintenance and, where feasible, expansion of an empire that differs from every other empire in history. This is hardly a matter for celebration; but neither is there any purpose served by denying the facts.'[4] More recent work has tended to confirm this notion, pointing out that the US is not only an empire, it is 'an aging empire watching dreadfully as rivals threaten to take their slice of the pie', as Julian Go puts it in his study *Patterns of Empire: The British and American Empires, 1688 to the Present* (2011).[5]

The relationship between imperialism, colonialism and culture has been investigated in many different ways. Previous research suggests that the gothic is a very informative form of writing especially when studied in relation to

1 William Appleman Williams, 'The Frontier Thesis and American Foreign Policy', *Pacific Historical Review* 24, no. 4 (1955): 379–95 at 379.

2 George W. Bush, 'Commencement Address at the United States Naval Academy in Annapolis, Maryland, May 25 2001' in *Public Papers of the Presidents of the United States: George W. Bush (2001, Book I)* (Washington, DC: United States Government Printing Office, 2001a), 579. http://www.gpo.gov/fdsys/pkg/PPP-2001-book1/pdf/PPP-2001-book1.pdf.

3 For a discussion of American military bases, see Chalmers Johnson, *The Sorrows of Empire: Militarism, Secrecy, and the End of the Republic* (New York: Metropolitan Books, 2004).

4 Andrew J. Bacevich, *American Empire: The Realities and Consequences of U.S. Diplomacy* (Cambridge, MA: Harvard University Press, 2002), 244. Cullen Murphy comes to the same conclusion in *Are We Rome? The Fall of an Empire and the Fate of America* (Boston: Houghton Mifflin, 2007).

5 Julian Go, *Patterns of Empire: The British and American Empires, 1688 to the Present* (New York: Cambridge University Press, 2011), 167.

imperial decline. In his seminal work *The Rule of Darkness: British Literature and Imperialism, 1830–1914* (1988), Patrick Brantlinger discusses the relationship between the British novel and the ascent, eclipse and decline of the British Empire. Brantlinger terms these stages 'dawn', 'noon' and 'dusk', where dusk designates the final and climactic stage of the British empire. In relation to this stage, Brantlinger argues that 'no form of cultural expression' traces the many anxieties that attended the climax of the empire as clearly as the gothic.[6] The gothic that most distinctly maps the decline of the British empire is termed the 'imperial gothic' by Brantlinger. This study employs this useful and influential concept in its examination of American gothic and its relationship to US empire.

Thus, this study investigates how a vast number of narratives negotiate the ascent, eclipse and decline of US empire through gothic images of conflict and disaster. It refers to these narratives as the *American imperial gothic* and notes that this form of culture has been especially prevalent and eloquent during periods of US imperial crisis. The study notes how certain tropes and imagery established in early American imperial gothic have come to structure later gothic narrative and also a great many other genres and forms of media. As I will argue, the American imperial gothic is concerned with the maintenance of the racial, sexual, cultural, political and territorial borders that have helped this form of culture to explain and even justify colonial expansion and the maintenance of empire. At the same time, it has given and gives expression to the many anxieties that accompany moments of perceived imperial decline.

The starting point of this study is the beginning of American literature in the late eighteenth century. From the vantage point of more than 200 years of gothic and horror culture, this study traces how the American imperial gothic understands colonial conflict, captivity, and the confrontation between modernity and the primitive that was typically imagined to inform colonial expansion. With this in mind, the study's primary focus is how the gothic negotiates the present decline in American power. In the wake of 11 September 2001, this study argues, the American gothic becomes increasingly imperial and frequently casts the United States as a vortex of modernity beleaguered by the gothic Other. This study thus aims to show how the American imperial gothic of recent years maps both the perceived need to aggressively defend, and at times even expand, the ideological and territorial boundaries the United States has established, and the profound anxiety connected to the experience that these borders are, indeed, constantly challenged, that the gothic Other is at the door, and that the apocalypse is imminent.

6 Patrick Brantlinger, *Rule of Darkness: British Literature and Imperialism, 1830–1914* (Ithaca: Cornell University Press, 1988), 228.

## The Gothic

In the study of literature, the gothic has often been understood as a relatively limited body of texts produced in the late eighteenth and early nineteenth century. David Punter has influentially established that this form of writing emerged as a revolutionary mode at the end of the Enlightenment.[7] Appearing in the wake of the French and American Revolutions, 'in the awful obscurity that haunted eighteenth-century rationality and morality',[8] to quote gothic scholar Fred Botting, the early gothic exposed through metaphors of death, decay, prophesy, captivity and haunting the several dark secrets of modernity: its feudal pasts, irrationality, religious superstition and, perhaps most importantly, the many terrible practices that helped support its expansion. These include the subjugation of the working classes, industrial pollution, genocide in the colonies, slavery and the neglect of the darker and more irrational aspects of the human psyche. From this perspective, the gothic appeared as modernity's and empire's dark doppelganger and the early gothic has frequently been understood as a truly rebellious mode of writing that enabled (and perhaps enable) radical and liminal positions through its display of transformative, haunted and tortured bodies, its constant border transgressions and its mapping of deviant behaviour. The gothic has retained this ability to query and queer dominant Enlightenment discourses. As Agnieszka Soltysik Monnet convincingly illustrates in *The Poetics and Politics of the American Gothic: Gender and Slavery in Nineteenth-Century American Literature* (2010), American gothic culture – from Edgar Allan Poe to Charlotte Perkins Gilman – demonstrates an unwillingness to get comfortable with racist and sexist discourses and practices that have permeated, and still often inform, American society.[9]

However, the gothic has also developed a more conservative slant and I will argue that it often supports rather than subverts official discourse. Indeed, a number of critics have remarked that the gothic has always been an unwieldy tool to disturb established discourse. Teresa Goddu has perceptively observed that 'the gothic can remain continuous with official narratives, even when it apparently contradicts them'.[10] This means that the 'gothic may unveil the ideology of official discourse, but its transformative power can be limited'.[11] From this perspective, the gothic does not automatically undermine our belief in reason or the practices of modernity even as they disrupt or question

7 See David Punter, *The Literature of Terror: A History of Gothic Fictions from 1765 to the Present Day*, 2 vols. (London: Longman, 1996).

8 Fred Botting, *Gothic* (London: Routledge, 1996), 1.

9 Agnieszka Soltysik Monnet, *The Poetics and Politics of the American Gothic: Gender and Slavery in Nineteenth-Century American Literature* (Farnham: Ashgate, 2010).

10 Teresa A. Goddu, *Gothic America: Narrative, History, and Nation* (New York: Columbia University Press, 1997), 2.

11 Goddu, *Gothic*, 2.

the worship of industrial, economic or imperial progress. Even the early gothic, as Andrew Smith and William Hughes argue in *Empire and the Gothic*, 'incorporated within its anti-Enlightenment fervour a set of complex views on the East, although often in order to consolidate rather than to question the kind of orientalist attitudes identified by Edward Said'.[12] With this in mind, Tabish Khair has made the crucial observation in *The Gothic, Postcolonialism and Otherness: Ghosts from Elsewhere* (2009) that gothic fiction was not simply a vehicle of enlightenment critique, it was more importantly a 'writing of Otherness' that helped the British empire define the borders on which it relied.[13]

As Catherine Spooner discusses in *Contemporary Gothic* (2006), and as Justin D. Edwards and Agnieszka Soltysik Monnet further explores in their collection *The Gothic in Contemporary Literature and Popular Culture: Pop Goth* (2012), the gothic has today transcended the old generic limitations. In the present moment, the gothic can be found not only in the novel, but in film, music, fashion, in comic books, in art, in performance and in street culture.[14] The gothic has also invaded other genres and modes of communication, from romance novels and Disney movies to political speeches.[15] For scholars of the gothic, this is a problematic development. Botting has argued that twentieth-century gothic has become so commercial, emaciated, self-referential and romantic it is no longer able to evoke either terror or horror. To Botting, this suggests that the gothic is now effectively dead.

If the gothic is understood as a literature or culture of terror that queries Enlightenment discourses, Botting may well be right. However, if gothic is instead understood as a mode, as suggested by Spooner, the gothic is in fact very much alive, albeit in a number of different guises. Thus, this study understands gothic not as a genre but as a mode capable of infecting and informing a number of media and genres. Defined in this way, gothic can be found in horror film, but also in romance novels, in super hero comics or in television commercials. This makes possible a scholarly engagement with a large number of cultural genres – nineteenth-century novels, Hollywood films of the Depression era, slasher and gore movies, science fiction computer games, and torture porn – as well as with other forms of public and political discourse such

12 Andrew Smith and William Hughes, *Empire and the Gothic: The Politics of Genre* (London: Palgrave Macmillan, 2003), 3. This is one of few anthologies that focuses on the gothic from a postcolonial perspective. However, despite its 2003 perspective, it disregards the American gothic.

13 Tabish Khair, *The Gothic, Postcolonialism and Otherness: Ghosts from Elsewhere* (London: Palgrave MacMillan, 2009).

14 See Catherine Spooner, *Contemporary Gothic* (London: Reaktion Books, 2006) and Justin D. Edwards and Agnieszka Soltysik Monnet, 'Introduction: From Goth/ic to Pop Goth' in *The Gothic in Contemporary Literature and Popular Culture: Pop Goth,* edited by Justin D. Edwards and Agnieszka Soltysik Monnet (London: Routledge, 2012).

15 Botting, *Gothic*, 180. Also, some recent gothic studies look for gothic as it has migrated to other genres. See, for example, Maria Beville, *Gothic-Postmodernism: Voicing the Terrors of Postmodernity* (Amsterdam: Rodopi, 2009).

as presidential speeches, news casts, and non-fiction writing. As I will argue, modernity remains a central concern in these different texts, but it cannot be argued that they aim to disturb a belief in the salvaging power of reason.

## The Imperial Gothic

Brantlinger dates the imperial gothic to the period 1880–1914. This was a very expansive and self-conscious era, but also a deeply anxious and often violent period. Imperialism was becoming not simply a project but also a form of creed that functioned 'as a partial substitute for declining or fallen Christianity and for declining faith in Britain's future'.[16] While bigger than ever, the empire as such had begun to fall apart and was besieged not only by its colonial subjects and by competing European nations but also by degeneration fears and by political turmoil.

Brantlinger describes the imperial gothic as a 'blend of adventure story with Gothic elements',[17] that served to bolster the ego of the empire by showing it as the only barricade against gothic and barbarian invasion but which simultaneously recognised the possibility of imperial collapse.[18] While often openly supportive of empire, this imperial gothic was ideologically complex and presented the reader with '[a]pocalyptic themes and images … in which, despite the consciously pro-Empire values of many authors, the feeling emerges that "we are those upon whom the ends of the world are come"'.[19] The writers who wrote within this genre include Rudyard Kipling, H. Rider Haggard, Bram Stoker, Arthur Conan Doyle and John Buchan, all of whom combined 'the seemingly scientific, progressive, often Darwinian ideology of imperialism with an antithetical interest in the occult'.[20]

The definition of the imperial gothic as an ideologically complex form of writing is crucial to this study. Brantlinger isolates three principal themes that suggest two different ideological vantage points. Brantlinger argues that the

---

16 Brantlinger, *Rule of Darkness*, 228.

17 Brantlinger, *Rule of Darkness*, 227.

18 Claims that the imperial gothic both charts and feeds the frenzy of empire by presenting it with its own worst nightmare have also been made by Elaine Showalter in *Sexual Anarchy: Gender and Culture at the Fin de Siècle* (New York: Viking, 1990), Daniel Pick in *Faces of Degeneration: A European Disorder, c.1848–c.1918* (Cambridge: Cambridge University Press, 1989) and Stephen D. Arata, in 'The Occidental Tourist', an essay that illustrates how *Dracula* participates in defending, and even assuaging, the general 'anxiety attendant upon cultural decay' that saturated Britain during the late nineteenth century. See Stephen D. Arata, 'The Occidental Tourist: *Dracula* and the Anxiety of Reverse Colonisation', *Victorian Studies* 33, no. 4 (1990): 621–45 at 623.

19 Brantlinger, *Rule of Darkness*, 230.

20 Brantlinger, *Rule of Darkness*, 227.

imperial gothic was concerned with: 'individual regression or going native; an invasion of civilization by the forces of barbarism or demonism; and the diminution of opportunities for adventure and heroism in the modern world'.[21] The focus on imperial adventure here forms an extrovert and exploratory narrative trajectory. Buchan's and Haggard's African fiction, where the continent looms as a vast repository of treasure and male adventure, are good examples of this extroverted type of gothic. By contrast, the stories that instead describe the invasion of civilisation (London) constitute an introverted and apocalyptic form of narrative. Stoker's and Marsh's urban gothic novels, revealing London in the throes of Oriental invasion, exemplify this type. These two narrative trajectories were capable of simultaneously supporting and disturbing colonial British imperialism by showing the empire as an important and civilising force in a world of primitive darkness, and by revealing the empire itself as besieged and invaded, or even (in some cases) as an orchestrator of unjust violence. These two trajectories existed side by side in Britain, even if the introverted and apocalyptic narrative became increasingly predominant before the outbreak of World War I in 1914.[22]

The point here is that the imperial gothic is capable of charting and expressing very different ideological positions. The imperial gothic is a form of culture that seeks to shore up support for imperialism by allegorising or gothicising colonial relations. In the imperial gothic, the Egyptian subaltern turns into a gothic other, a malign warlock or ancient mummy that threatens British society and the modernity on which it relies. However, at the same time the gothic metaphors and narrative trajectories of this form of writing are capable of housing the same kind of anti-Enlightenment or anti-imperial discourse as the early gothic. In the imperial gothic, British empire appears at the necessary bulwark but also, at times, as an unsustainable system.

From this perspective, the imperial gothic is an often problematic cultural mode tied to imperial, modernity and Enlightenment concerns. It is capable of assuming many different ideological positions and of inhabiting many different genres and media. As Justin D. Edwards observes in *Gothic Passages: Racial Ambiguity and the American Gothic* (2003) the gothic is a 'polyphonous' form of culture that 'can adapt to various political agendas'.[23] It is when viewed as such a polyphonous form of culture that has invaded a wide range of media that the gothic can be seen to simultaneously embrace and disturb modernity and empire.

---

21 Brantlinger, *Rule of Darkness*, 230.

22 See I.F. Clarke's survey of the British, pre-World War I invasion narrative in *Voices Prophesying War 1763–1984* (London: Oxford University Press, 1966).

23 Justin D. Edwards, *Gothic Passages: Racial Ambiguity and the American Gothic* (Iowa City: University of Iowa Press, 2003), xix–xx.

## The American Imperial Gothic

The usefulness of the term 'imperial gothic' in the American context depends to a great extent on the many similarities between the two nations. These similarities include a number of historical, linguistic and cultural denominators. This study will note a number of continuities between the two empires. As this study hopes to illustrate, Wells's *The War of the Worlds* (1898), Stoker's *Dracula* (1897), Stevenson's *The Strange Case of Dr. Jekyll and Mr. Hyde* (1886) and Haggard's *She* (1887) still make good (imperial) sense to a modern audience and thus exist in multiple reincarnations as part of the canon of the American imperial gothic.[24]

Brantlinger proposes that the imperial gothic is a form of writing encouraged by the eclipse of the British empire. The imperial gothic feeds off and feeds the prevalent sense that the territorial, ideological, moral and sexual borders that organise the empire are challenged. The imperial gothic is the literature of terror as it becomes obsessed with the perceived 'dusk' of an empire. The American imperial gothic, I argue, can be related to a similar – although not identical – historical development. The American imperial gothic also negotiates moments of imperial crises. Like the British imperial gothic, it is most usefully understood as a culture of competition and decline.

As mentioned, the idea that the US is not only an empire, but an empire in decline has been forwarded by a number of historians and sociologists. One of the more influential studies is Julian Go's aforementioned *Patterns of Empire*. Based on work done by world-systems scholars Immanuel Wallerstein, Terry Boswell and Christopher Chase-Dunn, Julian Go has mapped the phases of the hegemonic career of the United States. The United States, Go argues, began its ascent towards hegemony in 1776, but this phase did not become pronounced until 1873 and it lasted until 1946 when, in the wake of World War II, the nation achieved hegemonic maturity. In 1974, it entered the phase of competition/ decline, a phase it still inhabits.[25]

---

24 H.G. Wells, *The War of the Worlds* (London: Heinemann, 1898); Bram Stoker, *Dracula* (London: Archibald Constable, 1897); Robert Louis Stevenson, *The Strange Case of Dr. Jekyll and Mr. Hyde* (London: Longmans, Green and Co., 1886); H. Rider Haggard, *She* (London: Longmans, Green and Co., 1887).

25 World-systems theory is a form of inter-disciplinary analysis inspired by dependence theory, and Marxism and neo-Marxist theory. World-systems theory rethinks many of the tenets of the traditional empire model of centre and periphery and tends to emphasise how global power and hegemony is related to similarly global economic developments rather than to the politics of would-be empires. Wallerstein's and Boswell's mapping of US ascendancy from minor colony to global hegemon and its current decline is useful when contrasted with the different phases the British empire went through and, like Go, I rely on their research. However, it should be observed, as Go does, that world-systems theory does not equate hegemony with empire. Hegemonic nations are not necessarily empires and empires are not necessarily hegemonic nations. In fact, while world-systems theory sees economic hegemony and world empire as

The long sequences of American history mapped by Go with the help of world-systems theory are not homogenous and linear. Since the American Revolution, US history has been marked by sudden economic or territorial expansion but also by abrupt and sometimes profound crises. During the first few decades after the revolution, the United States faced many challenges to their increasingly expansive programme in the form of continued resistance from Native American nations, from Spanish and formerly Spanish colonies and from the competing imperial ambitions of Great Britain. Similarly, the Great Depression was an era of great anxiety as the economy ground to a sudden and catastrophic halt in the late 1920s. Even the period after World War II, the moment that world-systems studies describes as an era of undisputed economic hegemony, was, as this study will suggest, an era riddled with anxiety. The reading of the American imperial gothic performed in this study takes particular note of how this mode negotiates these moments. In particular, this study looks at the present as part of a long period of competition and decline, a period that, as I will attempt to illustrate, has many things in common with the 'dusk' of the British empire.

Having argued that the US is experiencing an imperial 'dusk' similar to that of Britain in the late nineteenth century, and presenting economic models that testify to a certain rise and fall trajectory, it is important to note that while the US may be in a phase of decline at the moment, it should not be assumed that the US empire is, in fact, about to collapse. Since the publication of Edward Gibbon's *The History of the Decline and Fall of the Roman Empire* (1776–89), historians have tended to look at historical development in terms of the ascent and descent of large powers.[26] Not only does this model direct attention away from the many important developments that occur outside the borders of imperial power, it tends towards a universalisation of historical development. As I will argue in this study, the US is currently experiencing an economic, military and ideological slump that can be referred to as a form of imperial 'dusk'. However, it is too early to say if this development is going to continue so that the US permanently loses its central global position, or if the rise and fall model is even useful during this particular phase of transnational capitalism.

compatible during certain historical phases, several of its proponents have argued that these two forms of global rule are incompatible today. This contention has been challenged, notably by Peter Gowan in 'Contemporary Intra-Core Relations and World Systems Theory' where he argues that the US constitutes precisely a world-wide empire that has seized control of the global capitalist market. See Peter Gowan, 'Contemporary Intra-Core Relations and World Systems Theory', *Journal of World-Systems Research* 10, no. 2 (2004): 471–500. http://www.jwsr.org/wp-content/uploads/2013/03/jwsr-v10n2gs-gowan.pdf.

26 Edward Gibbon, *The History of the Decline and Fall of the Roman Empire* (London: Strahan & Cadell, 1776–89).

## The Material

The definition of the imperial gothic as a mode rather than as a body of text presents this study with a methodological challenge. If the gothic today is everywhere, how can a certain text be identified as (imperial) gothic in relation to others? This study does not pretend that useful boundaries can be erected today that separate the gothic from the non-gothic. Instead, it isolates a number of gothic tropes that grow out of the early (American) gothic and traces them as they permeate different texts and media. As I have argued, this gothic mode is capable of permeating a vast range of culture and media and of inhabiting different ideological positions.

To limit the study, I focus on types of texts that have long been associated with the gothic and which can be said to have grown out of this genre: horror; science fiction; and more traditional gothic to the extent it still survives. As argued by Roger Luckhurst in his recent study of science fiction, '[c]ultural history needs to understand the appeal of breathlessly paced interstellar pulp fictions as much as the self-consciously Modernist prose adopted by counter-cultural SF in the 1960'.[27] However, I will also discuss how the tropes closely tied to the imperial gothic have permeated public and political discourse in general. Thus, like Justin D. Edward's examination of racial gothic in *Gothic Passages*, this study will at times move 'back and forth between what we conventionally call gothic fiction and what Sander Gilman has called the fictive discourses of the human sciences, particularly biology, anthropology, and nineteenth-century theories of heredity and evolution'.[28] In this way, this study shifts the attention away from many of the otherwise seminal works of the American gothic towards the more politically problematic and notoriously popular narratives, as well as other forms of texts, many of which unabashedly prop up the American empire and thus help to sustain, unmake and remake this entity.

These limitations and ambitions still leave a vast number of texts and media open for analysis. Here, it must be noted that an endemic problem to any study that assumes to survey the development of a mode of culture over time is the sheer impossibility of considering even a fraction of all texts produced during the time in question. When selecting particular texts out of the very large canon of American popular gothic and horror culture, the aim has been to focus on novels, films, games and other forms of culture that have been influential and that have attracted both large audiences and some critical attention. I cannot pretend that other choices could not have been made, but I believe that the texts that now make up the body of this study are representative of different directions of the American imperial gothic and that they allow for

27 Roger Luckhurst, *Science Fiction* (Cambridge: Polity, 2005), 9.

28 Edwards, *Gothic Passages*, xi.

fruitful discussions of this mode of writing and its relationship to American imperialism during different historical stages.

## Theoretical Departures: Postcolonialism, American Studies and the New Imperialism

More than any other scholarly field, postcolonial studies have explored the material and cultural strategies which empires have employed to maintain and justify their practices. Also, postcolonial scholars have been instrumental in uncovering the often submerged experiences and stories of the subaltern and have discussed how the encounter between coloniser and subaltern has led to the formation of hybrid identities and to the development of intercultural and transcultural societies.[29]

However, postcolonial theory has rarely been applied to the US context. In fact, it was not until the invasions of Afghanistan and Iraq that America attracted significant attention from the postcolonial field. In the introduction to *Postcolonial Studies and Beyond* (2006), the editors Ania Loomba, Suvir Kaul, Matti Bunzl, Antoinette Burton and Jed Esty observe that:

> The shadow the 2003 US invasion of Iraq casts on the twenty-first century makes it more absurd than ever to speak of ours as a postcolonial world. On the other hand, the signs of galloping US imperialism make the agenda of postcolonial studies more necessary than ever. In a context of rapidly proliferating defences of empire (not simply de facto but de jure) by policy makers and intellectuals alike, the projects of making visible the long history of empire, of learning from those who have opposed it, and of identifying the contemporary sites of resistance and oppression that have defined postcolonial studies have, arguably, never been more urgent.[30]

This is a call for a new direction in postcolonial inquiry, one that views the present as colonial rather than as postcolonial and which argues that the United States has

29 In 'Can the Subaltern Speak?' in *Marxism and the Interpretation of Culture Marxism and the Interpretation of Culture*, edited by Cary Nelson and Lawrence Grossberg (Urbana: University of Illinois Press, 1988), Gayatri Spivak famously stresses the importance of listening to the marginalised and often silenced voices of the subaltern. In *Imperial Eyes: Travel Narrative and Transculturation* (London: Routledge, 1992), Mary Louise Pratt discusses the way that the cultures of coloniser and colonised frequently transformed and merged in zones of contact.

30 Ania Loomba, Suvir Kaul, Matti Bunzl, Antoinette Burton and Jed Esty, 'Beyond What? An Introduction' in *Postcolonial Studies and Beyond*, edited by Ania Loomba, Suvir Kaul, Matti Bunzl, Antoinette Burton and Jed Esty (Durham: Duke University Press, 2005), 1. See also *New Formations*'s special issue *After Iraq: Reframing Postcolonial Studies*, no. 59 (2006) http://www.newformations.co.uk/abstracts/nf59abstracts.html for a similar discussion.

been the most important agent orchestrating this re-arranged colonial present.[31] This study is in part an attempt to respond to this call by making visible the long history of American empire as it manifests in the American imperial gothic.

This study is also postcolonial in the sense that it makes use of two different yet complementary strands of postcolonial inquiry. Literary postcolonial studies have focused both on how culture has lent support to the imperial project and how it has offered ways of resisting imperialism. In 1978, Edward Said's *Orientalism* investigated the ways in which European culture lent support and cohesion to the British colonial project. Said's influential contention was that European writing on the Orient constituted a Foucauldian discourse and that this discourse had little to do with the actual geographical and material space and the people who lived there, but everything to do with Europe's desire to rule this portion of the world.

A different strand of postcolonial cultural studies has focused on the ways in which literature has become a way to counter the destructive influence of imperial discourses and practices. As Bill Ashcroft, Gareth Griffiths and Helen Tiffin have influentially argued in *The Empire Writes Back* (1989), the novel became a way to negotiate the transition from forced dependency to independence.[32] Furthermore, Homi K. Bhabha has argued that the 'English book' is not homogeneous but disturbed 'by the uncanny forces of race, sexuality, violence, cultural and even climatic differences'.[33] In this way, Bhabha argues, even texts that clearly aim to further empire are ambivalent and fail to simply command authority.

This is an important observation in relation to the imperial gothic. As I have argued, this mode of writing is often openly supportive of American empire but it also testifies to the many anxieties that have gripped and grip the nation. Thus, while the American imperial gothic does map and even encourage the megalomaniac fantasies and desires that fuelled American imperialism it also reveals the monstrous form such fantasies and desires may take.

While greatly inspired by postcolonial inquiry, this book is also deeply informed by the revisionist historical and cultural body of work that has recently given a new direction to the field of American studies. One of the first studies to effectively call for such an understanding of American history and culture as

31 Edward Said makes this point as early as in 1978, in the concluding and often neglected section of *Orientalism* (New York: Vintage, 1978).

32 Bill Ashcroft, Gareth Griffiths and Helen Tiffin, *The Empire Writes Back* (London: Routledge, 1989).

33 Homi K. Bhabha, *The Location of Culture* (London: Routledge, 1994), 161. By 'English book' Bhabha appears to designate any form of religious, literary, technological, anthropological or medical writing that serves to try to explain and command the world outside of England.

related to empire was the influential *Cultures of United States Imperialism* (1993).[34] This important work argued that US history and culture must be considered in terms of empire and also suggested that US imperialism is not necessarily better than anybody else's.[35] This attempt has been followed by many other studies that also challenge the notion of American exceptionalism. Many of these have focused on the role culture has played. In *The Anarchy of Empire in the Making of U.S. Culture* (2002), Amy Kaplan traces the relations of canonical writers such as Mark Twain, and of less well-known texts such as semi-documentary film during the Spanish–American War, to imperial discourse and practice.[36] Similarly, Shelley Streeby discusses the relationship between early American imperial ambition and the sensationalist mass culture industry of the mid-nineteenth century in *American Sensations: Class, Empire, and the Production of Popular Culture* (2002).[37]

The endeavour to critique American imperialism and exceptionalism has put mainstream American studies in contention with a group of neoliberal and neoconservative writers who are concerned with salvaging the idea of American exceptionalism while at the same time promoting the concept of American empire. An important point here is that many of the most influential recent histories that have proposed that the US is, and has always been, an empire do not do this in order to object. In *Colossus: The Price of America's Empire* (2004), Niall Ferguson has famously suggested that what the world needs, and what the US could become, is a liberal empire, one that:

> not only underwrites the free international exchange of commodities, labor and capital but also creates and upholds the conditions without which markets cannot function – peace and order, the rule of law, noncorrupt administration, stable

---

34 Amy Kaplan and Donald E. Pease, eds, *Cultures of United States Imperialism* (Durham: Duke University Press, 1993). This text makes little use of postcolonial theory. Amy Kaplan acknowledges this absence in American studies in the 1990s, and, in turn, of the US in postcolonial studies, but also makes the observation that the postcolonial field has often been Eurocentric. Since then, there have been some attempts to apply postcolonial theory to aspects of American culture, as demonstrated in such works as Melani McAlister's *Epic Encounters: Culture, Media, and U.S. Interests in the Middle East since 1945* (Berkeley: University of California Press, 2001) and Amritjit Singh and Peter Schmidt, eds, *Postcolonial Theory and the United States: Race, Ethnicity, and Literature* (Jackson: University Press of Mississippi, 2000).

35 A number of recent American studies conferences, notably the American Studies Association's meeting, *Dimensions of Empire and Resistance: Past, Present, and Future* in Puerto Rico, November 2012, and publications have addressed the issue of American empire, the rise of new American imperial liberalism and the tenuous nature of American exceptionalism.

36 Amy Kaplan, *The Anarchy of Empire in the Making of U.S. Culture* (Cambridge, MA: Harvard University Press, 2002).

37 Shelley Streeby, *American Sensations: Class, Empire, and the Production of Popular Culture* (Berkeley: University of California Press, 2002).

> fiscal and monetary policies – as well as provides public goods, such as transport infrastructure, hospitals and schools, which would not otherwise exist.[38]

Similarly, neoconservative political commentator and historian Max Boot has argued that American imperialism has been 'the greatest force for good in the world during the past century' and that even if the US is reluctant to embrace the term 'empire', the nation must 'definitely embrace the practice'.[39]

The existence of a neoconservative body of historical and sociological texts that support the notion that US liberal imperialism has been the greatest force for good in the world during the nineteenth century, and that it constitutes the world's best (perhaps only) hope today, is interesting and important to the project of this study since the American imperial gothic sometimes argues the same thing. It is also interesting because it seems to echo many pro-imperial sentiments expressed during the late nineteenth century in Britain. Indeed, Boot frequently cites Rudyard Kipling and uses examples from British imperial history to make points about present day US foreign policy.

It should be added that the pro-imperial sentiment expressed by Boot and others have met with scathing criticism from a number of well-known sociological and historical scholars. David Harvey is deeply critical of this turn towards empire and the practices it condones and has termed it 'the new imperialism'.[40] Other studies that have taken critical positions on American empire include Chalmers Johnson's *Blowback* (2000), *The Sorrows of Empire: Militarism, Secrecy and the End of the Republic* (2004) and *Nemesis: The Last Days of the American Republic* (2006), Noam Chomsky's *Hegemony or Survival: America's Quest for Global Supremacy* (2004), Andrew Bacevich's *The Limits of Power: The End of American Exceptionalism* (2009) and Craig Calhoun, Frederick Cooper and Kevin W. Moore's collection *Lessons of Empire: Imperial Histories and American Power* (2006) which, like Julian Go's aforementioned *Patterns of Empire*, questions the idea of American exceptionalism by placing US imperialism side by side with former empires.[41]

---

38 Niall Ferguson, *Colossus: The Price of America's Empire* (New York: Penguin, 2004), 2.

39 Max Boot, 'U.S. Imperialism: A Force for Good', *National Post*, May 13, 2003, http://www.cfr.org/iraq/us-imperialism-force-good/p5959.

40 Harvey argues that the rise of this phenomenon works to simultaneously extend American global influence and divert the attention of US citizens from domestic economic problems. See David Harvey, *The New Imperialism* (Oxford: Oxford University Press, 2003). Harvey's choice of term in the title furthermore echoes scholarship on British empire where the self-conscious and often jingoistic phase of British imperialism (occurring during the period Brantlinger refers to as 'Dusk') is also referred to as 'new imperialism'.

41 Chalmers Johnson, *Blowback: The Costs and Consequences of American Empire* (New York: Metropolitan Books, 2000), *The Sorrows of Empire: Militarism, Secrecy and the End of the Republic* (New York: Metropolitan Books, 2004) and *Nemesis: The Last Days of the American Republic* (New York: Metropolitan Books, 2006); Noam Chomsky, *Hegemony or Survival: America's Quest for Global*

## Modernity and US Empire

As argued above, this study aligns itself with a number of postcolonial, historical and cultural studies that critically map the history and nature of American empire. A key concept in relation to this body of work is modernity. Modernity is interesting not only because it has been flaunted as a peculiarly American phenomenon by those embracing American liberal imperialism but also because the ways in which modernity and imperialism have been perceived as intimately connected in recent sociological theory. In addition to this, modernity is a crucial concept in gothic studies.

This study understands modernity as essentially the ideological, economic, scientific and industrial project enabled by the Enlightenment. The application of reason and the study of natural principles were thought to allow humankind to fashion a new kind of society. In the words of David Harvey:

> The scientific domination of nature promised freedom from scarcity, want, and the arbitrariness of natural calamity. The development of rational forms of social organization and rational modes of thought promised liberation from the irrationalities of myth, religion, superstition, release from the arbitrary use of power as well as from the dark side of our own human natures. Only through such a project could the universal, eternal, and the immutable qualities of all humanity be revealed.[42]

Modernity did indeed transform the social, economic, religious and geographical landscape of Europe. Industrialisation made possible the transition from a feudal and local economy to a capitalist and global one. It brought great wealth and prosperity to large portions of Europe and formed the foundation for the many new political systems and revolutions that emerged or took place during the late nineteenth century. It was also the prime motivator for advances in medicine and (military) technology, advances that now seem inseparable from our daily lives. In fact, as will be discussed in this study, the apocalyptic imperial gothic frequently describes not the end of the world but the end of modernity.

However, a number of studies produced after World War II have suggested that the many advances in science and technology and the global markets that liberal capitalism created and attempted to control were also the prime motivators for colonialism and for a view of the human being as primarily a

---

*Supremacy* (New York: Metropolitan Books, 2004); Andrew J. Bacevich, *The Limits of Power: The End of American Exceptionalism* (New York: Metropolitan Books, 2008); Craig Calhoun, Frederick Cooper and Kevin W. Moore, *Lessons of Empire: Imperial Histories and American Power* (New York: The New Press, 2006).

42 David Harvey, *The Condition of Postmodernity: An Enquiry into the Origins of Cultural Change* (Oxford: Blackwell, 1990), 12.

cog in a vast machine. The view of the human as not only rational but also subject to seemingly rational processes, a species (or a series of sub-species) that could be categorised and assigned different functions within the larger project of modernity, paved the way for what Walter Mignolo has termed 'coloniality' or 'the dark side of modernity'.[43] Mignolo makes the important point that the prosperity that modernity generated, and continues to generate, was dependent upon the subjugation of the working classes in Europe and the transportation and enslavement of millions in colonies all over the world. With this in mind, Gurminder Bhambra has argued in *Rethinking Modernity* (2007) that we must consider the 'histories of imperialism, colonialism, and slavery that enabled Europe and the West' to understand the technological and economic dominance that constitutes modernity.[44] In this way, modernity, colonialism and empire are intimately connected phenomena. The economic, industrial and material conditions that are associated with European modernity were also the conditions that global imperialism relied upon during the expansive phase of eighteenth- and nineteenth-century European colonisation.

As I will attempt to show, the ways in which modernity and imperialism accompany each other are crucial when studying the relationship between US empire and the American imperial gothic. An important observation here is that modernity is not just a practice or a system, it is also a discourse that helps justify imperialism. Dipesh Chakrabarty has argued in *Habitations of Modernity: Essays in the Wake of Subaltern Studies* (2002) that:

> Following the tenets of the European Enlightenment, many Western intellectuals thought of modernity as the rule of institutions that delivered us from the thrall of all that was unreasonable and irrational. Those who fell outside its ambit could be described as *premodern*. Western powers in their imperial mode saw modernity as coeval with the idea of progress. Nationalists saw in it the promise of development.[45]

Similarly, Bhambra has observed how modernity has been imagined as an exclusively Western project. Indeed, colonialism was often presented as the first and necessary step to modernising the non-Western world, turning imperialism into, to use Rudyard Kipling's words from 1899, a 'white man's burden', a gigantic

43 Walter Mignolo has discussed this in a series of texts. See, for instance, *The Darker Side of Western Modernity: Global Futures, Decolonial Options* (Durham: Duke University Press, 2011).

44 Gurminder K. Bhambra, *Rethinking Modernity: Postcolonialism and the Sociological Imagination* (London: Palgrave Macmillan, 2007), 145–6.

45 Dipesh Chakrabarty, *Habitations of Modernity: Essays in the Wake of Subaltern Studies* (Chicago: University of Chicago Press, 2002), xix, emphasis in original.

and essentially altruistic project of global social transformation performed by the West on primitive nations.[46]

As already observed, in the wake of the recent re-mobilisation of imperialism by neoconservative and neoliberal historians and political advisers, modernity has again become a way to explain and justify American global power. In particular, the conflict between the Middle East and the United States has been cast as a confrontation between modernity and the primitive. The War on Terror that former president George W. Bush's launched in 2001 relied on the binary tension offered by contrasting these two concepts. Shortly after 9/11, Max Boot collapsed the actual geopolitical complaints of al-Qaeda by referring to the Taliban as a group of 'homicidal mullahs driven by a hatred of modernity itself'.[47] The conflation of modernity and empire then became increasingly dominant in the discussion of the invasion of Iraq. In the words of Barbara Bush, the 'justification of the invasion of Iraq in 2003 was to bring the benefits of modernity to the Middle East according to the neo-conservative vision of free markets and democracy'.[48] The idea that the US has a sacred duty to civilise and modernise the (Middle) East characterises so much of this discussion that it must be described as one of its central features.

Because of this, the way the American imperial gothic understands the nature of and challenges to modernity are core components of this study. As I will argue, the American imperial gothic is saturated by the confrontation between modern and primitive and frequently identifies empire as an essentially modern institution. In many ways, the American imperial gothic maps the ascendancy of a specifically American form of modernity. This mapping pays less attention to concepts such as democracy and freedom, even if those notions are still operational, to focus more on the machinery and military technologies of modernity. At the same time, empire is frequently mirrored back to the audience of the American imperial gothic through images of reverse colonisation. Any form of power that commits to such practices as genocide, slavery and colonialism risks becoming subject to its own exercises and the American imperial gothic sometimes imagines modernity as an apocalyptic threat when wielded by non-American cultures or by other species.

46 This poem, written for the US in the immediate wake of the Spanish–American War that marked the point where the US embarked on the same type of colonial venture as the European empires of the late nineteenth century, has received new and disturbing currency, notably in texts such as Max Boot's *The Savage Wars of Peace: Small Wars and the Rise of American Power* (New York: Basic Books, 2002).

47 Max Boot, 'The Case for American Empire: The Most Realistic Response to Terrorism Is for America to Embrace Its Imperial Role', *The Weekly Standard*, October 14, 2001, 23. http://www.weeklystandard.com/Content/Public/Articles/000/000/000/318qpvmc.asp?nopager=1.

48 Barbara Bush, *Imperialism and Postcolonialism* (Harlow: Pearson, 2006), 99.

## Outlining the Chapters

This is a study of the American imperial gothic and its relationship to the expansion and decline of American power throughout history. Because of this, the structure of this study is essentially chronological. However, as the final chapters discuss basically the same era, these are more clearly organised around different themes.

The first two chapters map the ascendancy of US empire by looking at the cultural treatment of the colonial expansion of the first 13 colonies into the western frontier and then at how the imperial gothic informed the understanding first of slavery and then of Reconstruction after the Civil War. These chapters also discuss US ascendancy from local empire expanding westward, to global power in the wake of the closing of the western frontier, the Spanish–American War and the overtly colonial wars that the US fought within the Western hemisphere. In relation to these latter historical developments, the American imperial gothic enters into dialogue with the British imperial gothic. Chapter 4 then discusses how the imperial gothic grows increasingly self-conscious during the Cold War and how some of the most popular gothic narratives of the 1950s, 1960s and 1970s have as their aim a critical interrogation of the ideological foundation they inherited from the nineteenth and early twentieth centuries. This discussion continues in Chapter 5 that looks at the role of the imperial gothic in the period of time between the end of the Vietnam War and the events of 9/11.

While it is relatively easy to see how the American imperial gothic negotiates different historical sequences in Chapter 2 to 5, the short time spans covered by the final chapters make the chronological sequence a convenient rather than precise instrument. Thus, they rely on a thematic as much as a on a chronological structure. With this in mind, Chapter 6 focuses closely on the relationship between the imperial gothic and the immediate understanding and treatment of 9/11. Important here is how the Bush administration understood these events and how they imagined the US reply as an all-out confrontation with the powers of 'terror'. Chapter 7 examines how the invasions of Afghanistan and Iraq triggered the creation of colonial frontiers in the American imperial gothic. The chapter notes how gothic culture such as Peter Jackson's remake of *King Kong* (2005) and Stephen Sommers's *Van Helsing* (2004) recorded an extroverted and expansive movement, and it relates these films to the political rhetoric that permeated the invasions of Afghanistan and Iraq.

Chapter 8 turns its attention to a different form of cultural interrogation by exploring the American imperial gothic as it manifests not just in narratives but also as commodity and practice. This chapter specifically discusses the merger between military and gothic gaming and how gaming technology allows subjects not only to consume and observe but also to inhabit and perform what has been termed the 'military–industrial–entertainment complex'. Chapter 9 examines how the imperial gothic became more apocalyptic, introverted and defensive through a discussion first of a series of violent torture narratives set inside and outside American borders and then the gothic's preoccupation with images of insidious, military, alien or gothic counter-invasions. Chapter 10 then studies the narratives that continue the stories begun in the apocalyptic invasion narratives. This chapter thus focuses on texts that investigate what happens after the world has been consumed by fire and darkness and notes that the post-apocalyptic imperial gothic is the story of the collapse of modernity but certainly not of the end of humanity.

The study's concluding chapter summarises the most crucial points of this study and then discusses some of the continuities and discontinuities that exist between the American imperial gothic and the British imperial gothic it often emulates. Then, this chapter addresses some implications of the central tropes and foci uncovered by the study and discusses them in relation to concepts crucial to postcolonial and cultural theory: agency; borders; memory; and modernity.

# Chapter 2
# Imperial Frontier Gothic

What today is referred to as America was settled 40,000 to 15,000 years ago by peoples coming from Asia. This is the beginning of American history. When Columbus arrived in 1492, only some 500 years ago, America was a vast network of nations with ancient pasts, diverse cultures, various religions, different social and economic practices and multiple languages. Some of these nations were large even by European standards, with the Aztec empire estimated to comprise some 15 million people. Other parts of the continent were less densely peopled, but the land was not virgin. It did not await the Spanish, French, Portuguese and British colonisers. It had already been cultivated and settled.[1]

With this in mind, the early American imperial gothic is most importantly a set of narratives that negotiate, sometimes complicate but more often justify the violent, sometimes genocidal, processes by which the North American continent, and then other regions, were formally and informally colonised by the United States. In an effort to map the historical background to the current predominance of the American imperial gothic, this chapter focuses first on how the categories of settler and native antagonist and the trope of capture take gothic shape in Charles Brockden Brown's *Edgar Huntly* from 1799.[2] I argue that Brown's gothicisation of the relationship between Native Americans and the citizens of the newly formed republic introduced an already existing understanding of racial categories and the consequences of contact into a gothic genre that very quickly takes an imperial or colonial form. Similarly, the early American gothic is concerned with the presence of a large black community

1 In the years that followed Columbus's arrival, the Native American population was reduced by 70 to 80 per cent through disease, relocations, depletion of resources and, at times, campaigns of extermination. The tenets of American exceptionalism hold that because the British settlers eventually freed themselves from the jurisdiction of the British empire, the colonisation of America ceased to be an imperialist project. The fact that the territories conquered by the American republic after 1783 were made part of this republic suggests to historian Anthony Pagden that colonialism 'has never been an option for the United States'. Anthony Pagden, 'Imperialism, Liberalism, & the Quest for Perpetual Peace', *Daedalus* 134, no. 2 (2005): 54. http://www.jstor.org/stable/20027977. This, of course, disregards the glaring fact that the native population inhabiting these territories was denied citizenship and exposed to very traditional colonial practices including genocide, forceful transportation to and confinement in small reservations.

2 Charles Brockden Brown, *Edgar Huntly; or, Memoirs of a Sleep-Walker* (Philadelphia: H. Maxwell, 1799).

that is, in the American South, largely enslaved.[3] As much scholarly study of the American gothic has shown, the Native Americans and black Americans take gothic shape and give rise to conflict that demands a violent resolution. Depending on which group is being discussed, this violence takes different yet related shapes. The Native American situation is addressed with the help of an organised and paramilitary effort that often takes the shape of small wars. While this is sometimes the case also when confronting the black community, the military solution here often manifests as quasi-legal torture and execution in the form of lynching.

The first segment of this period belongs to what world-systems theory has termed the long ascent of American hegemony. This is the entire period before a state reaches maturity and it is seen to stretch from 1776 to the end of the Civil War in 1873. The period after the Civil War until the end of World War II in 1945 is described as the beginning of the short ascent, referring to a period when the state is one of several powers that battle for hegemony. As I will argue, the first decades of the nineteenth century were uncertain years for the new republic. While it expanded greatly during this period, the future of the nation was never certain. During the Napoleonic War, the British Navy shelled Washington, and Native American and formerly Spanish nations attempted to defend their territories against US colonialism. In addition to this, slavery was always a hotly debated and difficult subject that divided the nation. These issues were crucial to the early American imperial gothic.

## *Edgar Huntly* and Brown's Frontier Gothic

In an early and still tremendously influential study on the American gothic, Leslie Fiedler observes that the American 'land of light and affirmation' was never supposed to harbour a gothic impulse.[4] Taking cues from Fiedler, a number of critics have argued that the American gothic's concern with the past, the grotesque and the unknown makes the presence of the gothic in America 'paradoxical, since so much of American culture denies the possibility of the gothic experience'.[5] Of course, in the light of previous criticism on the gothic,

3 Some of the nominally gothic texts from this period, such as Harriet Ann Jacobs's *Incidents in the Life of a Slave Girl* (Boston: Thayer & Eldridge, 1861), were written by formerly enslaved black Americans. These, however, are not usefully defined as imperial gothic as they strive (with some success) to actively undermine the racial categories that inform this mode of writing.

4 Leslie Fiedler, *Love and Death in the American Novel* (1960; reprint, Champaign: Dalkey Archive Press, 1996), 29.

5 David Mogen, Scott P. Sanders and Joanne B. Karpinski, 'Introduction' in *Frontier Gothic: Terror and Wonder at the Frontier in American Literature*, edited by David Mogen, Scott P. Sanders and Joanne B. Karpinski (London: Associated University Presses, 1993), 13.

it would be seen that it is this denial of the gothic experience and the focus on the Enlightenment principle that form such fertile ground for gothic narratives. In the land of invention, reason, democracy and freedom, the gothic can been seen to operate as an insistent reminder of the many horrific practices that accompanied the carving out and maintenance of the republic.

However, these insistent reminders sometimes also explain away the horrors that they bring to the surface. When the Native American appears as gothic fiend, the violence with which this entity is managed becomes natural. This can be usefully illustrated through a reading of Charles Brockden Brown's fourth published novel *Edgar Huntly* (1799), one of seven novels that employed the European gothic genre to discuss the early American experience from the vantage point of the white settler.

Brown's use of the gothic was a very conscious effort. In his often cited preface to *Edgar Huntly* (1799), Brown declares that he will call 'forth the passions' and engage 'the sympathy of the reader by means hitherto unemployed by preceding authors'.[6] Previously, Brown argues, such sentiment has been aroused with the help of '[p]uerile superstition and exploded manners, Gothic castles and chimeras'.[7] His own writing took its materials from a more north American context, such as the 'incidents of Indian hostility, and the perils of the Western wilderness'. In this way, Brown's writing exists at the crossroads between British and American writing. His model is the British gothic, but he also relies upon tropes that have been even at this stage firmly cemented in America.

The novel, as if to illustrate the points made in the preface, provides two gothic plots, one European and one American. The protagonist and narrator is Edgar Huntly, a young American who sets out to investigate the murder of his friend Waldegrave on a farm in Philadelphia. First, Huntly's suspicions fall on the Irish farmhand Clithero who is seen sleepwalking, digging and crying underneath the tree where Waldegrave was killed. Huntly interviews Clithero and is told a story eminently gothic in the European sense. As a child, Clithero was adopted by a wealthy patroness as a companion to her son. Forever grateful for this opportunity, Clithero excels in her service and soon has her trust, a moderate fortune and the promise of her niece's hand in marriage. However, Clithero also learns that his protector has an inherently evil brother to whose destiny her life is mysteriously tied. This brother is assumed to be lost at sea but eventually shows up in the city where his sister lives. Driven by some evil impulse, the brother attacks Clithero who ends up shooting him in self-defence. Knowing that this is likely to be the end of his patroness, Clithero is tormented by a terrible sense of guilt and, in a fit of insanity, tries to kill her to keep her from the knowledge. Failing to do this, he must confess

6 Brown, *Edgar Huntly*, vol. 1, 3.

7 Brown, *Edgar Huntly*, vol. 1, 3.

to shooting the brother, a confession that seemingly leads to his patroness's sudden and inexplicable death.

In this way, the first section of the novel reads like a typical British gothic novel. Clithero is caught in a web of prophecy, convoluted personal history, and class and social conventions that he fails to negotiate properly. Clithero's story is furthermore mostly set in a dark and labyrinthine urban landscape, and violence, importantly, leads not to a resolution of the gothic crisis but to more misery. The pervading sense is one of terror rather than horror as Clithero desperately tries to understand the world into which he has been cast. His sleepwalking is a manifestation of his guilt but also of his failure to comprehend his own misfortune and to exorcise the terror he has experienced. This is the story you have been told in the past, Brown seems to be saying. Then, the author initiates a very different gothic plot.

This alternative gothic story begins when Huntly, after what appears to be an episode of sleepwalking of his own, finds himself bruised and famished beside a tomahawk in a cave. This dark and labyrinthine space imprisons him and seems to reflect the dark chaos of the story so far, so that the cave takes on many of the qualities of the haunted castle of the early British gothic. However, *Edgar Huntly* is not a novel that dramatises how the sleep of reason rouses monsters. Rather, the novel now records the break with the British gothic tradition that Brown outlines in his preface and which he allows to structure the first part of the novel.

In the novel, this break is illustrated through an ascent out of the dark and gothic space that harbours imaginary ghosts and fears into a decidedly American frontier twilight and a confrontation with the native monsters that take shelter there. As Richard Slotkin has argued in *Regeneration through Violence* (1973), the American frontier space is crucial in the creation of an American identity. It is a space that must be combated: 'the wilderness must be destroyed so that it can be made safe for the white women and the civilisation she represents'.[8] At the same time, as Slotkin claims, such violence is perceived to regenerate American masculinity. The frontier is not only a dangerous place, it is primarily a regenerative space capable of transforming the Old World immigrants into New World pioneers.

In this early example of the imperial gothic, this frontier is imagined not only as wild and therefore regenerative but also as gothic. As Jeffrey Weinstock argues, Brown's fiction produces the frontier as a 'liminal space between wilderness and civilization', 'the uncanny contact point at which self confronts other [,]… civilization shades into nature and linear time is interrupted'.[9] Huntly's first

8 Richard Slotkin, *Regeneration through Violence: The Mythology of the American Frontier 1600–1860* (1973; reprint, Norman: University of Oklahoma Press, 2000), 554.

9 Jeffrey Weinstock, *Charles Brockden Brown* (Cardiff: University of Wales Press, 2011), 30.

encounter with this haunted and regenerative frontier is a man-eating panther. While this animal is certainly terrible, it is not, of course, a supernatural being. It can be met with the tomahawk that Huntly has brought with him from the cave so that this haunting can effectively be resolved by violence. In addition to this, its dead body allows Huntly to slake his thirst and his hunger. This prepares Huntly and the reader for the next stage of his frontier exploration. Having made his way out into the open, Huntly is confronted with what the novel now positions as the real horrors of the new republic: a wandering group of Indians who appear 'brawny', 'gigantic' and 'terrific' with 'fantastic ornaments' and grotesquely adorned moccasins.

Like the panther, these Indians are part of the frontier space into which Huntly has sleepwalked. As Fiedler argues, the Indians of *Edgar Huntly* are 'treated essentially as animals, living extensions of the threat of the wilderness, like the panthers with whom they are associated'.[10] Like the panther, then, they can be exorcised through regenerative violence. Huntly surmises that these Indians are the true murderers of Waldegrave and he also concludes that they constitute an immediate threat to the nearby white community: 'Should they leave this spot without notice of their approach being given to the fearless and pacific tenants of the neighbouring district, they might commit, in a few hours, the most horrid and irreparable devastation.'[11] As soon as this thought has been formed in Huntly's mind, he discovers that the Indians have captured a young white girl whom they keep bound hand and foot and whose features denote 'the last degree of fear and anguish'.[12] This young and bound girl is perhaps a reference to the maiden in distress of the European gothic but is more directly related to the captivity narrative. This form of writing relies on a formula developed by Mary Rowlandson's *The Sovereignty and Goodness of God: Being a Narrative of the Captivity and Restoration of Mrs. Mary Rowlandson*, first published in 1682.[13] This narrative describes the experiences of Rowlandson while the captive of Native Americans during the long conflict between European settlers and indigenous inhabitants known as King Philip's War. The captive girl thus transforms Brown's novel into a gothic captivity narrative. The introduction of this girl into the story fulfils the dual purpose of justifying the (colonial) violence that is about to be performed by Huntly and providing this violence with a performative quality that is central to much subsequent imperial gothic in America.

10 Fiedler, *Love and Death*, 160.

11 Brown, *Edgar Huntly*, vol. 2, 160.

12 Brown, *Edgar Huntly*, vol. 2, 164.

13 Mary Rowlandson, *The Sovereignty and Goodness of God: Being a Narrative of the Captivity and Restoration of Mrs. Mary Rowlandson* (Cambridge: Samuel Green, 1682).

Amy Kaplan has discussed what she refers to as the 'spectacle of masculinity' in the popular historical novel of the 1890s.[14] In these often overtly imperial novels, women function as approving spectators as men perform rituals of violence to save them from whatever threat that looms over them:

> Violence in the romance … is always framed by the theatrical display of the hero in conspicuously staged scenes, where the heroine serves as the chief spectator. On this fictional new frontier, physical rejuvenation does not emerge from bloody contests with a native other; the novels instead offer regeneration through a spectacle before the female gaze. This performance engineers the final defeat of the native insurgent by effacing his contesting agency.[15]

This ritual of male violence is not only designed to divest the enemy of malign agency, it also fulfils the purpose of stripping the women themselves of self-determination: 'To be liberated … means … to submit to being rescued, not to make claims for self government.'[16] The rescued female in distress is as much the property of the rescuer as of those from whom she is rescued. In *The Terror Dream* (2007), Susan Faludi traces this fantasy back to the captivity narratives of the seventeenth and eighteenth centuries, arguing that this narrative increasingly became the story not of capture but of rescue. While Rowlandson's narrative records the failure of white society to effectively (violently) rescue her, latter captivity narratives depict the successful and violent retrieval of the captured female. In this way, the transformed captivity narrative or rescue narrative becomes a way for America to retrieve a lost manhood and erect firm barriers between white American masculinity and its many feminised Others.[17]

*Edgar Huntly* further gothicises the captivity narrative and also draws from its tradition of depicting violence as a form of regenerative masculine ritual. The frightened girl fuels and guarantees Huntly's righteous anger, and at the same time she functions as female spectator and witness as Huntly sheds the European self-doubt and lethargy that filled Clithero in favour of a virile

14 Amy Kaplan, 'Romancing the Empire: The Embodiment of American Masculinity in the Popular Historical Novel of the 1890s', *American Literary History* 2, no. 4 (1990): 659–90 at 675.

15 Kaplan, 'Romancing the Empire', 675.

16 Kaplan, 'Romancing the Empire', 674.

17 Faludi argues that the ultimate rescue narrative is John Ford's *The Searchers* (1954), a movie that not only distils the essence of the transformed captivity narrative but also informed the War on Terror in various ways. See Susan Faludi, *The Terror Dream* (New York: Picador, 2007), 205. Also, it should be pointed out here that captivity is most usefully described as a practice that deprives the captive of first ontological and then epistemological agency. The captive is initially deprived of control of her own body (and the captive is usually, although not always, imagined as feminine) and then subjected to a form of ideological captivity or brainwashing that deprives the captive of her own subjectivity.

American manliness. Huntly quietly kills one of the Indians, seizes a hatchet and a musket and frees the girl. The two escape from the encampment, make their way through the landscape and come across an abandoned house where they rest. There, Huntly discovers, to his great surprise, that the musket he has seized is his own:

> This piece was of extraordinary workmanship. It was the legacy of an English officer, who died in Bengal, to Sarsefield. It was constructed for the purposes not of sport but of war. The artist had made it a congeries of tubes and springs, by which every purpose of protection and offence was effectually served. A dagger's blade was attached to it, capable of being fixed at the end, and of answering the destructive purpose of a bayonet.[18]

While this passage serves to alert Huntly to the fact that the Indians must have raided his home, it is also a notable precursor to the obsession with the gun and the militarisation of the gothic that takes place not just in the early American imperial gothic but also in American culture in general. It should be noted here that while Clithero's use of violence in his European story only took him deeper into the gothic vortex of terror and guilt, Huntly's attempt to resolve the gothic crisis with the aid of the gun is successful. Armed with his musket, he kills three of the Indians that threaten the area. The young girl is then reunited with her father who leads a paramilitary posse of settlers against the rebellious Indians. After having fainted from the exertion and the wounds he has received, Huntly wakes up and, as he makes his way back towards his home, finishes off another Indian in an act that is described as merciful euthanasia. This done, Huntly takes the Indian's gun and plants it in the middle of the road.

This sequence of the novel has been a moment of great contention among critics of the novel. As Weinstock observes, many critics have been reluctant to read *Edgar Huntly* as a racist text.[19] Recent discussions of the novel have been vague even when making note of the violence that imbues this passage. Harriet Hustis has suggested a useful, if somewhat general, reading of this scene, arguing that it establishes 'a psychological and textual crossroads where masculinity, narrativity, and American national identity violently and memorably intersect'.[20] Similarly, Weinstock argues that the planting of the gun in the ground beside the corpse of the dead Indian suggests 'that what grows from this soil is violence'.[21]

---

18 Brown, *Edgar Huntly*, vol. 2, 192.

19 Weinstock, *Charles Brockden Brown*, 42.

20 Harriet Hustis, 'Deliberate Unknowing and Strategic Retelling: The Ravages of Cultural Desire in Charles Brockden Brown's *Edgar Huntly*', *Studies in American Fiction* 31, no. 1 (2003): 101–20 at 101.

21 Weinstock, *Charles Brockden Brown*, 43.

These are acute observations, but they skirt the racism that, I would argue, does permeate the novel in general and this moment in the story in particular. Certainly, what grows from the soil is violence, but this violence is perceived necessary when performed against animal-like savages. If the Indians that Huntly comes across have a language that the settler community can understand, the reader is never informed of this. The Native Americans communicate only in screams of anger or pain and through their tomahawks and muskets. When Huntly attacks them with his own tomahawk, shoots them with his musket or stabs them with the attached bayonet – which is how he euthanises the grievously injured final Indian – he is in a sense speaking to them in what is imagined to be their only tongue. The musket thus remains in the road beside the dead Indian as a form of writing, the only type of inter-racial communication Brown imagines possible in this text.

The precursor here is not primarily Rowlandson's captivity narrative but Daniel Defoe's *The Life and Strange Surprising Adventures of Robinson Crusoe* (1719).[22] One of the most influential British novels in history, this British colonial fantasy imagines gun violence as the most efficient antidote to native insurrection and as the quickest way to restore white order. From this perspective, *Edgar Huntly* is a three-way merger between Rowlandson's captivity narrative, Defoe's imperial adventure story and the British gothic novel. The binaries that are native to the gothic take the shape of Indians and settlers as defined by Rowlandson's narrative, but the resolution in the form of regenerative violence is deeply reminiscent of Defoe's colonial fantasy. This is the military solution: the resolution of the gothic crisis through violence.

Read as imperial gothic, *Edgar Huntly* thus describes a movement from old gothic conventions, the gothic castles and chimeras that Brown derides in his preface, into an equally dreadful but importantly different American landscape. The difference here is that American terrors can, in fact, be forcibly dealt with. Muskets and axes become tools with which terror can be held at bay. Huntly does not return from his confrontation with the American frontier to a terribly bright future, but he has survived his conflict with the gothic Other better than Clithero, whose gothic encounter has left him emasculated (indeed, he is for a while captured by Indians) and unable to read reality properly.

The gothic paradigm that *Edgar Huntly* provides lends crucial support to a colonial process that was still in its infancy at the time of its writing. In 1799, when *Edgar Huntly* was published, the United States had not expanded far beyond the 13 original colonies. In the years that followed, the United States added to its territory through the Louisiana Purchase in 1803, through the Mexican–American War of 1846–48 and through countless confrontations

22 Daniel Defoe, *The Life and Strange Surprizing Adventures of Robinson Crusoe* (London: W. Taylor, 1719).

with the Native American population, transforming it into something that is most usefully referred to as an empire spanning the entire continent. As I will argue, the military solution as enacted by *Edgar Huntly* becomes paradigmatic in the fiction that accompanies these historical sequences, and it also saturates much nominally gothic writing such as that of James Fenimore Cooper.

## Slavery, Reconstruction and the American Gothic

If the colonial frontier is the first obsession of the early American gothic, slavery and its legacy is the second. As Teresa Goddu has observed in her influential study *Gothic America*, 'slavery haunts the American gothic'.[23] As the frontier is pushed further and further to the West, slavery and relations between black and white become an increasingly important concern for gothic writers. As I have argued, the gothic has often been described as a poetics of the repressed, a literature of trauma and remembering. The injustices perpetrated on the Other appear in the form of some ghostly or monstrous presence out to exact just revenge.

In many texts from the nineteenth century, however, the black American often comes across as a savage monster, a gothic Other that requires first enslavement or, if this fails to pacify him, the immediate military attention of the (imperial) state as represented by its policing institutions or simply its courageous pioneers. From this perspective, many of the early American gothic writers must be understood as being informed by, and informing, racist understandings of local and global relations. As Toni Morrison has observed in *Playing in the Dark: Whiteness and the Literary Imagination* (1992), the first and second generation of American gothic writers, including Brown, Washington Irving, Herman Melville, Nathaniel Hawthorne and Edgar Allan Poe did gothicise racial relations in the United States.[24] As Agnieszka Soltysik Monnet in *The Poetics and Politics of the American Gothic* (2010) and Justin D. Edwards in *Gothic Passages* (2003) have demonstrated, Brown, Melville, Hawthorne and Poe, allow for a certain ideological discord so that the black or Native American population appears not only as demons but also as abused and haunted. In this way, there are certainly moments in the gothic where the Manichean binaries that separate white civilisation from its Others momentarily collapse, especially in the writings produced by former slaves such as Harriet Jacobs or Fredrick Douglass.

At the same time, as Goddu has argued, the gothic can easily come to obscure the very real horror that was slavery. While gothic terror should open up an abyss of unknowing, the narrative strategy of the gothic in itself becomes familiar

23 Goddu, *Gothic*, 3.

24 Toni Morrison, *Playing in the Dark: Whiteness and the Literary Imagination* (New York: Vintage, 1992).

and even comforting. Thus, the evocation of gothic terror in order to disturb racist assumptions may distract from the historical and very real violence these assumptions have in fact produced. In this way, the gothic 'can also erase, the horrors of a racial history',[25] so that while the 'gothic might offer useful metaphors for depicting the historical event of slavery … its narrative construction could also empty slavery of history by turning it into a gothic trope'.[26]

Thus, it is not always those that seek to critique the machinery of empire that make the most efficient use of the gothic. Edwards has discussed what he refers to as 'racial gothic', a discourse that 'employed striking and metaphoric images to filter and give meaning to the social hierarchies of racial domination and subordination institutionalized through slavery and maintained in the disenfranchising effects of the segregation laws and lynchings of the postbellum period'.[27] Indeed, the binary structure of the imperial gothic is typically evoked in order to erect and support racist systems. During the antebellum period, the gothic constantly informed the representation of different categories of people, and of black and white Americans in particular. Similarly, during Reconstruction, pro-slavery arguments and white supremacist violence were often informed and structured by the gothic.

This is demonstrated by a number of nineteenth-century gothic texts written in the United States. A useful example is Edgar Allan Poe's short (and only) novel *The Narrative of Arthur Gordon Pym* (1838), a story that records a series of confrontations between bestial black people and somewhat more civilised white travellers and which climaxes in an abstract seascape where a towering white figure causes the instant death of the only black person present.[28] Edwards has read *Pym* as a story about the anxiety that permeated white American society in the antebellum period, a fear of revenge from a group of people who refused to appear as the atavistic and pliable remnant that systematic racism imagined them to be. In this way, Edwards suggests that *Pym* is not only a text that rehearses racist discourse, it also 'disrupts antebellum fears of hybridity'.[29] Similarly, Monnet understands Poe's writing as being informed by a powerful ethics often ignored by critics. This ethics, Monnet argues, serves to condemn racist practices such as slavery, even if it does not collapse racism as such.[30]

Not all critics have been as generous. Toni Morrison has argued in *Playing in the Dark* that blackness in *The Narrative of Arthur Gordon Pym* serves to define such concepts as whiteness, freedom and individualism by posing as

25 Goddu, *Gothic*, 132.

26 Goddu, *Gothic*, 135.

27 Edwards, *Gothic Passages*, xi.

28 Edgar Allan Poe, *The Narrative of Arthur Gordon Pym* (New York: Harper and Brothers, 1838).

29 Edwards, *Gothic Passages*, 12.

30 Monnet, *The Poetics*, 53–4.

the Other of these concepts.[31] Furthermore, John Carlos Rowe argues curtly that: 'Poe was a proslavery Southerner and should be reassessed as such in whatever approach we take to his life and writings.'[32] Goddu takes issue with this somewhat simplistic reading but not in order to dismiss the assumption that Poe's writing is informed by racism. Instead, her argument is that while Poe may have been proslavery and from the South, racism was not (and is not) a Southern issue. Thus, Poe's gothic writing needs to be located within a 'network of multiple discourses on race' and *The Narrative of Arthur Gordon Pym* 'records a complex and often contradictory vision of race and sets in motion a national, not just a regional, racial discourse'.[33]

While Poe has been the object of many studies of the American gothic, as have Hawthorne, Melville and Irving, less scholarly attention has been given to how the racial gothic that informs much of this literary tradition permeates other media and forms of representation. Of particular importance to the relationship between black and white Americans is the way that white supremacy organisations, journalism and photography understood the Reconstruction process in the South. In view of what I have termed 'the military solution', this political movement's and these institutions' obsession with organised violence against the black community is important, especially as it informs more recent gothic narratives as well as colonial practice.

As argued, the primary point with this chapter is to show how early American culture is invaded by the imperial gothic mode. However, as this project is undertaken, it is important to remember the sheer brutality of the transatlantic slave trade and the practice of slavery in the US and in many other parts of the American continent. Millions were murdered, tortured, starved, hunted, maimed, worked to death and stripped of all the freedoms and human rights celebrated in the Declaration of Independence. As with the killing of Native Americans, the scope of the suffering is impossible to survey and comprehend, and while the institution of slavery that looms in the background of Poe's *Pym* was made unlawful in 1865, conditions for black Americans continued to be very difficult, especially in the South. While measures to keep black Americans in check through the courts and through economic means were always central to the segregation effort in the South, this effort also came to rest on the terrorism that white-supremacist organisations practised against primarily black communities but also versus any form of intervention that aimed to disrupt the post-antebellum apartheid system. The use and abuse of the (imperial) gothic in the period after the Civil War must be read against these repressive processes.

---

31 Morrison, *Playing in the Dark*, 33.

32 John Carlos Rowe, 'Poe, Antebellum Slavery, and Modern Criticism' in *Poe's Pym: Critical Explorations*, edited by Richard Kopley (Durham: Duke University Press, 1992), 117.

33 Goddu, *Gothic*, 82.

While journalism and photography concerning lynching have not received the same amount of scholarly attention as the nineteenth-century novel, these are certainly not unexplored areas. The history of lynching scholarship has been mapped by Amy Louise Wood in *Lynching and Spectacle: Witnessing Racial Violence in America, 1890–1940* (2009) and by W. Fitzhugh Brundage in 'Conclusion: Reflections on Lynching Scholarship', the concluding contribution to *American Nineteenth Century History*'s 2005 special issue on lynching in America.[34] A point made by another contributor to this issue, Susan Jean in '"Warranted" Lynchings: Narratives of Mob Violence in White Southern Newspapers, 1880–1940' is that 'white southern newspapers drew on highly developed narratives about lynching' when reporting them. Thus, journalistic narratives 'were part of an effort by white southerners to control the representation of the practice [of lynching]'.[35] Jean then focuses on how these narratives defined and fuelled mob violence and how they impeded anti-lynching movements. The discussion below builds on Jean's contention that white media encouraged lynching and makes the additional observation that the justificatory narratives and photographic depictions of lynching often connect with the imperial gothic for added emphasis.

To understand how the representations of lynching were channelled through the gothic, virtually any one of the 4,742 lynchings recognised by the Census Bureau during the period 1882–1968, and most likely thousands and thousands not recorded as part of official history, could be discussed. However, for the purposes of this investigation, the lynching of Sam Hose in Newman, Georgia, in April 1899 illustrates both the horror of the practice as such and the way that contemporary journalism gothicised these events. It should be stressed here that while the act of lynching is incomprehensibly horrific, the act of lynching itself should not be described as gothic. Just like the wars against the Native American populations, the lynchings that took place in the South were documented through newspaper articles, photography and even audio recordings. While these mediations sometimes take the form of the gothic, or even of the imperial gothic – which is what the discussion below will centre on – the events themselves must be considered first as sequences of very real violence and suffering.

While the lynching events themselves were described in great detail, the circumstances surrounding them are often hazy and difficult to ascertain. As far as can be determined, however, Sam Hose had quarrelled with his employer,

34 See Amy Louise Wood, *Lynching and Spectacle: Witnessing Racial Violence in America, 1890–1940* (Chapel Hill: University of North Carolina Press, 2009) and W. Fitzhugh Brundage, 'Conclusion: Reflections on Lynching Scholarship', *American Nineteenth Century History* 6, no. 3 (2005): 401–14.

35 Susan Jean '"Warranted" Lynchings: Narratives of Mob Violence in White Southern Newspapers, 1880–1940', *American Nineteenth Century History* 6, no. 3 (2005): 351–72 at 351.

the planter Alfred Cranford, prior to being lynched. Threatened by a gun, Hose threw an axe at Cranford, killing him. In the papers and in white public discourse, the events were quickly rewritten into a gothic horror story in which Hose, 'a monster in human form', secretly entered the Cranford house, attacked its master with an axe, stole what there was to steal and then raped Cranford's wife in the room where her husband lay dying.[36] The subsequent lynching of Hose was witnessed by more than 2,000 people, some of whom came all the way from Atlanta to view the public, and publicly advertised, event during which Hose was horrifically tortured to death. His ears, fingers and genitals were cut off, his face skinned, his body soaked in oil, and he was then burned to death. After his death, his body was cut into pieces, and a slice of his heart was taken to the governor of Georgia who referred to Hose's deeds, not the lynching, as 'the most diabolical in the annals of crime'.[37]

The imperial gothic is clearly discernible in the white journalism of the period. It was the newspapers of the South that communicated, and perhaps also invented, the gothic reading of the events that led to Hose's capture. It was the same papers that attended the lynching as such and afterwards described the awful torture endured by Hose in great detail.[38] These detailed accounts were followed with a request to view these horrors in relation to, as the paper would have it, the even more horrific deeds perpetrated by the black victim. When discussing the lynching of Sam Hose, one such article urges the white reader to, '[w]hen the picture is printed of the ravisher in flames, go back and view that darker picture of Mrs. Cranford outraged in the blood of her murdered husband'.[39] The story told here is oddly and uncomfortably reminiscent of the narrative of Edgar Huntly's gothic adventures. The same images inform the simple narrative: a dark and racial Other has disturbed the domestic peace, a white man lies dead in his house, a white woman is taken and molested. The extreme and ritualised violence that ensues becomes just vengeance for a diabolical crime.

The imperial gothic thus converts the lynching of Hose from horrific, abject slaughter into justified ritual. Again, this is the military solution in a different guise. The violence takes the form of ceremony where a large and predominately male group, sometimes consisting of thousands of people, publicly restores the manhood that the lynching victim has supposedly violently assumed through the rape of a white woman. The brutal torture and murder, often including the castration of the victim, is thus not only an attempt at controlling the

36 Leon F. Litwack 'Hellhounds' in *Without Sanctuary: Lynching Photography in America*, edited by James Allen (Santa Fey: Twin Palms Publishers, 2000), 9.

37 Litwack, 'Hellhounds', 9.

38 As Litwack explains, newspapers would typically describe 'in graphic detail the slow and methodical agony and death of the [lynching]' victim, 'Hellhounds', 10.

39 Litwack, 'Hellhounds', 10.

black community through a demonstration of the horrors that modern white society is capable of delivering, it is also a form of regenerative violence that symbolically and publicly strips non-white society of (sexual) agency.

The gothicising of sanctioned lynching violence plays a key role here as it helps to dispel the outrage and sheer nausea that these practices should evoke. When cast as gothic adventure, lynching can appear even as a form of judicial, enlightened practice.[40] By the time Hose was lynched, American culture often described lynching as a useful solution to black and gothic challenges to white predominance. An example is D. W. Griffith's influential, racist and often overtly gothic epic *The Birth of a Nation* (1915), a film that depicts formerly happy black slaves corrupted by political freedom. Transforming into lewd, violent and indolent subjects, they sabotage the democratic process and prey on the community's white women. The film's black characters are repeatedly shown in the thrall of sexual excitement, an excitement that transmutes their faces and visibly contorts their bodies in gothic fashion. In a prolonged chase scene halfway through the film, the freedman Gus has given in to these uncontrollable sexual appetites and pursues the white and virtuous Flora through a wild and overtly gothic wilderness very different from the ordered cotton fields, plantations or small-town settings that function as the outdoor backgrounds in most of the film. Flora prefers death to being ravaged by Gus and throws herself off the face of a high cliff. Rightfully indignant, the ghostly apparitions of the Klan members that join together as a direct response to this event seize Gus, declare him guilty, castrate him (in a scene eventually removed from the film) and kill him. Again, (ritualised) violence is the only way to exorcise the gothic Other. In other words, in *The Birth of a Nation*, Reconstruction transforms the South from a pastoral utopia into a gothic wilderness, prompting the forming of the Klan as a reincarnation of the white and noble pioneers that settled and civilised the nation according to official history. Consequently, the Klan practises the military solution both in its form as public ritual as Gus is lynched, and as large-scale battle as the rebelling freedman is confronted and routed.

40 It should be added that lynching, and the dissemination of it by white lynching photography and journalism, did cause an outrage in the US, fuelling anti-lynching sentiment in Washington and other parts of the US. Interestingly, this critique has sometimes taken shape as a different form of captivity narrative where white children are taken hostage by a discourse of violence. In a National Association for the Advancement of Colored People (NAACP) fundraising flyer that disseminated photographs of the lynching of Rubin Stacy in Florida in 1935, in an attempt to seek support for anti-lynching legislation, the viewer is asked to 'not look at the Negro. His earthly problems are ended. Instead, look at the seven WHITE children who gaze at this gruesome spectacle ... what psychological havoc is being wrought in the minds of the white children?' Jonathan Markovitz, *Legacies of Lynching: Racial Violence and Memory* (Minneapolis: University of Minnesota Press, 2004), 25.

## Violence and the Other: Towards an Assertive Imperial Gothic Culture

In *This Violent Empire: The Birth of an American National Identity* (2010), Carroll Smith-Rosenberg further develops the central argument made by Toni Morrison in *Playing in the Dark*.[41] Like Morrison, Smith-Rosenberg contends that the US's remarkably diverse and multicultural constitution, even at the time of the Revolution, encouraged the construction of a largely artificial and thoroughly Manichean project of identity construction. The Other, Smith-Rosenberg notes, constitutes an 'oppositional' force that designates that which we are not. At the same time, the Other 'beckons us' and points 'to forbidden possibilities'. At times, we seek to incorporate this Other, at 'other times, we turn from them in disgust, for, as often as not, they are imaginative projections of our own worst qualities'. Because the Other constantly challenges the borders and barriers we erect specifically to exclude them, 'we turn upon our Others with rhetorical and literal violence'.[42] The presence of so many Others in the US, so many cultures and skin colours, so many religions and ethnicities, has historically exacerbated 'the tendency to exclusion, violence, xenophobia, and paranoia all national identities harbor within themselves'.[43]

One aim of this book is to trace the construction of the US's many Others in American popular culture and it returns repeatedly to the violence that saturates this culture. When moving into the twentieth century, and then the twenty-first, this violence becomes less clearly connected to the imperial violence perpetrated inside the US and (increasingly) outside of its borders. It becomes seemingly more rhetorical and less literal. As this connection blurs, it is important to remember that rhetorical violence has its literal counterpart. This is one of the points that this chapter has made: the violence that is perpetrated in the American imperial gothic is premised on actual deeds of violence. The shooting of Indians in *Edgar Huntly* must be considered in relation to the killing of actual Native Americans as the US border moved westward. The lynching of Gus in *The Birth of a Nation* in 1915 informs the lynching of thousands in the US. These narratives gothicise history but not primarily so that it can haunt their American audience, but so that the horrors of the past become manageable and feasible. Not only does this allow for a less guilt-ridden relationship to the past, it also legitimises future acts of violence.

This process is aided by the establishment of a number of tropes that, as this book will endeavour to show, become key elements in subsequent imperial gothic. These tropes centre on the captivity, transportation and possible sexual

41 Carroll Smith-Rosenberg, *This Violent Empire: The Birth of an American National Identity* (Chapel Hill: University of North Carolina Press, 2010).

42 Smith-Rosenberg, *This Violent Empire*, 21.

43 Smith-Rosenberg, *This Violent Empire*, 21–2.

molestation of white women and on the military solution to the gothic crisis. This military solution may take the form of organised large-scale battle or manifest as the violence of the posse: the ritualised torture and death of the gothic Other.

It is not strange that the central tropes of the imperial gothic as well as the discourses that inform these tropes appear during the first few decades of the US's existence. The focus of this book is the current phase of competition and decline of United States empire and the gothic culture that tries to understand and explain it. An important point here is that early American empire was often more unstable and certainly much more beleaguered than it is even today. Settlement of the entire region between the East and the West Coasts was little more than a distant vision at the beginning of the nineteenth century, and competition from Europe was fierce. Such uncertainty encouraged visions of both powerful expansion and of pending doom and constituted a very fertile ground for the imperial gothic. As subsequent chapters will illustrate, this sense of possible collapse never left the American gothic, even if the early twentieth century did see a more assertive form of imperial gothic.

# Chapter 3
# The Gothic of Benevolent Assimilation

In 1893, Fredrick Jackson Turner presented what has become known as the Frontier Thesis. Noting that the Census Bureau had recently declared the closing of the western frontier in the wake of former US settlement all the way to the Pacific Ocean, Turner declared in his opening paragraphs that:

> Up to our own day American history has been in a large degree the history of the colonization of the Great West. The existence of an area of free land, its continuous recession, and the advance of American settlement westward, explain American development.
>
> Behind institutions, behind constitutional forms and modifications, lie the vital forces that call these organs into life and shape them to meet changing conditions. The peculiarity of American institutions is, the fact that they have been compelled to adapt themselves to the changes of an expanding people – to the changes involved in crossing a continent, in winning a wilderness, and in developing at each area of this progress out of the primitive economic and political conditions of the frontier into the complexity of city life.[1]

To Turner, then, a colonial imperative has directed the energies of all American institutions. In a manner of speaking, all (white) Americans have been settlers 'winning' the wilderness that is America. With the closing of this particular colonial enterprise, American identity and development face a crisis. Will the expansive energies that have guided both the westward movement and the 'complexity of city life' fade now that the continent does not allow for further expansion? Turner does not think so. The closing of the frontier is, to Turner, the opening up of new territories: 'the demands for a vigorous foreign policy, for an interoceanic canal, for a revival of our power upon the seas, and for the extension of American influence to outlying islands and adjoining countries, are indications that the movement will continue'.[2]

---

1 Fredrick Jackson Turner, *The Frontier in American History* (New York: Henry Holt, 1920), 1.

2 Turner, *The Frontier*, 1.

As discussed in the introduction, the US entered a phase referred to as the short hegemonic ascent in 1873.[3] This stage is perceived to last until 1947 when, at the end of World War II, the US became the one dominant nation. During the short ascent, then, the US developed into an economic and military superpower capable of dominating the global economy in the late twentieth century. This development was not necessarily smooth. As discussed in this chapter, the first half of the twentieth century is marked by a series of material and ideological crises that, as I will argue, had a profound effect on the imperial gothic.

In many ways, the closing of the western frontier was such an ideological crisis. In the years that followed, the continued movement outward that Turner perceives took the form of very traditional colonialism. At the end of the Spanish–American War of 1898, the United States acquired Guam and Puerto Rico, bought the Philippines for $20 million from Spain, and seized control of Cuba. The invasion and inclusion of the Philippines, in particular, provided the US with a new frontier, a new territory to explore and violently conquer as well as a new set of natives to pacify. When US President William McKinley issued a proclamation at the end of the Spanish–American War, he cast US colonialism in the Philippines as an attempt to bring modernity to the island. In this proclamation, he argued that he wished to assure the inhabitants of the Philippines 'that full measure of individual rights and liberties which is the heritage of free peoples, and by proving to them that the mission of the United States is one of benevolent assimilation substituting the mild sway of justice and right for arbitrary rule'.[4] At the end of the day, this process involved frequent and violent demonstrations of power. In the words of Gabriel Kolko, writing in 1976, the violence with which America expanded its borders during the latter part of the nineteenth century:

> reached a crescendo against the Indian after the Civil War and found a yet bloodier manifestation during the protracted conquest of the Philippines from 1898 until well into the next decade, when anywhere from 200,000 to 600,000 Filipinos were killed in an orgy of racist slaughter that evoked much congratulation and approval from the eminent journals and men of the era who were also much concerned about progress and stability at home.[5]

3 The US entered this phase in the wake of the sudden global depression known as the Panic of 1873. The depression that followed affected the global economy until the early 1880s, and the US was certainly not exempt. Even so, this date marks a transformation of and increasing centrality of the US in the global market.

4 William McKinley, presidential speech of 21 December 1898, quoted in Fabian Hilfrich, *Debating American Exceptionalism: Empire and Democracy in the Wake of the Spanish–American War* (Basingstoke: Palgrave Macmillan, 2012), 21.

5 Gabriel Kolko, *Main Currents in Modern American History* (New York: Pantheon Books, 1976), 287.

The Spanish–American War and the acquisition of colonies in the Pacific and the Caribbean mark a new phase of US imperialism. While the expansion into western territory was certainly a colonial process, something that Turner in fact acknowledges in his opening paragraph quoted above, it could be imagined by urban US society as a natural and politically unproblematic process. By contrast, the acquisition of new frontiers outside of the borders of the American nation-state made it clear that the United States had joined the ranks of the ambitious, overseas European empires, a project that was not formally abandoned until 1946 with the signing of the Treaty of Manila.[6] In this way, the period following the invasion of the Philippines marks a crucial moment in the ascendancy of American empire.

This chapter initially traces how the increasingly confident imperial gothic negotiated this ascendancy from local to global empire in the wake of the closing of the US frontier and the opening up of new imperial borders in the Pacific as well as in the Caribbean and in the 'banana republics' of Latin America. However, the chapter also notes that while the United States grew increasingly confident during this period, there were moments when this confidence was shaken. The great empire of the period was still Britain, a nation that during the first decades of the nineteenth century controlled more than 20 per cent of the world's land surface. During the late nineteenth and early twentieth centuries, British imperialism peaked in a flurry of acquisition of territory, colonial warfare and imperial confrontations with other European states. The expansive and self-conscious form of imperialism that the British practised generated the sense that imperialism was a stage of national evolution that the US had not yet attained. While the US ability to successfully interfere in World War I boosted US confidence (and sent Britain on its way to final imperial collapse), the Great Depression constituted a deeply felt national crisis.

To focus on the imperial gothic, the gothic narratives of this period were deeply influenced by the racist frontier mythologies inherited from the nineteenth century, with their attendant celebration of performative male violence. At the same time, this chapter also seeks to demonstrate how the American imperial gothic of the period was informed by the British imperial gothic. The British imperial gothic spoke eloquently and effectively of many of the issues that America also faced at this time and thus became immensely popular and influential in the US. When the US economy entered the Great Depression, the (re)appearance of the vampire as the atavistic and Oriental Other and the notion of invading and technologically advanced interplanetary intruders became seminal to the American imperial gothic.

6 This, of course, marks the transition of the Philippines from formal to informal colony, not the end of American imperialism.

## The American Imperial Gothic and the British Imperial Gothic

Many of the concerns that Turner outlines in his important essay were also discussed in Britain at the turn of the century. As historians of the British Empire have argued, British imperialism grew increasingly self-conscious in the late 1870s and 1880s until it was, to quote J.A. Hobson writing in 1902, 'on everybody's lips'.[7] The imperial British gothic of the time was concerned with the same problem as that which Turner now argued faced America: the closing of old frontiers and the need to open up new ones in Africa and Asia. In other words, the imperial gothic in Britain as well as in the United States operated in nation-states that were recognisably and officially colonial, and the governments of these states were both concerned with the creation of new frontiers and markets. It is thus no great surprise that the turn-of-the-century American gothic was greatly inspired by British writers such as Robert L. Stevenson, John Buchan, Henry Rider Haggard, Arthur Conan Doyle, Bram Stoker, H.G. Wells, Richard Marsh and Rudyard Kipling.

The British imperial gothic as defined by Brantlinger is described in some detail in the introduction to this book. As observed there, the imperial gothic is a 'blend of adventure story with Gothic elements'[8] produced by writers that combined 'the seemingly scientific, progressive, often Darwinian ideology of imperialism with an antithetical interest in the occult'.[9] At the same time, the imperial gothic was impregnated with '[a]pocalyptic themes and images … in which, despite the consciously pro-Empire values of many authors, the feeling emerges that "we are those upon whom the ends of the world are come"'.[10] As noted, this allows for two somewhat different narratives to surface, one extroverted, adventurous and self-confident and one introverted and apocalyptic. Buchan's and Haggard's African adventure fiction exemplifies the extroverted kind and the imperial ambitions that saturated the US at the end of the nineteenth and beginning of the twentieth centuries – the opening up of new borders and the energy provided by a seemingly ever-expansive economy – encouraged the American imperial gothic to emulate Haggard, Buchan and Doyle. Thus, the imperial gothic of the first three decades of the twentieth century is often an optimistic and adventurous narrative that takes place in a frontier landscape that offers opportunity for conquest and regenerative violence. The American writers that looked to Britain for this type of inspiration include Edgar Rice Burroughs, Abraham Merritt and Gertrude Barrows Bennett (writing as Francis Stevens). Burroughs's novels set in Barsoom, Merritt's South

7 J.A. Hobson, *Imperialism: A Study* (London: James Nisbet, 1902), v.

8 Brantlinger, *Rule of Darkness*, 227.

9 Brantlinger, *Rule of Darkness*, 227.

10 Brantlinger, *Rule of Darkness*, 230.

American adventure tales and Bennett's lost world stories are examples of the extroverted American imperial gothic.

As I have argued above, the Great Depression shifted the American imperial gothic towards a darker, urban and more invasive type of narrative. As David J. Skal has argued, the 'image of Bela Lugosis' *Dracula* ushered in the great depression'.[11] It did so in the company of other gothic fare such as *Frankenstein*, starring Boris Karloff as the monster (1931), *The Mummy* (1932) and *The Invisible Man* (1933). In fiction, Robert E. Howard's and H.P. Lovecraft's fiction is noticeably darker than anything produced by Burroughs. Howard certainly celebrates male regenerative violence in his stories of Conan the Barbarian, but Conan never becomes the channel for white empire that Haggard's Allan Quatermain or Burroughs's John Carter are (Conan is, after all, a barbarian). Similarly, Lovecraft's stories reveal a US beset by ancient demonic forces. Chaos is always ready to erupt, even in the quietest hamlets of New England. In this way, the imperial gothic of the Great Depression does not rehearse the optimism that saturates many of Burroughs's novels. Instead, they give shape to the same sense of beleaguerment that was native to the British at the end of the nineteenth century.

Brantlinger never directly observes that violence is the resolution to gothic crisis in many British imperial gothic novels, but this is often the case; Haggard's *King Solomon's Mines* ends with a cleansing war, the intrepid gentlemen of Stoker's *Dracula* pursue the vampire to his castle and drive a knife through his heart, and the death cult of Isis in Richard Marsh's *The Beetle* is obliterated through a large explosion.[12] As argued in the previous chapter, this resolution has been rehearsed by the American imperial gothic at least since the publication of *Edgar Huntly*. Moreover, this violence is perceived as a form of modern and enlightened practice as it rids the world of dark and primitive beings. It is with the aid of modernity (medical science, train timetables, flashlights, revolvers) that Dracula is finally vanquished in Stoker's novel. Similarly, the abject and anthropomorphic priestess of Isis of *The Beetle* is brought to her knees just by being given 'a little exhibition of electricity'.[13] As will be discussed below, the American imperial gothic often erects similar technological boundaries between the US and its primitive Others.

11 David J. Skal, *The Monster Show: A Cultural History of Horror* (London: Plexus, 1993), 119.

12 H. Rider Haggard, *King Solomon's Mines* (London: Cassell, 1885); Richard Marsh, *The Beetle: A Mystery* (London: Skeffington and Son, 1897).

13 Marsh, *The Beetle*, 131.

## Burroughs's Imperial Pulp Gothic

The historians of early twentieth-century American writing have typically filed Burroughs, Merritt and Howard under the 'pulp' and/or science fiction headings, but they also belong to a gothic tradition.[14] American pulp fiction has been recognised as having its roots in the British gothic and sensation novel of the nineteenth century as well as in the works of E.A. Poe and Ambrose Bierce.[15] Pulp refers to the low, wood-pulp quality of the magazines printed during this era, inaugurated by *Argosy Magazine* in 1896.[16] *Argosy* serialised stories by Haggard and became one of the most important outlets for the American imperial gothic of this period. The stories produced by Chambers, Burroughs, Merritt and their colleagues often explore the themes and discourses of the British gothic writers from an American perspective. Haggards's anthropological tales of African adventure – complete with discoveries of vast treasures and incomprehensibly beautiful women of lost civilisations – Doyle's prehistoric worlds that allow the revitalisation of overly civilised masculinities, the myth of the 'man who would be king' as explored by Buchan and Kipling and, finally, the threat of alien (Martian) invasion as imagined by Wells form the foundation for this first generation of American pulp fiction writers.[17]

In essence, these American writers mapped the imperial concerns of the British gothic onto an American context. While the British imperial gothic was often located in, or functioned in relation to, imperial frontiers in Africa, India and the Middle East, American writers turned to a different set of colonial frontiers. They found them sometimes in what had been inscribed by Turner as America's frontier past but often also in the Philippines, in the Caribbean or in Latin America – a region that the Monroe Doctrine had singled out as out of bounds for European imperial ambitions and which the Roosevelt Corollary of 1904 had declared as being within the jurisdiction of the international police power of the US. As an example, Abraham Merritt's *The Face in the Abyss* (1931) records the confrontation between the daring American adventurer and mining

14 As observed by Roger Luckhurst, gothic and science fiction share DNA: 'The sense of trauma induced in the subject by modernity means that Gothic and SF writing are constantly in dialogue.' *Science Fiction*, 5.

15 Charles L. Crow, *American Gothic* (Cardiff: University of Wales Press, 2009), 123.

16 *Argosy* was first published in 1882 and was geared towards children. Its readership, publication interval and appearance changed during the following years until it found its most successful form in the low-cost, pulp format.

17 'The Man Who Would Be King' is the story told by Robinson Crusoe of how the Anglo-Saxon finds his natural slot at the top of the social/racial hierarchy when transported to colonial settings. Kipling (and then Conrad in *Heart of Darkness*) complicates this narrative but does not collapse it; in Kiping's and Conrad's stories, the white European does assume his place on the throne of the native. Joseph Conrad, *Heart of Darkness* (1899; reprint, London: Dover Thrift, 1990).

engineer Nicholas Graydon and a South American snake cult in a tale very reminiscent of Haggard's fiction.[18]

At this point in time, the American imperial gothic increasingly turned to metaphor and myth to discuss the political issues of the period. This allowed imperial concerns to be mapped onto imaginary, allegorical landscapes. The most prolific writer of imperial gothic in this respect was Burroughs who located his stories on Mars (Barsoom), the centre of the Earth (Pellucidar) or the lost-world island Caspak. Mars, in particular, became a new frontier upon which the many imperial issues of the period could be projected. As Diane Newell and Victoria Lamont have noted, Mars:

> provided Burroughs and his immediate predecessors with a useable setting for colonial narrative at a time when political realities on Earth were testing the viability of such narratives ... Burroughs turned to Mars to help sustain a little longer the mythology of a nation predicated on expansion into alien territory. He chose Mars as his setting because, as fantastic a setting as it was, it was a *real* place and therefore a potential territory into which the empire could one day expand.[19]

In this way, Mars is at the same time a real and an unreal space, a potential colonial territory and a metaphor for an actual colonial geography.

Burroughs, inspired by a number of studies on Mars, and possibly also by H.G. Wells's influential *The War of the Worlds* (1898), managed to get *A Princess of Mars* serialised in 1912 in the pulp magazine *The All Story*.[20] The novel tells the story of former confederate officer John Carter who, when the war is over, moves on to make his fortune on one of the few remaining frontiers left in the country. Discovering gold in the still un-pacified state of Arizona, he is confronted with the Native American population described in the novel as 'vicious marauders' that take their toll in 'lives and torture of every white party which fell into their merciless clutches'.[21] In an attempt to escape his pursuers, he hides in a cave and is mysteriously transported to Mars. The lower gravity on Mars gives him superhuman strength so that he is now capable of gigantic leaps and extreme violence. The gigantic green, tusked and six-limbed Thark warriors that he is

18 Abraham Merritt, *The Face in the Abyss* (New York: Horace Liveright, 1931).

19 Diane Newell and Victoria Lamont, 'Savagery on Mars: Representations of the Primitive in Brackett and Burroughs' in *Visions of Mars: Essays on the Red Planet in Fiction and Science*, edited by George Slusser and Eric S. Rabkin (Jefferson: McFarland, 2011), 78, emphasis in original.

20 Interestingly, this novel, said to have functioned as an important inspiration for both the *Star Wars* universe and Cameron's blockbuster *Avatar* (2009), has experienced a renaissance in popular culture in recent years. In 2009, it was turned into the direct-to-DVD effort *Princess of Mars* and in 2012, Disney produced the big-budget *John Carter.*

21 Edgar Rice Burroughs, *A Princess of Mars* (1917; reprint, Rockville: Phoenix Science Fiction Classics, 2010), 17.

first confronted with are amazed by his martial prowess and quickly elevate him to a position of importance in the local hierarchy. Carter's position is further raised when he encounters the red-skinned and strictly humanoid citizens of Helium and their princess, Dejah Thoris. In a highly convoluted turn of events, Carter manages to liberate Dejah Thoris first from the clutches of the Tharks and then from the red-skinned Zodanga, finally becoming a prince of Mars.

Newell and Lamont argue that Burroughs's Mars novel 'was written in the tradition of American frontier narratives' and that 'Burroughs ... took for granted the imperialist values that are as pervasive in his Mars stories as they were in early 20th century American culture.'[22] Indeed, *A Princess of Mars* is in every way an inspired if sometimes ungainly reinvention of the imperial gothic that Haggard championed in Britain. Like Haggard's fiction, Carter's description of the alien biologies and customs of the Martians reads like nineteenth-century anthropology or travel writing. In this way, Mars fulfils the role of an imaginary frontier where American manhood can again perform the rituals of violence that certify its manliness while at the same time scientifically mapping the odd customs and biologies of this new frontier.

The violence that Carter so enthusiastically practices paves the way for a regeneration of the colonial space itself. In the wake of the violent pacification of the more unruly Martians, Carter's wise council brings an era of peace and prosperity during which Carter himself has the time to reproduce with his princess.[23] In this way, *A Princess of Mars* explores virtually all of the concerns of the British imperial gothic. Carter's constant consideration of his own customs in relation to those on Mars gives voice to the anxieties of 'regression or going native' that Brantlinger sees as one of the central elements of the imperial gothic. The pitting of the violent and unloving Tharks against the comparably civilised and humanoid citizens of Helium is yet another version of what Brantlinger terms the 'invasion of civilization by the forces of barbarism and demonism' and the novel as such constantly comments on the 'diminution of opportunities for adventure and heroism in the modern world'.[24]

Throughout the story, it is Carter's ability to perform heroic violence in front of the admiring eyes of Dejah Thoris that leads to his success. The performative nature of this violence is enhanced by the fact that Carter as well as most other characters in the story are mostly naked. This fetishised nakedness importantly connects violence and sexuality in the novel. Violence becomes not only a way to gain access to the women who observe the performance thereof, it becomes a displacement of the sexual act itself. This is also something that runs through

22 Newell and Lamont, 'Savagery on Mars', 73–4. It may be added that Burroughs's fiction became somewhat more nuanced towards the end of his life.

23 In the novel, the red and humanoid Martians lay eggs.

24 Brantlinger, *Rule of Darkness*, 230.

the imperial gothic of this period and which leaves an indelible mark on later texts. The prevalence of sexualised violence in later narratives will be further discussed in particular in Chapter 8.

## The Resurgence of the Yellow Peril

The first two decades of the twentieth century were a period of colonial, military and economic expansion, and as a result, the imperial gothic of the period was often extroverted and self-confident, as demonstrated by Burroughs's early writing. Even so, there were times when American empire was also imagined as unstable and under threat during this expansive period. Eugenics and degeneration theory imported from Europe and further developed in the US suggested to multi-racial America that miscegenation could erode society from within. Also, the influx of Asian immigrants from Japan and China in particular encouraged a particular kind of xenophobia that has been termed the 'Yellow Peril'. This also forms a parallel with the British imperial gothic of the late Victorian period, since this was at times concerned with distinctly Asian challenges to British imperial hegemony. During the late nineteenth and early twentieth centuries, the Chinese were thus at times cast as both military invaders and as gothic Others in British fiction such as Sax Rohmer's *Fu Manchu* series and in Richard Marsh's novel *The Joss: A Reversion* (1901).[25] Also, in a number of military invasion novels, it is the Chinese that plan to sack London and seize the empire.[26]

As Colleen Lye has observed in *America's Asia: Racial Form and American Literature* (2005), American society was similarly worried about the possibility of a Chinese invasion.[27] The 1882 Chinese Exclusion Act was an attempt to curb Chinese immigration not repealed until the Magnuson Act of 1943. In the literature of the late nineteenth century, writers such as Jack London worried that China might overwhelm the world through sheer numbers. In his most anti-Chinese story 'The Unparalleled Invasion' from 1907, London tells a story of how the nations of the West unite in the 1970s to secretly rid the world of the Chinese threat through a massive and complete genocide. This is accomplished through large-scale biological warfare where China is bombarded with 'plague-bearing germs'. In the wake of the almost total annihilation of the Chinese, the West resettles the now empty space. In this way, China becomes a new frontier landscape that is completely open to new colonisation but still

25 Richard Marsh, *The Joss: A Reversion* (London: White, 1901).

26 See, for example, M.P. Shiel, *The Yellow Danger* (London: Grant Richards, 1898).

27 Colleen Lye, *America's Asia: Racial Form and American Literature, 1893–1945* (Princeton: Princeton University Press, 2005).

dangerous because of the remaining germs. The small expeditions of 'scientists, and bodies of troops' that penetrate this frontier also find 'bands of wild dogs and bandits who had survived'. When these have been put to death and China is thus 'sanitised', a new and modern utopia created with the aid of 'a democratic American program' and characterised by 'splendid mechanical, intellectual, and art output' is established.[28]

London's short story of genocide is, of course, only marginally gothic and more usefully filed under science fiction, yet it illustrates the kind of anti-Asian discourse that saturated a great number of gothic novels and short stories from the period. Robert Sampson has observed that the Yellow Peril was a recurrent topic in post-1913 pulp writing and that '[p]opular literature prior to 1913 was already packed with menacing Far Eastern types, all representing a threat most dire to Western civilization'.[29]

## The First World War, Hollywood and the Imperial Gothic

1917, the year that *A Princess of Mars* was finally published in the form of a novel, was also the year when the US entered World War I. The reasons for this conflict were many. Certainly, there was a sense of Anglo affinity, a felt need to come to the aid of the nation that had spawned most of the powerful and ruling families of the US. Certainly, there was also a need to protect the many global British assets in which Americans had invested. Undoubtedly, the fact that Britain and the US perceived themselves involved in the same kind of modernising and civilising mission was important.

While Congress voted to join the war in April 1917, American forces did not see combat until November and the war was over about one year later. Indeed, the US experience of the war was very different from the European experience. The nation was never invaded or starved, and German hostilities inside US borders amounted to little more than sabotage and a U-boat attack on the New Orleans harbour. In the wake of the armistice in November 1918, the US found itself much closer to a position of global dominance. The nation's infrastructure had been bolstered by the war, and the economy was moving into an unprecedented period of growth. From a geopolitical perspective, the war had made it clear both to the world and to the nation itself that the US was now a dominant power.

---

28 See Jack London, 'The Unparalleled Invasion' in *The Complete Short Stories of Jack London*, vol. 2, edited by Earle Labor, Robert C. Leitz III and Milo Shepard (Stanford: Stanford University Press, 1993).

29 Robert Sampson, *Yesterday's Faces: A Study of Series Characters in the Early Pulp Magazines. Volume 3: From the Dark Side* (Bowling Green: Bowling Green University Popular Press, 1987), 8.

This provided the US with an increasingly central position from which to dictate global relations. One important item on the agenda was imperialism and the issue of self-determination. The peace negotiations were an opportunity to re-negotiate the global map and even to encourage the spreading of Republicanism. While Woodrow Wilson did indeed raise the issues of self-determination and democracy at these negotiations, his secretary of state Robert Lansing made it clear that such privileges should only be made available to 'peoples or communities … who do possess the intelligence to make a rational choice of political allegiance'. It was not to be extended to 'races, peoples, or communities whose state of barbarism or ignorance deprive them of the capacity to choose intelligently their political affiliations'.[30] As discussed by Julian Go, the US expanded even under Wilson's supposedly anti-imperial era through the acquisition of the Virgin Islands in 1917: 'Colonialism was hardly a passing phase; it was enduring rather than abjured.'[31]

## New Media: Hollywood, *Frankenstein*, *King Kong* and the Zombie

Alongside the prolific and popular pulp-fiction stage of the early twentieth century, the British imperial gothic left its mark on US culture with the aid of the budding movie industry. When Hollywood began to produce movies a few years into the new century, it was often upon the imperial gothic that studios relied, and Hollywood had some success with adaptations of texts such as *Frankenstein* (1910) and *Dr Jekyll and Mr Hyde* (1912 and 1913).

Much has been written about the emergence of the movie industry and Hollywood during this period. Fatimah Tobing Rony has made the important observation that cinema 'is not only a technology, it is a social practice with conventions that profoundly shape its forms'.[32] Mark Wheeler observes in *Hollywood Politics and Society* that 'the US film industry has and always will be an arena for political action and conflicts',[33] and Mark Lacy has similarly argued that 'cinema becomes a space where "commonsense" ideas about global politics and history are (re)-produced and where stories about what is acceptable behaviour from states and individuals are naturalised and legitimated'.[34] In this way, Rony argues, 'cinema has been a primary means through which race and gender are

30 Robert Lansing, *The Peace Negotiations: A Personal Narrative* (1921; reprint, Teddington: The Echo Library, 2007), 59.

31 Go, *Patterns of Empire*, 64.

32 Fatimah Tobing Rony, *The Third Eye: Race, Cinema, and Ethnographic Spectacle* (Durham: Duke University Press, 1996), 8–9.

33 Mark Wheeler, *Hollywood: Politics and Society* (London: BFI Publishing, 2006), 1.

34 Mark J. Lacy, 'War, Cinema and Moral Anxiety', *Alternatives: Global, Local, Political* 28, no. 5 (2003): 611–36 at 614.

visualized as natural categories; cinema has been the site of intersection between anthropology, popular culture, and the constructions of nation and empire'.[35]

It should also be noted that the major Hollywood studios seized control of the distributions channels of the era at an early stage. Already in the 1920s, it was difficult for production companies or film producers outside the big Hollywood studios to market, distribute and have their films shown. In the years that followed, the dreams that Hollywood produced became popular not simply because they were the most grandiose and appealing, but more importantly because they were often the only dreams to be had.[36]

From an artistic and technological perspective, Hollywood was in a constant state of transformation during the 1920s, 1930s and 1940s due to continuous technological innovation, the emergence of the movies as a potentially extremely profitable art form, the US's increasingly central position and the fluctuating economic climate within the nation. While the first three decades saw the production of a lot of interesting and gothic films, it is when the economy ground to a halt in the late 1920s that the imperial gothic came into its own in Hollywood. It was at this time that the concerns of the period – such as economic collapse, anxieties regarding the black community's bid for political and economic agency and competition from Europe and from Asia – are most clearly given shape by the Hollywood cinema industry. In many ways, the Great Depression marks a period of imperial crisis in US history, and as such it also produces some of the most important and influential imperial gothic narratives of the era.

## Hollywood's Imperial Gothic

Mary Shelley's 1818 novel *Frankenstein* is not, of course, an example of the imperial gothic but instead a still relevant anti-Enlightenment fable. If a novel ever illustrated how the sleep of reason begets monsters, it is Shelley's story of how a scientist's urge to create artificial life leads to utter destruction. However, in Universal Studios's 1931 *Frankenstein*, the many pertinent philosophical issues that the original gothic novel explores reshape into thinly veiled imperial gothic through the introduction of a eugenic and highly racialised discourse that changes the monster from a rightfully vengeful and eminently intelligent being into an atavistic criminal. In its Hollywood guise, the monster is not a tragic, lonesome and then understandably vengeful product of unethical science but instead a reincarnation of the degenerate criminal whose brain the monster

35 Rony, *The Third Eye*, 9.

36 For a discussion of this, see Geoff King, *New Hollywood Cinema: An Introduction* (New York: I.B. Tauris, 2002), 25.

is provided with in the film. This takes on a peculiarly American dynamics in the movie. As Elizabeth Young suggests in *Black Frankenstein: The Making of an American Metaphor* (2008), a connection between the monster and the supposedly primitive black American was made as early as during the immediate post-Civil War period when 'the "hideous progeny" of Shelley's novel was symbolically reborn in racist parody as the symbol of the miscegenated nation'.[37]

An important reference to American Reconstruction history is also the ending of the movie. Instead of escaping to the North Pole, as is the case in Shelley's novel, the monster is exorcised by what amounts to a lynch mob.[38] In *Frankenstein* the movie, as in the American South, justice is done by the people on the spot; by 'lynch law'. The violation of the sanctified space and body of Frankenstein's fiancée, Elizabeth, as much as the accidental drowning of the little girl, justifies this public rage in the eyes of the movie audience. This is the end that comes to those who dare violate the purity of white women, or oppose the progress of modernity in any form, be they black Americans in the South, Native Americans on the reservations or unruly natives in the Philippines. Like so many lynching victims, Frankenstein dies in flames.[39]

In this way, the discursive conditions that informed the British colonial enterprise as well as the racism that structured black and white relations in the US permeate *Frankenstein*. The childlike and aggressive monster is an example of the kind of human category that can never 'possess the intelligence to make a rational choice of political allegiance', as Lansing put it. In addition to this, the audience is also free to imagine an alternative narrative in which Fritz never drops the jar with the 'normal' brain to the floor. It is not science or faith in modernity that *Frankenstein* fears, it is atavism. The resolution to the crisis that atavism constitutes is the sad but necessary violence of the lynch mob. When the monster has been burned, the movie can end with the happy union of the film's central white couple.

The most successful and influential of all of Hollywood's imperial gothic narratives is not *Frankenstein*, however, but *King Kong* (1933). This movie relies on the same tropes as those employed in Haggard's anthropological adventure tales but also has many denominators in common with *Dracula*, *Frankenstein* (the movie) and numerous other imperial gothic texts. These denominators include the violated white female, performative and generative male violence within a colonial setting, the contrasting of Western modernity with primitivism and a final lynching scene that precedes the romantic union of the story's white heterosexual couple.

---

37 Elizabeth Young, *Black Frankenstein: The Making of an American Metaphor* (New York: New York University Press, 2008), 56.

38 A number of critics of the movie have made this point, see, for example, Ken Gelder, *The Horror Reader* (London: Routledge, 2000), 193, and Young, *Black Frankenstein*, 177.

39 Only to be resurrected, of course, in countless sequels.

There is also a clear genealogy from Arthur Conan Doyle's 1912 novel *The Lost World*, via Edgar Rice Burroughs's *The Land That Time Forgot* (1918), to *King Kong*.[40] These texts describe spaces where the prehistoric still exists in the form of dangerous jungles inhabited by fierce predatory dinosaurs. In Burroughs's *The Land That Time Forgot*, the humans that also exist within this territory represent different evolutionary stages, creating a spatial rather than chronological map of Darwinian evolution as imagined at this time. The challenge, then, is for the modern male explorer to locate himself in relation to these evolutionary categories. Can he survive the onslaught of dinosaurs and negotiate the brutal and primitive world of the Neanderthals? Can he somehow make sense of this world by finding a way to commodify these ancient beings? In this way, lost worlds take on the properties of many actual colonies and, as Noël Carroll has argued in an influential essay on *King Kong*, it 'is hard to resist seeing *The Lost World* as an apology for colonialism'.[41]

As Rony has noted, *King Kong* relies not only on lost world and imperial gothic tropes, the film is also based on, and even references, ethnographic cinema. In fact, the film tells a (meta)story where ethnographic filmmaker Carl Denham, famous for his pictures of 'jungles and places', teams up with down on her luck actress Ann Darrow to go in search of a mysterious island with hopes of filming the mythical creature 'Kong'. While posing as pure fantasy, the film is, as Rony has argued, 'one more manifestation of fascinating cannibalism: it explicitly recalls the historical practice of exhibiting humans at ethnographic expositions, and partakes of many of the defining traits of the "racial film" genre'.[42] Of course, ethnographic cinema was in many ways a modernised version of the anthropological writing that inspired both Haggard and Burroughs. Like this type of writing, ethnographic cinema sought to define the Other as the antithesis of the modern (white) citizen it imagined as its audience. In this way, *King Kong* is:

> part of a long line of films representing the person of African, Asian, or Pacific Islander descent as an ape-monster. In its construction of the *ethnographiable* monster, *King Kong* draws on discourses which equate the native with the pathological, as well as on discourses – mainly nativist – on the fear of the hybrid as monster. *King Kong* summons a notion of time that feeds into ideologies of survival of the fittest, and of the indigenous body as the site of a collision between past and present, Ethnographic and Historical, Primitive and Modern.[43]

---

40 See Arthur Conan Doyle, *The Lost World*. 1912, reprint. (London: Hodder & Stoughton, 2012) and Edgar Rice Burroughs, *The Land That Time Forgot* (Chicago: A.C. McClurg, 1918 and 1924).

41 Noël Carroll, 'King Kong: Ape and Essence' in *Planks of Reason: Essays on the Horror Film*, edited by Barry Keith Grant and Christopher Sharrett (Metuchen: The Scarecrow Press, 1984), 219.

42 Rony, *The Third Eye*, 15.

43 Rony, *The Third Eye*, 15, emphasis in original.

In the film, Denham sends the ship *Venture* in the direction of Indonesia (which is also, of course, the direction of the Philippines). There, they land on a hidden island and come across a tribe of worshipping natives gathered at a gigantic wall. The natives are mesmerised by Ann's white body and kidnap her with the intention of sacrificing her to their god Kong who turns out to be, of course, a gigantic gorilla. Kong takes Ann through a landscape littered with prehistoric dinosaurs that he fights. Having climbed to the clifftop that is Kong's home, the ape begins to undress the beautiful Darrow in a sequence that has been labelled the 'rape scene'. Here, King Kong transforms from lost world tale into captivity narrative. Darrow is then saved by Jack Driscoll, the first mate of the *Venture*. Kong pursues the couple down to the native village that he tears apart only to be sedated by grenades brought by Denham.

In the next sequence of the movie, Denham brings Kong back to New York. This is a new development of the lost world narrative. By inserting the atavistic monster into the modern setting, the movie highlights the city as also a jungle of sorts. In New York during the Great Depression, life was difficult and the streets were certainly sites of struggle. The modern marketplace is also a wilderness informed by a Darwinian economy. However, when Kong escapes, again captures Darrow and climbs to the top of the Empire State Building in one of the most iconic moments of Hollywood cinema, this reading of the film transforms into a Darwinian confrontation of another type. The question now is whether modernity or primitivism will rule the day. Kong's ascent of the newly constructed wonder of modern architecture – a tribute to the empire's empire state – white woman in hand, is an essentially evolutionary challenge. As Rony argues, to 'set evolution back on course in *King Kong*, the white man seizes upon war technology. The film moves into the future with its depiction of fighter planes as cutting-edge technological achievements.'[44] The planes are sent up into the sky and what follows is another lynching scene: public, prolonged and bloody.

As in *Frankenstein*, there is something sad about the destruction of Kong's body. While chained in the theatre, he resembles a slave up for auction. There is a sense of tragedy (and at the same time perhaps an uncomfortable feeling of nostalgia) to this shackled and commodified black body. In addition to this, Kong is primarily driven by an understandable love for Miss Darrow. Even so, the audience understands that the black ape must die once his chains have been broken. Like the atavistic, childlike and monstrous Frankenstein, the atavistic, childlike and monstrous Kong must be punished for his desire for white women. Society has a duty to exterminate him. It may be beauty that makes Kong break his chains, but it is not, contrary to Denham's statement in the final scene of the film, what kills him. What kills him is his insertion into a modern context; the machine-gun bullets of the fighter planes that symbolise this context. Once

44 Rony, *The Third Eye*, 188.

Kong has moved beyond his primitive reservoir and broken his chains, the logic of the imperial gothic makes gunfire the inevitable conclusion.

*King Kong* has continued to haunt American popular culture, the most recent instalment being Peter Jackson's nostalgic version from 2005, discussed in Chapter 7. While inspired by the British imperial gothic, *King Kong* contains a very American monster. As already suggested, it has often been read as expressing the prevalent anxiety related to black sexuality that saturated Reconstruction society. Through its Pacific setting, the film negotiates both the matter of colonial violence in the Philippines and racist anxieties within US borders. At the same time, the insertion of Kong's destructive force into New York constitutes a form of primitive invasion that highlights the sense of dejection and beleaguerment that accompanied the Depression. In this way, Kong's ascent of the marvel of the Empire State Building is a challenge to US imperialism, while the natives and Kong himself come across as symbols of the various threats that were assumed to assail US power, miscegenation but also working class disorder, and the politically incompetent native insurgent.

## The Zombie

The same period that spawned *Frankenstein* and *King Kong* also saw the creation of another central and very American monster: the zombie. The zombie's first appearance in Hollywood is not that of the ravenous undead but of an entranced, enslaved and silent Caribbean. As Kyle Bishop argues in the cleverly titled *American Zombie Gothic: The Rise and Fall (and Rise) of the Walking Dead in Popular Culture* (2010), the Caribbean was frequently imagined as gothic space in American narrative during the interwar years.[45] This territory consisted of what used to be Spanish, French and British colonies. Some of the Caribbean islands, such as Puerto Rico, were informal US colonies. Others, such as Jamaica, were still irritatingly part of the British Empire, and still others, such as Haiti and the Dominican Republic, were at times disturbingly independent and at times occupied by the US, ostensibly for their own protection against internal political turmoil or to defend them from European imperial ambition.

As once the hub of the transatlantic slave trade, the Caribbean is reminiscent of a still repressed history of slavery and violence.[46] In early Hollywood zombie films, the Caribbean became the location of a series of positively colonial

---

45 Kyle William Bishop, *American Zombie Gothic: The Rise and Fall (and Rise) of the Walking Dead in Popular Culture* (Jefferson: McFarland, 2010), 42.

46 Haiti became independent in 1804 during the Napoleonic Wars. During 1915–34, under the auspices of the Monroe Doctrine, the US occupied the island. Cuba became independent in 1902 after a brief period under US rule following the Spanish–American War.

narratives where 'eroticized black characters who challenged social and sexual taboos' were portrayed, allowing white America to 'sample the pleasures of colonization and imperialist exploitation'.[47] In the first zombie film, *White Zombie* from 1932 these desires are enacted through a story that centres on the transformation of the local population into docile and silent slaves (as Bishop observes, these are truly subalterns that cannot speak). The enslavement of the local black population in the hands not of the enterprising European but of the local Voodoo witch doctor, displaces the guilt of slavery and of the incomplete Reconstruction process. The film furthermore allows a white woman to be turned into a docile and compliant zombie, again enacting the fear that white women may be sexually colonised by enterprising and ungovernable black people.

*White Zombie* became a resounding success and spawned a number of zombie films. As in *White Zombie*, the affected are somnambulist, depersonalised victims rather than the cannibalistic predators popularised by George Romero in the 1960s (as discussed in Chapter 5). In many ways, the zombie films of the interwar period are more accurately termed 'Voodoo movies'. These movies explore and exploit the dual images of the free and enslaved Caribbean subject. Left to their own devices, the black Caribbean is pictured as resorting to suppressed and forbidden gothic rites that sometimes allow the now-defunct practice of slavery to resurface but which can be put to even more sinister use as they make it possible to exercise control also over white people. In this way, the Voodoo and zombie movies of the 1930s negotiate the same racial and imperial themes as much of the previous American imperial gothic. As discussed in Chapter 5, American independent film derails the conservative trajectory of these narratives in the 1960s and 1970s, turning the zombie into a very different form of creature. However, as discussed in Chapter 10, the most recent developments in the zombie genre once again cast the imperial and racial Other as an infectious and cannibalistic monster.

## The Imperial Gothic and the Displacement of Empire

The first four decades of the twentieth century was a time when America transformed from local empire to global hegemon. Considering the many territories that were added to its reach, most of which remained under the nation's control as informal colonies even after having been given the right to self-determination, it is strange how absent empire has been in the historiography of the US. This absence becomes even more peculiar when considering the culture of the period. Many of the most popular and cherished texts of the period are outrageously imperial and embrace the same Darwinian

47 Bishop, *American Zombie Gothic*, 66.

paradigm, the same racist eugenic theory and the same sexual tropes as the British imperial gothic.

The reasons for this myopia seem to be manifold. While many speak fondly of the projection of American power, few are prepared to pay the kind of homage to the concept as is paid in Britain during the late nineteenth and early twentieth centuries. In 1821, John Quincy Adams, still secretary of state to the Monroe presidency, imagined his nation as constantly offering a hand of freedom and 'generous reciprocity':[48] 'Wherever the standard of freedom and Independence has been or shall be unfurled, there will her heart, her benedictions and her prayers be',[49] he declared. However, Adams also argued that US general foreign policy should not be one of intervention: '[America] goes not abroad, in search of monsters to destroy.'[50] Through the application of gothic metaphor, Adams acknowledges that there are monsters out there. However, his fear is that America might become equally monstrous by involving herself in wars of avarice, envy and ambition, until she finds herself 'the dictatress of the world'.[51]

These words are wise, perhaps even prescient, yet they clash strangely not only with the concurrent displacement of Native Americans and the continued enslavement of a large portion of the population but also with the Monroe Doctrine that Adams penned for his president in 1823. This doctrine explains that the US will consider all attempts by European powers to colonise the Southern Hemisphere as an aggression against itself. This was not only an attempt at keeping Europe away from US neighbourhoods, it was also a declaration that the region was in fact a neighbourhood under US control.

In 1904, Roosevelt added his corollary to the Monroe Doctrine, making it clear to the empires of Europe as well as to Latin America, that the region was not only a neighbourhood but effectively a backyard that the US intended to police. The corollary states that should the US detect an 'impotence which results in a general loosening of the ties of civilized society',[52] this may 'force the United States, however reluctantly, in flagrant cases of such wrongdoing or impotence, to the exercise of an international police power'.[53] In this way,

48 John Quincy Adams, *An Address, Delivered at the Request of the Committee of Arrangements for Celebrating the Anniversary of Independence at the City of Washington on the Fourth of July 1821* (Cambridge: Hilliard and Metcalf, 1821), 31.

49 Adams, *An Address*, 32.

50 Adams, *An Address*, 32.

51 Adams, *An Address*, 32.

52 Theodore Roosevelt, 'Fourth Annual Message, December 6, 1904' in Lamont Colucci, *The National Security Doctrines of the American Presidency* (Santa Barbara, CA: ABC_CLIO, 2012), 241.

53 Roosevelt, 'Fourth Annual', 241. In 1928, Undersecretary of State J. Reuben Clark added the Clark Memorandum, declaring that the US need not even consider the Monroe Doctrine or the Roosevelt Corollary when dealing with Latin America. The nation had the right to intervene whenever it felt itself threatened.

American political discourse keeps talking about the practice of imperialism without having to subscribe to the notion of empire.

The American imperial gothic functions in a similar way but brings the discourse to a different set of people and into a different public arena. The imperial gothic's predilection for metaphor becomes a way for US citizens to talk about the nature and challenges of colonialism through myth and symbol. Thus, US empire exists in the imperial gothic as a displaced discourse, always there but rarely recognised for what it is. In the imperial gothic, Indians are slaughtered, but this is never genocide; black bodies are burned and mutilated, but this is never racist violence; natives are gunned down on tropical islands, and their treasures brought back to the urban centres, but this is never colonialism.

In addition to the above, the reliance upon metaphor and symbol allow a significant cross-feed between the different Others that prey upon the innocent in the imperial gothic. The Filipino rebel blends with the autonomous Haitian, with the Chinese immigrant and with the politically empowered black American, taking one monstrous shape or another, always recognisably Other but never spoken of as real. In the imperial gothic, they are thus made to rise together, their many forms crammed into one ghostly monster – a giant primate, an atavistic automaton, a stumbling zombie – that must then be violently exorcised.

# Chapter 4
# Cold War Horror

In *The Beast from 20,000 Fathoms* (1953), scientist George Ritchie is taken with the awesome power of the nuclear bomb test he has just observed: 'Every time one of those things goes off, I feel as if we were helping to write the first chapter of a new Genesis', he muses. The project's lead scientist, the handsome Professor Tom Nesbit, is more cautious: 'Let's hope we don't find ourselves writing the last chapter of the old one.' In the film, both possibilities are explored. The atom bomb test awakens a prehistoric and frantically dangerous and aggressive 'Rhedosaurus' that wreaks havoc first in the primitive geography of the Arctic and then in New York City. 'This is full scale war against a terrible enemy such as modern man has never before faced' the radio newscast explains. In gothic fashion, the dream of reason, of harvesting the power of nuclear technology, has, literally, begotten a terrible monster. However, the solution to the problem is the same as the cause: an experimental, nuclear weapon fired into the dinosaur.

According to the world-systems theory that provides one of the frameworks for understanding the development of US imperialism, the US became the dominant hegemonic power after World War II. This is the short eclipse of the American empire and it is perceived to last until 1973 when, at the end of the Vietnam War, US supremacy was challenged and the US economy began to falter. One would perhaps expect that these brief decades of dominance would generate an adventurous, self-confident and extroverted form of American imperial gothic. After all, America seems to have achieved its manifest destiny. American industrial strength, manhood and democratic principle have proven themselves in this global contest, a contest understood as a confrontation between good and evil.

Indeed, there are such texts as will be discussed below, but even during this stage of economic and military hegemony, the imperial gothic is often introspective and, like *The Beast from 20,000 Fathoms* (1953), deeply divided on issues of modernity and technology. There are many reasons for this, the most important being, perhaps, the unfathomable scale of the slaughter of the war not only on the battlefield, but also of the civilian population conducted with the help of conventional weapons and with the aid of the doomsday technology of the atomic bomb. Long before American power started to decline, the imperial gothic began to manifest symptoms associated with imperial collapse.

This study relies partly on certain similarities in the imperial practices and the cultural expressions of Britain and the US. I have argued that similar historical developments have generated and are generating similar stories. Here, it is necessary to note some crucial differences between the way that Britain and the US achieved their hegemonic statuses and the ideological contexts of these hegemonic phases. Britain arguably achieved hegemonic maturity in 1816, in the wake of the British defeat of the Napoleonic armies in Waterloo. While the Napoleonic Wars were certainly destructive and left great scars in their wake, they did not suggest that war was an impossible practice. By contrast, the end of World War II did not allow for the same type of triumphalism. While the US may have felt that it had, in fact, saved the world, new threats continued to emerge and grow after the armistice and the peace treaties. The hot war was supplanted by a Cold War that was, if anything, a more fertile context to the imperial gothic than the military confrontations of the previous years.

In addition to this, it is also important to note a crucial difference in imperial policy between the phases of hegemonic maturity of the US and Britain. As Go has observed, Britain kept adding formal colonies to its empire after the defeat of Napoleon. By contrast, the US changed its colonial policy after 1947: 'Whereas the British empire was formal and informal at once after 1815, the United States empire *shifted* from formal to informal after 1947.'[1] The move from hard to soft power at this period can also be assumed to discourage the type of imperial adventure gothic that characterises the extroverted type of this mode of writing.

This chapter first discusses how the imperial gothic negotiated the war itself and how the US state attempted to temper its influence at the time. Then, it addresses the ways in which the horrors of the war were slowly made into subject matter that the imperial gothic could somehow manage. As I will argue, this process is intimately related to the popularity of the (drive-in) horror movies of the 1950s. These narratives became important vehicles for the American imperial gothic and are useful examples of how the imperial gothic negotiated the horrors, ideological pressures and imperial ambitions of the United States at a time when the nation was dominant. There was room for a self-confident and extroverted form of imperial gothic amongst these narratives, but, as this chapter also exemplifies, the imperial gothic grew increasingly self-conscious and dark. There was an increasing sense, to again use Brantlinger's words, that 'we are those upon whom the ends of the world are come'.[2]

## The Holocaust, the Bomb and the Gothic

The US joined the Second World War after the bombing of Pearl Harbor on 7 December 1941. In 1942, Franklin D. Roosevelt invited the major filmmakers of

1 Go, *Patterns of Empire*, 133–4, emphasis in original.

2 Brantlinger, *Rule of Darkness*, 230.

Hollywood to the White House, including major directors John Ford and Frank Capra, to discuss how the film industry might aid the war effort.[3] Hollywood was already doing this work, of course. With films such as *Confessions of a Nazi Spy* (1939) and *The Mortal Storm* (1940), Hollywood had fuelled the interventionist fire for years before Pearl Harbor. Roosevelt's invitation formalised the relationship between this institution and the war by creating a number of different offices that were designed to help the media project a unanimous image of what the war was about. For Hollywood, the most important of those were the Office of War Information (OWI) and its Bureau of Motion Pictures (BMP).

A number of films attempted to explore and exploit the war effort through the gothic, including *King of The Zombies* (1941) and *Revenge of the Zombies* (1943), in which mad scientists attempt to create armies of the living dead in the service of the Third Reich, and *Return of the Vampire* (1943) in which Dracula is freed in London during the Blitz. However, as Rick Worland has observed in an important article, the wartime advisers of OWI did not appreciate the casting of the war and its stakes in gothic form.[4] They worried partly that the gothic would taint and confuse the message, and they were also noticeably alert to the American imperial gothic's tendency to embrace white-supremacist discourses. Such discourses would be detrimental to the recruitment of black Americans to the fighting forces. Thus, the BMP reviewer who read the script for *Revenge of the Zombies* remarked that the 'Negroes ... are presented as a strange, uncivilized and superstitious group of people living in a world quite apart from that of other Americans ... There is not one real Negro American in this story.'[5] While the purpose of this commentary is perhaps cynical, it evidences a striking familiarity with the operations of the imperial gothic and constitutes a form of ideology critique practised by very few literary or film critics at the time in question.

As a result of BMP's influence, horror cinema tended to stay strictly metaphorical and focused on recycling Frankenstein, zombie and vampire stories without overt reference to the Nazis or the Japanese.[6] Indeed, there seems to have been a limited demand for the dark terrors of the gothic during the period. The horrors of the war were either too present, through the bodies

3 Jean-Michel Valantin, *Hollywood, the Pentagon and Washington: The Movies and National Security from World War II to the Present Day* (London: Anthem Press, 2003), 6. Interestingly, the Bush administration did the same thing in 2001, as discussed in Chapter 6.

4 Rick Worland, 'OWI Meets the Monsters: Hollywood Horror Films and War Propaganda, 1942 to 1945', *Cinema Journal* 37, no. 1 (1997): 47–65.

5 Lillian Bergquist, 'Feature Script Review' quoted by Rick Worland, 'OWI Meets the Monsters', 53.

6 In fact, very few horror movies were made during the war. IMDb lists some 70 films issued during the period 1942–45. The big genres were war and western movies. Almost twice as many western movies were produced during any given year of the war as horror movies during the entire duration.

of people lost to the carnage, or too absent. The war and western movies of the period more easily recast combat as a patriotic duty and the essence of the American national identity.

As I have argued, the end of the war did not lift the sense of doom that the war had brought. The liberation of the Nazi extermination camps and the bombings of Hiroshima and Nagasaki left in their wake a sense of even greater horror. In the words of Skal:

> The new American prosperity of the early 1950s was won atop the largest bone pile in human history. World War II had claimed the lives of over 40 million soldiers and civilians, and had introduced two radical new forms of mechanized death – the atomic bomb and the extermination camp – that seriously challenged the mind's ability to absorb, much less cope with, the naked face of horror at mid-century.[7]

It proved initially difficult to produce any form of coherent, regular culture capable of addressing these horrors. James Berger has even argued that there was a great silence in the US on the Holocaust. When the Holocaust was discussed, it was described as a void exorcised by American power. Even 20 years after the war, as Berger argues, the 'salient fact about the camps was the liberation of the camps; for Americans, the discovery of that horror coincided with its ending'.[8] The first generation of Holocaust writers, the generation that inhabited the camps, found it difficult to testify or even to find an audience for their testimonies. It took Elie Wiesel 10 years to write about his experiences, and Primo Levi was not translated into English until 1959. It was not until what Berger refers to as the 'third generation' that the Holocaust is given form in culture and 'enters the autobiographies and bildungsromans of people who were never themselves in the camps; it enters comic books, pornography, movies about Vietnam, avant-garde experimentation, and postmodern parody'.[9]

One reason why the Holocaust was difficult to imagine and discuss in popular culture was possibly that fact that it was not easy to place in relation to the myth about progress, modernity, colonial frontier expansion and contest with the Other that Turner had argued steered the nation. The Holocaust was obviously a project of modernity of some sort, it even had a utopian rationale, but it also suggested the utter collapse of this project. In addition to this, Europe was no new frontier and, unlike the Native and black Americans who had been ground through the mill of American modernity, the victims of the Holocaust often

7 Skal, *The Monster Show*, 229.

8 James Berger, *After the End: Representations of Post-Apocalypse* (Minneapolis: University of Minnesota Press, 1999), 65.

9 Berger, *After the End*, xvi.

looked peculiarly white and European. Their abject suffering was caught on camera and disseminated through journalistic movies and newspapers. In the late 1940s and 1950s, this was a horror that was difficult to imagine as unreal, as inconsequential or even as gothic.

The atomic bomb was a somewhat different matter. Unlike the extermination camp, the bomb was an American technology, and a technology that ended the war, saving the lives of a great many American soldiers. In a 1945 Gallup Poll, 85 per cent of all Americans asked approved of atomic bombing of Japanese cities.[10] As discussed by Patrick Sharp in *Savage Perils: Racial Frontiers and Nuclear Apocalypse in American Culture* (2007), wartime propaganda resurrected the fear of the Yellow Peril by casting the Japanese as milling, aggressive and alien invaders. While Japan was undoubtedly an industrial imperial contender, it could be cast as an essentially primitive threat. The doomsday technology of the bomb could thus be imagined as another justified shooting of the ape who had dared to climb the pillar of modernity.

The publication of John Hersey's *Hiroshima* (1946), a text focusing on the suffering of civilians after the bomb had been dropped, made this discourse difficult to maintain.[11] Then, with the declaration that the new enemy, communist Soviet Union, had also acquired the bomb, the devastation and horror that the bomb was capable of producing saturated popular culture. It is this particular horror that gives the imperial gothic its direction in the years following the war. Skal argues that: 'Most Americans found it easier not to face invasion/annihilation anxieties directly; they found indirect expression in … the popular medium of lurid and sensational comic books that had been growing steadily in circulation since the end of World War II.'[12] In other words, popular culture became one of the sites where the invasion and annihilation fantasies of the Cold War were acted out.

## The Cold War

As argued, the 1950s, with its economic post-war boom and youthful culture, is often understood as the quintessential American era. At the same time, the 1950s was a time of frequent international confrontation as the US attempted to consolidate its role as global hegemon. This attempt took many forms. Rather than trying to control the territories that were now abandoned one by one by Britain and other former European powers, the US often practised a

---

10 Patrick B. Sharp, *Savage Perils: Racial Frontiers and Nuclear Apocalypse in American Culture* (Norman: University of Oklahoma Press, 2007), 124.

11 John Hersey, *Hiroshima* (New York: Alfred A. Knopf, 1946).

12 Skal, *The Monster Show*, 230.

combination of soft cultural and economic imperialism in combination with the (sometimes realised) threat of military intervention. This threat was made possible and practical through a construction of a network of military bases that historian Chalmers Johnson describes as crucial to the American imperial project after the war.[13] In many ways, these bases allowed (and allow) the US a similar kind of military leverage as that exerted by Britain in its colonies but without the need for the extensive administrative apparatus that the British employed.

The interventions of the 1950s were typically related to the fact that a number of nation-states (often but not always democratically) opted to disembark from the capitalist bandwagon. These confrontations took place primarily in what has been termed the US's backyard as described and created in the Monroe Doctrine and in Asia. In South America, the US typically preferred small-scale, low-cost CIA-led intervention campaigns. In Asia, these types of operations were less practical, and the embrace of communist doctrine here instead resulted in two large-scale military campaigns in Korea between 1950 and 1953 and in Vietnam between 1955 and 1975 (with large-scale American involvement being initiated in 1963 and ending in 1971).

The constant confrontations between the West, now often imagined as located in the US, and the new communist East, with its centre in the Soviet Union, suggest that 'Cold War' is a misnomer. Even so, the term remains useful especially when considering the internal situation of the US. Although no military forces invaded American territory, many Americans did feel that they were at war and that their way of life was under attack. In the words of David Skal:

> [O]nly five years after the fall of Germany and Japan, America was once again at war, this time a 'police action' in Korea haunted by the spectre of the H-bomb, a looming necro-technology now shared uneasily with the Soviets. If America in 1950 was filled with the smell of new cars, it was still permeated by the stench of mass death, and the threat of more to come.[14]

In addition to this, a number of minority groups were asking for the civil rights the Constitution claimed for all citizens of the republic. In particular, black Americans in the segregated South demanded access to the political process, to education and to economic and cultural equality.

---

13 Johnson, *The Sorrows of Empire*, 2.

14 Skal, *The Monster Show*, 229.

## Imperial Drive-In Gothic

Not surprisingly, and as much research into the period has shown, a number of narratives from the 1950s gothicise the Cold War, the anxiety of communist sympathies infiltrating North and South America, the military confrontations taking place in Asia and the increasingly vocal black American population. These anxieties took shape across several media such as pulp magazines, novels and movies. To look first at the fear of nuclear warfare and the Korean war, a number of deeply influential and iconic films refashioned the Hollywood gothic of the 1930s into what Jean-Michel Valantin has termed a 'national security cinema'[15] deeply influenced by the imperial gothic. These films cast anxieties related to the atomic bomb, the internal Cold War and the minor and major military conflicts in South America and Asia as monstrous invasions of the US. In this way, these films are fuelled by the same anxiety of reverse colonisation that Stephen D. Arata claims fuelled such British invasion novels as Stoker's *Dracula* (1897) and Wells's *The War of the Worlds* (1898) during the late nineteenth century.[16]

These monster movies can be roughly divided into two categories with the first category typically set in a politically liminal, hot or tropical Southern American environment where a small group of American scientists, adventurers and/or holiday-makers are confronted with atavistic breeds of monsters that seize their women and which the male protagonists then have to (violently) confront with little or no help from the local population. To these films belong *Monster from the Ocean Floor* (1954), set in Mexico, and the well-known *Creature from the Black Lagoon* (1954) which takes place in the Amazon. These films are good examples of an extrovert form of imperial gothic that imagines South America as a site of exotic beauty and pleasure suitable for US biological and anthropological attention. However, the films soon make it clear that this site also houses an atavistic evil, typically in the form of an ancient sea-creature that, like Kong, is somehow also a sexual predator. Thus, movie posters from the period typically show a young white woman in the claws of an abject monster. In most cases, the guns that the (modernised) American explorers have brought suffice to suppress this threat, and there is no need to engage the large-scale military fireworks that mark the second type of Hollywood monster movies discussed in this chapter.

This second category consists of paranoid, large-scale invasion narratives where the actual American military is mobilised to engage either a gigantic monster of Kong-sized proportions; a milling, atavistic multitude of faceless monsters; or an invasion from outer space in ways that have frequently been

15 Valantin, *Hollywood, the Pentagon and Washington*, x.

16 See Chapter 9 for a more detailed discussion of the invasion narrative.

parodied – and just as frequently updated – by later Hollywood productions. As a mode rather than a genre, the imperial gothic informs the very creation of these narratives. While often filed as science fiction, they have many things in common with previous imperial gothic, especially with the aforementioned introverted invasion narratives produced by Stoker or Wells in Britain during the turn of the century.

The space where these films take place is often liminal and consists of some kind of south-western border territory such as the deserts of New Mexico or the Californian seaboard. This territory is then discovered to house a form of large mutation that requires a massive military effort. To these films belong Oscar-nominated *Them!* (1954) which tells the story of how gigantic mutated ants invade Alamogordo, New Mexico, and *Tarantula* (1955) which articulates a similar story but with rodents and a giant spider taking on the roles of monsters. In both films, the insects are destroyed with the help of US armed forces who use the arsenal of the past war; machine guns, flame throwers and napalm bombs. Similar stories are told by *Beginning of the End* (1957) where giant locusts begin feeding on the Chicago population and infrastructure and *The Monster That Challenged the World* (1957) in which an army of giant molluscs invade California.

Like *The Beast from 20,000 Fathoms*, these movies typically explain the sudden emergence of the abnormal multitude with radiation. By making the monsters that appear in these movies the products of radiation, the films furtively discuss the atomic bombs dropped on Japan in 1945 and also comment on subsequent atomic-bomb testing in the Pacific. Valantin has argued that the message these films send out is that 'nuclear weapons are a perversion of power … expressed through the transformation of Nature into dangerous and grotesque objects' and that the monstrous creatures themselves 'defy all control, putting in danger the material framework of American urban civilization, the symbol for US citizens that they have left the world of Nature and therefore the Frontier'.[17] The appearance of enormous and atavistic creatures created or enhanced by radiation certainly encourages such a reading, yet these films often argue that the threat can be managed in the same way as it was created: through military confrontation and nuclear technology. The pre-historic 'Rhedosaurus' can only be stopped by firing a radioactive weapon into its body, suggesting that 'nuclear weapons can resolve the problems they create', as Ronald Davis has observed.[18]

In other words, the gothic Other can, again, only be exorcised through violence. In the wake of two World Wars, the dropping of the atomic bomb and the war in Korea, it is perhaps natural that this violence takes on large military proportions. The drive-in monster movies of this period almost invariably end

17 Valantin, *Hollywood, the Pentagon and Washington*, 15.

18 Ronald L. Davis, *Celluloid Mirrors: Hollywood and American Society since 1945* (Forth Worth: Harcourt Brace College Publishers, 1997), 51.

in large-scale battles where the military arsenal of modernity hammers the primitive Other into oblivion. In this way, as Scott Pole has argued, 'the vast majority of "creature features" proffered parables of American righteousness and power'.[19] The endings of these narratives are not, then, the apocalypse but instead the 'full restoration of a secure, consumer-oriented status quo'. The paranoia the films furtively acknowledge is thus offered 'quick and easy relief'.[20]

At the same time, the ending of the 1950s monster movie is often ambiguous and open. Eggs remain hidden to hatch in the future, aliens retreat into space but do not go back to their home planets, radiation keeps mutating insects and seamonsters into new horrific species. The violent eradication of one giant monster is the rise of another. To keep these terrors at bay there is a demand for constant vigilance and a need to repeatedly exercise the violence used to repress the gothic threat. This in turn suggests that the war on monsters will never cease, that the gothic and monstrous Other can never be completely pacified. This does not mean that American righteousness and power are problematised to any great extent. Instead, the war on the gothic Other takes on an Orwellian, permanent quality. Rather than appearing as a violent and tragic anomaly, war is (re)integrated as a natural component of the historical trajectory of the US. The location of these conflicts in liminal, formerly frontier territory reactivates this territory as again a conquerable space that requires constant military intervention. While the drive-in theatre largely disappears in the 1970s, the notion of permanent war and a need for constant vigilance, remain central to the imperial gothic.

## Introspective Imperial Gothic – *The Body Snatchers* and *I Am Legend*

The testing of the first Soviet atomic bomb in 1949 increased both the intensity and the stakes of the Cold War. It was clear to the United States that the rapid development of the bomb could not have been accomplished without intelligence being transferred from the Manhattan Project to the USSR. This suggested the operation of a substantial network of Soviet spies and a willingness even among Americans to embrace communist ideals and Marxist ideology. This in turn triggered an increasingly intensive campaign aimed at uncovering the organisation not only of communist espionage but also of general Marxist sympathies within the US. This campaign took visible shape in the McCarthy trials between 1950 and 1954, strongly supported by FBI

---

19 W. Scott Poole, *Monsters in America: Our Historical Obsession with the Hideous and the Haunting* (Waco: Baylor University Press, 2011), 113.

20 Poole, *Monsters in America*, 113.

director J. Edgar Hoover, and also in the trial and subsequent execution of the Rosenberg couple in 1953.

In the imperial gothic of the post-war period, the ideology of communism is often cast as a form of invasive infection. The most famous of these narratives is Jack Finney's novel *The Body Snatchers*, first serialised in *Colliers Magazine* in 1954.[21] The novel spawned any number of pulp-fiction copies and four official Hollywood adaptations entitled *Invasion of the Body Snatchers* (1956 and then in 1978), *Body Snatchers* (1993), and *The Invasion* (2007).[22] Published in the immediate wake of the Korean War, the Rosenberg trials and the McCarthy witch hunts, this novel and its first film version have been read as gothic expressions of the communist fears that imbued the US at this time.[23] The novel is an interesting and inventive revision of Wells's *The War of the Worlds*. As in Wells's original, Earth is subjected to an invasion from space – the colonial paradigm thus saturates the story – but Finney conflates this very violent invasion narrative with gothic invasion novels such as Stoker's *Dracula*, making the invasion clandestine, insidious and infectious. Thus, the novel tells the story of how spores from outer space invade the small town and citizens of Santa Mira in California. Resistance in the novel is put up by local physician Miles Bennell and his love interest, Becky Driscoll, who discover that the odd transformation of their fellow citizens is due to an extra-terrestrial invasion strategy that replaces actual humans with identical copies. The townspeople that come into contact with the seeds at night while sleeping trigger the growth of a pod that then produces an identical copy of the host. The copy continues to live the life of the original human, but they are unable to experience true emotion and they lose their essential identities. It should be noted that the replacement of individual identity with a type of hive consciousness is endemic of the imperial gothic, a type of going native cemented in such novels as Stoker's *Dracula*. Furthermore, the lifespans of the pod-people are short, only some five years, and they cannot procreate. Their intention to eventually replace all human beings with alien pod people is therefore apocalyptic. When the invasion is finally completed, the

21 Jack Finney, *The Body Snatchers* (1954; reprint, New York: Scribner, 1998).

22 The story has also spawned numerous copies and rewrites including Scott Sigler's *Infected* (New York: Crown Publishing, 2008) and *Contagious* (New York: Crown Publishing, 2008), Dean Koontz's Frankenstein series, consisting of *Prodigal Son*, co-written with Kevin J. Anderson (New York: Bantam Books, 2005), *City of Night* (New York: Bantam Books, 2005), *Dead and Alive* (New York: Bantam Books, 2009), *Lost Souls* (New York: Bantam Books, 2010) and *The Dead Town* (New York: Bantam Books, 2011), and Guillermo del Toro's *Mimic* (1997).

23 This has been discussed by many critics, including Cyndy Hendershot in *Anti-Communism and Popular Culture in Mid-Century America* (Jefferson: McFarland, 2003), and Fraser A. Sherman in *Screen Enemies of the American Way: Political Paranoia about Nazis, Communists, Saboteurs, Terrorists and Body Snatching Aliens in Film and Television* (Jefferson: McFarland, 2011).

Earth will be devoid of human life, and the pods will leave and move on into space in search of another planet to invade.

The couple that uncovers the plot soon become the hunted. Escaping and then confronting the pursuing pod-people with fire bombs, the two human protagonists manage to stave off the pod invasion through what comes across as the sheer will to resist. Seeing the pods depart up into the atmosphere, Miles remembers Winston Churchill's famous words:

> *We shall fight them in the fields, and in the streets, we shall fight in the hills; we shall never surrender.* True then for one people, it was true always for the whole human race, and now I felt that nothing in the whole vast universe could ever defeat us.[24]

Passages such as this, where the military solution guarantees the universal predominance of the human race, effectively align the narrative with the imperial gothic. As in the drive-in gothic that maps the Korean War and anxieties regarding the atomic bomb, the solution to the gothic crisis in *The Body Snatchers* is military both in the sense that Miles and Becky violently confront the pod-people and in the way that Miles imagines the confrontation as a military battle of the same epic proportions as the recent global conflict. This is the preferred solution of (Anglo) imperialism to any gothic challenge. In the words of Priscilla Wald, then, the 'triumph of the human spirit [in the novel] is a victory for a white America'.[25]

In many ways, *The Body Snatchers* remains a gothic celebration of white, independent, individualistic, middle-class America. Yet, as with so many invasion narratives published after Wells's *The War of the Worlds*, there is an implicit critique of the colonial process and perhaps also of the rabid anti-communist sentiment that saturated the United States at the time. In the novel, one of the alien impostors observes that human civilisations have also been in the habit of destroying native populations and eco-systems as they have expanded. Similarly, the novel and the subsequent films have been read as critiques of the McCarthy trials undertaken in the US during this period. In this way, *The Body Snatchers* is certainly a polyphonous novel that balances on the edge that separates the anti-enlightenment gothic and the imperial gothic. While obviously informed by the imperial gothic, the novel sometimes reforms as a critical text that uses the gothic to query the discourse that informs it. Regardless of how the novel is positioned, however, it remains a testament to an increasingly anxious and introverted form of imperial gothic culture.

---

24 Finney, *The Body Snatchers*, 214.

25 Priscilla Wald, *Contagious: Cultures, Carriers, and the Outbreak Narrative* (Durham: Duke University Press, 2008), 198.

If *The Body Snatchers* is furtively critical of colonialism even as it embraces the categories upon which the imperial gothic relies, Richard Matheson's short novel *I Am Legend* (1954) is openly dismissive of these categories.[26] This is another central gothic narrative that has inspired countless adaptations and copies, including *The Last Man on Earth* (1964), *The Omega Man* (1971), *I Am Legend* (2007) and the mockbuster *I Am Omega* (2007), as well as *Night of the Living Dead*, George A. Romero's 1968 reinvention of the zombie narrative discussed in the next chapter.

*I Am Legend* tells the story of Robert Neville, seemingly the one survivor of a vampire pandemic that has swept the across the United States. Neville is now boarded up in the house he once shared with his small family, fending off nightly attacks by the local and exclusively nocturnal vampire population while researching the disease and killing off vampires during the day. Struggling with periods of alcoholism and depression, Neville survives three years in isolation to discover what appears to be an uninfected woman, Ruth. She runs frightened from him, but he manages to catch her and brings her back to his house. At the same time elated and suspicious, Neville quickly forms an emotional attachment to her. Realising this, he decides to test her blood for the virus just to make sure that she is truly human. When the test turns out to be positive for a vampire infection, Ruth beats him senseless and flees the house, leaving a note that explains that she is part of an evolved vampire breed capable of existing in the daytime and intent on rebuilding society. There is no place in this society for Neville, Ruth explains. He has killed countless vampires, including Ruth's husband, and will probably be hunted down unless he flees his house and takes refuge somewhere else.

Neville decides not to heed this warning and is eventually caught and imprisoned by the new vampires. In a final conversation with Ruth, Neville is told that he is 'the last of the old race' and that when he is gone, there will be nobody like him left. The realisation that he may be the only human left jars Neville to the core: 'I'm the abnormal one now. Normalcy was a majority concept, the standard of many and not the standard of one man.'[27] The reader realises that Neville's house was not the last civilised abode, but a Dracula's castle from which he has schemed the overthrowing of the dominant species. In other words, Neville is the actual vampire of the novel: 'To them he was ... an invisible spectre who had left for evidence of his existence the bloodless bodies of their loved ones … he knew he did not belong to them; he knew that … he was anathema and black terror to be destroyed.'[28]

26 Richard Matheson, *I Am Legend* (1954; reprint, New York: Tor, 2007).

27 Matheson, *I Am Legend*, 156.

28 Matheson, *I Am Legend*, 156.

In this way, Neville is transformed from righteous human crusader to gothic monster. This dislocation of normalcy, from the white male with both a military and scientific pedigree to that of a new and abject human species, is what turns *I Am Legend* from yet another vampire narrative into a subversive text. Obviously, the military solution does not resolve the gothic crisis in Matheson's novel. Instead, Neville's insistence on violently confronting the vampires that surround him eventually leads to his own demise at the hands of the judicial system of a new world order. This conclusion testifies to a discursive and ideological discord, a haunting suspicion, or even bold declaration that the values society (and the imperial gothic) has taken for granted may fold in on themselves.

## Empire and Superpower

If the 1950s and 1960s constitute the eclipse of American (economic) power, the narratives discussed in this chapter testify to a prevalent sense that this power is already under siege. While many of the texts discussed here celebrate American power and modernity, few view the ideological and territorial borders that surround the nation as impossible to transgress. America is open to many different types of invasion, and while the military solution might serve to defend the nation at least temporarily, the sense emerges that power must be constantly defended precisely because it is constantly challenged.

This is perhaps not surprising in the aftermath of a war when so many territorial, moral, ideological and technological borders were traversed, yet it seems that it is not the war as much as the centrality of American power that encourages the transgressions that these narratives record. While the US arguably did not think of itself as an empire at this time, there was a keen awareness, locally and globally, that the US was indeed an immensely powerful nation. In *The Super-Powers: The United States, Britain and the Soviet Union – Their Responsibility for Peace* (1944), William T.R. Fox first discussed the superpower as a nation-state capable of decisive global influence.[29] The fact that Fox argued, as Nicholas Spikeman had done before him, that Britain was the original European superpower in fact suggests a great similarity between empire and this designation. However, unlike 'empire', superpower became a concept that the US could be comfortable with. There was no denying that the US was a very powerful nation and that it was quite prepared to wield this power in different forms, but at the same time, both Spikeman and Fox argued that superpowers ought to be concentrations of power actively working to ensure global peace.

29 William T.R. Fox, *The Super-Powers: The United States, Britain and the Soviet Union – Their Responsibility for Peace* (New York: Harcourt, Brace, 1944).

There is an important and noticeable difference here between the culminations of American and British hegemony. As discussed, Britain became hegemonic in the aftermath of the Napoleonic Wars. After the signing of the peace treaty, the supremacy of the British navy allowed the British to build and maintain their colonies in relative peace. While Britain was involved in numerous small wars as their colonial empire grew, only the Crimean War (1853–56) involved a confrontation with a comparatively well-armed European enemy. It was not until the unification of Germany under Bismarck and the Franco-Prussian War in the early 1870s that Britain needed to start considering challenges to its own central position. By contrast, the short period of American hegemonic dominance was marked from the very beginning by fierce challenges from the thoroughly industrial and communistic Soviet Union and by a series of large-scale conflicts in Asia.

From this perspective, it is not strange that a sense of beleaguerment saturated the imperial gothic even at that stage of American global dominance. At the same time, the realisation that the nation was indeed a super-powerful state allowed for a more self-conscious wielding of power. Beside a rapidly crumbling British empire, the US often viewed itself as a nation that must aggressively project its economic, cultural and military power globally not only to protect its own interests and those of the West in general but also to ensure future peace and freedom. The need for such constant policing of ideological and territorial borders, and sometimes for the expansion of these borders, set the stage for the imperial gothic narratives of the post-Vietnam era.

# Chapter 5
# Post-Vietnam Gothic

In *Night of the Living Dead*, flesh-eating zombies close in on Ben, the only black character trapped with an assortment of panicking white people in a similarly white farmhouse somewhere in rural Pennsylvania. Ben is decisive, resourceful and strong, but he fails to sway the group. The frightened crowd desperately try to either escape the besieged house or barricade it. An attempt to flee the zombies results in some of the escapees getting burned and eaten. At the end of the movie, Ben, the only survivor, stumbles into the morning sunlight only to be gunned down by a posse that mistakes him for yet another zombie. As the credits roll, Ben's body is burned with those of the undead. Nobody gets out alive, and the final exercise of violence ends in Ben's tragic death.

According to several film critics, modern American horror film begins with George Romero's *Night of the Living Dead*.[1] This may be true, but if so, it is a beginning inspired by an already accomplished revolution in horror writing. As Romero has himself acknowledged, his film is essentially an adaption of Matheson's *I Am Legend*, discussed in the previous chapter. Of course, the two narratives are also very different; the undead in Romero's film are not vampires but 'ghouls' who have been reanimated as a result of radiation. Ben is never alone and beleaguered in quite the way that Neville is, and the ghouls do not constitute a new competitive species. However, as will be discussed below, the film seems to embody the same kind of critique of American power. The violence that first the predominately white and middle-class zombies, and then the similarly white posse, perpetrate asks questions about the persistent belief in white supremacy and about the war in Vietnam.

This chapter first discusses the relationship between the decline of American hegemony that began in the early 1970s and the seemingly paradoxical expansion of American global influence. Then, the chapter traces the emergence of a set of seemingly radical horror films that appear to be set on disrupting the capitalist and imperial logic that have informed many of the previous narratives discussed in this study. As Christopher Sharrett has observed, the horror films of the late 1960s and early 1970s became 'steadily more progressive, constantly

1 See Gregory A. Waller, 'Introduction to *American Horrors*' in *The Horror Reader*, edited by Ken Gelder (London: Routledge, 2000), 256.

challenging the legitimacy of capitalist, patriarchal rule'.[2] This development transformed the notion of monstrosity so that the gothic Other was 'no longer metaphysical or the product of a lab experiment gone awry, but instead an emblem of the upheaval in bourgeois civilization itself'.[3] From this perspective, this often anti-capitalist, anti-imperial, anti-enlightenment, and anti-modern wave of horror is reminiscent of the first gothic narratives of the the late eighteenth and early nineteenth centuries. In many ways, these narratives cannot be termed imperial gothic.

However, as I will argue, the anti-modern element is often misunderstood or lost as the gruesome violence rather than the social critique that these narratives explore is that which is celebrated by audiences. In addition to this, these films deserve scrutiny because of the way that the critique inherent in them is transformed by what Sharrett terms the 'neoconservative culture' of the 1980s and 1990s (and then, as will be discussed in later chapters, by the even more politically rigid and xenophobic cultures of the post-9/11 era). It is difficult to understand how the gothic produced during these and the following decade reinvests in the original binaries of the imperial gothic without an understanding of how these radical narratives first attempt to sabotage the basic structure of the imperial gothic.

## Competition, Decline and the Assertion of American Power

As argued, American hegemony began to decline in the early 1970s. In a number of articles (usefully located and organised by Julian Go in *Patterns of Empire*) Christopher Chase-Dunn, Andrew K. Jorgenson, Thomas E. Reifer and Shoon Lio, and Terry Boswell have mapped the economic development of the US as a dominant capitalist power within the capitalist world system. With the help of GDP figures, Chase-Dunn et al. have charted the hegemonic rises and declines of the US, finding that the US economy peaked as early as in 1945 (due to the fact that it is the only major Western industrial nation not to have been bombed during the war) and that it has been in steady decline since the late 1960s.[4]

The decline in economic importance is, interestingly, accompanied by a number of statements that testify to an *increased* centrality of American power. This may be attributed to a great extent to the end of the Cold War and the

2 Christopher Sharrett, 'The Horror Film in Neoconservative Culture' in *The Dread of Difference: Gender and the Horror Film*, edited by Barry Keith Grant (Austin: Texas University Press, 1996), 254.

3 Sharrett, 'The Horror Film', 254.

4 Christopher Chase-Dunn, Andrew K. Jorgenson, Thomas E. Reifer and Shoon Lio, 'The Trajectory of the United States in the World-System: A Quantitative Reflection', *Sociological Perspectives* 48, no. 2 (2005): 233–54.

failure of the Soviet Union. Thus, Henry Nau, Samuel P. Huntington and Joseph S. Nye, Jr, argued during the 1990s that American power and influence had grown since the 1970s and that, with the fall of the Soviet Union in the late 1980s, the nation had become a 'hyperpower', a lone superpower in a 'uni-multipolar' world. Of course, this analysis of American preponderance did not build on the same type of economic statistics and analysis as that of Chase-Dunn and Boswell. Rather, Nau, Huntington and Nye focus on the actual and perceived impact of the United States in global matters.

In this way, the final years of the twentieth century were at the same time a period when the US began to economically deteriorate and, in the wake of the collapse of the Soviet Union, when it transformed into a 'hyperpower' with a reach that transcended all previous states, a nation that held 'sway over the world as no empire has ever done before in the entire history of humankind' as Ignacio Ramonet put it in 1998.[5] These two movements seem incompatible, but this is not necessarily the case. In fact, the American case parallels that of the British empire as it entered its phase of competition and decline in 1873. In the years that followed, Britain became increasingly central on the world stage. It was not until this time that many Brits became conscious of the fact that the nation had a formal empire. To John Robert Seeley, the British empire was acquired in a 'fit of absence of mind', and it was not until the 1870s that it was openly discussed as a political and material entity.[6] From then on, and until the cataclysm of World War I, economic competition and decline (as mapped by world-systems theory), imperial expansion and imperial awareness went hand in hand. Between 1880 and 1900, Britain added large parts of Africa to its dominion, and attempted to consolidate their hold of many other regions. At the same time, the notion that Britain had an empire, and that this empire was crucial to the nation's well-being, began to permeate the national consciousness.

In many ways, the American development 100 years later seems to mirror the British trajectory. Although the circumstances are very different, as discussed above, the period of economic competition and decline is marked by an increasingly more aggressive and assertive foreign policy, the belief that America is an 'indispensable nation' with the right to exercise force globally, as Madeleine Albright argued in 1998. In 2003, Michael Ignatieff noted that if the British absentmindedly acquired their empire, the US did so in 'a state of deep

5 Ignacio Ramonet quoted by Kim Richard Nossal, 'Lonely Superpower or Unapologetic Hyperpower? Analyzing American Power in the Post-Cold War Era', paper for presentation, biennial meeting of the South African Political Studies Association, Saldanha, Western Cape, June 29–July 2, 1999, http://post.queensu.ca/~nossalk/papers/hyperpower.htm.

6 John Robert Seeley, *The Expansion of England: Two Courses of Lectures* (1883; reprint, New York: Cosimo, 2005), 8.

denial'.[7] As will be discussed in latter chapters, it is when this state of denial fades, in the wake of the wars in Iraq and Afghanistan but also following the many sociological, historical and political science interventions discussed in the introduction, that 'imperialism' again becomes a word on many people's lips.

## Collapse of the Modern: *Night of the Living Dead* and *The Texas Chain Saw Massacre*

To return to the late 1960s, it should be noted that while the US was growing increasingly sure of its place in the world, the West experienced a form of ideological transformation, causing a partial change of the US through a reordering of the ideological borders that organized American society. A number of interrelated movements enabled new ways of thinking and an actual relocation of normalcy. The intensification of the civil rights movement, the women's liberation movement, the new left, the hippie movement and the sexual revolution, including the decriminalisation of homosexuality, had a profound political and cultural effect on the US.

However, it must again be stressed that these movements did not arrest continued American empire-building. The 1960s and early 1970s may have been times of internal social transformation in many of the large metropolitan areas, but it was also the time when the US launched and sustained one of the largest war efforts in history. While the Vietnam War grew increasingly unpopular among US citizens, it was the prohibitive costs rather than internal criticism that brought it to an end. In addition to this, the period was marked by continuous and often escalating intervention in Latin America. In short, the US may have been reinventing itself, but this reinvention did not deeply permeate the nation's foreign policy at the time.

The collision between a shifting ideological landscape, the still on-going Cold War and frequent US global involvement encouraged a widely discordant gothic. Hollywood and many pulp fiction magazines kept retelling the British and American imperial gothic where the borders between good and evil, and black and white, remain relatively intact. What is known as the first splatter movie, *Blood Feast* (also billed as *Egyptian Blood Feast*) was released in 1963 and features the Egyptian caterer Fuad Ramses who kills young (white) women so that he can use their body parts in a lavish meal in honour of the Egyptian goddess Ishtar. When attempting to escape the police at the end of the movie, he climbs into a garbage truck and is crushed to death. The final verdict rings of the same turn-of-the-century racism that permeated the British imperial gothic:

7 Michael Ignatieff, 'The Burden', *New York Times Magazine*, January 5, 2003, http://www.nytimes.com/2003/01/05/magazine/05EMPIRE.html?pagewanted=all.

'he died a fitting end, just like the garbage he was'.[8] Similarly, a number of the canonical horror films that Alfred Hitchcock produced during the period (including *Psycho* [1960] and *The Birds* [1962]), show the torture, rape and murder of notably independent young women, recalling the problematic attitude to the 'new woman' in much British (and American) turn-of-the-century culture.

At the same time, the gothic appears increasingly aware of the binaries that have structured the genre and frequently manipulates them to allow for potentially anti-imperial sentiments to surface. This is where Romero's *Night of the Living Dead* comes in. Released at the culmination of the efforts of the civil rights movement in the US, it shows black actor Duane Jones as Ben trying to survive the attack of the reanimated and cannibalistic undead. Not only does this film mark the introduction of the flesh-eating, mindless zombie that has been revived for reasons not involving the use of Voodoo, the undead clearly become a vehicle for social critique in the film. The ending with Ben's dead body being dragged to a large bonfire and burned with the zombies – 'one more for the fire' – transforms the film into a long lynching sequence that, unlike in many previous gothic narratives, comes across as utterly tragic.[9]

Romero's provocative film left an indelible mark on American culture. As Skal has observed, horror films of the 1970s and 1980s 'began exhibiting symptoms remarkably similar to some of those suffered by victims of posttraumatic stress syndrome: startle reactions, paranoia, endless scenes of guerrilla-like stalking, and, like traumatic flashbacks, endlessly repeated images of nightmare assaults on the human body, especially its sudden and explosive destruction'.[10] The seminal film in this tradition is Tobe Hooper's *The Texas Chain Saw Massacre* (1974). This is one of many extremely violent films that have been read by critics as a scathing critique of the capitalist society which produced the Vietnam conflict. In the film, a group of hippies, three men (one of whom is paraplegic) and two young women travel across the US in a van. This Scooby Doo-like outfit moves through a landscape that is at the same time occult, apocalyptic and industrial. The slaughter of livestock has been mechanised, one of the characters observes, and before long, he is similarly

8 *Blood Feast* is the first of a trilogy known as the *Blood Trilogy*. The second instalment is named *Two Thousand Maniacs* (1964) and describes a very different set of anxieties. The film tells the story of how a white redneck community tortures, murders and consumes a group of Northern tourists in an attempt to avenge the loss of the Civil War. The final piece, *Color Me Blood Red* (1965), deals with a crazed artist who uses blood from young white females to paint and who is eventually shot in the face. *Blood Feast* was given a belated sequel in 2002 (*Blood Feast 2*) while *Two Thousand Maniacs* was remade as *2001 Maniacs* in 2001.

9 Romero has stated that he did not set out to make a film about the civil rights movement and that Jones was hired simply because he made the most convincing audition. Yet, the film is typically understood as, in many ways, a comment on the state of civil rights in the US at the time.

10 Skal, *The Monster Show*, 311.

slaughtered by the chainsaw-wielding Leatherface. One by one, the small group is murdered, sawed to pieces and consumed by a dysfunctional and motherless family that inhabits a house littered with human remains. Leatherface himself wears a mask made out of the faces of previous victims. If the post-Holocaust era was built on a pile of bones, these form the architecture of this setting.

As one of the most controversial but also critically acclaimed movies of the decade, *The Texas Chain Saw Massacre* has received a great deal of critical attention. While the film has been criticised for its brutality, and for depicting severe violence against women in particular,[11] few critics today take issue with Robin Wood's early assessment of the movie as bringing to focus 'a spirit of negativity, and undifferentiated lust for destruction, that seems to lie not far below the surface of the modern collective unconsciousness'.[12] Thus, the film can be seen to invert the paradigm of the imperial gothic where the champion of goodness is always the white and armed male. In this way, as Mark Bould has argued, *The Texas Chain Saw Massacre* 'is a story told from a perspective sympathetic to the Monster (the young travellers) caught in the grinding wheels of Normality (the slaughterhouse family and the bourgeois capitalist order they represent)'.[13] In this useful reading of the film, Leatherface manifests not as gothic monster but as white order. He wears the equally white faces of his former victims in whose name he kills his next victims. He commands a technology of murder (the chainsaw), and he kills in order to feed and preserve his family. When he runs out of the house in the movie's final sequence, chainsaw in hand and in pursuit of the surviving hippie, he is dressed in the uniform of the middle-class: the suit, the white shirt and the tie.

In this way, the movie's powerful images of the mechanised slaughter of the innocents and the pervading sense of social and moral collapse into unfathomable horror and carnage launch a powerful critique against a society that is somehow able to accommodate the killing of (at least) hundreds of thousands of civilian Vietnamese in the name of democracy. Thus, *The Texas Chain Saw Massacre* draws from footage coming out of Vietnam at the time; images of dead and dying civilians, of children running, burned and crying from bombed-out villages, and of American soldiers not as liberators and defenders of freedom but instead as 'child killers'. In the television images, the military

11 On the other hand, Carol J. Clover has argued in *Men, Women and Chain Saws: Gender in the Modern Horror Film* (Princeton: Princeton University Press, 1992) that the slasher genre's insistence on a lone female survivor empowers women.

12 Robin Wood, 'An Introduction to the American Horror Film' in *Planks of Reason: Essays on the Horror Film*, edited by Barry Keith Grant (1984; reprint, Oxford: The Scarecrow Press, 2004), 133.

13 Mark Bould, 'Apocalypse Here and Now: Making Sense of *The Texas Chain Saw Massacre*' in *Horror at the Drive-In: Essays in Popular Americana*, edited by Gary D. Rhodes (Jefferson: McFarland, 2003), 100.

solution – aided by the de-leafing Agent Orange, long-range bombers, grenade launchers and all other modern tools of warfare imaginable – was stripped of its comforting gothic form and projected by television into people's homes by a generation of journalists that had not yet been brought in line by the Pentagon. It is this sense of moral dissolution, of visceral and unpredictable horror and violence that *The Texas Chain Saw Massacre* arguably seeks to conjure. Thus, the explosion of slasher, splatter and gore movies in the 1970s and early 1980s can be seen as a general comment on the state of US society during and after the Vietnam War. Films such as *The Last House on the Left* (1972), *Black Christmas* (1974), *Halloween* (1978), *Dawn of the Dead* (1978) and *Friday the 13th* (1980) build on the same sense of moral dissolution and societal collapse. The ambiguous endings of these films – the killer is rarely captured or destroyed – also deny the audience the sense of closure that may allow them to put the horrors dramatised behind them.

However, the horror movies of this era are also polyphonous. The frequent violence directed against (independent and sexually liberated) women suggests that these narratives can also be read as very conservative statements of what happens if you stray beyond the confines of the political and sexual main stream. The splatter and gore genres balance mayhem and social critique uneasily. As will be discussed further in Chapter 9, the fact that capitalist modernity is cast as a mechanised, chainsaw-wielding madman does not mean that the audience prefers identifying with the beleaguered young men and women who seek to escape him. Wood describes the experience of seeing *The Texas Chain Saw Massacre* in a movie theatre: 'Watching it recently with a large, half-stoned youth audience who cheered and applauded every one of Leatherface's outrages against their representatives on the screen, was a terrifying experience.'[14]

From this perspective, even the movies that position modernity as a meat grinder reshape into conservative stories as audiences celebrate the effect and affect of violence. Two hundred years of the imperial gothic have taught the audience to always identify with the person holding the gun (or the chainsaw), to cheer this person on regardless of what he (or in rare cases she) is doing. As I will discuss below and in subsequent chapters, later remakes of slasher films with large, Hollywood budgets testify to an attempt to appropriate the genre for conservative ideologies while at the same time desensitising the audience.

## The Return of the Imperial Gothic: The Reagan Years' *Alien* and *Aliens*

Despite the innumerable sequels generated by the *Friday the 13th* and *Halloween* franchises, the most influential gothic horror series spawned in the 1970s

14 Wood, 'An Introduction to the American Horror Film', 133.

remains Ridley Scott's *Alien* films, the first of which appeared in 1979. This seminal horror movie is in many ways a distillation and a reinvention of the American imperial gothic of the past 170 years. The *Alien* franchise revitalises the xenophobic, colonial, post-Darwinian and military discourse that structures much of the conservative imperial gothic but also echoes some of the critical, self-reflective concerns of texts such as *I Am Legend* and *The Body Snatchers*. Just like *Apocalypse Now* (1979), Francis Ford Coppola's Vietnam remake of Joseph Conrad's *Heart of Darkness*, it can be read as a comment on the Vietnam War and on the general commodification of human life in the wake of an increasingly cynical and militarised form of modernity.[15] While set in space, *Alien* is in every way a gothic narrative that relies upon the basic dichotomy between primitive and modernity, light and darkness, and open and labyrinthine spaces, and later imperial gothic narratives continually reference it.

The film takes place on the gigantic mining vessel and space freighter the *Nostromo*. The crew of this ship awakens to a distress call emanating from a nearby planetoid. Tracing the call to its source, the small team comes across a gigantic, stranded spaceship unlike anything they or the ship's computer, nicknamed Mother, have seen before. Obeying protocol, the crew send out an exploration party to locate and respond to the distress call. The slow journey into the belly of this spaceship is visually and viscerally stunning. The humans in their spacesuits are dwarfed, literally and metaphorically, by the sheer size of the technology that surrounds them. Clearly, the spacecraft they are traversing is much more advanced than the bulky and unwieldy mining vessel in which they have arrived. The penetration of the foreign vessel is in some ways a penetration of modernity itself, of the ultra-modern rather than the postmodern, of the future of technology.

At the heart of this great belly of modernity, the exploration party encounters the skeleton of an enormous extra-terrestrial strapped to what looks like a gigantic cannon that points erectly yet impotently into space. In the being's chest is a large fracture, a hole as if some strange progeny has forced itself out. Evidently, the remarkable technological and military equipment that surrounds the fossilised being has not managed to save it. Daunted but still curious, the explorers investigate a hole in the floor that leads down to an equally large and overtly gothic sublevel. This level hides the utterly primitive and fundamentally biological organism that has caused the demise of the petrified pilot attached to the enormous gun, the alien life form that proceeds to impregnate – through a form of oral rape performed by insect-like face-huggers – and invade the small group of humans aboard the *Nostromo*. After the half-formed foetus has made its bloody escape from the belly of the impregnated human, it grows quickly in

15 Also like Coppola's film, *Alien* references Conrad in various ways, the most obvious being the name of the space ship *Nostromo*, the name of a 1904 novel by Conrad.

the spaceship's dark corners. Fully adult, it kills with the help of a long, toothed appendage that can be extended from its mouth; all humans are female to the alien's primitive and utterly virile body.

This is the sort of story that would have coalesced into an orgy of regenerative, military violence during the 1950s. However, the constant sexual references that inform the alien, designed by surrealist H.R. Giger, and the fact that the multinational company that the crew works for wants to harness the alien's weaponised anatomy, makes the creature into something of a floating signifier. The black and violent alien does manifest as a black, repressed, voracious subaltern Other but also as male sexual violence. It's abject, hostile and overtly sexualised body may call for male, regenerative violence, but the film never supplies it. The homemade flamethrowers (certainly a Vietnam War reference) with which the ship's crew attempts to fight the alien have little effect. As in *The Texas Chain Saw Massacre*, it is impossible to exorcise the carnivorous Other through violence, and, as in this movie, the one survivor of the film is a young woman. In the final scenes of the movie, the alien dies almost by accident, by climbing into the boosters of the escape pod just before the heroine ignites them.

The fact that the first *Alien* movie does not tell the story of a decisive and creatively violent male who can meet the challenge that the monster, as a representative of an ultra-primitive, ultra-male and extremely competitive species, constitutes, marks *Alien* as indeed an introverted form of imperial gothic. It is not that violence is ineffective against the alien. Indeed, like the Indians in *Edgar Huntly*, violence is the only language with which it is possible to communicate with this species. The problem is that there is nobody aboard the ship capable of practising this violence. This is a horror from which the humans can only escape. In addition to this, the crew discovers that they too are merely expendable cogs in the machinery of the company for which they work. Like *The Texas Chain Saw Massacre*, then, the film leaves the audience with a feeling of uncertainty and ideological instability.

This changes with James Cameron's 1986 sequel *Aliens*. In this movie, the company who owned the mining ship on which Ripley works has colonised the planetoid where the crew of the first film encountered the face-hugger that evolved into the original alien. Now, the company is having problems with the natives and the solution is, this time, to send in the cavalry. Tim Blackmore has argued that Cameron's film is essentially 'a war film about Vietnam … and colonialism'.[16] As in *Alien*, there is room for a critical reading of these enterprises as the company is still trying to harvest the aliens at the expense of the humans that fight them. However, the heroes of Cameron's *Aliens* are the

16 Tim Blackmore, '"Is This Going to Be Another Bug-Hunt?": S-F Tradition versus Biology-as-Destiny in James Cameron's *Aliens*', *Journal of Popular Culture* 29, no. 4 (1996): 211–26 at 211.

brave marines and the military hardware they command. In many ways, this film reinstates the military solution as the only way to come to terms with the gothic Other. Unlike *Alien*, the threat is imagined not as a single individual impervious to regenerative violence but as a black, writhing and relentless horde that must be met with constant gunfire. Together with Ripley, the audience learns how to operate the complex military machinery that is surprisingly effective against the alien monsters and offers the main characters a way to temporarily resist the invasion. The final solution is, with a nod to the monster movies of the 1950s perhaps, a nuclear explosion.

The two *Alien* movies take the gothic out of the still radical 1970s into Ronald Reagan's 1980s. As Sharrett has suggested, the horror film of this era is often characterised by a neoconservative discourse that rewrites and reimagines the provocative narratives of the previous decades. This gothic is fundamentally nostalgic and imperial and either avoids the gory and nihilistic images introduced by the splatter genre or frames this violence within narratives that seek to reinforce the binaries that the horror movies of the late 1960s and 1970s attempted to query.

A useful example of the type of film that avoids the nihilism of the 1970s is Steven Spielberg and George Lucas's utterly nostalgic *Raiders of the Lost Ark* (1981). This film, further discussed in Chapter 6, is perhaps the most obvious reincarnation of the traditional, Orientalist British imperial gothic to be produced in Hollywood since the 1940s.[17] Examples of movies that transform the violence explored by previous horror include the *Predator* movies (1987, 1990), *The Silence of the Lambs* (1991), *Bram Stoker's Dracula* (1992), and *I Know What You Did Last Summer* (1997), films that are, Sharrett argues 'emblematic of capital's ongoing attempts at refurbishing its democratic façade by acknowledging the cynicism of the population while simultaneously emphasizing an ersatz liberalism, and by making use of a variety of progressive discourses current in academe that inevitably appear transmuted within the commercial entertainment industry'.[18]

Sharrett's observation is important. These horror narratives commented on a shifting societal climate where the US is transformed into hyperpower while at the same time becoming increasingly conscious of this new central position. With the nomination of Mikhail Gorbachev as general secretary of the Communist Party in 1985, the era of *Perestroika* and *Glasnost* was initiated, leading in 1989 to the fall of the Berlin Wall and the dissolution of the Soviet State.[19] The

17 This film is also an example of the third generation of Holocaust depiction, as described by James Berger, a type of depiction that explores the war and its horrors in the form of entertainment.

18 Sharrett, 'The Horror Film', 254.

19 An important preliminary to this transformation was the 1979–1989 war in Afghanistan during which the US lent significant financial and military support to the mujahedin that resisted the Soviet invasion. In the revels that followed Soviet withdrawal not only from Afghanistan but also from most of Eastern Europe, Afghanistan was largely forgotten.

US appeared, in Madeleine Albright's words, the 'indispensable nation', seeing further and understanding better than other nations, slowly but surely realising their manifest destiny. With the fall of the 'evil empire' as Reagan had termed the Soviet Union, the US seemed to have an opportunity to make the American way of life, their ideals of democracy and individual freedom into permanent global ideals. In the influential essay 'The End of History' from 1989, Francis Fukuyama even suggested that the liberal democracy that the US appeared to champion was the final stage in the evolution of human government.[20]

Yet the years that followed were often as fraught with conflict as the preceding period. The US attempt to help accelerate global liberalisation and consolidate their command of global natural resources led to a series of conflicts that, even when successfully concluded, as in the case of the first Persian Gulf War, led to much anti-American sentiment. Already, on 26 February 1993, the first World Trade Center bombing planned and executed by al-Qaeda took place. While the plan to topple one tower into the other failed, it did show that the US was not as invulnerable, or as universally popular, as was imagined after the end of the Cold War. The bloody Battle of Mogadishu between US Rangers (represented by a series of narratives known as *Black Hawk Down*) and local warlords in Somalia on 3–4 October the same year was another confrontation that further challenged the notion that the US was capable of policing the world and ensuring order. Also, the Waco Siege of 1993 and the 1995 Oklahoma City bombing suggested that the US was itself still a divided and vulnerable nation.

In this way, the closing years of the second millennium can be described as a period of increasing apprehension regarding the global role and stability of American power and society. Sarah Dunant and Roy Porter termed this era *The Age of Anxiety* in a book from 1996, arguing that '[as] we inch closer to a dark new millennium, anxieties rise. The sense of progress and promise that prevailed so powerfully in the 1960s has been replaced by a nervous pessimism, centering chiefly around uncertain realities – economic, political, environmental'.[21] Out of this anxiety grew increasingly assertive projects that looked back to the Cold War as an era of moral clarity. A number of neoconservative political organisations, headed by the Project for a New American Century (PNAC), clamoured for a much more aggressive foreign policy, one that would ensure lasting American global dominance in the face of future challenges.[22]

It is against these sentiments and against the very real US bid for global control that the neoconservative horror narrative of the end of the millennium needs to be understood. If the role of Self and Other were reversed in the late 1960s and 1970s, so that the monster of ideological progression (the civil rights

20 See Francis Fukuyama, 'The End of History?', *The National Interest* 16, no. 3 (1989): 3–18.

21 Sarah Dunant and Roy Porter, *The Age of Anxiety* (London: Virago, 1996), 1.

22 See Chapter 8 for a discussion of the PNAC.

champion, the hippie) is suddenly the hero beleaguered by the violent terror of modernity (the hungry, white middle-class zombie, the chainsaw-wielding cannibalistic capitalist), the old roles are surreptitiously restored during the 1980s and 1990s. The hero once again becomes an agent of modernity who, gun in hand, is capable of restoring order by putting bullets into the invasive Other. The victims of slasher narratives become increasingly combative; the heroes of gothic science fiction tales increasingly well armed.

## Setting the Stage for the Twenty-first Century

The final few decades of the twentieth century were as ambiguous as the gothic culture that they produced. This was a period of virtually constant economic decline as argued by world-systems scholars. Yet it was also a period during which the US perceived itself as finally victorious in its global struggle against communism, and when the kind of liberal democracy that the US saw itself the foremost champion of was perceived to become a global ideal. The time of US hegemonic decline was also the moment at which the US fully assumed global leadership.

The imperial gothic of this period traces both of these movements. It metaphorically recognises the ruthlessness with which the US asserted its power in Asia during the final years of the 1970s and points to the moral void that this ruthlessness opened. The gore and sadism that saturates the American horror film of the 1970s gives it a positively apocalyptic dimension. It is not the primitive subaltern that threatens to throw the world into chaos but the voracious nature of modernity itself. At the same time, the exploration of increasingly more extreme violence is capable of encouraging identification with the perpetrator rather than with the victim.

However, as American power grew increasingly more assertive, even as its relative economic power declined, the American imperial gothic also grew more conservative. The horror, slasher and gore films as well as the gothic science fiction movies of the 1980s and 1990s began policing the borders that the gothic culture of the 1970s had attempted to dissolve. In the neoconservative horror movie, Leatherface takes off his suit and becomes yet another primitive redneck. The bodies of the sleek black aliens are shredded by automatic fire. Gender and race are disciplined by countless slasher movies where the promiscuous female and the solitary black friend are the first to succumb to the murderous intent of the villain. The sense of apocalypse remains in these narratives, even the feeling that the human species is under threat, but sticking to the tenets of American society – freedom, democracy, chastity and the right to resolve disputes with guns – may still supply a form of salvation. The stage has been set for the cataclysmic events, and the imperial gothic, of the twenty-first century.

# Chapter 6
# 11 September and the Gothic War on Terror

> This is a war where we're fighting tough people, smart killers, who hide in dark caves or who kind of slither into shadowy recesses in large cities and parts of the world and then send youngsters to their suicidal death.[1]

It has been pointed out that New York skies were clear and tranquil on the morning of 11 September 2001.[2] The US had survived the millennium and a very close and complicated presidential election. Head of the US state was born-again Christian George W. Bush, son of George Bush who took the US to war in the Persian Gulf in 1990–91. During the election campaign, Bush had promised to focus on domestic issues rather than intervene in global developments. During the first few months of his presidency, Bush had engineered a massive, 10-year tax cut in an attempt to stimulate the waning economy, and in the summer of 2001, he had sent 43 million dollars, rather than missile strikes, to the Taliban regime in humanitarian aid and to award their efforts to curb poppy farming in Afghanistan.[3] The US was certainly still in the grip of an age of anxiety, but that clear sky did not testify to it. The attacks that followed seemed to many as inexplicable as lightning from that blue sky, acts of terror not only terrible but also illogical and incomprehensible. Television images from New York streets showed distraught people looking towards Manhattan where the towers were burning, shouting the crucial question: 'Why?'

This is still a good question. Unfortunately, in the immediate aftermath of the attack it received few good answers. The tendency of media and of official channels was to mobilise a rhetoric insisting on absolute political, moral and religious boundaries. This was a conflict between good and evil, between modernity and

1 George W. Bush, 'Remarks to the Community in South Bend, Indiana September 5, 2002' in *Public Papers of the Presidents of the United States: GEORGE W. BUSH (2002, Book II)* (Washington, DC: United States Government Printing Office, 2002b), 1547. http://www.gpo.gov/fdsys/pkg/PPP-2002-book2/pdf/PPP-2002-book2.pdf.

2 'Blue: What Everyone Would Remember First', *New York Magazine*, August 27, 2011, http://nymag.com/news/9-11/10th-anniversary/blue-sky/.

3 Elise Labott, 'U.S. Gives $43 Million to Afghanistan', CNN, May 17, 2001, http://articles.cnn.com/2001-05-17/us/us.afghanistan.aid_1_ban-on-poppy-cultivation-afghanistan-afghan-refugees?_s=PM:US.

barbarity, between democracy and fanaticism. With little experience or interest in foreign policy, and with no definite knowledge of who had actually engineered the attack, Bush simply repeated these arguments, saying that 'America was targeted for attack because we're the brightest beacon for freedom and opportunity in the world. And no one will keep that light from shining.'[4]

As evidence pointed increasingly towards an enemy outside American borders, the rhetoric became more inflamed. The attack became a moment when 'war was declared on the United States of America', a war initiated by a 'group of barbarians'[5] who 'can't stand freedom'.[6] As days progressed, the official rhetoric and the media's image deteriorated even further. In an often-discussed press conference held on 17 September, Bush enforced the notion that this was not a political conflict but a battle between good and evil, and he also envisioned this conflict as a 'long-term battle–war' with no end in sight.[7] When asked about bin Laden specifically, this long-term battle–war reshaped into a nostalgic frontier confrontation: 'I just remember – all I'm doing is remembering – when I was a kid, I remember that they used to put out there, in the Old West, a wanted poster. It said, "Wanted: Dead or Alive." All I want – and America wants him brought to justice. That's what we want.'[8] While this rambling and confusing statement makes little sense as foreign policy, it signals a reliance upon the binaries of the same frontier myth, and the same lynch law, as structured the imperial gothic of the nineteenth and early twentieth

---

4 George W. Bush, 'Address to the Nation on the Terrorist Attacks September 11, 2001' in *Public Papers of the Presidents of the United States: GEORGE W. BUSH (2001, Book II)* (Washington, DC: United States Government Printing Office, 2001b), 1099. http://www.gpo.gov/fdsys/pkg/PPP-2001-book2/pdf/PPP-2001-book2.pdf.

5 George W. Bush, 'Remarks in a Meeting with the National Security Team and an Exchange with Reporters at Camp David, Maryland September 15, 2001' in *Public Papers of the Presidents of the United States: GEORGE W. BUSH (2001, Book II)* (Washington, DC: United States Government Printing Office, 2001d), 1113. http://www.gpo.gov/fdsys/pkg/PPP-2001-book2/pdf/PPP-2001-book2.pdf.

6 George W. Bush, 'Remarks on Arrival at the White House and an Exchange with Reporters September 16, 2001' in *Public Papers of the President of the United States. George W. Bush (2001, Book II)* (Washington, DC: United States Government Printing Office, 2001e), 1116. http://www.gpo.gov/fdsys/pkg/PPP-2001-book2/pdf/PPP-2001-book2.pdf.

7 As Peter Singer points out in *The President of Good and Evil: The Ethics of George W. Bush* (New York: Dutton, 2004), Bush invoked the notions of good and evil more often than any other president 'in living memory' (p. 1). A quick look at his first four years reveals that Bush 'has spoken about evil in 319 separate speeches, or about 30 percent of all the speeches he gave between the time he took office and June 16, 2003. In these speeches he uses the word "evil" as a noun far more often than he uses it as an adjective – 914 noun uses as against 182 adjectival uses' (p. 2).

8 George W. Bush, 'Remarks to Employees in the Pentagon and an Exchange with Reporters in Arlington, Virginia September 17, 2001' in *Public Papers of the Presidents of the United States: GEORGE W. BUSH (2001, Book II)* (Washington, DC: United States Government Printing Office, 2001f), 1120. http://www.gpo.gov/fdsys/pkg/PPP-2001-book2/pdf/PPP-2001-book2.pdf.

centuries. The 'coalition against terrorism' that Bush loosely organised became a wildly potent Wild West posse. 'From the ashes of September 11, arise the manly virtues', as the *Wall Street Journal* declared on 21 September.[9]

Susan Faludi has studied the emergence and proliferation of this frontier myth in great detail, noting that even Ground Zero became the site of a frontier struggle. The image of an inevitable confrontation, the 'battle–war', Faludi convincingly argues, sprang from the captivity narrative:

> Our cultural response to 9/11 brought into play many forces disinterred from our distant past. Prominent among them was a renewed subscription to an abiding American security myth that has its roots in the captivity narrative of our earliest national experience. The kinship between that myth and our reflexive reaction to the 2001 terrorist attacks is apparent in the genetic code shared by both. After September 11, our recovery passed through a series of phases that uncannily recapitulated the metamorphosis of captivity literature into the comforting myth of American impregnability.[10]

This chapter first discusses how the frontier metaphor saturated much political and historical writing at the time but then makes the point that it was not to the western that readers, moviegoers and gamers turned in the years that followed. Instead, the predominant genre of the post-9/11 era is the imperial gothic. Of course, the imperial gothic builds on the same frontier mythology as the western. The difference is that it raises the stakes by depicting the Other that inhabits the frontier space as not only a primitive barbarian but also a gothic and monstrous creature. As I will argue, to bring this image of monstrous evil across, the imperial gothic frontier narrative is often fused with the looming threat of the Nazi.

This chapter initially focuses on the political rhetoric of this period rather than on specific narratives produced at the time. It argues that this rhetoric, as evinced in public statements, in media and in culture, revolves around images popularised by the imperial gothic and observes that these images are crucial to shore up support for the War on Terror. It is not until a year or two after the attacks that imperial gothic culture has had time to digest the events of 9/11 and Bush's violent response to them. This chapter discusses one such response, the Hollywood adaptation of *The League of Extraordinary Gentlemen* (2003), and places it in relation to both the long heritage of the imperial gothic and to the political and historical development after 9/11.

---

9 Faludi, *The Terror Dream*, 4. In the same newspaper, Robert Kaplan noted after the invasion of Iraq that the 'overlooked truth about the war on terrorism' is that 'the American military is back to the days of fighting the Indians'. See Robert D. Kaplan, 'Indian Country', *Wall Street Journal*, September 21, 2004, http://online.wsj.com/article/0,,SB109572689960923141,00.html.

10 Faludi, *The Terror Dream*, 215.

## The War on Terror

When the Bush administration launched its countermeasure to the attacks, they termed it not the 'war on terrorism' but, significantly, the 'War on Terror'. Bush first described this war as intangible and clandestine, suggesting on 15 September that it 'will be a different kind of conflict against a different kind of enemy. This is a conflict without battlefields or beachheads, a conflict with opponents who believe they are invisible.'[11] This is a description of a war that no American can be expected to fully understand but which all can somehow comprehend. As George Lakoff has observed, the choice of the term 'war' in this phrase evokes:

> the idea that the nation is under military attack – an attack that can only be defended militarily, by use of armies, planes, bombs, and so on. The war frame includes special war powers for the president, who becomes commander in chief. It evokes unquestioned patriotism, and the idea that lack of support for the war effort is treasonous. It forces Congress to give unlimited powers to the President, lest detractors be called unpatriotic.[12]

Even more crucial from the perspective of this study is the notion that this war is not waged against particular terrorists or even against the practice of terrorism but against Terror itself.[13] As Lakoff argues, terror 'names not a nation or even people, but an emotion and the acts that create it. A "war on terror" can only be metaphorical. Terror cannot be destroyed by weapons or by signing a peace treaty. A war on terror has no end.'[14] This observation is important for several

11 George W. Bush, 'The President's Radio Address September 15, 2001' in *Public Papers of the Presidents of the United States: GEORGE W. BUSH (2001, Book II)* (Washington, DC: United States Government Printing Office, 2001c), 1113. http://www.gpo.gov/fdsys/pkg/PPP-2001-book2/pdf/PPP-2001-book2.pdf.

12 George Lakoff, 'War on Terror, Rest in Peace', *AlterNet*, July 31, 2005, http://www.alternet.org/story/23810/war_on_terror,_rest_in_peace.

13 It should be observed here that the gothic has often been considered a literature of 'terror' rather than of 'horror'. Terror, here, is understood as an emotion of dread in anticipation of a horrific experience. This is part of the appeal of terror. Botting has argued that terror 'marks the uplifting thrill' like 'the dilation of the pupil in moments of excitement and fear', while 'horror distinguishes a contraction at the imminence and unavoidability of the threat'. Botting, *Gothic*, 10. While critics such as Dani Cavallo have argued that the gothic achieves its effect through horror as well as terror, this separation between the two emotions is telling in this instance. In view of this discussion, what Bush claims his war is going to combat is not terrorism or the horror produced by terrorist action but instead the anticipation of terrorist horror. At the same time, the perceived need for a long-term War on Terror can be said to create a climate of fear where the entire world reshapes into a gothic castle.

14 Lakoff, 'War on Terror'.

reasons. The concept of a 'war on terror' sanitises the notion of perpetual military conflict, obscures the very real political motives behind the terrorist attacks and the US response, and – most importantly for this particular study – it encourages an understanding of American foreign policy as being structured by the same binaries and tropes as those informing the imperial gothic. As Richard Devetak observed in 2005, 'a particular type of international relations narrative has emerged with greater distinction after the traumatic experience of September 11: the gothic narrative'.[15]

The War on Terror was the cornerstone that Bush's post-9/11 international relations narrative came to rest on. It became what Lakoff has termed a 'metaphor we live by', an image that pervades our understanding of the world to such an extent that it eventually becomes part of it.[16] This metaphor was furthermore fuelled from the very beginning by the already existing and fundamentally imperial gothic narrative that insisted that dark and dangerous beings always seek to topple civilisation and that they must be resisted through the application of military violence.[17] In this way, the War on Terror both justified and enabled the very material and violent acts of power that were conducted in its name. Cast in a more Foucauldian terminology, the concept of the War on Terror encouraged and legitimised the discursive and material demolition of any insurrective politics or project. Thus, the War on Terror was not just a metaphor, of course, it quickly became also a military practice.

## Representing the Horrors of 9/11 and the War on Terror

To move from Bush's declaration of a War on Terror to the representation of this war in media and culture, the first reaction to 9/11 was similar to the first reaction to the horrors of the Holocaust: the impossibility of representing it. The burning of several thousand people who had been quietly pursuing their jobs in the Twin Towers of Manhattan, the smoke and ash that covered the island, the people jumping from the burning architecture, the trauma of it all,

15 Richard Devetak, 'The Gothic Scene of International Relations: Ghosts, Monsters, Terror and the Sublime after September 11', *Review of International Studies* 31, no. 4 (2005): 621–43 at 621.

16 See George Lakoff and Mark Johnson, *Metaphors We Live By* (Chicago: The University of Chicago Press, 1980).

17 This does not mean that the War on Terror constituted or constitutes an inescapable ideological vortex, a master discourse that determines everything. Many were and certainly are capable of deconstructing Bush's binary politics as it appears in his speeches or in the imperial gothic. In fact, this book is in itself an intervention that aims to enlarge that pre-existing discursive space where the ideology, cultures and practices of American imperialism are critiqued. In addition to this, as I will discuss in subsequent chapters, many gothic texts are discordant and temper their patriotic zeal with a concurrent critique of the American imperial project.

seemed impossible to depict properly. In *The New Yorker*, film critic Anthony Lane argued in an article named 'This Is Not a Movie' that 'Hollywood should no longer try to match' the circumstances of 9/11.[18] The very real horror of 9/11 was at the same time too public and horrific and too private and traumatic to allow for mediation. To some, this entailed the (temporary) demise of the horror film as such. As Aviva Briefel and Sam J. Miller observe in their introduction to *Horror after 9/11*, the question was asked:

> How could American audiences, after tasting real horror, want to consume images of violence on-screen? The omnipresent posttraumatic response of 'it was like a movie' seemed to herald the death of a genre that would either remind viewers of catastrophes they wanted to forget or pale in comparison to the terrors of the real thing.[19]

If many called for the end of representation in the immediate aftermath of 9/11, the Bush government wanted to direct it as the War on Terror grew into a large-scale invasion during the month of October 2001. There was little doubt that culture would play a major role in the years ahead and that a prolonged War on Terror could not be funded and fought without the popular support engineered, in particular, by Hollywood. In other words, what Lane had stressed was not a movie had to become one, and it needed direction from the White House. To aid in this enterprise, Bush adviser Karl Rove did what Roosevelt had done in 1942 and called Hollywood to a meeting. On 11 November 2001, Rove convened with more than 40 of the Hollywood elite at the Beverly Peninsula Hotel in Beverly Hills. When asked about the meeting, Rove stressed that the purpose was not to ask Hollywood to begin censoring entertainment or to produce propaganda. Instead, the idea was to guide entertainment in the same way as had been done during World War II. This included the idea that the invasion of Afghanistan was not a war against Islam (despite Bush's unfortunate reference to a 'crusade' in one of his speeches), but rather against 'evil'. Bryce Zabel, then CEO of the Academy of Television Arts and Sciences, attended the meeting and said that '[t]he word I like is advocacy. We are willing to volunteer to become advocates for the American message.'[20]

However, Rove's invitation was not readily accepted. As Terence McSweeney observed some years later, 'Hollywood initially refused to explore the turbulent political aftermath of the destruction of the Twin Towers in New York

18 Anthony Lane, 'This Is Not a Movie', *The New Yorker*, September 24, 2001, 79–80.

19 Aviva Briefel and Sam J. Miller, 'Introduction' in *Horror after 9/11: World of Fear, Cinema of Terror*, edited by Aviva Briefel and Sam J. Miller (Austin: University of Texas Press, 2011), 1.

20 Marc Cooper, 'Lights! Cameras! Attack! Hollywood Enlists', *The Nation*, November 21, 2001, http://www.thenation.com/article/lights-cameras-attack-hollywood-enlists#.

directly.'[21] It was not until early 2002 that tentative attempts at representation beyond the documentary were made. Such attempts included special edition comic books such as *9–11: Artists Respond*, where well-known comic book artists memorialise, rather than represent, the events of the day. Some films that had had their release dates pushed forward as a result of the attack, such as the Arnold Schwarzenegger feature *Collateral Damage*, premiered in edited form to relatively small audiences. While Bush had called upon consumerism as a way to dispel the national crisis, it seemed difficult, or indeed immoral, to make a buck off 9/11.

When major Hollywood films arrived that attempted to openly engage with 9/11, such as Paul Greengrass's *United 93* (2006) and Oliver Stone's *World Trade Center* (2006), they resisted the neo-conservative attitudes of the Bush government. Films that focused on the War on Terror, meanwhile, emphatically did not agree with the state-sanctioned agenda. Thus, *Rendition* (2007), *In the Valley of Elah* (2007), *The Hurt Locker* (2008), *The Men Who Stare at Goats* (2009) and *Green Zone* (2010) portray the War on Terror as, at best, a confused and largely failed attempt to wreak vengeance and protect the American way of life and, at worst, as a criminal and inept grab for the resources of the Middle East – or even a terrorist action in its own right.

The reluctance of these and many other films to depict a clear-cut battle between good Americans and evil Islamic terrorists caused consternation in pro-war media. Struck by this reluctance, Michael Fumento declared in *The New York Sun* in 2007 that 'Hollywood truly has declared war on the global war on terror.'[22] Similarly, Andrew Klavan complained in *The Wall Street Journal* in 2008 that the 'direct and realistic' (and financially unsuccessful) films of 'left-wingers', 'preach moral equivalence and advocate surrender', and that they thereby 'disrespect the military and their mission'.[23]

At the same time, there was a set of narratives comprising a wide range of media that already did support the notion of good and evil as Bush described it and which cast the confrontation between these two entities as a violent battle. As McSweeney argues, 'a diverse range of films tackled these issues through subtext and allegory'.[24] In many cases, these films were imperial gothic fantasies, something Klavan notes in his article when he asks why:

21 Terence McSweeney, 'The Land of the Dead and the Home of the Brave: Romero's Vision of a Post-9/11 America' in *Reframing 9/11: Film, Popular Culture and the 'War on Terror'*, edited by Jeff Birkenstein, Anna Froula and Karen Randell (New York: Continuum, 2010), 107.

22 Michael Fumento, 'Hollywood Goes to War', *New York Sun*, October 25, 2007, http://www.nysun.com/opinion/hollywood-goes-to-war/65253/.

23 Andrew Klavan, 'What Bush and Batman Have in Common', *The Wall Street Journal*, July 25, 2008, http://online.wsj.com/article/SB121694247343482821.html.

24 McSweeney, 'The Land of the Dead', 107.

> Hollywood conservatives have to put on a mask in order to speak what they know to be the truth? Why is it, indeed, that the conservative values that power our defense – values like morality, faith, self-sacrifice and the nobility of fighting for the right – only appear in fantasy or comic-inspired films like '300,' 'Lord of the Rings,' 'Narnia,' 'Spiderman 3' and now 'The Dark Knight'? [25]

Klavan's turn to the imperial gothic here for the kind of moral stance he considers patriotic is important. I have described the imperial gothic as an ideologically problematic mode capable of expressing a variety of discordant positions.[26] From Klavan's observation, it seems that the period after 9/11 encouraged a conservative form of imperial gothic, a gothic that centres on a confrontation between civilisation and 'evil' in its most basic meaning, and which engages in a process of displacement and forgetting of the actual, complex political, ideological and moral stakes. Zack Snyder's *300* can comment upon the invasion of Iraq and Afghanistan without having to engage in a discussion regarding, for instance, US support for Israel or for India in the Kashmir conflict, US dependency on oil from the Middle East and its role in North and East Africa. Similarly, Christopher Nolan's *The Dark Knight* (2008) has no need to review several hundreds of years of European colonialism in the Middle East or in Africa. The displacement of these historical and political vectors allowed for the basic binaries of good and evil that inform these gothic stories to remain intact. It is arguably this that makes the imperial gothic into a useful vehicle for 'Hollywood conservatives' and for the discourses they champion.

As I will discuss, the imperial gothic did indeed turn increasingly conservative during this period. While there were certainly gothic horror movies that queried the War on Terror during the first few years after 9/11, many imperial gothic narratives continued the conservative tradition of the 1980s and 1990s. This will be one of the most important foci of this and the following chapters.

## The New Imperial Gothic in 2001 – Think about the Nazis

The renaming of a confrontation between US geopolitical interests and Islamic extremist terrorism into a conflict between good and evil, freedom and totalitarianism that the Bush administration undertook in late 2001 can be viewed as a form of ideological and political remapping that is endemic of the imperial gothic. As I have argued, the imperial gothic during this period encouraged a

25 Klavan, 'What Bush and Batman'.

26 Of course, it can be argued that some of these films do not celebrate the Bush and the War on Terror in the ways that Klavan takes for granted.

dismissal of the political issues and gothicises the actual geopolitical stakes into simple binaries of unquestioned good and terrible evil.

In this way, even films produced and edited before the events of 9/11 could somehow be seen as commenting on the current conflict as long as they pitted monstrous evil against the power of some white, Western authority. The two top-grossing films released in 2001 were *Harry Potter and the Sorcerer's Stone* and *The Lord of the Rings: The Fellowship of the Ring*. Both are notably gothic in terms of plot and iconography, featuring relentlessly evil villains whose monstrous and terrible armies must eventually be violently confronted by eerily white champions against the backdrop of dark and forbidding forests and soaring gothic architecture. The sixth best grossing film of the year was Stephen Sommers's *The Mummy Returns*, a movie that is in many ways a reincarnation of the British (Egyptian) imperial gothic of the late-Victorian period with an American hero inserted to boost the movie's appeal.

In these films, terror takes the faces of Voldemort, of Sauron and of the Egyptian mummy Imhotep.[27] However, when Bush wanted to somehow ground the image of sheer evil that his rhetoric rests upon he turned not to Hogwarts or to Middle Earth but instead to the Nazis. Bush made this connection only a few days after the attacks, arguing that the terrorists of al-Qaeda are 'the heirs of all the murderous ideologies of the twentieth century. By sacrificing human life to serve their radical visions, by abandoning every value except the will to power, they follow in the path of fascism and nazism and totalitarianism.'[28] This is certainly an example of the rhetorical strategy Leo Strauss has termed 'Reductio ad Hitlerum', and Bush was not the only one to resort to it. Only days before the invasion of Afghanistan was initiated, the award winning television series *West Wing*, set in the White House, aired their widely discussed 9/11-episode 'Isaac and Ishmael'. While this show provided a more complex understanding of the terrorist attacks than the Bush government ever did, it resorted to the same kind of political comparison, asking its audience to, 'When you think of Afghanistan, think of Poland. When you think of the Taliban, think of the

27 The connection between bin Laden and al-Qaeda and these villains has been made explicit in a number of different ways in popular media. See Gregg Kilday, 'Eerie Links between "Harry Potter," Osama bin Laden: Why Movie May Benefit', *Hollywood Reporter*, May 2, 2011, http://www.hollywoodreporter.com/news/eerie-links-between-harry-potter-184109; Lynnette R. Porter, *Unsung Heroes from the Lord of the Rings: From the Page to the Screen* (Westport: Greenwood Publishing, 2005), xii.

28 George W. Bush, 'Address before a Joint Session of the Congress on the United States Response to the Terrorist Attacks of September 11 September 20, 2001' in *Public Papers of the Presidents of the United States: GEORGE W. BUSH (2001, Book II)* (Washington, DC: United States Government Printing Office, 2001g), 1142. http://www.gpo.gov/fdsys/pkg/PPP-2001-book2/pdf/PPP-2001-book2.pdf.

Nazis. When you think of the citizens of Afghanistan, think of the Jews in concentration camps.'[29]

From a historical perspective, this comparison makes very limited sense. As totalitarian as the Taliban regime was at the time, there are numerous examples from history that are a better fit. In this way, to ask the American people to think about the Nazis when they think about the Taliban is (again) a request to disregard the historical specificity of the Taliban in favour of metaphor. At the same time, the comparison between the Taliban and Nazi Germany also makes the Taliban appear as expansive: a 'Fourth Reich' or a new Ottoman Empire. If the Taliban are like the Nazis, their intention must be to dominate. If Afghanistan is Poland, the next step is the rest of the Middle East and then the world. In this way, 9/11 takes shape not as an act of vengeance and anger, the obscene gesture of a group of reasonably well-organised and well-funded fanatics, but as a first step towards a new global hegemony. The obvious answer to such ambitions is the pre-emptive and punitive war that Bush launched in October 2001.

To return focus to the imperial gothic, it should be noted that the Nazi era had been thoroughly gothicised in popular culture by 2001. This process began with the aforementioned 'third generation' of Holocaust fiction as described by James Berger,[30] a generation that not only wrote about the events but also began to explore the connection between occultism and Nazism.[31] As the utter horror of the extermination camps faded, this connection was investigated by Dennis Wheatley's *They Used Dark Forces* (1964), Trevor Ravenscroft's *The Spear of Destiny* (1973) and James Herbert's *The Spear* (1978).[32] These texts form much of the background for Spielberg's and Lucas's nostalgic *Raiders of the Lost Ark* (1981), the first instalment of the enduring *Indiana Jones* franchise. In *Raiders of the Lost Ark*, Nazis pursue the Ark of the Covenant but are terribly punished by what appears to be ghosts or angels of vengeance when they open the chest containing the stone tablets (a fate the small contingent of allied archaeologists and adventurers escape by cleverly shutting their eyes to the spectacle). These and many other narratives gothicise Nazism so that the very real, destructive and racist ideologies that informed Nazi politics become obscured by an obsession with the occult. Thus, *Raiders of the Lost Ark* is in many ways a film

29 Jack Holland, '"When You Think of the Taliban, Think of the Nazis": Teaching Americans "9/11" in NBC's *The West Wing*', *Millennium: Journal of International Studies* 40, no. 1 (2007): 85–106 at 96.

30 See Berger, *After the End*, 67.

31 Nicholas Goodrick-Clarke's *The Occult Roots of Nazism: Secret Aryan Cults and Their Influence on Nazi Ideology* (New York: New York University Press, 1985) is both an example and a useful mapping of this tradition.

32 Dennis Wheatley, *They Used Dark Forces* (London: Hutchinson, 1964); Trevor Ravenscroft, *The Spear of Destiny: The Occult Power behind the Spear Which Pierced the Side of Christ* (London: Neville Spearman, 1973); James Herbert, *The Spear* (London: New English Library, 1978).

that resurrects the gothic colonial and Orientalist attitudes that inform the works of Haggard and Buchan and combine them with the American gothic pulp and adventure films of the 1930 and 1940s.

Since *Raiders of the Lost Ark*, the connection between Nazism and the occult has informed much popular culture and a great deal of the gothic. In 1992, the seminal first-person shooter game *Castle Wolfenstein 3D* put the gamer into the shoes of an allied soldier who infiltrates a German castle during World War II and there discovers an occult programme to resurrect and weaponise the dead. In 1993, comic book artist Mike Mignola placed the Nazis within Lovecraft's Cthulhu mythos in *Hellboy*, a story that was turned into a major Hollywood movie in 2004 by Guillermo del Toro. In *Hellboy* as well as in *Raiders of the Lost Ark*, the stakes are imperial. The Nazis ally themselves with the powers of supernatural evil and chaos and seek to bring about an absolute and global reign of darkness. With the very real horrors of their actual racist politics lost in this gothic vortex, they come to symbolise evil in disturbingly uncomplicated terms.

In this way, there is, in 2001, a multitude of imperial gothic texts that describe Nazism as an occult form of evil that can be effectively combated with military violence. The insistence that the Taliban are like the Nazis then allows for a certain confusion between the two. If the Taliban are like the Nazis, fighting the Nazis is like fighting the Taliban. The form of imperial gothic that most readily allows for such an engagement is the computer game *Return to Castle Wolfenstein*, released for Microsoft Windows in late November of 2001. This computer game is essentially a remake and technical update of the 1992 game. Like *Hellboy*, the plot and iconography of the game relies heavily on Lovecraft's Cthulhu mythos. In terms of cultural engagement, however, the game is different from *Hellboy* through its performative, first-hand perspective. The gamer must literally fight his way through the combined forces of the living SS and the undead and modified 'Übersoldaten' that threaten the civilised world. Each infested game map must be cleansed through extensive military violence. As the gamer moves through the map, not unlike a pioneer that pacifies an unruly frontier space, the weapons she or he gets access to become increasingly more effective and modern. In this way, the game is also a progressively more advanced journey through modernity, from the knife that the gamer's avatar, an American Special Forces soldier, uses to kill his first guard to the Tesla gun that electrocutes all those who stand before it. At the same time, because of the connection between the Taliban and the Nazis, *Return to Castle Wolfenstein* makes it possible to engage in a War on Terror. When you think of the Taliban you can think of the Nazis, but when you think of the Nazis you can also think about the Taliban.

## Modernity and Empire

The confusion of the Taliban religious and political agenda with Nazi totalitarianism and the conflation of the Invasion of Afghanistan with World War II warfare helped the image of a general War on Terror seem sensible, even a potentially hopeful and generative enterprise. In many ways, the World War II conflict with Nazi Germany has been imagined as a crucial point in the becoming of the US. Bush made this clear in a number of speeches after 9/11. In a long remark made on 22 July 2002, Bush explained that:

> [h]istory has called each of us to defend America. That's what's happened. History has called us into action in a time of great peril. The struggles against nazism and communism helped to define the 20th century. The war on terror will be the defining conflict of the 21st century. It's our solemn duty, it's our responsibility, and it's our great privilege to help America prevail in this war.[33]

This reading of America's past and current predicament taps into the notion of manifest destiny and American exceptionalism. The Nazi comparison in particular invited Americans to imagine the clandestine spy war, the invasions of Afghanistan and Iraq, the battle against this new breed of gothic savage, as part of the new becoming of America. If the US rises to this particular occasion, there is the promise of global renewal, of an even stronger US steering the ship of liberal capitalism into an ever brighter future.

Tied to this reading of America's past and present duties is the notion that America is somehow uniquely modern. As I have suggested, the notion that modernity is always pitted against different forms of primitive darkness has a distinct imperial genealogy that imbues early American historiography as well as the imperial gothic. Bush did not invent or even reinvent the binaries that he uses to describe the nature of American power. Obviously, and perhaps naively, Bush tapped into these ready-made binaries to simplify and contain a very complex global development. However, it may be argued that Bush lent this old imperial discourse new vitality by insisting that the events of 9/11 must be understood as a conflict between US modernising endeavours and the hatred of fanatic barbarians – a conflict that evidently is best addressed through a War on Terror: 'The war on terror is not just an American war on terrorists; it's a civilized government war on terror that we're talking about here.'[34]

---

33 George W. Bush, 'Remarks at the Argonne National Laboratory in Argonne July 22, 2002' in *Public Papers of the Presidents of the United States: GEORGE W. BUSH (2002, Book II)* (Washington, DC: United States Government Printing Office, 2002a), 1281. http://www.gpo.gov/fdsys/pkg/PPP-2002-book2/pdf/PPP-2002-book2.pdf.

34 George W. Bush, 'Remarks Welcoming General Tommy R. Franks and an Exchange with Reporters in Crawford, Texas December 28, 2001' in *Public Papers of the Presidents of the United States:*

Bush studiously avoids mentioning the notion of empire in any formal speeches during the first year after 9/11.[35] It is not until November 2002, when preparing the US and the rest of the world for the invasion of Iraq, that he is finally compelled to publicly dismiss the idea that the US may have imperial inclinations: 'We have no territorial ambitions. We don't seek an empire. Our Nation is committed to freedom for ourselves and for others.' Bush concludes this anti-imperial stance by again reminding his audience of the nation's role during World War II: 'We and our allies have fought evil regimes and left in their place self-governing and prosperous nations.'[36]

As previously discussed, not everyone agrees with this clearly ahistorical reading of America's history. The liberal left, including intellectuals such as Noam Chomsky and historians such as Chalmers Johnson, had argued long before 9/11 that the US certainly had imperial ambitions. From this perspective, the events of 9/11 are best understood as a form of 'blowback' resulting from the violence with which these ambitions were pursued. That the Bush administration would disagree with Chomsky's and Johnson's analyses comes as no surprise. What is interesting is that Bush's disclaimer also clashes with statements made by the neoconservative movement to which many of his advisers adhere. In the year after 9/11, neoconservative historian Max Boot published *The Savage Wars of Peace: Small Wars and the Rise of American Power.*[37] The notion of 'Savage Wars of Peace' comes from Kipling's aforementioned poem 'White Man's Burden' and Boot's thesis is that America needs to be considered an empire that has kept the nation expanding through a long history of small-scale, para-colonial warfare. Where he differs from Chomsky and Johnson is in his adamant assertion that America has the duty and obligation to operate as imperial 'globocop'.

As early as 1999, Boot drew numerous parallels between American foreign policy and British imperialism on the pages of the neoconservative magazine

---

*GEORGE W. BUSH (2001, Book II)* (Washington, DC: United States Government Printing Office, 2001h), 1548. http://www.gpo.gov/fdsys/pkg/PPP-2001-book2/pdf/PPP-2001-book2.pdf.

35 As will be discussed in later chapters, Bush never directly embraced the notion of US empire, but his administration did award conservative historians Paul Johnson and John Lewis Gaddis the Presidential Medal of Freedom and the National Humanities Medal, respectively. Both Johnson and Gaddis have claimed that the US has the right, perhaps even the obligation, to be a liberal empire.

36 George W. Bush, 'Remarks at a White House Reception for Veterans November 11, 2002' in *Public Papers of the Presidents of the United States: GEORGE W. BUSH (2002, Book II)* (Washington, DC: United States Government Printing Office, 2002c), 2060. http://www.gpo.gov/fdsys/pkg/PPP-2002-book2/pdf/PPP-2002-book2.pdf.

37 Boot is a senior fellow at the *Council of Foreign Relations* and a regular contributor to the neoconservative *The Weekly Standard.* In 2004, the *World Affairs Councils of America* named him one of the 500 most important people in the United States in the field of foreign policy, see Donald A. Yerxa, ed., *Recent Themes in Military History: Historians in Conversation* (Columbia: University of South Carolina Press, 2008), 133.

*The Weekly Standard.* Discussing the events of the Battle of Mogadishu in 1993, Boot praised the 'bravery' and 'gallantry' of the American Rangers and Delta Force soldiers during this conflict and suggested that their remarkable heroism should recall the 'outnumbered British garrison at Rorke's Drift, which won a record eleven Victoria Crosses for holding off thousands of Zulu warriors on January 22–23, 1879'.[38] To Boot, the tragedy of Mogadishu is not the 18 dead American soldiers (and certainly not the approximately 1,000 killed or wounded Somalis) but the fact that the Somalis were not properly punished for daring to attack the US soldiers who had landed in the midst of the city: 'Any self-respecting imperial power would have exacted a terrible vengeance for the death of its soldiers, as the British did after the massacre at Isandhlwana.'[39]

On 15 October 2001, Boot argued in the same magazine not only that the 'most realistic response to terrorism is for America to embrace its imperial role' but that 'Afghanistan and other troubled lands today cry out for the sort of enlightened foreign administration once provided by self-confident Englishmen in jodhpurs and pith helmets.'[40] In addition to this, Boot began paving the way for a continued excursion into the Middle East by suggesting that the time has come to depose Saddam Hussein and turn Iraq into 'a beacon of hope for the oppressed peoples of the Middle East'. In this way, Boot envisions the same kind of nation-building project that Bush does, the manifest destiny of America extended to the rest of the world. Like Bush, he also sees the conflict as essentially one between US modernity and Taliban primitivism. Boot is very specific on this point, describing the Taliban as a number of 'homicidal mullahs driven by a hatred of modernity itself' and bin Laden as a 'holy warrior who rejects the Enlightenment and all its works'.[41] However, unlike Bush he does recognise the imperial ambitions of the US, and in his view, US imperialism is the most effective agent of modernity and therefore the best countermeasure against the barbaric project upon which the Taliban has embarked.

Boot was not the only one to make this point. A number of historians and political commentators began to build bridges between the British and the American imperial contexts and to cast American empire as a salvaging, civilising, modernising and democratising force. The most prominent were the British historians Niall Ferguson and Paul Johnson. Paul Johnson argued in 2003

38 The comparison is exceedingly poor. The American soldiers invaded a densely populated part of a large city and were cut off when professional soldiers and civilians began shooting at them from the surrounding buildings. The British, by comparison, resisted an organised Zulu attack from within a rural and fortified garrison.

39 Max Boot, 'Imperial Misadventure: What Went Wrong in Somalia', *Weekly Standard*, March 28,1999,http://www.weeklystandard.com/Content/Protected/Articles/000/000/010/351llyyx.asp?page=1. It should be added that figures on the number of Somali casualties vary greatly.

40 Max Boot, 'The Case for American Empire', 23.

41 Max Boot, 'The Case for American Empire', 23.

that 'America is becoming [an Empire of Liberty] again, in fact if not in name. America's search for the security against terrorism and rogue states goes hand in hand with liberating their oppressed peoples.'[42] Similarly, Ferguson argued in *Colossus: The Price of America's Empire* (2004) that America has the potential to become a 'liberal empire – that is to say, one that not only underwrites the free international exchange of commodities, labor and capital but also creates and upholds the conditions without which markets cannot function – peace and order, the rule of law, noncorrupt administrations'.[43] As in Britain during the turn of the nineteenth century, 'imperialism' and 'empire' are concepts openly embraced and recognised as a forces capable of positively steering global development.

## Post-9/11 Imperial Gothic – *The League of Extraordinary Gentlemen*

Bush may have denied that the US had any imperial ambitions, but his description of US history, his casting of the War on Terror as a frontier battle with the forces of barbarity and his insistence that such a conflict may pave the way for a new American century belies his protestations, as both Chomsky and Boot (in agreement on this matter, if nothing else) observe. This forms the most fertile soil imaginable for the imperial gothic, a cultural mode that has often been involved in justifying spoken and unspoken imperialism. In particular, the extroverted type of imperial gothic has always been about a War on Terror. The military solution embraced by so many of the narratives belonging to this form of culture casts the confrontation between the West and terror in its many guises as precisely a military battle. The gothic Other and the terror that is associated with its presence is most effectively exorcised with the help of violence in these texts. The world of the imperial gothic, then, is typically a space where such violence is the only solution to any crisis.

To turn to imperial gothic film, 2002 is, in fact, a good year for horror and the gothic. *Eight Legged Freaks* (2002) is a semi-parodic reference to the monster movies of the 1950s and to *Tarantula* (1955) in particular. In the same year, the slasher franchises *Halloween* and *Friday the 13th* receive sequels in the form of *Halloween Resurrection* and *Jason X*, the first instalment in the action zombie franchise *Resident Evil*, Guillermo del Toro's *Blade II*, Eli Roth's *Cabin Fever*, Steve Beck's *Ghost Ship* and *The Ring*, the American version of the Japanese *Ringu*. Relevant here is also the equally retrospective Shekhar Kapur rendition of A.E.W. Mason's 1902 non-gothic, but very imperial, British adventure novel

---

42 Paul Johnson, 'From the Evil Empire to the Empire for Liberty', *The New Criterion*, June 2003, http://newcriterion.com:81/archive/21/jun03/johnson.htm.

43 Ferguson, *Colossus*, 2.

*The Four Feathers*, a story of British courage during the late nineteenth-century Madhist Sudanese uprising against British forces.[44]

Many of these can be discussed from the perspective of the imperial gothic, but the most nostalgic and most imperial of all the gothic fare that Hollywood puts out at this period is Stephen Norrington's *The League of Extraordinary Gentlemen* from 2003, a loose adaptation of a (far superior) Allan Moore comic book series by the same name. If someone did lend a sympathetic ear to Karl Rove during his briefing at the Beverly Hills hotel in November 2001, it was quite possibly Norrington. In addition to this, the scriptwriters seem to have read their Boot and Ferguson, as the movie transforms from imperial gothic romp into a story that describes the transfer of the burden of empire from British to American agents.

The movie begins with a prologue that shows one of the film's villains attempting to provoke war between Germany and Britain. Then, the audience is brought to the Kenyan countryside where Sanderson Reed of the Foreign Office is looking for H. Rider Haggard's Allan Quatermain in a lavish club house filled with black servants and very aged British adventurers. Allan Quatermain, of course, is a central character in the extroverted British imperial gothic and the hero of several of Haggard's novels, most notably *King Solomon's Mines* (1885). In the film, Quatermain is persuaded that the empire needs him, and that even the Africa he loves may be transformed by a World War. He agrees to lead a team made up of canonical characters from the British imperial gothic, including a vampiric (and now leather-clad and martial-arts trained) Mina Harker from Bram Stoker's *Dracula*, H.G. Wells's invisible man, R.L. Stevenson's Hyde/Jekyll (here in the form of a gigantic, deformed Hulk-like creature) and (oddly) Oscar Wilde's Dorian Gray.[45]

Soon, the group is joined in their efforts by Special Agent Tom Sawyer of the American Secret Service. Sawyer explains that his government also wishes to preserve world peace. The odd gathering of British gothic characters are at first reluctant to admit Sawyer as a member of their team, but Quatermain notes the American's deft handling of his weapon as well as the weapon itself, a Winchester rifle.[46] He plucks the gun from Sawyer's hands and Sawyer explains: 'It's modified, American style.' 'American-style shooting too', Quatermain concludes and Sawyer is brought into the group.

What is interesting about the movie is not its convoluted plot, which records a series of terrorist actions (half of Venice is blown up) and the creation of

44 See A.E.W. Mason, *The Four Feathers* (London: Macmillan, 1902).

45 To avoid copyright infringement, the character of the invisible man in the film is that of a thief who has stolen the invisibility potion from Wells's original story.

46 As the 'gun that won the West', Winchester is, of course, intimately associated with the frontier.

weapons of mass destruction, but more importantly the film's function as an almost formal handing over of the practice of empire from Britain to America. The parade of British gothic heroes and villains is a tribute not only to the imperial gothic but also to the British empire as provider of global stability and order. The film thus tells the story of how an aged but still vital Quatermain, willing to shoulder the white man's burden one final time, transfers this encumbrance from the British context to the American. This is told through the trope of an inheritance, symbolised by a powerful gun.

Halfway through the film, the audience discovers that Quatermain has lost his son during a mission in Africa. In the course of the movie, the young and eager Sawyer is able to step into the shoes of this lost offspring. This actual transfer of paternal affection occurs during a shooting lesson where Quatermain teaches Sawyer to shoot (the most important skill for any imperial agent). The transfer of imperial legitimacy and filial feelings is completed during the obligatory end battle. Seeing that Sawyer is likely to be killed, Quatermain sacrifices himself to save his substitute American son. To avenge the dying Quatermain, Sawyer picks up Quatermain's gun and, encouraged by his British mentor's assertion that he is 'ready', kills the villain with a shot to the back. Pleased with Sawyer's proficiency with the weapon, Quatermain's final words to his protégée are: 'May this new century be yours, son … as the old one was mine.' With these words, Quatermain transfers both his fatherly affections and the burden of empire to Sawyer's shoulders. Formally taking place in 1899, the film clearly locates the beginning of the twentieth century as the moment when the US takes up the white man's burden.

In this way, *The League of Extraordinary Gentlemen* is a modern and retrospective rewrite of Rudyard Kipling's poem 'White Man's Burden', published in 1899 at the conclusion of the Spanish–American War and the moment when the US acquires a number of formerly European colonies. *The League of Extraordinary Gentlemen* forges Anglo-Saxon ties by casting this transfer as a form of inheritance, a father passing on his birthright to his son. As in Kipling's poem, the film suggests that the maintenance of global stability requires significant personal sacrifice. This celebration of Anglo-Saxon empire is furthermore strikingly reminiscent of Boot's neoconservative assertion that the American people must accept, and perhaps even be proud of, the indisputable fact that they have become an empire.

In this way, *The League of Extraordinary Gentlemen* is a perfect vehicle for disseminating the War on Terror as imagined by the Bush administration. It historicises the US's rise to power during the turn of the nineteenth century as a form of handing over imperial power from Britain to the US. At the same time, the film is littered with references to global terrorism and insists that such terrorism can only be addressed with the help of violence.

## Towards a Renaissance of the Imperial Gothic

In 2001, the US had moved far into the era of competition and decline as described by world-systems theory. As discussed, this era is characterised both by a sense of pending decline and by the perceived need to aggressively defend the central global position of the US. Like Britain after the initial disasters of the Boer War, there is a sense that the nation is under siege, and there is also a similar turn to empire and imperialism as an antidote. Like in Britain, the imperial gothic negotiated this development and the sentiments that rose to the surface at this time. Bush's insistence that the events of 9/11 must be seen as a conflict between modernity and primitivism, a conflict that can be best resolved through a War on Terror itself, makes the imperial gothic into an increasingly central form of culture. Bush remembers the Nazis and the imperial gothic remembers the Nazis – not as a specific ideology but as an emblem of evil that, when it was destroyed by the US, enabled America to assume its current economic and military position.

As I will argue, the imperial gothic experienced a renaissance in the years that follow. The imperial gothic in both its extroverted and its introverted forms is a mode of writing capable of supporting the building of empire and the fortification of imperial borders with the help of gothic metaphor. It imagines global conflict as a Manichean struggle between good and evil and in its American guise, it typically suggests that the gothic Other must be contained through perpetual military violence. It is this structure that makes it possible also for popular culture produced prior to 9/11 to address a war that the Bush administration depoliticised into a struggle between good and evil, modernity and barbarity, progress and totalitarianism. It is this structure that makes the imperial gothic into one of the few forms of culture that can exist easily alongside the binaries with which the Bush administration explained the event of 9/11 and the war it launched in its wake.

# Chapter 7
# Afghanistan, Iraq and the New Frontiers of the Imperial Gothic

In *Exorcist: The Beginning* (2004), Father Merrin cannot shake the horrors he experienced in Holland during World War II. In the village where Merrin served, an SS soldier was shot and killed. In retribution, the local SS officer first shoots a small girl in the head and then threatens to kill everyone else present on the snowy square. However, Merrin is given the option to save most of them by instead telling the officer who he should execute. Merrin suggests himself, but the officer does not accept his sacrifice. Merrin is then made to point randomly at his congregation and watch as the officer shoots his parishioners. His faith in God shaken, Merrin has relinquished his profession and turned to the frontier science of archaeology. Based in Cairo, in British-controlled Egypt, Merrin is approached by a collector of antiquities who wants him to go to Kenya where the British are excavating an ancient Byzantine church and retrieve an ancient relic. In Africa, Merrin has to confront an ancient evil that resides in the very land itself. The church that is excavated is not an actual church but a kind of guardian relic in its own right, built on the site where Satan supposedly struck the Earth after having been hurled from heaven. Statues of warrior angels with spears line the inside of the church, their weapons directed down into the ground. Even so, evil emanates from this place and infects everyone who wanders into the vicinity. Hyenas stalk the excavation site and attack a young child in a scene that is gruesome despite the poor CGI. Diggers have seizures, the British and local tribes clash violently, and the chief archaeologist is 'touched' by the demon Pazuzu, carves a swastika into his chest and cuts his own throat.

*Exorcist: The Beginning* was one of two attempts at making a prequel to the classic horror movie *The Exorcist* from 1973.[1] The other version, *Dominion: Prequel to the Exorcist* by Paul Schrader, uses essentially the same script, was made before *Exorcist*, but was not released until 2005. Of course, both films are sequels rather than prequels in the sense that they seek to commodify the nostalgia for

---

1 *Dominion* ended up too psychological and bloodless to suit the producers who had Harlin reshoot it. It should be added that the original movie was based on a novel by the same name, written by William Peter Blatty (*The Exorcist* (New York: Harper & Row, 1971)) who then wrote the screenplay and produced the movie.

effective and yet commercially viable horror. As the US invades Iraq, and as it attempts to consolidate its command of the country, this is what a great many big-budget Hollywood movies try to do.[2] Following sequels to *Halloween*, *Friday the 13th* and *Nightmare on Elm Street* in 2002 and 2003, the big horror remake of 2003 is *The Texas Chainsaw Massacre*, an adaption that removes the critical and anti-capitalist subtext that saturated the original.[3] Gone is the reference in the beginning to the mechanised slaughter of livestock. Gone is also Leatherface's business suit; in the final scene he appears as yet another crazed Southern blue-collar redneck. It is not Leatherface, his voracious chainsaw and his cannibalistic family that represent modernity in this movie but the young and decisive woman who, in the final scenes, cuts off Leatherface's arm with a meat cleaver, runs over the corrupt sheriff with his own car and, with an untidy reference to the captivity narrative, saves a small child supposedly threatened by the inbred community. In the end, she is driving, dazed but somehow still confident, away from the mayhem. The final image is thus not, as in the original, of Leatherface, chainsaw in hand and dancing in his crumpled suit in the sunset, but of the battered heroine, driving towards dawn in the car she has appropriated. In this way, the horror remakes of the early Iraq era often adapt previous gothic and horror to the discourses that saturated the time in which they were made. Film critics are disappointed, but the audience is enthusiastic and *The Texas Chainsaw Massacre* is very successful at the box office.

To return to *The Exorcist*, the two sequels produced for 2004 are well suited to speak about the ongoing invasion since the original movie opens not in the urban, middle-class home in which most of the film is set but at an excavation site in northern Iraq. With the invasion, the entire nation is also returning there on live television in a war that is, like *Exorcist: The Beginning* or *The Texas Chainsaw Massacre*, also a remake: the Invasion of Iraq, Part 2, sequel to the Gulf War of 1990–91. *Exorcist: The Beginning* avoids being too obvious and moves the setting from Iraq to Egypt and Africa. However, the desert landscape that forms the visual backdrop is generic. This may be eastern Africa, but it might just as well be northern Iraq or Fallujah, a place where violence indeed did seem endemic in late 2003 and early 2004. This desert space is inherently evil in the two movies. Mindless violence is destined to erupt here, a violence that can only be (temporarily) kept in check by Christian intervention.

As if to hammer in the point, *Exorcist: The Beginning*, also makes the connection between evil in its Eastern guise and Nazism that permeated the immediate 9/11 understanding of the conflict between Islamic extremist terrorism and the

---

2 When Hollywood was not reinvesting in old franchises from the 1970s and 1980s, it remade Asian films such as Hideo Nakata's *Ringu* (1998).

3 The 2003 movie *Freddy vs. Jason* is a crossover film that functions as a sequel to both the *Friday the 13th* and *A Nightmare on Elm Street* franchises.

US. In addition to this, *Exorcist: The Beginning* is also and importantly a captivity narrative. At the end of the film, the beautiful, young female Holocaust survivor and physician Sarah is possessed by the demon Pazuzu. She becomes venomous and murderous. Her face grows pale, she speaks in voices and withdraws into a system of caves, retreating into the dark Earth itself. Merrin must now invade these caves in an attempt both to stop the demon and rescue Sarah's possessed mind through an on-the-fly exorcism. He succeeds and frees Sarah's body from the torment of the demon, and even though Sarah does not survive the exorcism she is thankful. It is better to die in this way than to live in a body possessed by the Other. The world needs such brave men as Merrin, those who will walk into the very heart of darkness and face the evil that resides there. Merrin then climbs out of the darkness, through the sand and the Earth that marks the boundary between the evil he has confronted and the faith he has regained.

The nostalgic and often unabashedly imperial gothic of 2003, 2004 and 2005 is full of such white men who dare to cross into the liminal frontier space of the Other to perform powerful and violent rituals of cleansing. In this way, Bush's War on Terror also becomes an expansive War on Horror in much American imperial gothic. This chapter discusses the construction of a (metaphorical) colonial frontier in the American imperial gothic and the War on Terror that must be conducted there. By focusing on two big-budget movie remakes: Stephen Sommers's *Van Helsing* (2004) and Peter Jackson's *King Kong* (2005), this chapter seeks to illustrate how the expansive movement these narratives record is reminiscent of the British imperial gothic set in Africa or Asia as well as of the frontier gothic of Burroughs and the popular culture of the 1930s and 1940s. The outward, essentially colonial movement that these forms of imperial gothic describe demands a certain form of imperial confidence. While the imperial gothic is a form of culture encouraged by imperial crisis, its extrovert forms chart the need to respond to such crisis through expansive gestures; through consolidation of imperial creeds and the actual territorial extension of imperial borders.

## Invading Iraq

The sense that the US had the ability, perhaps even the obligation, to free Iraq and turn it into a 'beacon of hope' in the Middle East was indeed dominant for a short while in the spring of 2003. The official reason for the invasion of Iraq was, of course, that the nation was still manufacturing and storing weapons of mass destruction and that it was likely to peddle these to terrorist organisations. In addition to this, Hussein himself was described as a dictatorial fiend who tortured, murdered and starved his own people. In this way, Hussein became a monster that the US had a duty to destroy not only to protect itself but, as Josh Smicker has observed, also to assist a beleaguered Iraqi people imagined to clamour for democracy and freedom.[4] Thus, the invasion was named Operation Iraqi Freedom.[5]

The lack of hard evidence that Hussein actually constituted a threat to the US meant that the invasion and occupation hinged on a rhetorical as much as on a judicial process. To take command of the image that was created by the media, the Bush government founded and made effective use of a number of institutions that were designed to manipulate public opinion. Apart from sending Karl Rove to Beverly Hills in November 2001, the Bush administration created such institution as the Pentagon's controversial Office of Strategic Influence – which employed the large public relations firm the Rendon Group[6] – and the White House's own 'Office of Global Communications' (formerly announced in January 2003 but active as early as in October 2001 in the form of the Coalition Information Center).[7]

One of the missions of these offices was to sell the notion of American democracy and enterprise in the Middle East. While this mission failed spectacularly, a carefully staged media campaign kept the American public optimistic about both the reasons for and the development of the invasion of Iraq. The media campaign and the support for the war culminated in May 2003 when Bush landed in a jet on the aircraft carrier the *USS Abraham Lincoln* in order to declare the first part of the mission accomplished. In the US, there was indeed a sense that the nation had actually completed an important and just mission and that the War on Terror, even when taking the form of a major military invasion, was truly able to address the problem of international terrorism. A number of polls have shown that during the preparatory stage of the invasion and during the initial surge, US media coverage was overwhelmingly supportive of the war.[8] While there was certainly great resistance against the US invasion also within the nation's borders, as manifested in a number of marches, public demonstrations and editorials, a well-designed PR apparatus, a partisan media and, as this book suggests, largely co-operative popular culture

4 Josh Smicker, 'Future Combat: Combating Futures' in *Joystick Soldiers: The Politics of Play in Military Video Games*, edited by Nina B. Huntemann and Matthew Thomas Payne (New York: Routledge, 2010), 118–19n.

5 In fact, in a colossal Freudian slip, the invasion was initially named Operation Iraqi Liberation, but this was changed as soon as the Bush administration realised what the acronym would be. See http://georgewbush-whitehouse.archives.gov/news/releases/2003/03/20030324-4.html.

6 Elvira Classen, 'Media Transmitted Values Transfer: The US at "War Against Terrorism" and Its Implications for the Information Society' in *Cultural Imperialism: Essays on the Political Economy of Cultural Domination*, edited by Bernd Hamm and Russell Smandych (Ontario: Broadview Press, 2005), 142–146n.

7 Julia Day, 'US Steps Up Global PR Drive', *The Guardian*, July 30, 2002, http://www.guardian.co.uk/media/2002/jul/30/marketingandpr.terrorismandthemedia.

8 http://www.fair.org/index.php?page=1145.

industries still generated an essentially supportive American audience. On the eve of the invasion, 19 March 2003, 75 per cent of all Americans were largely supportive of the war.[9] In another poll, taken 5–7 May, immediately after the Bush presentation aboard the *USS Abraham Lincoln*, 86 per cent of all people interviewed felt that things were going very well or moderately well for the US in Iraq.[10] There was certainly a sense during these spring months of 2003 that the US could use its military powers for global transformation, and that order could be brought by going abroad and destroying monsters.

## *King Kong*

This sense was recorded and disseminated in different ways by the imperial gothic. One of the most vocal, complex, expensive and financially successful movies that can be said to map the developments of this era with the aid of the imperial gothic is Peter Jackson's *King Kong* (2005). This film had been in production hell since 1997, when Jackson's *The Frighteners* did poorly in America. However, after the phenomenal success of Jackson's *The Lord of the Rings* trilogy, the film was not only green-lit in 2003 but also given one of the biggest budgets in history.[11] At 187 minutes – 201 in its extended, director's cut version – it is about twice the length of the original, 100-minute version. When making the movie, Jackson had to negotiate a number of conflicting narratives and discourses. One such discourse was obviously the 2003 invasion frenzy that saturated the US as Jackson began rewriting the original script he had penned with his wife in the mid-1990s. Other discourses to consider included the often blatant racism that permeates the original *King Kong*, as discussed in Chapter 3, and also the awkwardly revisionist remake of the movie from 1976.

The 1976 version, it should be noted, was produced in the wake of the Vietnam War and the American civil rights movement. A much more conscious and modern version of the story, this film seeks to subvert the racism latent in the original story in various ways. Set in the mid-1970s, the villain of the piece is not Kong but the cynical oil-prospecting company that has come to the island to look for natural resources. Stowaway palaeontologist Jack Prescott (Jeff Bridges) keeps telling the manager of the operation that 'This is no longer the nineteenth century, you cannot just go in and take their island' and to not fire the rifles they have brought directly at the primitive natives. Furthermore, what amounts to a sacrifice in the 1933 version is described as a marriage ceremony in

9 http://www.gallup.com/poll/1633/iraq.aspx.

10 http://www.gallup.com/poll/1633/iraq.aspx.

11 Ray Morton, *King Kong: The History of a Movie Icon from Fay Wray to Peter Jackson* (New York: Applause Theatre & Cinema Books, 2005).

the 1976 film. In many ways this is precisely what occurs when Kong eventually seizes the kidnapped white woman (named Dwan in this version) from the altar. What is typically referred to as the rape scene in the original *King Kong* is recast as an oddly tender and even mildly erotic scene as Kong carefully washes Jessica Lange under a waterfall and dries her with his warm breath. The meeting between the affectionate, smiling ape, significantly more upright and humanoid than the original Kong, and the white Dwan, seems to encourage rather than discourage inter-racial union. At the same time, of course, it posits such a union as precisely inter-racial (in fact, inter-species), in the process reinforcing absolute notions of black and white.

There are no dinosaurs and little action in the 1976 version. Apart from Kong, the only abnormally large creature is a gigantic snake with which Kong wrestles. When Kong has been captured, he is placed in the gigantic tank that the prospectors hoped to fill with oil, making Kong's status as now merely a commodity within capitalist society clear to the audience. When Kong has been transported in chains over the ocean, he is exhibited from inside a gigantic petrol pump. The ending of the movie, in which Kong climbs the newly constructed World Trade Center rather than the Empire State Building, references the Vietnam War as first soldiers with flame throwers and then military helicopters move in for the kill. Kong dies in a hail of bullets, his body riddled with wounds and bleeding profusely. In the final scene, the heterosexual union that serves as climax to the original is never accomplished; Dwan stands crying at the dead body of Kong, surrounded by photographers, but Prescott stalks angrily away.

With the 1976 remake in mind, it comes as a surprise that Jackson's 2005 version is considerably more racist and imperial than even the 1933 version and just as reliant on the British and early American twentieth-century imperial gothic.[12] The reason for this is, arguably, Jackson's nostalgic relationship to the original but, as I will return to, perhaps also the movie's reliance on Joseph Conrad's complex novella *Heart of Darkness*. Jackson deeply admired the 1933 version and wanted to bring to his own audience the same kind of thrill and excitement he experienced when first seeing it.[13] The problem is, of course, that this excitement is intimately related to the pro-colonial discourses that inform the imperial gothic. What makes the original *King Kong* into an exciting and reassuring movie is not just its visual magic but also the colonial mythologies that argue that the Pacific is a place of dangerous adventure where white explorers can re-connect with their own primitive natures, engage in revitalising

---

12 It deviates also from the original script, written by Jackson and his wife in 1996. In this script, the party of white explorers is a very unsavoury and often unsympathetic crowd, Ann is a driving force and the daughter of a British anthropologist rather than the hapless and unemployed vaudeville performer of the 1933 and 2005 versions and Jack Driscoll is a fighterpilot who struggles to fight off the attacking planes at the end of the movie.

13 Morton, *King Kong*, 581.

rescue operations, and gather long lost treasures. In this way, Jackson's film rekindles not just the roller-coaster ride of the original but also the imperial discourses upon which the original *King Kong* relied.

True to the original, Jackson's film charts a journey from a Great Depression-ridden New York to a lost island in the southern seas. The location of the mysterious, dangerous and potentially rich island in the Pacific revives the image of the region as essentially a troublesome but profitable colonial territory. As in the original, the crew aboard the ship *Venture* is armed to the teeth and one can understand why. Their mission is similar to those of countless intrepid British explorers moving into the bountiful yet utterly hostile terrain that Africa represented during the late nineteenth century. This is a paramilitary excursion into the hostile and colonial periphery, a periphery that is unlikely to want to yield its treasures without a struggle.

The first such struggle occurs as the adventurers reach the island. In Jackson's *King Kong* the island is a chaos of hostile, jagged rocks and the native village is little more than a graveyard with decomposing bodies strung up on barren wooden structures. The natives that eventually emerge from dark caves are supremely hostile, with black grinning faces that show filed teeth. They quickly overpower the first small party of explorers and begin to sacrifice them by dashing out their brains on a black, wet altar. So aggressively primitive do they appear that it is impossible to understand their relationship to the remarkable ruins that are all over the island. Surely, they cannot be related to the people who once built these enormous structures. In fact, it is difficult to understand how such a predatory group of people can even survive as there seems to be nothing to eat on their side of the great wall, except, of course, other people. In many ways, these wild savages are relatives not of the dancing natives of the 1933 version but of the Orcs of Jackson's *Lord of the Rings* trilogy. When Captain Englehorn suddenly arrives with reinforcement and machine guns, it is a relief to see the natives fall to the hail of bullets or to scurry away, their savagery finally tempered by Western military technology.[14]

As in the previous versions, a white woman remains the most precious and desirable object imaginable in Jackson's film. If the natives understand anything, they understand this and after having kidnapped Ann, they offer their price to the giant ape they worship. For the second time, the ship's crew lands with guns blazing, again scattering the frenzied natives. Of course, Ann has already been captured by Kong, forcing the rescue party to enter the jungle in search of their lost, white maiden. In this territory they encounter, as in the 1933

---

14 Before the end of the movie, this scene is repeated, only this time Engelhorn's rescue party shoots spiders, giant cockroaches and enormous, carnivorous worms that have attacked the party. The two sequences are eerily similar, and the insects elicit the same kind of fear and revulsion as the natives do in the first scene.

version, a lost and primitive world right out of the imperial gothic as presented by Arthur Conan Doyle and E.R. Burroughs. Here, Darwin's law rules supreme and everything is trying to eat everything else. Just like in the early twentieth-century imperial gothic, the movie places a group of predominately white Anglo-Saxons within a fundamentally primitive and evolutionary context and forces them to survive using their wits, their reawakened male virility and their superior technology. It should be added that halfway through their trek through the hostile landscape, all non-white Americans (the Chinese Choi, the black Ben Heyes) and most (working-class) sailors of the original party have been devoured by dinosaurs or gigantic insects.[15]

As observed, Jackson's *King Kong* is not simply a remake of the original *King Kong*, it is also an adaptation of Joseph Conrad's novella *Heart of Darkness*, first serialised in *Blackwood's Magazine* in 1899. Conrad's influential story resembles the British imperial gothic in many ways but contains no actual supernatural elements. More importantly, Conrad's story was written as an indictment of Belgian predatory colonialism in the Congo and inspired, as discussed in Chapter 5, Francis Ford Coppola's *Apocalypse Now* (1979).[16] Just like *Heart of Darkness* opens on the Thames and makes the point that London was once in the periphery of a vast (Roman) empire, *King Kong* opens in New York. The opening shot of a monkey in Central Park's zoo, a zoo surrounded by the loitering, cold and hungry unemployed, further positions New York as a wilderness of sorts. In addition to this, Jackson has his characters quote extensively from Conrad's novel, after which the director Karl Denham (Jack Black) is seized by predatory desires as palpable as those of Kurtz, the pan-European villain of Conrad's novel, and proceeds to walk over the corpses of the natives, of his own camera crew and, finally, of Kong.

Jackson perhaps intended the *Heart of Darkness* references to fortify his otherwise nostalgic movie against accusations of racism and colonial romanticism.[17] If so, this is a failed effort for many reasons. Even though Denham's progressively muddied appearance and his increasingly dark obsession with commodifying Kong is reminiscent of Kurtz embracing the horrors of African tribal culture while accommodating the European appetite for ivory, the violence perpetrated against the indigenous population is never seen as unjust

15 It needs to be pointed out, though, that while Adrian Brody's Jack Driscoll was based on a young Arthur Miller (Morton, *King Kong*, 325), Brody's physical appearance may not bring the typical Anglo-Saxon to mind.

16 It should be added that *Heart of Darkness* has inspired a great number of post-9/11 narratives on American empire. Some of the most recent are the claustrophobic and surreal first-person shooters *Far Cry* (2004) and *Spec Ops: The Line* (2012).

17 Dutch colonisation of the Congo was initially run as a private enterprise by King Leopold II. Before long, the brutality by which the project was pursued earned a lot of attention from other nations and the Congo was often perceived as an example of how colonialism should not operate.

in Jackson's movie. Also, while Conrad's novella may have launched a powerful critique against (Belgian) imperialism by showing the utter greed and brutality of the process itself, Chinua Achebe has argued in his seminal essay 'An Image of Africa: Racism in Joseph Conrad's *Heart of Darkness*' that Africa comes across as a 'metaphysical battlefield devoid of all recognisable humanity' in Conrad's novel.[18] In other words, Africa remains a heart of darkness in Conrad's story, the antithesis of the veneer of civilisation that importantly separates the Dark Continent from Europe. In the same way, Kong's Pacific island and its inhabitants, whether humanoid, dinosaur or ape, are primitive, dark and Darwinian. It is little more than a savage playground where some white explorers get eaten in atrocious ways by the forbidding territory and some survive.

Because of this, the fact that Jackson truly wants us to root for Kong does not do much to alleviate the sense that this film relies upon contrasting white modernity with black primitivism. Jackson's giant gorilla may be less obviously a reincarnation of the anxiety over America's black population than the original. Naomi Watts's Ann forms a genuine friendship with Kong, the type of friendship that only comes from being saved, literally, from the jaws of three frenzied Tyrannosaurus rexes. Even so, the film establishes, in the fashion of the imperial gothic, a colour divide that leaves no doubt that their love is doomed. There is no place for Kong on this modern island even if it takes on the characteristics of a jungle at times. After a brief and dreamlike sequence where Kong and Ann play on the ice of Central Park, Kong must die. This is the logic of the story and of the discourse that helped spawn it. Furthermore, the audience (the frightened Broadway viewers in the film as well as the actual spectators) demand it. The most nostalgic moment of this exercise in nostalgia features a dead Kong on the concrete below the Empire State Building and Denham uttering the line: 'It was beauty that killed the beast.'

In this way, the commodity that Jackson's film peddles most effectively is the reinstatement of the simple, imperial structures that informed the original movie. Just like this movie, Jackson's *King Kong* is precisely a 'blend of adventure story with Gothic elements' as Brantlinger has defined the imperial gothic.[19] In Jackson's *King Kong* there are again white places on the map, places that need to be discovered and explored, at great personal risk, for the mystery and wealth that they hold to become realised. Again, *King Kong* romanticises and commodifies the process of colonial adventure. This makes Jackson's *King Kong* a reassuring film that suggests that it is important for the enterprising West to also explore the most hostile places of the Earth. This process enriches society

18 Chinua Achebe, 'An Image of Africa: Racism in Joseph Conrad's *Heart of Darkness*' in *Reclaiming the Human Sciences and Humanities through African Perspectives*, Volume II, edited by Helen Lauer and Kofi Anyidoho (Accra: Sub-Saharan Publishers, 2012), 935.

19 Brantlinger, *Rule of Darkness*, 227.

in a very literal way, and this movement into forbidding colonial territory is also the moment when the West comes into being. It is through the encounter with the frenzied natives, their muscular black bodies sleek with rain and blood, with the even more primitive dinosaurs, or with Kong's body, tumbling from the Empire State Building, that the West becomes the West, and the Anglo-Saxon, again, the fittest race on Earth.

## *Van Helsing*

If Peter Jackson's *King Kong* was the first post-invasion, big-budget adaptation of the American imperial gothic, *Van Helsing* was the first post-invasion, big-budget rendition of the British imperial gothic as mediated by Hollywood in the 1930s. Directed by Stephen Sommers, *Van Helsing* is also a deeply nostalgic film by a director who made the first part of his career out of the imperial gothic but who has recently moved on to the *G.I. Joe* franchise, a series of movies with a more direct relationship to the Pentagon. As discussed by Roberto González in *Militarizing Culture: Essays on the Warfare State* (2010), Stephen Sommers's recent *G.I. Joe* films are intimately related to the military–industrial–entertainment complex.[20] Although these films sometimes make use of the gothic, they are essentially science fiction stories where the real heroes are the Special Forces and the technological inventions of the Pentagon.

Sommers's move from imperial gothic spectacle to adolescent war action is perfectly natural. Following in the footsteps of the *Indiana Jones* franchise, Sommers launched his career in 1999 with the aforementioned overtly imperial gothic adventure *The Mummy*, a film that may be said to help re-install, in the wake of the *Indiana Jones* movies, a very traditional, main-stream form of Orientalism within the American movie industry.[21] Wildly reminiscent of Arthur Conan Doyle's and Richard Marsh's imperial gothic, *The Mummy* and its sequel *The Mummy Returns* (2001) describe how courageous Western archaeologists, gun rather than shovel in hand, struggle to contain Oriental demons in Egypt. These films thus imagine the East as a place of boundless treasure where different laws (sexual, judicial, natural) apply and where the gothic Other is ever prepared to devour you. To get access to the wealth that surely belongs to the one able to seize it and cart it back to civilisation, you first have to vanquish this gothic Other. In this way, the Mummy films are logical precursors to Sommers's 2004 post-invasion movie *Van Helsing* as well as to his later *G.I. Joe* movies.

---

20 Roberto J. González, *Militarizing Culture: Essays on the Warfare State* (Walnut Creek: Left Coast Press, 2010).

21 Douglas Little, *American Orientalism: The United States and the Middle East since 1945* (London: I. B. Taurus, 2003), 39.

Just like *The League of Extraordinary Gentlemen*, *Van Helsing* relies upon the British imperial gothic for its menagerie of monsters and heroes as perceived through the nostalgic lens of Hollywood in the 1920s and 1930s. Thus, Frankenstein, Mr Hyde, Dracula and Van Helsing have a very tenuous connection to their British originals. In particular, the film's eponymous hero Van Helsing has little in common with the aged, Belgian doctor of Stoker's novel. This reincarnation presents instead a young, dashing, leather-clad, gun-wielding secret agent with inexplicable amnesia and a Stetson hat that is as wildly anomalous as it is fitting for this frontier hero. While his hatred of the atavistic vampire ties him to the original, his weapons are physical strength and a surprising array of strikingly sophisticated weapons such as the automatic crossbow and the anti-vampire light bomb. As previously demonstrated, this reliance on superior, Western technology is central to many gothic narratives, both British and American: Western heroes combat evil with the aid of advanced weaponry.

During the film's opening sequence, strangely reminiscent of a sequence in *The League of Extraordinary Gentlemen*, Van Helsing dispatches a large and computer-animated Mr Hyde on the gothic rooftops of Paris. This job completed, Van Helsing is sent to Romania, a nation or area described in telling terms: 'You need you to go to the East, to the far side of Romania. An accursed land ... terrorised by all sorts of nightmarish creatures lorded over by a certain Count Dracula.' Thus, the territory that Van Helsing is sent to visit is depicted as a liminal and transcultural frontier space where the East comes into contact with the West. In addition to this, the notion that Dracula's reign is one of terror is crucial. Importantly, Van Helsing's mission, like that of the US army marching into Iraq as the movie was produced, is to free a suffering people from the terrors inflicted by a tyrannical and imperious ruler.

Not surprisingly, the Transylvania that Van Helsing travels to is clearly reminiscent of a barren, cold and hostile Afghanistan inhabited by suspicious natives who are less than amused by Van Helsing's arrival. They are also very little help in fighting Dracula, forcing Van Helsing to work deep within enemy territory to expel the ancient evil and make the country safe if not for democracy then at least for the Western traveller. This is a difficult mission since Dracula's actual whereabouts cannot be discovered. The situation is becoming critical since Dracula's plans are predictably apocalyptic. He aims to launch his own biological weapon of mass destruction in the form of a mass of undead, atavistic foetuses, his progeny that will fill and consume the world.

In this way, this gothic narrative conjures an essentially gothic image of the current historical situation as constructed by 9/11 discourse. Dracula in *Van Helsing* is an anti-Christ who distinctly recalls the popular image of both Saddam Hussein and Osama bin Laden. Like bin Laden or Hussein, Dracula is in hiding from the justice Van Helsing intends to mete out with his crossbow loaded with silver arrows. Similarly, like bin Laden or Hussein, Dracula is plotting the destruction of the civilised world through his legion of vampire offspring.

The moral stakes of this battle are further emphasised by the revelation that Van Helsing is the archangel Gabriel, the left hand of God come to Earth to combat the Devil's offspring. Interestingly, being an angel does not give Van Helsing the power to finally vanquish Dracula in his own form. The vampire can only be killed by another monstrous being: a werewolf. Even as an angel, Van Helsing is apparently bound by certain moral and ontological restraints. To kill Dracula, Van Helsing must himself become a monster. Fortunately, the liminal space of Transylvania teems with monsters and Van Helsing is soon bitten by a werewolf. In this way, *Van Helsing* constructs the East not only as an infected locale but also an infectious one. Its surplus of gothic Others makes it an unusually risky place for the Western champion. If the native gothic Other does not consume you, a single bite will force you to join this entity.

The crossing over to the gothic Other that occurs in *Van Helsing* is a crucial element of many imperial gothic narratives. A number of popular gothic franchises, including *Blade* (1998), *The League of Extraordinary Gentlemen* (2003), *Resident Evil* (2002), *Hellboy* (2004) and *Underworld* (2003), feature heroes and heroines who are capable of effectively combating evil precisely because they are themselves part monster. The acquisition of a monstrous nature is in many ways a metaphorical yet limited way of joining the Other. Those that do so 'go native', as the British colonisers described those European subjects who took too readily to the customs and habits of the colonised. In other words, the imperial gothic recasts the process of going native into a monstrous transformation.[22] This is obviously highly undesirable not only because the hero literally becomes a monster but also because such transitions signal a possible lack of the absolute categories upon which imperial discourses rely.

Yet, as the gothic franchises mentioned above suggest, the crossing over to the monstrous Other is at times perceived as useful. It is as part native – part Other, part monster – that the Western champion gains access not only to the gothic spaces where evil resides but also to monstrous strength and to gothic practices such as deceit and murder that are at times necessary to fulfil the mission at hand. At the same time human and monstrous, Self and Other, the gothic hero/heroine benefits from a double moral nature. His or her firm grounding in the metropolitan West guarantees the morality of the invasive project with which he or she is involved, while his or her monstrous nature allows, even enforces, conduct incompatible with the official standards of the

22 Brantlinger argues in *Rule of Darkness* that 'individual regression or going native' is endemic in the imperial gothic and provides Kipling's 'Mark of the Beast' as an example, 230. For the full short story, see Rudyard Kipling, 'Mark of the Beast' in *Life's Handicap* 1899, reprint. (London: Macmillan, 1991).

West. Thus, it is only in his werewolf form that Van Helsing can shred Dracula's equally monstrous forms to pieces and it is only when assuming the guise of the torturer that the CIA agent can gather information from the subaltern terrorist.

The imperial gothic allows these transgressions into the monstrous to be temporary. After having accomplished his mission, the Western champion can often (but not always) change back into his true and civilised identity, making him safe for the society that sent him out in the first place. Van Helsing is cured from his werewolf state at the end of the movie. His monstrous transformation was necessary only while the source of terror still existed. With Dracula, all his vampire children also die. Order is restored.

With this conclusion, Sommers's movie unfolds as a thinly disguised gothic allegory that speaks clearly, if metaphorically, about the invasions of Afghanistan and Iraq and the hunts for Osama bin Laden and Saddam Hussein. By using the imperial gothic to speak about these invasions and manhunts, the moral boundaries are firmly established. There can be no gray zones in the battle between Dracula and Gabriel the Archangel. Van Helsing's one-man invasion of Eastern territory is perfectly justified. In fact, this Eastern space comes across as in dire need of some sort of (military) incursion not only because it is primitive but also because it is, like Dracula himself, dangerously transformative.

## Captivity, Crisis, and the Extroverted Imperial Gothic

On 23 March 2003, only four days into the invasion, Private Jessica Lynch was knocked unconscious when her convoy was ambushed after having become lost in the city of Nasiriyah. When Lynch woke up a few hours later, she was first a prisoner of war of the Iraqi army and then found herself being sent to the city's hospital. Attempts were then made to return Lynch to the invading army, but the ambulance that carried her was shot at by US troops. She was taken back to the hospital, and a number of sources reported her location to the US military in the area. On 1 April, marines and Special Forces staged a video-recorded, night-time raid on the hospital to retrieve Lynch from a building that had by then been completely abandoned by the Iraqi military.

The successful and unopposed raid turned the hospitalisation and retrieval of Jessica Lynch into the capture and rescue of Jessica Lynch. As Faludi observes, the 'story of a helpless white girl snatched from the jaws of evil by heroic soldiers was the story everybody wanted'.[23] The Lynch incident was one of the few that made good sense to the American audience during the invasion. Here was evidence that this was indeed a frontier confrontation, a desperate rescue attempt to retrieve a bruised and brutalised young white woman from

23 Faludi, *The Terror Dream*, 166.

the clutches of the Other. However, Jessica Lynch was never captured. She was never tortured, stabbed, raped or mistreated as Pentagon sources suggested at the time. She was never rescued either; there was nobody to rescue her from except medical staff that had already attempted to return her.

The Jessica Lynch incident is interesting because it represents the war as captivity narrative. It is not a gothic story, of course, but it shares more rhetorical DNA with *Exorcist: The Beginning* or with *King Kong* than with the actual progress of the war at that stage. Like these films, the rescue of Jessica Lynch was a staged media event, not an actual act of war. It was for the benefit of an expectant audience who had paid a high admission price, around 100 billion dollars of their tax money in the summer of 2003.[24]

*King Kong*, *Van Helsing* and many other imperial gothic tales from this period speak to the same audience by romanticising colonialism as explorative (and sometimes exploitative) adventure. The films' deeply nostalgic evocations of moments of exploration, gothic rescue and confrontation with guns blazing at a time when the US was venturing into the Middle East are informative. The increasingly violent incursions into the jungles of Skull Island, the deserts of Eastern Africa, the mazes of Eastern Europe or into the urban labyrinths of Fallujah blur easily. Both the actual war and the metaphorical conflicts of these two films speak about the need to aggressively defend ideological and territorial boundaries through expansive, exploratory and colonial projects. These assertive and often self-confident films thus testify to the same concerns as those that gripped Britain during what Brantlinger has referred to as the 'dusk' of the nation's imperial project. Hollywood turns to the imperial gothic for the same reasons British novelists did, and as it does so, it resurrects the gothic heroes and villains of the late-Victorian period. In this way, the extroverted imperial gothic is a form of text born out of a need to encourage colonial expansion at times of imperial crisis. However, as later chapters will argue, the modern extroverted imperial gothic that Hollywood produces at this juncture has no more success stemming this crisis than did the British.

---

24 The total cost for the invasions of Afghanistan and Iraq is difficult to estimate and many different figures circulate. The Center for American Progress states that the war had cost American taxpayers 144.4 billion dollars by 25 August 2004, see http://www.americanprogress.org/issues/military/news/2004/08/25/1009/the-opportunity-costs-of-the-iraq-war/. The Costs of War Project, based at Brown University, suggests that the two wars have today, in the spring of 2013, comprised costs of 4 trillion dollars, see http://costsofwar.org/.

# Chapter 8
# Militarising the Virtual Gothic

'People are dying. We need guns'
*Aliens vs. Predator: Requiem*

Once upon a time, Batman was 'the world's greatest detective'. Intelligent and independent, he was different from common detectives because he did not use (or need) a gun and because he wore a mask and a dark suit. In Tim Burton's popular *Batman* from 1989, the Batmobile is still essentially a form of police car: a black, sleek cruiser built on a Chevy Impala chassis. By contrast, the Batmobile that Batman drives in Christopher Nolan's *Batman Begins* (2005) is an urban battle tank, the result of research conducted by Wayne Enterprises's Applied Sciences Division. Nicknamed the Tumbler, it was developed for the army as a bridging vehicle; it can jump without the assistance of a ramp, it is heavily armoured and thoroughly weaponised. The same goes for the Batman's other modes of transportation: the Batpod that can be extracted from the Tumbler and the airborne Bat that appears in the final instalment of Nolan's Batman trilogy and which, according to the marketing material, was 'created as a tool for urban pacification'.[1] Similarly, Nolan's Dark Knight uniform is essentially a form of military grade, high-tech kevlar, 'for advanced infantry'. Even his cape is a form of militarised cloth capable of forming a glider on which he sails around crime-ridden Gotham city. In many ways, the military gear Batman uses plays as important a part in the film as the hero himself. It is Batman's suit and weapons and his command of cutting-edge military technology that make him a modern hero, even a soldier of modernity, capable of tremendous yet surgical interference and violence.[2]

This makes Nolan's Batman uniquely placed among the many reincarnations of the 70-year-old franchise to literally fight a war against crime. However, the plot that frames Nolan's three films is, in fact, not that Batman must protect Gotham against organised crime, it is instead that he must confront another

1 http://batman-news.com/2012/12/03/the-dark-knight-rises-vehicles-infographic/.

2 As Caren Kaplan has discussed in 'Precision Targets: GPS and the Militarization of US Consumer Identity', *American Quarterly* 58, no. 3 (2006): 693–713, the notion of surgical strikes has structured the discourse on modern warfare since the first Gulf War. As Justine Toh has observed, this discourse is crucial also to Nolan's vision of Batman and the violence he practises. Justine Toh, 'The Tools and Toys of (the) War (on Terror): Consumer Desire, Military Fetish, and Regime Change in *Batman Begins*' in *Reframing 9/11: Film, Popular Culture and the 'War on Terror'*, edited by Jeff Birkenstein, Anna Froula and Karen Randell (New York: Continuum, 2010).

group of vigilantes, the League of Shadows, that seek to overcome the societal corruption by utterly destroying the city. To the League of Shadows, Gotham has been so thoroughly infected by crime that it is beyond saving. Batman is actually a product of this secret society, having been trained by its leader, Ra's al Ghul. In the end, the difference between Batman and the League of Shadows is Batman's arsenal of advanced military weaponry, an arsenal that allows him to micromanage, rather than generally exterminate, the criminals of Gotham.

As critics have pointed out, the League of Shadows shares many similarities with al-Qaeda.[3] They come from the East, they have vast resources and their desire for justice is perverted by a form of fanatical fundamentalism. They seek to indiscriminately destroy Gotham and with it, the capitalist fabric that fuels both Bruce Wayne's immense corporation and the criminals that are locked up in Arkham Asylum. As discussed in Chapter 6, Andrew Klavan noted with considerable approval that *The Dark Knight* (2008) can be read as 'at some level a paean of praise to the fortitude and moral courage that has been shown by George W. Bush in this time of terror and war'.[4] Certainly, Nolan's *Batman* trilogy tells the story of a man who uses violence to make the world a better place, who batters and abuses his prisoner to get information, who uses advanced technology to spy on the population of Gotham and who regularly transgresses the boundaries of national and international law.

However, *Batman* can also be usefully read as a critique of US imperial violence in the Middle East. In *Batman Begins*, the League of Shadows operates more like the CIA than al-Qaeda, infiltrating Gotham from within, encouraging the practices they mean to eradicate with the hope that this will make Gotham destroy itself. In the final film, *The Dark Knight Rises* (2012), the league seizes control of the island centre of Gotham and introduces simultaneous anarchy and a form of fascist rule that brings the American occupation of Afghanistan and Iraq to mind. The two villains, Ra's al Ghul himself in *Batman Begins* and Bane in *The Dark Knight Rises*, with their uncompromising and expansive ideals, actually bring George Bush, Sr, and George W. Bush to mind, Ra's al Ghul being the more sophisticated operator, while Bane, relying on brute force, encourages only the parody of justice in the city that crumbles around him.

These two readings of Nolan's trilogy both make sense. Which one the audience prefers depends more on the position of the individual than on the films themselves. To understand the impact of the trilogy – its relation to the invasion of Iraq and to US imperial ambitions – close reading is a blunt tool. A more useful approach in this case is to read the trilogy not as a narrative but as a product of what has been termed the military–industrial–entertainment

3 See, for example, W. Bryan Rommel-Ruiz, *American History Goes to the Movies: Hollywood and the American Experience* (London: Routledge, 2011), 254.

4 Andrew Klavan, 'What Bush and Batman'.

complex. Nolan's *Batman* trilogy is not only a conflicted narrative, it is, equally importantly, part of a franchise consisting of a multitude of products, games, toys, amusement parks, action theatres, comics and novels. The trilogy is furthermore deeply concerned with weapons that make it possible to imagine urban warfare as effectively surgical. Building on this observation, Justine Toh perceives 'Batman's Batsuit and the Batmobile as emblems of the military–industrial–entertainment complex, arguing that their transformation into desirable consumer items encapsulates the militarisation of popular culture'[5] and that Nolan's 'Hollywood adaptations of *Batman* promote a matrix of consumer desire, military fetish, and an ultimate reliance on force, not only feeding a taste for the tools and the toys of war but the desire to see them engaged in action'.[6]

This chapter argues that the post-9/11 American imperial gothic is intimately connected with the military–industrial–entertainment complex. The chapter seeks to outline first the way in which the military, industry and the media have converged in recent years. This chapter then discusses how imperial gothic film advertises the complex both by marketing the tools of current and future warfare and by constructing gothic spaces where the military solution is the only viable, even the only imaginable, solution. Then, the chapter discusses the specific merger between military gaming and gothic gaming and how gaming technology allows subjects not only to consume and observe but also to inhabit and perform the world of the imperial gothic. A crucial point here is that the complex in itself can be considered a stage in the evolution of modernity and, at the same time, part of an effort to stave off the 'dusk' of US power. Thus, some of the imperial gothic culture that is produced in the wake of 9/11 not only condones modernity, it is often produced in symbiosis with the complex and attempts to consolidate US empire.

The military–industrial–entertainment complex constitutes a new development in the way in which empire interacts with culture. Rituals such as film premiers, the placement of actual or imaginary tools of war in novels, films or games, and the mobilisation of former gothic villains as champions for the West in imperial gothic narratives can all be seen as aspects of this complex. Because the military–industrial–entertainment complex manifests in so many different ways, the analysis of its nature and its interaction with culture is not a straightforward process. It can comprise a close reading of a narrative and a discussion of the discourses that this narrative espouses, but it should also include a study of how narratives become narratives in the first place, how they are funded, produced, censored, manipulated and marketed. Furthermore, as will be discussed below, the military–industrial–entertainment complex produces culture but it actually also helps engineer wars and the tools of these wars. The culture that

5 Toh, 'The Tools and Toys', 127–8.

6 Toh, 'The Tools and Toys', 127.

the military–industrial complex generates showcases these tools – advanced weapons systems as well as guns readily available to the consumer – and it also creates imaginary spaces and situations where these weapons and guns become absolutely essential instruments, the only tools with which the gothic Other can be addressed; even the only way in which history can progress.

## Bush's *Top Gun* Moment and the Military–Industrial–Entertainment Complex

As discussed in the previous chapter, Bush landed in an overtly staged and wildly premature performance on the aircraft carrier *USS Abraham Lincoln* on 1 May 2003 to declare the end of major combat operations. The press, at the same time excited and bewildered by this spectacle, called the incident a '*Top Gun* moment'. This was a very appropriate observation. From the Bush government's point of view, the *Top Gun* reference provided yet another rhetorical context and even a form of imagined closure for a war that was, of course, anything but over. At the same time, describing the landing as a *Top Gun* moment recognises the staged quality of this media event and illustrates how interdependent the institutions of politics, military and entertainment had become at this stage. In other words, when landing on the aircraft carrier, Bush not only performed a scene from a seminal movie, he simultaneously condoned and inhabited the intimate relationship between the military, the military–industrial complex and the entertainment industry that has been given a number of different terms such as the Military–Industrial–Media–Entertainment Network (MIME-NET), the military–industrial–entertainment complex, the military–industrial–educational complex or, simply, the Complex.[7]

*Top Gun* (1986) is one of the most useful examples of how this complex operates. As discussed by David L. Robb in *Operation Hollywood: How the Pentagon Shapes and Censors the Movies*, this movie changed the way Hollywood produced narrative.[8] Made with significant financial and material support from the air force, *Top Gun* was not only a financial success, it also boosted confidence in

7 See James Der Derian, *Virtuous War: Mapping the Military–Industrial–Media–Entertainment Network* (Boulder: Westview Press, 2001); Timothy Lenoir and Henry Lowood, 'Theatres of War: The Military–Entertainment Complex'. http://www.stanford.edu/class/sts145/Library/Lenoir-Lowood_TheatersOfWar.pdf; Nick Turse, *The Complex: How the Military Invades Our Everyday Lives* (New York: Metropolitan Books, 2008); and C. Richard King and David J. Leonard, 'Wargames as a New Frontier: Securing American Empire in Virtual Space' in *Joystick Soldiers: The Politics of Play in Military Video Games*, edited by Nina B. Huntemann and Matthew Thomas Payne (New York: Routledge, 2010).

8 David L. Robb, *Operation Hollywood: How the Pentagon Shapes and Censors the Movies* (New York: Prometheus Books, 2004).

the military and in the air force in particular. Recruitment booths were set up in theatres and Hollywood producers told screenwriters and directors to get the military on board or 'forget about doing the picture'.[9] Today, as argued by Robb, Hollywood routinely allows the Pentagon to censor and edit their scripts in exchange for access to costly hardware.

The film industry is not the only institution to have been permeated by the military–industrial–entertainment complex. In *Militarizing Culture* Roberto J. González discusses how militarism is 'designed, manufactured, packaged, and marketed in America today',[10] arguing that 'today's military–industrial complex is powerful and sophisticated enough to infiltrate and mediate intimate social relationships – between parent and child, between family and community, between civilian and soldier – while exploiting those who can help it further its own ends'.[11] González discusses military historian Richard H. Khon's assertion that in the past 70 years, American society has experienced an unprecedented degree of militarisation and he also addresses the possibility that this militarisation will evolve into *militarism*, a state where war becomes the dominant force in American thinking, policy and society.

The engine in this process is not so much the military itself or the White House but is instead the neo-liberal market. The US military is increasingly privatised so that independent contractors supply weapons, vehicles, uniforms, food and in-field entertainment. Even soldiers are for sale by large and profitable corporations such as Blackwater. In this way, private businesses also become stakeholders in global conflict. At the same time, the militarisation of the civilian market place involves the marketing and consumption not only of military narrative, but of all things military: Humvees, G.I. Joe dolls, camouflage fatigues and assault rifles.[12] The consumption of these and other military-related paraphernalia comes with a narrative that suggests that consuming these tools of war is not only a patriotic duty but also a way to stabilise an increasingly unstable world. These narratives, as rehearsed in countless Hollywood movies and, in particular, in the imperial gothic, can also be consumed. The consumption of both items and narratives further feeds the complex that produced these guns and these narratives. In other words, going to the movies to watch Robin gun down criminals with his Glock 17 or his Remington 870 in *The Dark Knight Rises* feeds the complex by advertising both actual weapons and a discourse that imagines them as necessary. Even if someone begins to shoot people with his own Smith and Wesson MP15 assault rifle, his own Glock 22 and his own

9 http://articles.washingtonpost.com/2011-08-26/opinions/35271385_1_pentagon-brass-military-budget-top-gun.

10 González, *Militarizing Culture*, 15.

11 González, *Militarizing Culture*, 19.

12 As Nick Turse observes in *The Complex*, it is actually difficult to consume products that are not somehow produced by or in relation to the complex.

Remington 870, as happened in the 20 July 2012 Aurora shooting during the premiere of *The Dark Knight Rises*,[13] this also feeds the complex, because as the sense of insecurity grows, more guns are consumed. The American imperial gothic continually emphasises how guns is the last best hope to meet any form of challenge. In *Aliens vs. Predator: Requiem*, Ridley Scott's Alien from 1978 has finally reached the Earth and begun slaughtering the inhabitants of a small rural town. The hero quickly diagnoses the situation and recommends the remedy: 'People are dying. We need guns.'

The logic of the complex suggests that the solution to all disruption, be it local violence in the form of school shootings or terrorism, global or international conflict, or abject gothic terror, is more (gun) violence. This logic can be said to inform both the neoconservative Project for the New American Century's (PNAC) assertion that 'we need to increase defense spending significantly if we are to carry out our global responsibilities today and modernize our armed forces for the future',[14] and the National Rifle Association (NRA) declaration that the 'only way to stop a monster from killing our kids is to be personally involved and invested in a plan of absolute protection. The only thing that stops a bad guy with a gun is a good guy with a gun.'[15] Both of these assertions serve to instil a longing for security (rather than a sense of actual safety), to legitimise the use of violence to satisfy this longing and to feed the increasingly ubiquitous market that produces these guns.[16] By this logic, even social problems such as poverty or drug addiction appear as hostile entities that can be addressed through what I have termed 'the military solution'.[17] Similarly, terror can only be addressed with a *War* on terror, just as the challenge that the gothic Other represents can best be resolved with the aid of the assault rifle. The very consumption of guns

13 See http://www.guardian.co.uk/world/aurora-shooting for an account of this shooting.

14 See PNAC, 'Statement of Principles' at http://www.newamericancentury.org/statementofprinciples.htm.

15 Wayne LaPierre quoted by David Nakamura and Tom Hamburger in 'Put Armed Police in Every School, NRA urges', *The Washington Post*, December 12, 2012, http://articles.washingtonpost.com/2012-12-21/politics/35950179_1_gun-regulation-national-school-shield-program-gun-violence.

16 The Project for the New American Century or PNAC is a now defunct neoconservative think tank founded in 1997 by Bill Kristol. The organisation's members included Donald Rumsfeld, Paul Wolfowitz, Jeb Bush, Frances Fukuyama and Dick Cheney. This organisation understood the US as the very centre of modernity: 'The United States is the world's only superpower, combining preeminent military power, global technological leadership, and the world's largest economy.' At the same time, the organisation encouraged increased military spending and a more forceful and interventionist foreign policy to preserve and extend American hegemony. See http://www.newamericancentury.org.

17 Lyndon B. Johnson launched the 'War on Poverty' in 1964 and Richard Nixon the 'War on Drugs' in 1971.

becomes a way to prevent darkness from spreading. The more guns you buy, as a private person or as a nation, the safer from terror you are.[18]

Because of the ability of the military–industrial–entertainment complex to commodify military practice, to generate (new and more modern) tools of war in the form of actual hardware, and to produce the narratives that make these tools seem essential, it can be described as part of the most recent stage of modernity in the US. The complex connects with the central processes and concerns of modernity. Like modernity, it is not only fuelled by capitalism, capitalism is part of its very fabric, a beating heart that sustains it. It is expansive and military in nature, demanding new markets and battlefields, both which feed each other and the complex. It tells citizens that they are safe in its technological embrace and it drives scientific innovation. It informs the citizens that it holds on to that this embrace is necessary, that such innovation is necessary, because the alternative is chaos and disorder, an invasion of the (gothic) savages that flock outside the borders of civilised society or which may grow inside the subject like an infection.

## Cultures of War and Cultures of the Gothic – Recruiting and Arming the Gothic Other

The imperial gothic thrives on the military–industrial–entertainment complex. While the complex as such is a relatively new phenomenon, this study suggests that the imperial gothic has been military in its nature since its inception. It can be argued that the technological and military advances of modernity and a willingness to make use of these advances to eradicate the gothic Other have been a core aspect of the American imperial gothic since Edgar Huntly made use of his exquisite rifle to bring order to the particular liminal territory of the new and unruly American continent he inhabited. What is different in the most recent American imperial gothic is that this process has become even more formalised through the merger between the military, the military–industrial complex and the entertainment industry. Thus, while the American imperial gothic has long been military in nature, the ubiquitous and interdependent structure of cultural sponsorship, industry, military and technology that now increasingly informs it is, in fact, a new development.

18 Adam Lanza's mother Nancy had seven guns at home and was shot with one of them before her son drove to the Sandy Hook Elementary School with another four: a 10 mm Glock handgun, a Sig Saur P226 handgun, an Izhmash Saiga-12 combat shotgun and the .223-caliber Bushmaster XM15-E2S assault rifle that he used to kill 20 school children and six adults at the school. Following this horrific school shooting, the demand for military-style assault rifles soared.

In the imperial gothic, this complex manifests in many different ways. As I have argued in 'Militarizing the Vampire: Underworld and the Desire of the Military Entertainment Complex', the gothic figure of the vampire has been transformed by the military–industrial–entertainment complex into a militarised champion of the West.[19] In other words, modern vampires like Selene in the movie *Underworld* (2003) represent not the gothic, Oriental Other, but the warlike and overtly sexual desires of the complex. The same transformation occurs in a lot of gothic movies from this period. In *The League of Extraordinary Gentlemen*, discussed in Chapter 6, the villains of the British imperial gothic team up to fight for Anglo-Saxon empire. Mina from *Dracula* may be a vampire, but she is still happy to lend her considerable dark powers, her substantial intellect and her martial arts skills to the service of the British empire. Similarly, the invisible man and even the brutal and enormous Mr Hyde toe the line of patriotism to fight the good fight in the movie. A great many narratives of the post-9/11 period, including *Blade II* (2002) and *Resident Evil* (2002), also mobilise the formerly gothic Other for patriotic duty in this way.[20]

As suddenly Western champions, these characters are equipped with a number of easily identifiable guns from manufacturers Heckler and Koch, Smith & Wesson, Beretta, Desert Eagle, Glock and Remington.[21] Often, as when Quatermain handles Tom Sawyer's Winchester 1873 in *The League of Extraordinary Gentlemen*, guns are named and play a role in the film.[22] The prominent positions of guns in these and many other films turn them into advertisements for the weapons industry and the military. In the hands of sexually desirable, rubber-clad heroines such as Selene or Alice in *Resident Evil*, guns become sexual objects and the exchange of violence a form of carnal intercourse where blood serves as bodily fluid and the groans of the dying often sound disturbingly orgasmic.

The transformation and mobilisation of the former gothic Other into Western champion forces the invention of a new gothic Other that can take its place, and the natures of these reinvented gothic Others also emphasise

19 See Johan Höglund, 'Militarizing the Vampire: Underworld and the Desire of the Military Entertainment Complex' in *Transnational and Postcolonial Vampires: Dark Blood*, edited by Johan Höglund and Tabish Khair (London: Palgrave Macmillan, 2012).

20 A theme here, discussed also in Chapter 6, is how soldiers of the West must somehow cross over the borders that separate Self and Other, not to bridge this gap but in order to gain access to the deadly and amoral practices that the Other commands. Bounded by the moral and ontological restraints of Western civilisation, the Western champion cannot effectively combat the gothic Other. Thus, many imperial gothic narratives describe an often sacrificial transformation of the Western body and psyche to allow for a less restricted engagement with evil.

21 The Internet Movie Firearms Database (http://www.imfdb.org) records in painstaking detail the plethora of guns used in these and other films.

22 The Winchester Model 1873 has featured prominently in other films too, notably the 1950 western *Winchester '73* by Anthony Mann.

the sexual subtext that informs the violence of these narratives. When the vampire becomes your friend and champion, a new breed of vampire or a new set of monsters must step up and take the place of the previous gothic Other. Often, as in *Underworld* or *Resident Evil*, this refigured gothic Other will again be fundamentally primitive and use its powerful, abject, atavistic and transformative body as a weapon. In *Resident Evil*, the highly infectious T-virus transforms people into raging zombies, Doberman Pinschers into fast and relentless canine killing-machines and some individuals into horrifically powerful agile and aggressive 'lickers', a type of fast predator with large claws, sharp teeth and a long and penetrative tongue. Similarly, in *Blade II* (2002), the militarised vampire hunter Blade teams up with the (similarly militarised) vampires he has always hunted to fight a new and increasingly atavistic form of vampire caused by a new strain of vampire virus named the 'reaper virus'. To again emphasise the sexual context, these vampires have long and protruding tongues that accentuate their sexual natures, as do the vampires of Guillermo del Toro and Chuck Hogan's *The Strain* trilogy of novels (2009–11).[23] Like the face-huggers of the *Alien* films, the lickers and these new vampires threaten men and women alike with a form of perverted gothic rape. The penetrative tongues of these monsters are not only instruments of forced intercourse, however, but also of impregnation. People subjected to their sexual violence will be transformed into similar atavistic and primitive Others.

## Electronic Gaming and the Complex

While imperial gothic Hollywood movies are typically intimately linked to the military–industrial–entertainment complex, the forms of new media most directly related to the complex are video and computer games. There are many reasons for this, one being the technology as such. While the novel and the movie are arguably civilian technologies in the sense that they were not first created as military applications, the computer was developed in close relationship with the military. Computerised gaming technology is no exception here. The first computer and console games made use of hardware and software protocols first developed by the US Army.[24] In addition to this, the military has always been keen to employ games and simulators in order to train their personnel.

23 See Chuck Hogan and Guillermo del Toro, *The Strain* (New York: HarperCollins, 2009), *The Fall* (New York: HarperCollins, 2010) and *The Night Eternal* (New York: HarperCollins, 2011).

24 See John Naisbitt, *High Tech/High Touch: Technology and Our Accelerated Search for Meaning* (London: Nicholas Brealey, 1999); Sebastian Deterding, 'Living Room Wars: Remediation, Boardgames, and the Early History of Video Wargaming' in *Joystick Soldiers: The Politics of Play in Military Video Games*, edited by Nina B. Huntemann and Matthew Thomas Payne (London: Routledge, 2010).

In a recent development the Pentagon has even sponsored a project that aims to treat soldiers suffering from post-traumatic stress disorder with the help of immersive, digital simulators.[25]

From this perspective, it is not surprising that many contemporary war games, such as the immensely popular *Call of Duty: Modern Warfare* (2007) or *Medal of Honor: Warfighter* (2012), were produced in co-operation with the Pentagon, Hollywood and the gun industry. As an example, in 2012 EA games formed a partnership with weapons manufacturer and supplier Magpul and furnished the home page of the recent *Medal of Honor: Warfighter* game with links so that gamers that visited could easily acquire some of the actual weapons and gear used in the game. Furthermore, this game was subsequently provided with a *Zero Dark Thirty* map add-on, connecting the game to Kathryn Bigelow's Hollywood version of the hunt for bin Laden. In addition to this, EA has created Project Honor, a campaign tied to the Special Operations Warrior Foundation 'dedicated to raising awareness and generating charitable contributions for fallen warriors from the Special Operations Community in honor of the sacrifices they and their families have made for their country'.[26]

As I have discussed in 'Electronic Empire: Orientalism Revisited in the Military Shooter', some games such as *Full Spectrum Warrior* (2004) and *America's Army* (2002) were produced not only with the help of the Pentagon but also by the Pentagon as training or recruitment tools.[27] In this way, the consumption of these games feeds the complex while they simultaneously teach the gamer to both appreciate the mechanics of being a soldier and the discourses that make war possible, even desirable. In the words of Richard King and Justin Leonard, video games are a 'powerful pedagogical vehicle, providing youth, and perhaps all users, with ideological, political, historical, and racial lessons that guide U.S. hegemony around the globe'.[28] A crucial point here is that games allow the consumer not only to observe the rituals of colonial expansion but also to actually perform them within spaces designed to make an always virtuous war always possible. It is these qualities that make them, again in the words of King and Leonard, a 'crucial space of articulating American empire, providing a vehicle of interactive dissemination that allows for the transportation of citizen bodies from their homes onto battle fields, into political struggles, and into a

25 Jay Dixit, 'The War on Terror', *Wired Magazine*, August 2006, http://www.wired.com/wired/archive/14.08/warterror.html.

26 Heather McLellan, 'Devs Announce *Medal of Honor: Warfighter* Charity Project', *The Escapist*, last modified June 13, 2012. http://www.escapistmagazine.com/news/view/117891-Devs-Announce-Medal-of-Honor-Warfighter-Charity-Project.

27 Johan Höglund, 'Electronic Empire: Orientalism Revisited in the Military Shooter', *Game Studies* 8, no. 1 (2008). http://gamestudies.org/0801/articles/hoeglund.

28 King and Leonard, 'Wargames as a New Frontier', 94.

global theatre where U.S. efforts to secure power is normalized and justified'.[29] It is the military paradigm – the sense that the world is always hostile and must be always and forever controlled through extensive (and frequently sexualised) gun violence – that makes the first person shooter the pre-eminent vehicle of the military–industrial–entertainment complex.

## Performing the Complex

The step from war gaming to imperial gothic gaming is notoriously short. As discussed in Chapter 6, the first widely popular and disseminated first-person shooter was *Wolfenstein 3D* published in 1992, while the real breakthrough for the genre of the first-person shooter was *Doom* in 1993. Both games conflate the military with the gothic by allowing the gamer to perform military violence in response to a gothic threat. This threat is produced by Nazis in *Wolfenstein 3D* and by the fictional Union Aerospace Corporation in *Doom*. What was revolutionary about these games was their 3D interface. The gamer does not observe and control the action from the traditional 2D, third-person perspective. Instead, he or she inhabits the body of the avatar, looking out through the avatar's eyes. The only portion of the avatar's/gamer's body that is actually seen is that of the hand holding the weapon he or she is currently using, thus the designation first-person shooter. In this way, the gun becomes the only tool with which the world around can be engaged. Many first-person shooters will not allow the gamer to drop the gun. In the cases where this is possible, and the hands become instruments of unarmed combat, there is a pervading sense of being lost, of being unable to effectively communicate with the game world.[30]

The military soon recognised the ways in which games such as *Doom* could be used not only to recruit and train soldiers but also to disseminate the notion that war is the only viable way to manage global crises. This has led to a deeply problematic blurring of the borders that separate virtual war and the actual practice of war. James Der Derian has influentially argued that the diplomatic and military policies of the United States are increasingly based on 'technological and representational forms of discipline, deterrence, and compulsion' that are best described as 'virtuous war'.[31] 'Virtuous' here connotes 'virtual' because of

29 King and Leonard, 'Wargames as a New Frontier', 102.

30 Having a gun not only empowers the gamer, it is what makes the game possible. It should be noted that the gun is a phallic object also in computer games. The first-person shooter typically equips the gamer with a number of increasingly potent weapons. This structure was firmly established by *Doom*. The final and most powerful weapon that the gamer is given access to in this game is named the BFG or the Big Fucking Gun. Not only is this a big gun, it is a gun that fucks.

31 Der Derian, *Virtuous War*, xxxi.

the way that war has been mediated for Western audiences and because the interfaces with which war is actually fought (computers, screens, joysticks) remove the soldier from the carnage they cause. At the same time, 'virtuous' connotes 'clinical' since this type of war allows the pretence that military violence is precise and clinical. Virtuous war thus refers to precision bombing imagined to surgically remove the bad combatants while sparing the civilians next door. It may also refer to Navy Seals infiltrating the home of bin Laden and gunning him down without the need for collateral damage, or to the military-grade violence that Batman dishes out only to criminals in Nolan's trilogy.

At the same time, virtuous war is a form of practice enabled by computer technology. As King and Leonard argue, computerised gaming is the ideal space for virtual/virtuous war. Here, war is 'without bloodshed, carnage, or destruction or the personal stories and experiences that make it tragic'.[32] Essentially, the military first-person shooter makes it possible for the individual to not just observe virtuous war being played out on the movie or television screen but to actually perform it. In the *Call of Duty: Modern Warfare* series, the gamer performs surgical bombing with the aid of greenish, thermal interfaces identical to those seen on television. The games *Kuma War* (2004) and the previously mentioned *Medal of Honor: Warfighter* make it possible to download maps where the gamer actually guns down (a suddenly very combative) bin Laden and exchanges gunfire in some locations that were associated with him in the film *Zero Dark Thirty* (2012).

## Taking the Fight to Them: *Quake 4* and the Colonial Boundaries of Electronic Warfare

In the wake of the invasion and occupation of Iraq, technological and virtuous war was evoked through imperial gothic games that fuse science fiction and war into their narratives: *Doom 3* (2004) and *Quake 4* (2005). Both games were developed by id Software (in the case of Quake 4 in connection with Raven Software) and build on the same narratives and interface as were adapted into combat simulators by the US military in the early 1990s, in the wake of the first *Doom* game. In both games, the gamer takes on the role of a marine who has to fight the gothic Other in the liminal frontier territory of Mars or in outer space. These games thus re-enact operations of colonial pacification and missions of conquest, while at the same time referencing the expansive colonial gothic of Burroughs's Barsoom stories from the early twentieth century. The fact that the gamer not only observes this narrative but actually performs it helps the gamer to internalise the discourse that informs the games.

32 King and Leonard, 'Wargames as a New Frontier', 96.

The game that most interestingly casts the invasion of enemy territory as gothic/military frontier adventure is *Quake 4*. The opening sequence of this game shows the face and upper torso of a space marine slowly revolving against the vastness of space. The face looks collected and tranquil, but as the soldier's body keeps turning the gamer discovers that most of him is gone. Half of his face has been eaten away, and his eviscerated abdomen marks the end of his torn body. He keeps turning, surrounded by debris and other dead and mutilated bodies. Out of this chaos of dead flesh and metal scraps, a number of ships appear, moving inexorably through anti-spacecraft fire towards a reddish planet. On board of one of these ships, marines are seen to board a transportation vessel. The third-person perspective is replaced by the first-person view as the gamer finds himself or herself in a small transportation ship, in the body of soldier 'Kane' who has just sat down beside a number of gung-ho marines. The context and conversation is military and the uniforms reminiscent of actual army or navy fatigues. On the transportation ship, the gamer is informed that the war against the Strogg, the alien race that the gamer is about to confront, is going well. The Strogg planetary defence guns have been disabled and it is now time to invade the planet itself: 'it's a ground-pounders war from here on out'.

In this way, the first few seconds of *Quake 4* merge military, gothic and science fiction themes in ways that are typical of both the first-person shooter and the imperial gothic and places them within the context of an invasion. The game does not describe the stakes of the invasion in great detail, but as in the prequel *Quake 2* (1997), the invasion of the Strogg world is in response to an attack on the Earth.[33] The Strogg are tough and industrialised enemies. They command a complex technology and, in gothic fashion, actively seek to transform the people they capture into Strogg warriors through brutal, industrial surgery and computerised brainwashing.

If the cold and barren landscape and hostile natives of *Van Helsing* remind its audience of Afghanistan, the military and heavily industrialised Strogg home world recalls the significantly more developed state of Iraq. The gamer traverses a heavily industrialised landscape, large military installations and factories that typically transform into dark, dangerous and labyrinthine spaces when the gamer enters them. The marine avatar Kane is called upon to disrupt communications and to engage the enemy with the assistance of his comrades. Unlike in the early first-person shooters, Kane completes his missions as a part of a military team. It becomes as important to keep teammates alive as killing opposing Strogg since fulfilling missions becomes virtually impossible without help. Again, this is an element introduced by the tactical military first-person shooter, a genre that places great emphasis on squad interaction and co-operation.

33 *Quake 3 Arena* (1999) is a multi-player game that lacks the story-driven content of single-player campaigns.

As in *Van Helsing*, the avatar of *Quake 4* is eventually transformed into the Other, allowing him to fight the Strogg more effectively. In this case, however, the transformation is mechanised rather than occult: Halfway through the game, the gamer's avatar infiltrates the medical facilities of the Strogg. Knocked out during combat, Kane wakes up on a moving trolley, strapped down and naked with the exception of his camouflage underwear. Kane, and by extension the gamer, can only move Kane's head and must now watch as first the person on the trolley in front of him, and then Kane himself, are subjected to various violent procedures including having his legs circle-sawed off at the knees. This industrialised surgery is not primarily an elaborate form of torture but a preliminary to fusing Kane's body to the technology of the Strogg. Piece by piece, his human body is merged with Strogg parts. The final operation is the reprogramming of Kane's identity, a process that will make him part of the Strogg, but at the last minute, Kane is saved. His body has merged with that of the gothic Other, but since the chip that obliterates free will is never activated, Kane's mind remains intact. This hybrid state provides him with access to the weapons of the Strogg, making him a much more effective soldier. In this way, his transformation has revitalised him, turning him, like the werewolf Van Helsing, into a being that is part human and part virile weapon.

As part Strogg, Kane plays an increasingly offensive role in the war against the enemy. The lack of free will means that the Strogg must be controlled by a master entity, a hive mind that has taken the place of individual decisions. This is, of course, a common gothic trope. Those who are transformed into the gothic Other frequently fall under the spell of a hive mind. The destruction of this mind means that the remaining soldiers will be leaderless and disoriented, drastically reducing the threat that the Strogg represent. This again positions the game as an allegory of the invasion of Iraq as imagined by the Bush government. With Saddam Hussein captured or at least ousted, the Iraqis would cease resisting the American invaders. A new period of transformation would begin, converting the militant and hostile nation into a new Germany or Japan, eager to adopt the tenets of liberal capitalism.

In this way, *Quake 4* lets the gamer perform an all out 'ground-pounders' war, and portrays the partial transformation of the Western champion into the gothic Other. This transformation gives the avatar access to practices necessary to combat the gothic enemy. The final destruction of the gothic Other paves the way for a new world order. The vanquished Strogg planet is now amenable to positive change. In addition to this, the game actually teaches the gamer the grammar of modern combat. What the gamer does is what soldiers actually do, regardless of the political context. Flanking movements work in the game, ammunition must be saved, tactics must be adapted to the opponents, and the Geneva Convention must be studiously ignored.

## The Modernity Engine

In popular culture, not just gothic or imperial gothic culture, but in general action and thriller narratives, the concept of the self-perpetuating energy source is commonly occurring. This self-perpetuating or super-economic energy source is typically described as the great secret of the future, a secret engineered by the good agents of modernity. In the thriller or action movie, all sorts of villains want this self-perpetuating device, some – oil tycoons, agents of destructive forms of modernity – want to destroy it; others – rival governments – want it for themselves.[34]

In many ways, the military–industrial–entertainment complex is self-perpetuating (although certainly not super-economic). One element of the complex feeds and encourages the next one in an accelerating process. It is 'our daily bread and nightly circus', as Der Derian observes.[35] The institutions that sustain it and are sustained by it – the Pentagon, Hollywood, the military gaming companies, the civilian and military weapons industry, several Washington lobbyist organisations and the NRA to mention just some of the central players – are so much a fabric of the US economy and society that it seems impossible to sever the ties that now bind them to each other and to the economy.

From this perspective, the military–industrial–entertainment complex is a form of modernity engine. It drives technological innovation, it fuels the marketplace, it creates occasions where the investments in military hardware can be put to use, creating a demand for new innovation and industrial production, and it encourages narratives – the imperial gothic is one of the foremost forms – that enable and legitimise this process. There is no simple way, perhaps no way at all during this particular phase of capitalism, to break this spiral of financial transaction, cultural production, industrial manufacture and military intervention. Yet the process is a spiral and not a circle. If the war in Iraq testified to anything, as will be discussed in the next chapter, it is that the modernity this complex engineers is not viable. The complex may be self-perpetuating, but it is not sustainable. It does not engineer a future, but, as Josh Smicker has argued and as subsequent chapters will illustrate, a war on the future.[36]

34 Nolan's *The Dark Knight Rises* is a good example of this kind of narrative.

35 Der Derian, *Virtuous War*, 243.

36 Smicker, 'Future Combat'.

# Chapter 9
# Tales of Torture and Invasion

On 11 March 2004, just 10 days before the first-year anniversary of the invasion of Iraq, an independent terrorist cell set off a bomb on a Madrid commuter train, killing 191. At the same time, fighting erupted in the city of Fallujah following the shooting of a number of Blackwater employees. In April, *60 Minutes* aired pictures of torture and murder conducted by American prison guards in the Abu Ghraib prison. On 19 May, US troops bombed a wedding in Mukaradeeb, killing 42. Sectarian violence in the form of suicide and car bombings became more and more common during the spring and summer and seemed to target civilians as often as police or invading soldiers. In October, the respected British medical journal *The Lancet* published a survey that estimated that the invasion and occupation of Iraq had caused 98,000 excess Iraqi deaths, not counting the dead that were amassing as a result of more intense fighting in Fallujah.[1] While this survey caused significant controversy, it paled in comparison to the study published two years later, which suggested an excess death toll of 654,965 people up to that date.[2] In December 2005, George W. Bush admitted that the decision to invade Iraq was based on faulty intelligence but maintained that it was right to invade.

Most Americans disagreed.[3] At the time, it had become clear that if there were weapons of mass destruction in Iraq, the US had brought them. If Iraq was a hotbed of international terrorism set on slaughtering civilians by the thousands, it was because they had been attracted to the nation by the US presence. If people were tortured and murdered in prisons, it was because the US allowed it or actually performed it. The war in Iraq was not going well.

---

1 Les Roberts, Riyadh Lafta, Richard Garfield, Jamal Khudhairi and Gilbert Burnham, 'Mortality before and after the 2003 Invasion of Iraq: Cluster Sample Survey', *The Lancet* 364, no. 9448 (2004): 1857–64.

2 Gilbert Burnham, Riyadh Lafta, Shannon Doocy and Les Roberts, 'Mortality after the 2003 Invasion of Iraq: A Cross-Sectional Cluster Sample Survey', *The Lancet* 368, no. 9545 (2006): 1421–8.

3 In June 2004, the first Gallup that indicated that more Americans were thinking that the invasion was a mistake than otherwise was presented. In the years that follow, up until March 2013, 14 Gallup polls showed the American public in favour of the war while 54 showed them as thinking the invasion was a mistake. After August 2005, no Gallup poll revealed majority support of the war. See http://www.gallup.com/poll/1633/iraq.aspx.

It was not just the war that was perceived as going badly. The notion that America was indeed an empire capable of positive global transformation, as argued by Ferguson and Boot, began to collapse at this time. If America was indeed an empire, or at least a hegemon, the spring of 2004 and the years that followed testified to its failure to constructively project its power globally. When the economy showed signs of failing in 2007, and then fell apart completely in 2008, this sense of a hegemony in rapid decline permeated many discussions and representations of the US. World-system research may indicate that the US has been in decline since the early 1970s, but it was arguably at this point in time that the possibility of an American imperial collapse was widely discussed and experienced.

This sense of collapse also left its mark on the imperial gothic. Justin Cronin, author of the successful and critically praised gothic and post-apocalyptic vampire epic *The Passage* (2010), discussed in Chapter 10, has stated that he began writing the novel in late 2005, 'about the time the war in Iraq was really going badly. It seemed to have a crescendo of gore and confusion.'[4] This gore and confusion is at the heart of much gothic culture produced after 2005. Few gothic narratives embrace the optimism and the frontier spirit prevalent in *Van Helsing*, *King Kong* or *Quake 4* in the years after 2006. Instead, gothic culture became increasingly concerned with the body in pain and the acts inflicting this pain. Films occupied with these concerns were termed 'torture porn' by film critic David Edelstein in 2006,[5] a designation that suggests that plot is of secondary importance in these films, that what the audience comes to see is the human body in pain. Indeed, the torture films depict limbs sawed off, the flesh rent by power tools in ways that make the original *The Texas Chain Saw Massacre* seem coy and timid by comparison.[6] Torture is also common in more conventional gothic narratives. In a series of films, Western champions have to make use of torture to save civilisation, and in many ways the genre at this stage comments on what may be described as a 'culture of torture'.[7]

4 Justin Cronin, *The Passage* (2010; reprint, New York: Ballantine Books, 2012). Quotation from: http://www.powells.com/blog/interviews/justin-cronin-the-powells-com-interview-by-jill/.

5 Adam Lowenstein is one of many critics to have suggested the term 'spectacle horror' instead of 'torture porn'. This term may help steer the reader clear of the instinctual distaste that critics such as Edelstein attempt to generate for films such as *Hostel* (2005) and *Saw* (2004), but at the same time it disregards what these films are actually about: torture. See Adam Lowenstein, 'Spectacle Horror and *Hostel*: Why Torture Porn Does Not Exist', *Critical Quarterly* 53, no. 1 (2011): 42–60.

6 In *The Texas Chain Saw Massacre* from 1974, the camera turns away from the act of sawing the human body apart, to instead focus on the victim not being butchered, but who observes the butchery.

7 See, for instance, *The Torture Debate in America*, edited by Karen J. Greenberg (Cambridge: Cambridge University Press, 2006).

In addition to this, the apocalyptic invasion narrative popular in Britain during the late nineteenth century and in the US during the 1950s experienced a renaissance at this time. In these texts, the US is no longer seen as an invader destined to pacify and transform liminal frontier spaces. Instead, these narratives show the US as the object of alien and gothic invasion and colonisation.

This chapter discusses the relationship between the US's increasingly desperate attempt to consolidate global hegemony through the invasion of Iraq and the torture and invasion narratives that characterise the imperial gothic at this time. The two genres are very different but in fact offer quite similar perspectives on the nature and legitimacy of American empire. Torture porn relies on images of pain and murder rather than on narrative, even if the narrative is far from inconsequential. The invasion narrative focuses on a different iconography, but it is even more a staple of the imperial gothic. This chapter traces the genealogy of the twenty-first century invasion narratives back to British late-Victorian and early-Edwardian fiction and argues that, like these previous novels, the post-9/11 invasion narrative is informed by geopolitical concerns, and by a feeling that the American empire is utterly vulnerable. In ways that directly recall the introverted and apocalyptic British imperial gothic as defined in the introduction to this book, the torture films and the invasion narratives mirror an increasingly anxious society that has lost faith not only in the invasion of Iraq and the administration that engineered it but also in America's ability and right to project power across the globe. In relation to this, this chapter also discusses the clandestine invasion narrative modelled on such novels as Dracula, and on the outbreak narrative that reframes the invasion as a form of viral yet gothic contagion.

## Torture

In *Hostel* (2005), the two young Americans Paxton and Josh backpack through Europe and end up in Slovakia at an unregistered hostel full of beautiful and strangely willing women. There, Paxton and Josh enjoy the sexual favours of local natives Natalya and Svetlana. On the morning after, when the two friends meet for breakfast, Paxton turns to Josh with the words: 'Mission accomplished.' As Adam Lowenstein notes in 'Spectacle Horror and *Hostel*', this is a subtle reference to George W. Bush's premature announcement on the *USS Abraham Lincoln* in May 2003.[8] In the throes of the same 'delusional arrogance' as the US president and blind to his status as 'American imperialist victimiser' Paxton thinks he deserves the satisfaction these women grant him.[9]

8 Lowenstein, 'Spectacle Horror and *Hostel*', 56.

9 Lowenstein, 'Spectacle Horror and *Hostel*', 56.

But the hostel is not a transnational harem where Paxton and Josh rise to the surface because of their status as white, middle-class American males. Before the evening is over, they have been sedated and taken to secluded torture chambers. Josh is the first to go as a Dutch businessman he has previously encountered begins to cut him up and eventually kills him in a prolonged and increasingly gory scene involving drills and knives. The camera never shuns from the act of torture itself. This is, after all, what the audience has paid the price of the admission ticket to watch. Paxton is next, but the German who has paid good money to butcher him is sloppy. When cutting fingers off Paxton's hand, he accidentally frees him. Then, he slips and cuts his own leg with the chainsaw he is using to torture Paxton. Paxton manages to escape, kills several people and finally makes his way out of the facility. Dressing up in the business suit of another torturer, Paxton discovers evidence of a global torture ring – Elite Hunting – where the wealthy can pay to torment citizens of different nationalities. The most expensive type is, not surprisingly, Americans.

*Hostel*'s novelty is not that it describes torture in graphic detail. This has been done before. What is new about *Hostel* is that it depicts the torture of young American men in a liminal Eastern European setting. Just like Transylvania is the place where East meets West in Stoker's *Dracula*, this run-down region of Slovakia is a form of transitional frontier space where East and West collide. Catherine Zimmer has argued that the ultimate absurdity and horror of films such as *Hostel* is the fact that Americans are not imagined as exempt from torture:

> The emergence of these narratives of American youth, frequently men, going abroad and finding themselves immersed in what often amounts to an economy of torture must, I believe, be read as a tremendously projective fantasy – one in which American youth are figured as the victims rather than the perpetrators of this kind of organized violence.[10]

Indeed, there is something perverse about the very presence of Josh and Paxton in the torture chamber. Like the frontier women of America's past, they have been captured by vicious marauders who, like the Indians in Burroughs's *A Princess of Mars*, delight in the 'torture of every white party which fell into their merciless clutches'.[11] As young, white, American males, Josh and Paxton have no business getting captured and tortured.

Indeed, most other texts from this period insist, like the images coming out of Abu Ghraib, that American males are the ones who orchestrate

---

10 Catherine Zimmer, 'Caught on Tape? The Politics of Video in the New Torture Film' in *Horror after 9/11: World of Fear, Cinema of Terror*, edited by Aviva Briefel and Sam J. Miller (Austin: University of Texas Press, 2011), 84.

11 Burroughs, *A Princess of Mars*, 17.

torturous violence. In the television series *24* (2001–10), torture is an often clinical and always morally legitimate and effective interrogation technology performed by American agents. In *The Dark Knight*, Batman beats up the Joker in an interrogation room, and in Frank Miller's short graphic novel *Holy Terror* (2011),[12] first conceived of as a Batman story in 2006, the superhero the Fixer tortures Islamic terrorists in ways that directly reference the images of torture coming out of Abu Ghraib.

*The Dark Knight*, *24* and *Holy Terror* are narratives that represent torture as an inevitable aspect of power but they also function as attempts to justify the practice by presenting it as an ultimately necessary, effective, patriotic and modern practice. As violence becomes the only way for Edgar Huntly to communicate with the Native Americans he encounters, as discussed in Chapter 2, torture is represented as the only way to communicate effectively with the secretive terrorist. This category of person will only divulge matters of importance while in pain. In this way, torture is not an abject ritual, but a form of explanation, even a translation from plain English into an even plainer language that the terrorist can comprehend.

From this perspective, torture porn re-imagines torture not only by subjecting Americans to it but also by transforming it from a rational and effective method used to extract vital information into a sadistic and self-indulgent ritual. As observed by Zimmer, *Hostel* portrays torture as a new capitalist frontier, the ultimate indulgence of the wealthy, a portrayal seemingly designed to cast further doubt on the sustainability of this system. Furthermore, in *Saw* (2004), where a serial killer places victims inside torturous traps that they can only escape by mutilating themselves or others, torture is always monitored, turning it into also a sadistic surveillance game. Finally, these films deny firm borders between the perpetrators and the victims. In virtually all films, the tortured change place with the torturers at some point during the narrative so that they 'posit every character as both guilty and innocent'.[13] Indeed, Paxton rises from his chair to trade places with the people who have been torturing him. The same thing happens in many other torture-porn movies such as *Captivity* (2007), *Hostel: Part II* (2007) and in the *Saw* series.

The emergence of these films in the immediate wake of Abu Ghraib is no coincidence. The images of tortured or dead Iraqi prisoners that found their way into the media in 2004 frequently show smiling American men and women standing behind their victims. The evident delight or (at times) boredom that the prison guards show in these photographs does not bring counterterrorist Jack Bauer's stern face in *24* to mind. The Abu Ghraib images reveal torture not as a clinical and efficient practice but rather as an imperial way of life.

12 Frank Miller, *Holy Terror* (Burbank, CA: Legendary Comics, 2011).

13 Zimmer, 'Caught on Tape?', 85.

In this way, they are reminiscent of the lynching narratives and the lynching photography of the early nineteenth century. Just like the victims of lynching were rarely tried in a court of law, and never punished by one, the victims of Abu Ghraib were not put on trial. Just like the actual guilt of those lynched in the late nineteenth and early twentieth centuries was never an important issue, guilt seems to have been of little concern in Abu Ghraib. As numerous studies show, and as Naomi Klein has forcibly argued, torture is notoriously ineffective as a practice with which to acquire information but very efficient as an instrument of social control.[14] Thus, in 2004 as well as in Reconstruction USA, torture must be advertised. It must be described in the newspapers; it must be photographed and disseminated.

From one perspective, torture porn seeks to interrogate and critique this function of torture. When the *Hostel* and *Saw* series present torture as the ultimate indulgent capitalist practice, they uncover a society where humans have been reduced to (screaming) and interchangeable commodities. The awful violence practised in the films is thus descriptive of the violence that capitalist societies at times direct not only at the imperial periphery but also at their own citizens. In *Saw* and *Hostel*, as in Iraq, torture is an indulgent, surveilled and networked practice, a manifestation rather than an accident of power. This makes it possible to read the *Hostel* and *Saw* movies into fiercely critical, anti-capitalist texts in the same vein as the original *The Texas Chain Saw Massacre*.

At the same time, the torture films repeat some of the tenets of the conservative imperial gothic. While these movies are significantly more nihilistic and less assuring than many of the other narratives discussed in this study, it is still possible to escape the torture chamber by embracing manly virtues. Evangelos Tziallas observes in 'Torture Porn and Surveillance Culture' that in *Captivity* (2007), the beautiful model Jennifer, horribly tortured throughout the movie, finally manages to turn the tables on her tormentor, picks up a large (and phallic) gun and uses it to castrate him.[15] Similarly, young Beth in *Hostel: Part II* manages to overcome her torturer Stewart at the last minute. Her way out of the dungeon is also to symbolically assume his masculinity. This is accomplished first by offering to pay the member's fee of Elite Hunting, taking Stewart's place in the capitalistic order, and then castrating her male tormentor with a sharp knife. In most torture porn movies, there is a way out for the strong, resourceful and symbolically masculine.

---

14 This argument is forcefully presented by Naomi Klein in *The Shock Doctrine: The Rise of Disaster Capitalism* (New York: Knopf Canada, 2007).

15 Evangelos Tziallas, 'Torture Porn and Surveillance Culture', *Jump Cut: A Review of Contemporary Media* no. 52 (2010). http://www.ejumpcut.org/archive/jc52.2010/evangelosTorturePorn/index.html.

In addition to this, it is important to observe that these films also commodify the suffering they depict. Even those in the audience that 'get' the not always transparent criticism that informs them do not necessarily watch in order to fuel their latent dislike of an oppressive capitalist society. As discussed in Chapter 5, Robin Wood makes a crucial point just after defining *The Texas Chain Saw Massacre* as a collective nightmare: 'Watching it recently with a large, half-stoned youth audience who cheered and applauded every one of Leatherface's outrages against their representatives on the screen, was a terrifying experience.'[16] In other words, torture porn may reveal the brutality of a voracious and capitalist society, but it also peddles this brutality to an enthusiastic audience. Edelstein, deeply dejected by the extreme sadism that he is confronted by on the screen, complains that he does not 'want to identify with the victim *or* the victimizer'.[17] The audience that watched Leatherface cut his way through the young men and women of the story seems less reluctant.

From this perspective, *Hostel* and *Saw* are certainly polyphonous gothic texts. They simultaneously condemn and encourage the horrors they seek to interrogate. As texts, they query the voracious nature of capitalist society. As commodities, they inspire and feed off of the same system. It is in this way that they remain imperial gothic. The many straightforward, visual references to the horrors of Abu Ghraib that form part of the subtext of the *Hostel* and *Saw* franchises become part of the perverse affect of pleasure and disgust that these films generate and, as affect, they are peddled to a society that may detest the actual practice of torture but that will still, paradoxically perhaps, pay to see it performed.

## 'Right Now, We Are Being Colonised'

In *Battle: Los Angeles* (2011), the viewer is first met by confused news footage and the voices of concerned reporters. They speak against a background of green and grainy images that show anti-aircraft fire, rockets and artillery lighting up the city skyline. 'One thing is clear', an anonymous reporter tells us, 'the world is at war'. Explosions rumble and civilians flee past running soldiers down streets pockmarked by gunfire. A sergeant major on television explains the hostilities to the general public and to concerned men and women in army fatigues: 'This is a textbook military invasion.' The point of view shifts from chaos on the streets, from fleeing civilians and stock imagery, to a number of worried-looking marines running into a troop transport helicopter. The hand-

16 Wood, 'An Introduction to the American Horror Film', 133.

17 David Edelstein, 'Now Playing at Your Local Multiplex: Torture Porn', *New York Magazine*, February 6, 2006, http://nymag.com/movies/features/15622/index1.html, emphasis in original.

held camera photography is shaky and realistic. The soldiers look frightened yet determined as the helicopter takes off through a barrage of explosions. Smoke, fire and shrapnel make it difficult to see out of the transport's window.

The audience is familiar with this way of depicting war, with the aesthetics of the movie: it is the face of urban warfare from the 1991 Persian Gulf War to the more recent invasions or Afghanistan and Iraq. In fact, what we see in the beginning is probably archival footage from these wars. The shaky photography depicting soldiers under fire comes from actual war photography and is also copied from films such as Ridley Scott's *Black Hawk Down* (2001) which chronicles US fighting in Somalia in 1993. The similarities between these images and archival footage from Afghanistan or Iraq are not coincidental. When recruiting actor Aaron Eckhart for the lead role, director Jonathan Liebesman showed YouTube clips of marines fighting in Fallujah and explained that this was the look he was aiming for.[18]

However, in *Battle: Los Angeles* the gunfire that envelops the people in the streets and the audience is not directed at invading American forces fighting Islamic rebels in Iraq but at marines *defending* an American city. This is the US being invaded. The city burning and crumbling to ruins below the troop transport helicopters is, as the title of the movie informs the viewer, Los Angeles. In the middle of this invasion of the American city is the reluctant marine veteran Michael Nantz (Aaron Eckhart's role in the movie). Nantz helps lead a platoon of brave soldiers into the thick of the fighting to stall the invading aliens and save a handful of civilians. The point of view from now on is this small group of soldiers, a few civilians and the choices and sacrifices that they have to make as they confront the technologically superior, yet strangely inept, alien invaders. The reason for the invasion is hastily sketched: 'There has been no communication so, obviously, they are here for our resources. When you invade a place for its resources, you wipe out the indigenous population. Those are the rules for any colonisation. And, right now, we are being colonised.'[19] In this way, the violence that is colonisation in action is being visited upon the American people. Soldiers and civilians lie dead in the streets. Earth's resources are harvested by occupying forces.

The invasion and colonisation of the Earth by an alien intelligence as told by *Battle: Los Angeles* is one of the most popular and commercially viable plots

---

18 See http://screenrant.com/battle-los-angeles-comiccon-2010-robf-69613/.

19 One could take issue with this description, of course. In many historical cases, colonisers have made use of the indigenous population as a labour force. In Africa, Dutch, Belgian, British and French colonists were absolutely dependent on the local population. The description may not be entirely wrong when considering the North American context however. The treatment of the Native American population, refusing to be used as a labour force by the European colonisers, did resemble the type of genocide described here. Of course, slave labour was imported from Africa in this case.

of post-9/11 culture. The first truly big-budget Hollywood movie to explore the invasion narrative after 9/11 was Steven Spielberg's *War of the Worlds* (2005). Since then, similar stories have been told by the *Transformers* franchise (2007–11), the most recent remake of the *Body Snatchers* simply called *The Invasion* (2007), *Cloverfield* (2008), *Skyline* (2010), *Monsters* (2010), *Super 8* (2011) and *The Darkest Hour* (2011). On television, the reboot of *V* (2009–11) and *Falling Skies* (2011–) have also depicted humans resisting the military arsenal of various alien species. In 2012, *Battle: Los Angeles* was followed by *Battleship* and the major blockbuster *The Avengers*, a film also telling the story of an alien invasion of the Earth. Similarly, the game industry has produced a series of games, such as the *Crysis* and *Resistance* series, where the gamer must defend the Earth against an intergalactic enemy.[20] In fiction, Scott Sigler's *Infected* (2006, 2008) and *Contagious*, as well as J.L. Bourne's zombie series *Day by Day Armageddon* (2004, 2007), *Beyond Exile* (2010) and *Shattered Hourglass* (2012) make use of gothic imagery to describe how alien invasion transforms people into predatory creatures.[21] In addition to this, non-alien and non-gothic invasions of the American homeland were explored in the remarkably successful game franchise *Call of Duty: Modern Warfare*, in the best-selling *Battlefield 3* and in *Homefront*, the latter game accompanied by a much delayed remake of the 1986 invasion movie *Red Dawn* (2012).[22] Thus, the invasion narrative became one of the most important vehicles for understanding a world in which the US appears as not only post-9/11 but also post-popular and, perhaps, post-powerful.

## Imperial Genealogies

Narratives of foreign or alien military invasion have a distinctly imperial genealogy. The original invasion narrative, the story that virtually all alien invasion stories that will be discussed here look back to, is H.G. Wells's *The War of the Worlds* (1898). Few turn-of-the-century novels have had such an impact on modern popular culture as this novel. It was not, however, the first story to describe the violent invasion and colonisation of (British) society. Wells's

20 *Battle: Los Angeles* was marketed with its own limited first-person shooter by the same name. In addition to this, the film advertises the game *Resistance 3*, like *Battle: Los Angeles*, a Sony product (Sony owns Columbia Pictures, the producer and distributer of *Battle: Los Angeles*).

21 Sigler's *Infected* was first released as a free audiobook in 2006. In 2008, it was published by Crown Publising. J.L. Bourne, *Day by Day Armageddon* (Nashville: Permuted Press, 2007), *Day by Day Armageddon: Beyond Exile* (Nashville: Permuted Press, 2010), *Day by Day Armageddon: Shattered Hourglass* (Nashville: Permuted Press, 2012).

22 It should be noted that many of these stories are typically filed as science fiction or future war story rather than gothic, but, as discussed in the introduction, the borders separating science fiction and the (imperial) gothic are notoriously permeable.

novel belongs to a long tradition of invasion writing that comprises gothic forerunners such as Stoker's *Dracula* and Richard Marsh's *The Beetle* but also a number of non-gothic, military invasion narratives. As I.F. Clarke in *Voices Prophesying War 1763–1984* (1966) and Cecil Eby in *The Road to Armageddon: The Martial Spirit in English Popular Literature, 1870–1914* (1987) have argued, the invasion trope structured a large number of British novels, short stories, historical writing, theatre, music, and political writing during the late nineteenth and early twentieth centuries.[23] These narratives began to appear following the unification of Germany and the Franco-Prussian War of 1870–1871. This conflict, which denoted a central shift of power on the European continent from France to Germany, inspired Lieutenant C.G. Chesney to write the novella *The Battle of Dorking* for *Blackwood's Magazine*.[24] Conceived only days after the armistice between France and the new Germany in 1871, it describes how Germany manages to thwart the powerful British navy and land a significant army on British shores. In the battle that ensues, the vast and effective German army has no problems dealing with the disorganised and ill-prepared British infantry that stands in its way. While the Germans are uninterested in Britain as territory, the British lose their fleet and their world-wide empire in the peace agreement that follows.

This story was the first of many to describe an actual military invasion of the British Isles by a foreign power. It paved the way for a jingoistic, xenophobic and increasingly paranoid wave of spy and military invasion novels that climaxed in 1914 when the war they had long predicted, perhaps even paved the way for, finally broke out.[25] Between 1871 and 1914, Germany was not always perceived as the most likely imperial contender and invader. Depending on the political climate, the French, the United States, Japan, China or a confederation of hostile states were cast as the attacker of the British isle. However, as the century drew to a close, Germany, supporting the Boers in South Africa and constructing a navy capable of threatening the British, became the focus of these military invasion narratives.

---

23 For useful overviews of these novels, see the aforementioned I.F. Clarke, *Voices Prophesying War* and Cecil Degrotte Eby, *The Road to Armageddon: The Martial Spirit in English Popular Literature, 1870–1914* (Durham: Duke University Press, 1987).

24 See G.T. Chesney, *The Battle of Dorking: Reminiscences of a Volunteer* (1871) in I.F. Clarke, *The Tale of the Next Great War: Fictions of Future Warfare and of Battles Still-to-Come* (Liverpool: Liverpool University Press, 1995).

25 It can be argued that these novels assisted the British war effort along by insisting that military confrontation with Germany, or other foreign powers, was the only way to ensure lasting imperial predominance. Also, the kind of discourse and sentiment that the novels helped create may have boosted the number of volunteers that the British army saw arriving after the declaration of war. See Johan Höglund, 'Mobilising the Novel: The Literature of Imperialism and the First World War', PhD diss., Acta Universitatis Upsaliensis, Studia Anglistica Upsaliensia, Uppsala, 1997.

The invasion novel accompanies the period when British imperialism was at its most conscious and expansive phase. This was the time of the scramble for Africa, when the technological advances of the Industrial Revolution in the form of steam engines and machine guns allowed for a relatively quick conquest of territory. However, the period 1880–1914 was also, as has been discussed, a period of competition and imperial decline. In the face of this competition, the British became involved in a number of confrontations with indigenous populations in Africa and with other European settlers, as in the prolonged Boer War in South Africa.

The imperial gothic (invasion) novel was thus produced during a period of often violently extroverted imperial decline. Thus, Stephen D. Arata has argued that the invasion novels from the period express 'the anxiety of reverse colonisation' so that late-Victorian fiction was 'saturated with the sense that the entire nation – as a race of people, as a political and imperial force, as a social and cultural power – was in irretrievable decline'.[26] At the same time, Arata argues, the invasion narratives were 'responses to cultural guilt. In the marauding, invasive Other, British culture sees its own imperial practices mirrored back in monstrous form'.[27] In other words, the invasion narrative dramatised (and often gothicised) a sense of failure and pending doom, but it also expressed a form of imperial remorse or perhaps a guilty conscience. There is indeed a sense in much British imperial gothic, as in the new American imperial gothic, that the gothic invasion, whether insidious or direct, is a payback, the wretched of the Earth striking back in monstrous form, imperial practice hideously mirrored. In the narratives discussed in this chapter, this sense often drowns in spectacles of gunfire and righteous anger at the sudden reversal of the practice, but all the same it is there, visible under the surface like a poorly drowned corpse.

## The Spectacle of Invasion: Military Confrontation

One thing that this book seeks to demonstrate is how American popular gothic culture converges on themes similar to those of British popular culture of the late-Victorian period and that it does so for very similar reasons. The prevalence of the invasion narrative in contemporary American culture is one of the most striking connections between the cultures of the British and the American empires. As illustrated in Chapter 4, the invasion narrative has been an important part of American gothic culture since the Cold War. However, it has arguably never been as widely disseminated, or as legitimate, as it is today when invasion films attract the biggest Hollywood budgets, stars and directors.

26 Arata, 'The Occidental Tourist', 622.

27 Arata, 'The Occidental Tourist', 623.

Like the British invasion narrative, the American invasion narrative comes in different forms. Following the example of H.G. Wells (or the prolific British invasion writer William Le Queux), invasion narratives such as *Battle: Los Angeles*, *Battleship* or *Red Dawn* depict a large-scale military invasion of apocalyptic proportions engineered by alien or foreign nations. This makes for invasion spectacles encouraged by, and encouraging, the military–industrial–entertainment complex as discussed in Chapter 8. Thus, *Battleship* comes with an assortment of toys and games from Hasbro; it was named after one of the company's most popular board games and features a sequence where a variant of this game is played for real against the alien invaders. At the same time, the film is an opportunity for the navy to showcase some of its advanced weaponry and to celebrate, in a striking sequence, the role the navy played in conflicts such as World War II. At the end of the film, the intrepid heroes have to take command of the World War II battleship *USS Missouri* and they do so assisted by actual World War II navy veterans.[28] In a sequence that seeks to place the film within a historical and patriotic tradition that understands any current American pre-eminence as directly related to American participation in global warfare, the veterans are informed that 'You men have given so much to your country, and no one has the right to ask any more of you ... but I'm asking'.

*Battle: Los Angeles* also references World War II but is more directly related to the invasions of Afghanistan and Iraq. The hero of the film is the Marine Corps as much as the brave Nantz. When civilian Michael Peña picks up a gun and then takes a bullet for the soldiers who have come to save him, his adolescent son is told to wipe away his tears. This accomplished, the son is promptly adopted by the corps and taught to repeat their mottos: 'Marine's never quit' and 'Retreat Hell'. When the monster's lair in the form of a massive, mobile command centre has been blown to pieces and the few remaining soldiers have returned to the base, they stand dazed and drained for only a few minutes before again loading up on ammunition to return to the fighting. As in late-Victorian fiction, a good soldier is always ready to die for his or her country. National unity, patriotism, courage and sacrifice come across as the virtues most necessary not only to confront the alien invaders but also to shore up the anxiety that has taken hold of the American nation after the invasions of Iraq and Afghanistan.

In this way, many military or science fiction invasion narratives can be said to attempt to amend the failures of these invasions by displacing the politics involved in these endeavours. Like George W. Bush argued in multiple speeches, the battle depicted is always and only a conflict between good and evil. Once these absolute borders have been established, there is no longer any reason to discuss the political rationale behind the confrontation depicted. The only thing

28 In a similar sequence, astronaut Buzz Aldrin has a cameo role as himself in *Transformers: Dark of the Moon* (2011).

left is the need to respect the courage and sacrifice of America's fighting forces: war is just in these narratives simply because American men (and women) die fighting it.

## Clandestine Invasions

While Hollywood does excel in extravagant and apocalyptic images of military invasion, many narratives explore invasion not as a large-scale battle but as an essentially clandestine affair. As previously discussed, the War on Terror was initially described by Bush as something going on behind the scenes. He argued on 17 September 2001 that in the past '[w]e've been able to watch on our television screens sophisticated weaponry find a building, and we've seen dramatic reports from the front where Pulitzer-Prize-to-be-winning reporters stood up and declared, "The United States has attacked," and all that'.[29] Perhaps already contemplating the invasions of Afghanistan and Iraq, Bush acknowledged that there 'may be some of that', but then assured his audience that most of this new war was going to be fought without cameras against an elusive enemy, someone who fights unfair, who hides and burrows, who obeys no rules. As if commenting on and conforming to this vision, many invasion narratives explore the clandestine hunt for the cowardly burrower, the terrorist in hiding, the monsters who 'kind of slither into shadowy recesses in large cities', as he put it in 2002.[30]

The secretive struggle with the 'slithering' Other is, of course, also an undertaking with which the imperial gothic is intimately familiar. The British imperial gothic was very concerned with the clandestine policing of the gothic Other. The gathering of white men who oppose the vampire count in *Dracula* is a useful example. Although only consisting of five people (counting Van Helsing), they are imagined as a form of enlightened, underground military resistance to Dracula's gothic invasion of London. They provide a model for a number of similar groups that, with time, become more and more directly associated with the government.

An influential television series here is *The X-Files* (on television 1993–2002 and in the form of Hollywood movies in 1998 and 2008). As Heidi Kaye has argued, this series 'reworks the Gothic for the 1990s. In place of power-hungry aristocrats and evil monks, its villains are authoritarian government bureaucrats and secretive army officers. Ghosts are replaced by aliens and castles by government installations, but the expected dangerous scientists and

29 Bush, 'Remarks to Employees in the Pentagon', 1119.

30 Bush, 'Remarks to the Community', 1547.

the weird monsters appear much as usual in the Gothic'.[31] The protagonists of the series are FBI agents Mulder and Scully who investigate a great number of extra-terrestrial and supernatural phenomena inside US borders. Mulder and Scully have a hard time finding anyone who is ready to believe in their mission. Indeed, Scully is herself full of doubt. In addition to this, the government has been infiltrated by people who participate in one or many of the multiple plots against the nation's well-being. In *The X-Files*, government agencies are already involved in a War on Terror and constitute, paradoxically, both the greatest hazard to the nation and its only real hope.

After 9/11, the secretive government organisation that fights gothic terrorist invasion in the dark became common in the American imperial gothic. In many cases, these organisations are described as having been forced to recruit some of the monsters that they seek to destroy. Another model here is *Hellboy*, also discussed in Chapter 6. As described, the *Hellboy* saga tells the story of how Nazis summon an infant demon to Earth during World War II. This demon, the eponymous Hellboy, becomes the first and most important member of the Bureau of Paranormal Research and Defence (BPRD). This government agency is in fact an operational task force comprising a number of paranormal agents as well as the usual paramilitary enforcers with machine guns and uniform clothing.

Christopher Farnsworth's novels about vampire-turned-government-assassin Nathaniel Cade employ the government model established by the *Hellboy* franchise and take place in essentially the same Lovecraftian universe but are at the same time a patchwork of the gothic. A great many classic gothic and horror stories, from Mary Shelley's *Frankenstein* to *Halloween*, are somehow related to the Cade mythos in the novels.[32] The series is particularly interesting as it makes the relationship between the struggles with the gothic Other and the War on Terror as outlined by the Bush administration absolutely explicit. In the novel, White House employee Zach Barrows is introduced to the vampire Cade and the work he performs with the words: 'Forget the War on Terror, Zach. This is the War on Horror.'[33] The stakes of this war are high:

> There are worse things in this world than al-Qaeda and North Korea, Zach. And they are just waiting for their chance at us … Humanity will not survive that. They're an infection, and they spread like Ebola. Whatever it takes, we have to keep that border between light and dark. Or we lose. Everything. Every one of us will die.[34]

---

31 Heidi Kaye, 'Fin-de-siècle Fears: *The X-Files* as Contemporary Gothic' in *Fictions of Unease: The Gothic from Otranto to* The X-Files, edited by Andrew Smith, Diane Mason and William Hughes (Bath: Sulis Press, 2002), 202.

32 Mary Shelley, *Frankenstein* (London: Lackington, Hughes, Harding, Mavor & Jones, 1818).

33 Christopher Farnsworth, *Blood Oath* (London: Hodder & Stoughton, 2010), 22.

34 Farnsworth, *Blood Oath*, 22.

While Griffin seems to be turning Zach's and the reader's eyes away from the political and material threat that al-Qaeda and North Korea constitute, Zach soon discovers that what Griffin is really telling him is that the War on Horror *is* the War on Terror. Al-Qaeda and North Korea operate simultaneously as geopolitical and as gothic entities, and as the latter, al-Qaeda is, in fact, the worst thing in the world. This becomes clear when the reader is told that Cade took part in an assassination attempt on bin Laden in November 2001 only to discover that the al-Qaeda leader is not simply a terrorist but also a shape-changing monster:

> His head and jaw jutted forward as black bile dribbled from his mouth. His skin shredded as muscle and bone moved beneath it like snakes under a tarp. He locked eyes with Cade, and Cade saw his pupils had become diamond-slitted. His mouth gaped like a fish, revealing dozens of cruel, piranha-like teeth. The new flesh under his torn skin was dark green, almost black, and covered in scales.[35]

In this way, Islamic fundamentalism is directly linked to gothic horror; the War on Terror is the War on Horror is the War on Terror.[36]

Similar stories are also told in Jennifer Rardin's *Jaz Parks* novels and Jonathan Maberry's *Joe Ledger* series. These also centre on government agencies that fight the War on Terror by combating supernatural terrorists. In Rardin's *Once Bitten, Twice Shy* (2007), CIA assassin and former Special Forces soldier Jaz Parks, joined by ancient vampire Vayl, uncovers a plot by the Arabic terrorists Sons of Paradise to release the soul-eating demon Tor-al-Degan.[37] In Maberry's *Patient Zero* (2009), Baltimore detective, martial arts expert and former US soldier Joe Ledger is recruited to the secretive Department of Military Sciences.[38] This clandestine organisation is then tasked with the job of preventing Islamic fundamentalist El Mujahid from unleashing a zombie virus on the American population.

In all of these novels, it is imperative to keep the nature or even the presence of the gothic/Islamic Other from the public. The American people must be kept in blissful darkness, never confronted with the actual horrors that are always infiltrating the suburban landscape they inhabit. The knowledge that evil truly exists might be almost as devastating as any project this evil undertakes.[39]

---

35 Christopher Farnsworth, *The President's Vampire* (New York: Putnam, 2011), 8.

36 It should be added that in this passage bin Laden denounces the Prophet Mohammed. Even so, the connection remains, especially since the central plot of the nation involves another set of Islamic fundamentalists who conduct an attack on the White House with the help of American soldiers who have been killed in action and transformed into 'unmenschsoldaten' by a still living Dr Frankenstein.

37 See Jennifer Rardin, *Once Bitten, Twice Shy* (London: Orbit Books, 2007).

38 See Jonathan Maberry, *Patient Zero* (New York: St Martin's Griffin, 2009).

39 The logic is partly Victorian as expressed by Marlow in *Heart of Darkness*. At the end of this novella, Marlow explains why women must not be made aware of what goes on in the

The realisation that this is not a beautiful world may in itself become an invasion of apocalyptic dimensions. Thus, these undercover governmental organisations must keep the nature of the gothic threat from the public to avoid the panic and civil unrest that may result if they understand that the actual and symbolic borders of empire are hopelessly permeable. A symptom as well as an engine of imperial decline, such unrest may be as detrimental to modernity and the maintenance of empire as any gothic infection. Thus, these agencies exist as much to keep the knowledge of evil from the public as to combat evil.

## The Imperial Gothic and the Outbreak Narrative

In a number of invasion narratives, the invasion is cast as an actual viral or bacterial infection. In the Cade novels, Griff's admonition that the powers of evil that threaten the world is an infection that spreads like Ebola is not simply a metaphor, although it is this too. Many of the threats that Cade has to confront are, in fact, viral and infectious by nature. Post-9/11 discourse as expressed by the Bush administration allows metaphorical connections between terrorism, viral infection and gothic challenges. All of these constitute a painful and potentially lethal contest, all disregard the borders erected to keep the West separate from its many Others, all have the ability to transform body and psyche, to make the infected monstrous in some way, and all pit a primitive and relentless entity against the machinery of modernity. Thus, it is not surprising that many of the most effective and influential gothic texts have made use of imagery and modes of contagion that have their roots in what Priscilla Wald has called the 'outbreak narrative'. This narrative has in itself a long genealogy. As Wald argues, it became firmly entrenched in the West through the case of 'Typhoid Mary', an Irish cook and asymptomatic typhoid carrier who caused a number of outbreaks in New York at the turn of the twentieth century. It was further accelerated by the global spreading of a number of flu strains during the twentieth century and in particular by the HIV virus that surfaced in the 1980s.

Indeed, many British and American imperial gothic texts can be defined as outbreak narratives. As observed by a number of critics, Bram Stoker's *Dracula* furtively discusses the spreading of syphilis and also imagines the construction of various modern/medical barriers (most importantly the blood transfusion) to keep Dracula's vampirism from taking hold in its victims.[40] Similarly, the increasingly

colonies and how thin the line between coloniser and colonised is: 'They – the women, I mean – are out of it – should be out of it. We must help them to stay in that beautiful world of their own, lest ours gets worse.' Conrad, *Heart of Darkness*, 44.

40 See, for example, Carol Margaret Davison, 'Blood Brothers: Dracula and Jack the Ripper' in *Bram Stoker's Dracula: Sucking through the Century 1897–1997*, edited by Carol Margaret Davison (Toronto: Dundurn Press, 1997).

influential zombie narrative casts viral disease as monstrous by depicting the carrier as overtly abject. In fact, any ideology hostile to the American capitalist project can be made to take on the nature of a monstrous infection. During the height of the Cold War, as 'viruses became increasingly sinister and wily, sneaking into cells and assuming control of their mechanisms, external agents, such as Communists, became viral, threatening to corrupt the dissemination of information as they infiltrated the nerve center of the state'.[41] As discussed in Chapter 4, these images were disseminated by such texts as Jack Finney's *The Body Snatchers*, a text that 'brought monstrous aliens to medical science and the language of virology into a battle for the survival of the human race'.[42]

During the final three decades of the twentieth century, the metaphorical connections between the carrier of disease and the political Other became increasingly important and surfaced in a series of gothic texts. Following Matheson's *I Am Legend*, Stephen King's *Salem's Lot* (1975) describes vampirism as a kind of germ that spreads with the bite of the vampire; quick application of a disinfectant can prevent it from spreading throughout the body.[43] It is at the same time that the zombie reforms from stumbling Voodoo marionette into aggressive carnivorous viral super-spreader with Romero's *The Crazies* (1973).[44] By the final decade of the twentieth century, few narratives about the undead imagine them as something other than walking spreaders of viral disease.

When viruses take gothic shape in the form of vampires or zombies, this allows for these viruses to more effectively inhabit different political positions. As Mark Dery has argued, the:

> zombie is a polyvalent revenant, a bloated signifier that has given shape, alternately, to the repressed memoirs of slavery's horrors, white alienation from the darker Other; Cold War nightmares of mushroom clouds and megadeaths; the posttraumatic fallout of the AIDS epidemic; and, in movies like *28 Days Later* and books like Max Brook's faux-historical *World War Z: An Oral History of the Zombie War*, free-floating anxieties about viral plagues and bioengineered outbreaks. These days, visions of a zombie apocalypse look a lot like the troubled dreams of an age of terrorism, avian flu, and H1N1, when viruses leap the species barrier and spread, via jet travel, into global pandemics seemingly overnight (which may be why the infected, as they're called in both *28 Days Later* and *Left 4 Dead*, move at terrifying, jump-cut speed, unlike their lumbering, stuporous predecessors).[45]

---

41 Wald, *Contagious*, 159.

42 Wald, *Contagious*, 160.

43 Stephen King, *Salem's Lot* (1975; reprint, New York: Anchor Books, 2011).

44 *The Crazies* (remade in 2010), is not a zombie movie per se but is often seen as belonging to the same tradition.

45 Mark Dery, *I Must Not Think Bad Thoughts: Drive-By Essays on American Dread, American Dreams* (Minneapolis: University of Minnesota Press, 2012), 11.

As 'troubled dreams of an age of terrorism', the modern zombies are, as Aalya Ahmad has observed, 'redolent of the subaltern'.[46] More aggressive, fast, hostile and hungry than previous generations of zombies, they can be said to personify fears of bioterrorism that were redolent after 9/11 and after the anthrax letter attacks of November 2001. In other words, the post-9/11 zombie is often a form of weaponised subaltern and emerges less as the undead and more and more as an alternative new species, a new Darwinian challenge for the West to meet.[47]

The personification of disease as a (political) monster makes it possible, even necessary, to confront the disease in the same way as the imperial gothic imagines all forms of gothic conflict: with violence. In non-gothic invasion narratives, the infected are dangerous but pitiful. They demand that the agents who attempt to preserve them be careful, and they require our pity and sympathy. These diseased remain within the confines of the West. By contrast, the person infected by a zombie virus crosses into the ontological and epistemological territory of the Other. The zombie is a gothic being; often an utterly primitive and voracious cannibal without language, exactly the kind of being that early European anthropology located in the colonial territories they sought to exploit. In this way, contracting the zombie virus is to 'go native', to cross over a border made permeable by the virus into the territory of the subaltern.

It is not strange that the post-apocalyptic landscape that follows in the wake of a vampire or zombie infection is a territory of perpetual war and conflict. This landscape turns into a space where violent conflict is not simply endemic; constant violence has become so completely a part of society that it now constitutes normality. It is the primeval jungle of Kong's island where something is literally always trying to eat you, only this something is not a dinosaur but your neighbour who has been made to join the other side, who has gone native.

## The Girding and Cutting of Loins

The post-9/11 torture and invasion narratives map the military, economic and ideological challenges that America is perceived to have faced after the invasion of Iraq deteriorated into gore, confusion and moral uncertainty. This was also the period when the decline that US hegemonic ambition had in fact experienced since the early 1970s became too obvious to ignore. In the days after 9/11, Bush encouraged citizens to return to the marketplace, to continue

46 Aalya Ahmad, 'Gray Is the New Black: Race, Class, and Zombies' in *Generation Zombie: Essays on the Living Dead in Modern Culture*, edited by Stephanie Boluk and Wylie Lenz (Jefferson: McFarland & Company, 2011), 130.

47 Chapter 10 discusses a complementary reading of the fast, post-9/11 zombie as manifesting fears about internal social unrest.

using their credit cards, and he assured the world that the US was still 'open for business'.[48] In 2007, it became increasingly difficult for the administration to make such assurances. As will be discussed in more detail in the next chapter, the notion that US empire had run its course had begun to permeate public discourse. America was understood as not simply Rome or Britain, but as 'Rome in 200AD or Britain at the eve of the first world war: an empire at the zenith of its power but with cracks beginning to show'.[49]

It is against this historical and economic backdrop that the invasion narrative asks that US citizens have faith in modernity and presents all challenges to its many faces as deeply troubling. It also wants the audience to have unquestioned belief in the military as the only effective solution to global crisis. Like the invasion novels of the late-Victorian period, the torture and invasion narratives that lay claim to large audiences after 2005 map a loss of imperial confidence but also, to an even greater extent, an immediate need to consolidate imperial practice and discourse. The Darwinian challenge that alien invasion constitutes can only be accepted after a shedding of the veneers of civilisation. In the face of an allegorical apocalypse, before the possibility that the 'dusk' of the empire is turning into endless night, loins must be girded, courage gathered and lives put on the line. Only by embracing the masculine virtues of strength and self-sacrifice can the gothic tides be stemmed.

In the invasion narratives discussed in this chapter, the apocalypse (moral or material) is either averted or postponed. The plucky marines find a way to hurt the seemingly invincible armies of the alien invaders. Antidotes are invented, portals are closed, weapons systems are modified and odd weaknesses are discovered. The invasion is stopped in its tracks and the guilt that perhaps informs the story is alleviated. The torture narrative presents a grimmer picture of the present. The pervading sense of ontological and moral upheaval does not allow for the same redemptive trajectory. Even if it is possible to escape the torture chamber and even to avenge the horrors performed there, the chamber remains. What complicates even this critique of modern society, however, is the fact that these films also commodify the atrocities they purport to query. Just like the implicit critique of all colonial practice is engulfed by the celebration of heroics, exploding buildings and space ships, death rays and CGI in the invasion story, the implicit criticism of the torture movie drowns in a carnival of blood and gore.

---

48 Bush, 'Address to the Nation', 1099.

49 Larry Elliott, 'Decline and Fall of the American Empire', *The Guardian*, June 6, 2011, http://www.guardian.co.uk/business/2011/jun/06/us-economy-decline-recovery-challenges.

# Chapter 10
# The Imperial Gothic of the Post-Apocalypse

London art gallery Tate Britain's 2011–12 exhibition *John Martin Apocalypse* was advertised with the help of a short film.[1] Amid thunder and darkness, a beautiful young woman wakes up in some grimy and mostly unlit underground structure. The world around her begins to shake and complain like some gigantic beast. She leaves the haggard and dirty people that surround her and that look worriedly up at the trembling stone that forms their ceiling. She finds her way up to the surface only to be faced with an animated version of Martin's painting *The Great Day of His Wrath*: amid lighting and tempestuous skies, the Earth has cracked open and is in the process of folding into itself. Two gigantic ridges are closing, like enormous jaws, while entire cities perched upon them like teeth tumble into a burning abyss. In the foreground, human bodies lie sprawled out on the ground, limbs stretched to the heavens while at the same time they too tumble into the open gorge below them.

Martin's painting does not, in fact, depict the apocalypse, but the fall of Babylon. However, just like in Tate's short advertisement – which, it turns out, does not describe the end of the world but a woman daydreaming of it while looking at Martin's gigantic canvas – the apocalypse has often been imagined like this. The world will die in a cataclysm of fire and brimstone. Frank Kermode has influentially claimed that images such as these provide (Western) culture with a 'sense of an ending'.[2] Without this sense, Kermode argues, it is impossible to imagine a beginning or a middle so that time appears disjointed and chaotic. From this perspective, apocalyptic texts such as *Hostel*, *Saw*, *War of the Worlds*, *Battle: Los Angeles*, *Cloverfield*, and *Transformers: Dark of the Moon*, ones that linger on images similar to those captured by Martin's painting, lend a certain cohesion to the present. Images of pending apocalypse make us more rather than less comfortable with the specific historical trajectory we inhabit, a trajectory that, I have argued, is still essentially that of modernity and empire.

---

1 See http://www.youtube.com/watch?v=814ll2oPevo.

2 See Frank Kermode, *The Sense of an Ending* (1966; reprint, Oxford: Oxford University Press, 2000).

However, in these Hollywood movies, the apocalypse is more or less successfully resisted. As in Stoker's *Dracula*, the white and male champions, often in their modern shape of heavily armed marines or Special Forces soldiers, manage to halt the powers of darkness. The war may not be over (in the imperial gothic, it never is), but the empire does not fall. Modernity is still in place at the end of the narrative. In this way, these narratives provide a sense of ending but never the end in itself. Lives move on, and it is just like life before the catastrophe, only with even more soldiers. Revitalised by the Darwinian challenge, these soldiers watch the skies or the dark earth below us.

This chapter focuses on a complimentary set of texts that initially read very much like the apocalyptic stories of invasion discussed in the previous chapter. The difference is that in these narratives the bravery and technology of the military and the fabric of modern society do not have the ability to resist gothic Armageddon. Modernity cannot keep the sky from falling. Society collapses. In *After the End*, James Berger has argued that the focus on the post-apocalypse, rather than the apocalypse, is a general tendency in modern culture: '[the] visions of the End that Frank Kermode analyzed in terms of a sense of an ending have increasingly given way to visions of after the end, and the apocalyptic sensibilities both of religion and of modernism have shifted toward a sense of post-apocalypse'.[3]

These post-apocalyptic narratives come in two very different versions. As Teresa Heffernan has argued, the post-modern and post-apocalyptic (and typically non-gothic) text describes the present world 'as exhausted, but there is no better world that replaces it – these narratives refuse to offer up a new beginning or any hope of rebirth or renewal; the end is instead senseless and arbitrary'.[4] The other version, to which the imperial gothic belongs, does offer up a world after the apocalypse that is not only possible to inhabit, it may even have utopian qualities. As Claire P. Curtis has argued, the destruction of modern society, of the world as we know it, sends us back to the world as we imagine it once was, to a new beginning, to a pre-governmental 'state of nature' that allows for the reinvention, or more properly renovation, of society. Post-apocalyptic fiction thus 'focus[es] on the very idea and possibility of starting over, with all of the potential hope and utopian imaginings that starting over implies'.[5]

This chapter first discusses how society is imagined to break down in the post-apocalyptic imperial gothic and how this breakdown reflects the political and economic climate of the time. Essentially, I argue, these narratives describe

---

3 Berger, *After the End*, xiii.

4 Teresa Heffernan, *Post-Apocalyptic Culture: Modernism, Postmodernism, and the Twentieth-Century Novel* (Toronto: University of Toronto Press, 2008), 5.

5 Claire P. Curtis, *Postapocalyptic Fiction and the Social Contract: 'We'll Not Go Home Again'* (Lanham: Lexington Books, 2010), 2.

a society that is falling apart at the seams and which has begun to besiege itself. Thus, these narratives to some extent suggest that the US is susceptible to the same social and sectarian disorder that has shaken Northern Africa and the Middle East. At the same time, they explore the class and racial conflicts that have always haunted the US and which have erupted regularly during its history. It is not necessarily the subaltern that takes gothic form and stalks the apocalypse, it may be the equally frightening image of the Western citizen stripped of his or her economic privileges.

The chapter then discusses the various societies that the imperial gothic sees growing out of the ruins of civilisation. The depiction of the collapse of modern society, of the military that should protect us, encourages a less conservative and more polyphonous imperial gothic. As I will argue, many post-apocalyptic gothic narratives imagine the fall of mankind to the forces of darkness as a self-engineered flood of biblical proportions. In this way, the completed apocalypse is a just punishment for a society that has become too voracious, too self-confident and too morally ambiguous. Not all post-apocalyptic narratives are as dismissive of modernity, however, and this chapter also discusses representation of a post-apocalyptic society where endemic war is a platform for a virtually utopian society where the warriors of the future can excel. In these narratives, the military solution is elevated from intervention into a form of permanent utopian social order.

## Societal Breakdown and *The Walking Dead*

I have suggested that once the US turns outward, to Afghanistan and then to Iraq, to manage the national crisis of 9/11, this first generates an extroverted form of imperial gothic. It is when the invasion of Iraq begins to falter and fold in on itself in the 'crescendo of gore and confusion'[6] that Justin Cronin notes that the gothic too becomes introverted and gory. This is, of course, a general tendency rather than a precise development. Even after Bush rallied and assured the world and the American public that the US was 'still open for business', 9/11 remained a moment of symbolic apocalypse. Similarly, the invasion of Iraq was to many a sign of imperial desperation rather than consolidation even when Bush landed on the *USS Lincoln* under the 'Mission Accomplished' banner. The British film *28 Days Later* (2002), Zack Snyder's remake of George Romero's *Dawn of the Dead* (2004) and the zombie action *Resident Evil: Apocalypse* (2004) are examples of apocalyptic narratives produced before the general public lost faith in the wars in Iraq and Afghanistan.

---

6 http://www.powells.com/blog/interviews/justin-cronin-the-powells-com-interview-by-jill/.

It is interesting to note that *28 Days Later, Dawn of the Dead* and *Battle: Los Angeles* as well as the first-person shooter *Crysis 2* discussed below are all prefaced by very similar archival footage depicting global social unrest.[7] These images are not situated by any coherent commentary, but the viewer may still make some kind of political sense out of them, as most seem to depict rioting in the Middle East. Angry mobs chant in unison, riot police fire tear gas and bullets into large groups of people, limp bodies are dragged through the streets. These films transplant images of global unrest, the breakdown of society as it occurs outside of the US, into Western society. In the narratives that follow, the societal chaos routinely reported by media as endemic to 'failed' or 'rogue' states suddenly paralyses US urban spaces. This is especially obvious in Snyder's remake of *Dawn of the Dead*, where fast, aggressive and ferocious zombies besiege a large shopping mall where a handful of human survivors have made their stand. The hungry undead want in. The living want to keep them outside. In the end, the inside of the mall turns into chaos and carnage.[8]

While apocalyptic texts certainly haunted the American imagination in the years immediately before and after 9/11, imperial gothic narratives depicting social unrest became increasingly more frequent and more relevant after the invasion of Iraq lost both its momentum and its moral foundation in the eyes of the public. This process became further accelerated by the Bush administration's feeble response to hurricane 'Katrina' that hit New Orleans and the Gulf Coast in August 2005 and by the financial crisis that began in late 2007 and accelerated in 2008. In the wake of this depression, homelessness and poverty rose drastically until, at the time of writing, 46.2 million people in America are estimated to live below the poverty line, the highest number in the 53 years in which the Census Bureau has measured poverty in the nation.[9] Poverty is not just private and individual. Entire cities has lost the ability to provide some of the most basic services. In 2010, on the pages of *Salon*, Glenn Greenwald lists some of these and also connects the depression with American global ambition:

> Does anyone doubt that once a society ceases to be able to afford schools, public transit, paved roads, libraries and street lights – or once it chooses not to be able to afford those things in pursuit of imperial priorities and the maintenance of a vast Surveillance and National Security State – that a very serious problem has

7 See Charles Derry, *Dark Dreams 2.0: A Psychological History of the Modern Horror Film from the 1950s to the 21st Century* (Jefferson: McFarland, 2009), 244.

8 As Christian Thorne has argued, this is one of the most important differences from Romero's original movie. In Romero's version, the undead are already in the shopping mall, stumbling mindlessly around the aisles. In Snyder's version, the mall instead becomes a permeable fortress that separates the surviving middle class from the symbolic subaltern. See http://sites.williams.edu/cthorne/articles/the-running-of-the-dead-part-2/.

9 http://www.nclej.org/poverty-in-the-us.php.

arisen, that things have gone seriously awry, that imperial collapse, by definition, is an imminent inevitability?[10]

Sentiments such as these created a fertile ground for a different kind of gothic narrative, one that gothicises the spectre of poverty and the possibility of social unrest. As I will argue, it was poverty and unrest, perhaps even a fear of revolution, as much as the sense of failure in Iraq, that turned the gothic towards more introspective and social subject matter after 2006. As in *28 Days Later*, *Dawn of the Dead* and *Resident Evil: Apocalypse*, the gothic monster that takes on the burden of representation of the impoverished rioting society member is often the zombie. Unlike many other gothic monsters, the zombie inhabits the dual positions of Self and Other. The zombie is not an Egyptian warlock or the black, monstrous body of Ridley Scott's space alien; the zombie is your neighbour deformed by cuts and bruises, your wife or husband who wants to eat you.

Few zombie narratives make this as clear as the AMC television series *The Walking Dead* (2010–13). In the first episode of this series, police officer Rick Grimes wakes up abandoned in a hospital bed after having been comatose for an undetermined period of time. Rick staggers out into the streets of a small town that has been completely transformed by incomprehensible violence and carnage. The street is littered with the debris of war and dead bodies lie strewn across the urban landscape. Not all dead bodies remain dormant though. In a park, a legless, eviscerated, impossibly decomposed body stretches its arms out after Rick who hurries from the scene only to be knocked unconscious by a young boy. Again, Rick wakes up but now under the attention of an anxious but decisive black man named Morgan Jones. Morgan explains the new world that Rick now inhabits: the dead do not sleep any longer. They shamble across the earth and feed on the living. Those bitten are infected with what is assumed to be a deadly virus. After a terrible fever, the infected person dies and is reanimated. Severe trauma to the head is the only way to kill them.

Rick is given a baseball bat by Morgan and is sent out into the yard to dispatch a zombie who lies slumped against a fence post. Fortunately for the still dazed Rick, this zombie is not entirely uncanny, not a young girl or a mother, but a somewhat brawny young man, the kind of figure that Rick has no doubt packed into his squad car many times before. Thus, Rick does not hesitate for long and cracks the man's skull with a few well-aimed swings. Back in the house with Morgan and his adolescent son Duane, Rick is told that Morgan and Duane are still haunted by the zombie apparition of the wife/mother of the family. At night, she wanders by the house with a group of

10 Glenn Greenwald, 'What Collapsing Empire Looks Like', *Salon*, August 6, 2010, http://www.salon.com/2010/08/06/collapse/.

other zombies. Sometimes she even comes up to the door, furtively trying the doorknob, perhaps somehow remembering that she sheltered there for a while with her family before becoming infected and joining the zombies. Seeing her mindless corpse in the streets is torture for Morgan and Duane. Whenever she appears, Duane becomes terribly agitated and Morgan must hold and calm him. 'I should have put her down', Morgan explains. 'I just didn't have it in me. She's the mother of my child.'

Accepting the reality of the world that now surrounds him, Rick goes with Morgan and Duane to the police station to pick up guns and ammunition. Rick hands a rifle to Morgan with the comment: 'Take that one. Nothing fancy. The scope's accurate.' Morgan's serious face tells the audience he has understood. This is a useful gun if he means to kill what used to be his wife. Rick and Morgan then separate, both with the intention of euthanising a particular zombie: Morgan, his wife; and Rick, the eviscerated corpse he encountered in the park. The two attempts are juxtaposed in a long sequence set to sad music: Rick tracks the mangled corpse through the park where birds are singing in the sunlight while Morgan attracts his wife by shooting other zombies through the window of the house he now occupies. Rick finds the barely animated remains of the zombie under a giant tree and makes a short statement: 'I am sorry this happened to you.' Then, he dispatches it with a shot to the head from his powerful revolver. Meanwhile, Morgan locates his former wife in the crosshairs of the gun's scope and takes a deep breath, but his wife raises her gaze and looks back at him through the crosshairs. Morgan starts to cry and shake. 'Come on', he tells himself, choking on tears. But he cannot pull the trigger.

Why is it so important for Morgan to kill his wife? She may be a cannibal now, but the viewer never sees her practising this ghastly habit. When spotted through the peephole of the door behind which Morgan and his son have barricaded themselves or through the lens of the riflescope, she does not seem to be suffering. She is very different from the vibrant woman that the audience sees in a photograph that Morgan holds on to. Her zombie reincarnation has a vacant expression, mouth hanging open and hair in disarray, but she does not seem to be in pain. She does not appear to constitute a threat either. Although she seems to have located her family, her attempts to enter the house where they hide from her and from the other zombies are conventional and unaggressive; she turns the locked doorknob, but there is no hammering and no snarling like in most other zombie narratives. One answer, of course, is that Morgan's wife is now uncanny, that she has irrevocably joined the other side. In a world of humans and the reanimated dead, she has involuntarily joined the hostile Other and in the imperial gothic, death is often the only remedy for such crossings of borders.

For this to make sense, however, it is necessary to consider precisely what sort of otherness Morgan's wife has been made to inhabit. It should be noted here that when bitten by a zombie, the subject transforms into a creature uncomfortably similar to the stereotypical image of the poor. The modern zombie hobbles down the street with greasy hair, ragged and dishevelled clothing, hollow cheeks, driven by an insatiable hunger. In other words, what Morgan's wife looks like is the homeless poor. The apparition is frightening when encountered in small numbers, but the single zombie can quite easily be overcome. It is when their numbers rise, when they form large groups and overwhelm you, that they become truly frightening and dangerous. Morgan tells Rick that 'They may not seem like much one at a time … but in a group all riled up and hungry … Man, you watch your ass.' Single zombies thus appear as the impoverished homeless. They are abject and frightening, possibly even contagious, but you can defend yourself from them. Large groups of zombies, however, bring to mind the anarchy and chaos that accompany violent social revolution. In large numbers, the zombie will not simply bite you, it will indeed consume you.

In this way, the zombie is a reminder of how easy it is, especially in times of economic turmoil, to fall on the social ladder, to find yourself on the street, another poor, hungry subject on the fringe of society. It only takes a bite and you resemble not only the third-world refugee, the Mexican illegal alien trying to scale the wall that separates the US and Mexico, but also the impoverished US citizen. You are homeless on the street, and all your former friends, even your family, will barricade doors and windows to keep you outside the civil society that they, with increasing desperation and artificiality, try to uphold. You will have no choice but to join the ever-growing army of the famished undead, walking side-by-side into the gunfire with which the Other is addressed in the imperial gothic. By the same logic, all remaining human survivors must become violent enforcers of (imperial) order. All those who cross the border into the ontological and epistemological territory of the Other are legitimate targets, even if it is your wife. Again, the solution to the gothic crisis is violence; Morgan must shoot his wife in the head because that is what people do to the Other in the post-apocalyptic imperial gothic. No other recourse can be imagined.

## *The Passage*: Apocalypse and the New Frontier Gothic

This, of course, is only the beginning of the end. The post-apocalyptic imperial gothic imagines also the next step, the utter abandonment of urban spaces and a return to a (highly temporary) state of nature. In *The Walking Dead*, the few survivors that made it out of Rick's small town have set up camp in the forest outside the city. They literally live in nature and off of nature as they try to figure out how life is supposed to move on now and in what kind of authority they can invest their trust.

In Justin Cronin's aforementioned and truly post-apocalyptic *The Passage*, this has been sorted out. Almost 100 years after a vampire apocalypse that has completely destroyed civilisation, life continues in small and well-defended rural colonies. *The Passage* is an unusually rich and complex example of the imperial gothic that has already received critical scrutiny for the ways in which it negotiates post-9/11 and post-Iraq-War USA.[11] This includes Glennis Byron and Aspasia Stephanou's timely 'Neo-Imperialism and the Apocalyptic Vampire Narrative: Justin Cronin's *The Passage*' to which my analysis below is indebted.[12] Also, as acknowledged by Byron and Stephanou, Christian Thorne has written interestingly of *The Passage*, and on many other horror narratives too, in his blog the 'Commonplace Book'.[13] *The Passage* is a sprawling, epic and multi-layered story, consisting, in the vein of Stoker's original *Dracula*, of a number of different third-person narratives and also of letters, e-mails, conference extracts and journals. *The Passage* is the first of a trilogy, and like its sequel *The Twelve* (2012)[14] it is divided into two parts where the first describes the apocalypse caused by a viral vampire plague and the second a small group of survivors 100 years into the post-apocalyptic future.

The apocalyptic, rather than post-apocalyptic, section is set only a few years into the future, in a world that is effectively imperial. In the novel, America has seen a drastic increase in war and terrorist activity. Foremost on people's minds are the horrors of the '"Mall of America" Massacre – three hundred holiday shoppers gunned down by Iranian jihadists, all the horror captured by security cameras to be replayed in painstakingly gruesome detail on CNN.'[15] This event is apparently just one of many confrontations that have put the US and the world into a state of permanent warfare. The War on Terror has become ubiquitous and constitutes the only paradigm for international interaction. The reasons for this development and state of affairs are traced back to 9/11 but also to an already existing Manichean mind-set: 'The war – the real war, the one that had been going on for a thousand years and would go on for a thousand thousand more – the war between Us and Them, between the Haves and the Have-Nots, between my gods and your gods.'[16]

In this state of perpetual and clearly imperial warfare, the American military is looking for a game-changer, something that will give them a permanent edge. They find this in project Noah. Initially civilian, it soon turns military: 'This

11 A number of reviewers have pointed to similarities between Cronin's and Stephen King's fiction. In fact, King called Cronin up to congratulate him while Cronin was being interviewed on 'Good Morning America'.

12 Glennis Byron and Aspasia Stephanou, 'Neo-Imperialism and the Apocalyptic Vampire Narrative: Justin Cronin's *The Passage*' in *Transnational and Postcolonial Vampires: Dark Blood*, edited by Johan Höglund and Tabish Khair (London: Palgrave Macmillan, 2012).

13 http://sites.williams.edu/cthorne/.

14 Justin Cronin, *The Twelve* (New York: Ballantine Books, 2012).

15 Cronin, *The Passage*, 37.

16 Cronin, *The Passage*, 98–9.

was the new Manhattan Project. This was bigger than that. Cole couldn't go into details, not yet, but for the sake of context, think of the human form itself, weaponized. Think of the American Way as something truly long-term. As in permanent.'[17] The Faustian pursuit of a weaponised body capable of sustaining American global leadership into eternity predictably leads to the complete collapse of American society. Rather than furnishing the American government with the perfect weapon, the 12 death-row-test-subject-inmates-turned-vampires escape the military facility, turn on their previous handlers and initiate the apocalypse.

This background and plot development seem to offer a rather straightforward critique of American empire and modernity. Indeed, American empire comes across as an unsustainable system, seemingly programmed to produce its own demise. Thus, the US may be seen to deserve the apocalypse that the vampires initiate and all but complete. Following through on the story of Noah, this apocalypse is not simply imagined as terrible, it is also a cleansing flood, a just punishment for a modernity gone impossibly voracious. However, the post-apocalyptic society that replaces the imperial/colonial paradigm is not a society where empire and modernity are dismantled. Instead, the second part of the novel, set 92 years after the vampire apocalypse, is more appropriately described as initially a transcultural accident where modernity commands significant nostalgia and then the foundation of a new form of empire.

The setting is a fortress, appropriately referred to as an 'Ark' but also importantly termed a 'colony'. The enclosed community is inhabited by the descendants of a handful of survivors who, isolated from modern society and even from history itself, have become effectively if inadvertently transcultural and transracial. After a couple of generations of intermarriage between the racially mixed survivors, nothing remains of the racial and sexual hierarchies that used to saturate pre-apocalyptic US society. The small population is now effectively hybrid.

However, the reader is soon informed that a new hierarchy informs this setting. The more closely associated to the original settlers of this utopia you are, the higher your place in society is. Similarly, this post-apocalyptic society is governed by the Document of One Law, a new instrument of government that clearly and harshly structures life in the small community by describing the jobs possible, the communication with the outside world allowed and the severe punishments inflicted should you break any of its instructions.

From this perspective, the small and enclosed fortress society has much in common with the first Puritan settlements, isolated from their geographical and historical roots, surrounded by, and challenging, the Native Americans that actually inhabit the landscape. Not surprisingly, as Byron and Stephanou observe, the second part of *The Passage* soon merges gothic post-apocalypse

17 Cronin, *The Passage*, 100.

with the western, the frontier gothic and the captivity narrative. A group of prospective colonist/explorers strike out into the vampire-infested lands that surround them. This journey increasingly reads like an attempt at reconquering a continent that again has become possible to conquer. America is now inhabited by bloodthirsty vampires rather than bloodthirsty Indians so the novel allegorically plays out a confrontation with wild and unruly frontier spaces.[18]

However, in the trilogy's second instalment, *The Twelve*, the metaphors used to designate Self and Other, empire and subaltern are again reversed. In *The Twelve* the vampire population is thinning. The human food supply has dwindled, and the 12 original vampires force their vampire hordes to collectively kill themselves by staying out in the sun. To ensure that they will remain well fed, the remaining vampires ally themselves with deputy director of the Department of Special Weapons, Horace Guilder, who has survived the apocalypse by feeding on the blood of one of the Twelve's human familiars. With the aid of other familiars and the vampires they control, Guilder has created his own colony and refers to it as Homeland. This machine-like, fascist society operates essentially in the manner of a Nazi concentration camp or, for that matter, a slave plantation.[19] Rape, starvation, beatings and even murder are commonplace. Yet Guilder expects the members of his colony to be grateful that they are not the prey of vampires. Every morning the members of the ironically named Homeland have to line up and sing the colony's anthem: 'Homeland, our Homeland, we pledge our lives to thee. Our labors do we offer, without recompense or fee. Homeland, our Homeland, a nation rises here. Safety, hope, security, from sea to shining sea.'[20]

Opposed to this society is an underground resistance movement that has resorted to seemingly random acts of terrorism. Termed 'the insurgence', this resistance movement clearly references the Iraq War. The protagonists of the first novel soon join this terrorist organisation in an effort to rid the world both of Guilder and the 12 head vampires that are converging on the Homeland. As insurgents, their methods are identical to those of the terrorist: they drive trucks

---

18 It should be added that *The Walking Dead* also imagines the post-apocalypse as a (terrible) event that is able to resurrect the gun-slinging pioneer. The posters advertising the first and second seasons frequently display the lone gunslinger.

19 Many other gothic narratives also imagine fascism as a consequence of the post-apocalypse and pose terrorism as a first remedy to this development. In *The Night Eternal* (New York: HarperCollins, 2011), the final novel of Chuck Hogan's and Guillermo del Toro's *The Strain* Trilogy, the ancient vampire Josef Sardu reorganises post-apocalyptic America by setting up 'blood camps' where surviving humans are drained of blood for himself and his vampire legions. The initially predatory and insatiable vampires become the fascist police of this new state.

20 Cronin, *The Twelve*, 478.

laden with explosives into the crowds of people who help guard or otherwise serve the oppressive regime.[21]

Again, the narrative seems to encourage a very straightforward critique of American colonial practice. Homeland appears like the bizarre merger between Abu Ghraib and the Bagdad Green Zone. Yet this analysis also collapses. The Homeland anthem speaks not of freedom but of safety and security. This rhetoric and the organisation of Homeland are reminiscent of three very different historical and political sequences: the political tyranny of the British empire after the French and Indian War in 1754–63; the Nazi regime of the mid-twentieth century; and, finally, the system of socialism as demonised by the Republican Right during the Obama campaigns.[22] Thus, while *The Twelve* does ask interesting questions about what the difference between terror and fighting for freedom is, it reads as a very American saga. To re-establish America, the new set of colonists must first confront and overcome the new natives of the virgin land of America. This time, the genocide on which they embark is perfectly justifiable. The natives may be reluctant killers, transformed family and friends, but bloodthirsty killers they are. When this has been firmly established, and ways of dealing with the vampire explored, the new colonists are instead made to face the political darkness of colonial, fascist totalitarianism and socialism.

To further emphasise their righteous cause, events mysteriously, even religiously, conspire to aid those who keep resisting the gothic Other. God is on their side as they pursue, as in all imperial gothic, the military solution. The messianic Amy is, in the first novel, a tormented child who gets infected with the final-stage virus and then develops into a quiet and introverted 100-year-old teenager. In the second novel, Amy further transforms, or perhaps evolves, into a ruthless warrior, the weaponised body desired by the former empire. As the terrorist efforts culminate in *The Twelve*, she becomes, finally, a soldier. Similar to all other imperial gothic texts, (military) violence is the only conceivable solution. In this way, *The Passage* and its sequel *The Twelve* oscillate between two different positions. Both novels launch a potent critique of American colonial practice in the Middle East, a critique that even seems inspired by postcolonial inquiry. At the same time, these narratives reinvest in the colonial/imperial model. Post-apocalyptic society never becomes effectively post-colonial or post-imperial even if the post-apocalyptic process has transformed, or rather obliterated, the racial and ethnic boundaries that characterise our own society.

---

21 Stephen King's 2006 novel *Cell* (New York: Scribner, 2006) operates in a similar way. This book pits 'phone-crazies', people driven aggressively insane by a cell-phone signal, against the few remaining 'normies' that remain. In an effort to rid the world of the increasingly well-organised phone-crazies, the normies resort to setting off car bombs.

22 As observed by many reviewers, and as acknowledged by Cronin, *The Twelve* is deeply informed by George Orwell's *1984*.

## 'Welcome to the Future, Son. Welcome to the War.' – Utopia and the Post-Apocalyptic Imperial Gothic

As described above, the first-person shooter and invasion game *Crysis 2* prefaces violence by seemingly authentic footage of social unrest. Before the game even begins, the gamer is presented with the voices of two news anchors who discuss the prospect of New York, San Francisco and Los Angeles in relation to some undetermined sport. Then, the attention shifts to the 'health desk' which briefly tells us of the spreading of an 'alien' virus. Again, archival photography of kids playing in parks, fire trucks arriving and people on stretchers being taken away by ambulances is used. The gamer will have seen these images a thousand times on television. He or she probably has seen them often enough in reality. They are common, yet there is a sense that in this case they describe the first stages of a society about to fall apart. Actual photography and computer-generated images are then mixed as the game depicts the crash of the stock market and the beginning of civil unrest on the streets. Sirens and people are heard wailing, and the fabric of society begins to break apart. The final introductory sequence, again told mainly through archival footage, shows panicking people running and clashing with riot police and heavy, unconscious bodies being dragged through the streets. 'Civilians take the law into their own hands', one headline informs us. Modernity no longer rules. New York has become Cairo or Bagdad or Mogadishu.

As in *The Twelve* or Hogan and del Toro's aforementioned *The Night Eternal* (2010), the immediate resolution is the creation of a fascist state. In *Crysis 2*, the private military contractor Crynet Enforcement & Local Logistics, or CELL, brings civil unrest to a violent end and starts policing New York. As in *The Twelve* and *The Night Eternal*, two hostile forces thus besiege the remaining citizens: the fascist police of the future and a gothic/alien threat in the form of the Ceph from the first *Crysis* (2007) game. On the surface, the society that surfaces is essentially dystopian. The fascist government of this future version of New York is not much better than that of 'a state of nature' as defined by Hobbes in *Leviathan*. Even with this form of totalitarian government, New Yorkers live in 'continual fear and danger of violent death, and the life of man [is] solitary, poor, nasty, brutish, and short'.

A number of critics have argued that the post-apocalyptic gothic narrative often dramatises a longing for the authoritarian government Thomas Hobbes imagined as the only antidote to the violence of the state of nature. Christian Thorne has observed that films such as Snyder's *Dawn of the Dead* daydream of the destruction of society so that the audience is able to appreciate the (increasingly) totalitarian US government apparatus that surrounds it – not just the electric lights that illuminate the highways or the convenience store still open across the street, but the very fact that the US is not in the middle of a terrorist attack, a South American drug war or a Chinese military invasion. In this way, Thorne argues, the fast and post Romero-era zombie narrative encourages US citizens to embrace authority even when exercised by George W. Bush. Thorne is not the only one who has seen post-apocalyptic narrative in this light. Claire P. Curtis has made a similar claim in *Postapocalyptic Fiction and the Social Contract*.[23] Also, Claudia Aradau and Rens van Munster, with reference to Étienne Balibar, have observed in *Politics of Catastrophe: Genealogies of the Unknown* that:

> the post-catastrophic Hollywood worlds of social breakdown, struggle for survival and violence appear reminiscent of Hobbe's fictional state of nature where the creation of the Leviathan served to guard civilization through a 'system of preventive defence against the mass movements that forms the basis of civil wars (or classes and of religions) and of revolutions'.[24]

Much apocalyptic imperial gothic discussed in the previous chapter makes sense when understood in this way. However, many post-apocalyptic gothic narratives do not imagine the authoritarian and fascist states that fill the post-apocalyptic political void as being any better than the state of chaos that preceded them. The fascist police are not the solution. The solution, in the post-apocalyptic gothic, is the soldier. In fact, the future that much post-apocalyptic imperial gothic desires is not, in fact, the restoration of (authoritarian) society after the war, it is the war itself.

In *Crysis 2*, this becomes clear when the cut scenes end and the gamer finds himself or herself in the body of Force Recon marine Alcatraz, sitting in a military submarine that has been sent out to help retrieve a scientist who might assist in creating a cure for the alien virus that has caused the breakdown of society. Minutes into the game, the submarine is attacked and sunk. The few marines that make it to the surface are met with images of a New York on fire. A damaged Statue of Liberty still stands guard at the inlet, and it becomes clear to the gamer, as a strange flying vehicle begins to spray bullets from the sky, that the alien Cephs from the island of the first game have mobilised and are now demolishing New York even as New York is demolishing itself. A single US soldier remains, clad in the nanosuit he is soon to abandon so that Alcatraz/the gamer can use it. He greets the dazed marine with words that could introduce a great many imperial gothic invasion narratives: 'Welcome to the future, son. Welcome to the war.'

---

23 Curtis, *Postapocalyptic Fiction*.

24 Claudia Aradau and Rens van Munster, *Politics of Catastrophe: Genealogies of the Unknown* (London: Routledge, 2010), 2. Part of the sentence is a quotation from Étienne Balibar's *Masses, Classes, Ideas: Studies on Politics and Philosophy before and after Marx* (New York: Routledge, 1994), 16.

The point here is that this greeting is not, in fact, a sarcastic remark. The future here is indeed war, and it is an essentially Darwinian conflict were virtually everyone is an enemy.[25] It is a simultaneous confrontation with both the new dominant species on the block, the Ceph, and the fascists that govern humanity now. Competent agents of empire are indeed welcome and at home in a post-apocalyptic reality. This is the future for which such agents were made, an agent that is in fact not the virtual marine Alcatraz but the gamer who assumes control of his body and the nanosuit that covers it.

In this way, the invasion narrative paves the way for a future that is always and forever warlike. The Darwinian struggle in which empire ultimately engages has become the only paradigm, and the imperial invasion narrative centres on those that excel and seize the right to exist within this new and hostile world. What *Crysis 2*, *The Twelve* and *The Night Eternal* record then is not the creation of a new government, or even the reinstatement of the old one but the war that occurs between different forms of governments against the backdrop of the vicious and Hobbesian 'state of nature'. In many ways, these texts are inherently suspicious of all forms of government and focus primarily on the Darwinian violence that is, again, imagined as a regenerative process, the becoming of the protagonist-as-soldier.

The consequence of this is that war gains a distinctly utopian quality. When equipped and programmed for conflict, the intense violence that threatens in the post-apocalypse gothic landscape is not the end of the world as we know it, it is the world becoming. The same narrative trajectory becomes apparent in *The Walking Dead* which shifts focus from the undead towards the humans who become more and more proficient soldiers, honed by the constant strife of the post-apocalypse. From this perspective, the nightmare that this type of imperial gothic imagines is not the vampires, the zombies or the aliens rising in the dark, it is humanity rising only to find that there is no vampire, no zombie, no gothic Other there to challenge it. If you are not a soldier, who are you? If there is no war, where is the narrative, the story, that makes sense out of existence?

## The End of the World as We Know It

The post-apocalyptic imperial gothic is potentially more ideologically disruptive than most other texts that this book discusses. The notion of a post-apocalypse demands that the forces the US invests in today, the military–industrial complex, government, medical science, have been unable to protect the world. In fact, some of these narratives suggest that these institutions have caused the

25 The permanent Darwinian nature of conflict is made even more obvious in *Crysis 3* (2013) where New York has partially transformed into a jungle landscape.

apocalypse. Infected by greed, by poor judgement, ineptitude and by a general paranoia, modernity collapses in on itself. The powers that caused the chaos are often seen to erect totalitarian systems in the ruins. These societies pretend to be the old civilisation but are little more than concentration camps where the strong rule over and feed on the weak.

It should be noted that a few very bleak post-apocalyptic novels actually stop there. Cormac McCarthy's Pulitzer Prize-winning and post-apocalyptic *The Road* (2006) shows only a continuing spiral into death and destruction.[26] Although a realistic story, this novel is powerfully gothic at moments, especially when depicting how many of the survivors turn to cannibalism in order to survive. When everything else is gone, this is the only means of sustenance left. Similarly, Alden Bell's *The Reapers Are the Angels* (2010) shows a society without hope, and while the reader may be comforted by its attractive and combative heroine, the 15-year-old Temple, she too is eventually devoured by the post-apocalyptic world into which she has been born.[27] In this way, some post-apocalyptic novels consider the ways in which modernity and its attendant ideologies are not what keep terror at bay but instead are what triggered it. Even the most pro-imperial and xenophobic texts studied in this book contain moments of polyphony and discord when the core values and systems of US empire are (if only momentarily) called into question and the text is cut through by concurrent voices that speak from and for a different perspective.

However, most imperial gothic insists on re-erecting the borders they have torn down. In an interview about *The Twelve* in *The Independent*, Justin Cronin argued interestingly that '[e]very novel of this type – everything that deals with "the end of the world" – is actually a creation story … Otherwise, it's completely nihilistic and nobody would read it.'[28] This statement expresses succinctly the challenge that the imperial gothic faces: it is a popular genre, as Cronin well knows and it must offer the reader some hope. In an effort to supply hope, the possibility of positive closure, the post-apocalyptic landscape often reforms into a new frontier landscape where conflict is regenerative. New champions appear, revitalised by this new frontier. Their (terrorist) tactics may be problematic, but the violence they perpetrate is finally constructive partly because it does form the foundation for yet another beginning, a beginning after the beginning, so to speak, but also because violence when perpetrated by the US agents of war is constructive by definition.

26 Cormac McCarthy, *The Road* (New York: Alfred A. Knopf, 2006).

27 Alden Bell, *The Reapers Are the Angels* (New York: Henry Holt, 2010).

28 Justin Cronin quoted by Stephanie Cross, 'Justin Cronin: "It's Not the End of the World, You Know ..."', *The Independent*, October 28, 2012, http://www.independent.co.uk/arts-entertainment/books/features/justin-cronin-its-not-the-end-of-the-world-you-know-8229142.html.

# Chapter 11
# Conclusion

This study has examined how images of gothic and apocalyptic confrontation and catastrophe produced in American popular culture negotiate the concept and the practices of US empire. Adapting Patrick Brantlinger's concept of the imperial gothic, the study has argued that the American gothic narrative has accompanied and mapped the development of the American imperial state since the late eighteenth century. In the early American imperial gothic, modernity is constantly confronted with a primitive and barbaric, yet virile and competitive, Other that threatens to unmake it. Similarly, the genocide of Native Americans, the enslavement of Africans and the grab for new territories in the Caribbean and the Pacific were remembered but also re-imagined with the aid of the imperial gothic. This re-imagining importantly helped to justify the often brutal process of colonial expansion.

At the same time, the American imperial gothic also mirrors the anxieties and guilt that these violent historical sequences inevitably produce as well as the fear that the power that makes expansion possible is waning. As this book has argued, the imperial gothic has been especially relevant and popular at times of imperial opposition and crisis. Such crises have occurred with regularity during the history of the United States. Recent historical and sociological studies and world-systems research argue that the US began its ascent towards hegemony after the American Revolution, that this ascent was accelerated in the early 1870s in the wake of a global depression that left the European empires weakened, and that the US became dominant in 1945, after World War II. While this development may have been relatively constant, it was not smooth or straightforward. This study has noted that the first uncertain and conflict-ridden decades after the Revolution, the Great Depression and the early Cold War period were times when the US ability to continue expanding and to defend the territorial ideological borders that fenced it in were moments of imperial crises that encouraged the sometimes extroverted and expansive, but more often introverted and anxious, imperial gothic.

The main focus of this study has been the period after 1970, a time when the US entered the period of economic competition and decline that it still inhabits. However, while the US economy has been struggling at least since the Vietnam War, as illustrated by several world-systems studies, the US was perceived, and perceived itself, as increasingly central and powerful towards the end of the late twentieth century. In the early twenty-first century, historians such as Andrew Bacevich, Chalmers Johnson and Niall Ferguson described it as just as powerful, and as imperial, as Rome in 200 AD or Britain before World War I. This study suggests that the imperial gothic of the final decades of the twentieth century reflects this sense of increasing global importance, but it also argues that the imperial gothic charts, through a number of discordant narratives, the decline and sense of anxiety that also characterise this period.

Such anxieties permeated US society even in the 1990s and exploded in the wake of 9/11. The War on Terror and the invasions of Afghanistan and Iraq forced the notion of US empire to the surface and intensified fears regarding the nature and sustainability of American global power. The idea of US empire transformed from the submerged and unspoken entity it often was prior to 2001 into a hotly debated and often criticised concept. However, there were also those, such as Ferguson or Boot, who described US imperialism as a force for good in the word. To these neoconservative historians, US empire was the only entity capable of ensuring global stability in the face of what Samuel P. Huntington has termed the 'clash of civilizations'.[1]

As this study has endeavoured to illustrate, the military invasions of Afghanistan and Iraq, the prevalence of the concept of empire and the increasing feeling that American hegemony may be in decline formed very fertile ground for the imperial gothic of the immediate post-9/11 period. During this period, the American imperial gothic, as a mode rather than as a genre, became increasingly central to American culture and permeated novels, horror movies, science fiction-themed computer games, comics, public discourse and presidential speeches to an even greater extent than before. As part of these different texts and media, the imperial gothic sometimes queried but ultimately encouraged imperial practice, and much imperial gothic popular culture produced in the immediate wake of the US invasion of the Middle East is in fact extroverted and expansive. Like the early American imperial gothic, these narratives imagine what I have termed the military solution – the exorcism of the gothic Other through extensive violence – as regenerative, practical, clinical and successful. The gothic threat is effectively routed from its lair. The agents of empire may be temporarily tainted by their confrontation with the gothic Other, but this passes when order has been restored.

It is in connection with this development that American popular culture again connects with the British imperial gothic that is the focus of Brantlinger's study. As discussed in the first chapters of this study, the resurrected villains of this genre became especially prominent during the Great Depression. In their nostalgic twenty-first-century reincarnations, discussed in the later chapters

1 Samuel P. Huntington, *The Clash of Civilizations and the Remaking of World Order* (New York: Simon & Schuster, 1996).

of this book, they are noticeably more inclined to violence on a large scale than their early-twentieth-century counterparts. However, while these villains might have become even more menacing and the violence more explicit, the narratives rely upon the same logic and perform essentially the same function. As in the British novel, the gothic Other must be annihilated in order to restore order in the Anglo universe. Also as in the British gothic, the hero routinely accomplishes this annihilation through the military solution as enabled by superior, Western technology. In addition to the above, this study notes new forms of relationships between imperial gothic narratives and institutions of power such as the entertainment industry, the Pentagon, Washington and the weapon manufacturers. This relationship has been termed the military–industrial–entertainment complex and it informs much of the more expansive, expensive and extroverted imperial gothic of the post-9/11 period.

At the same time, the imperial gothic also encourages a less confident narrative trajectory that suggests to an increasingly concerned Western public that 'we are those upon whom the ends of the world are come', as Brantlinger describes the British imperial gothic.[2] As the wars in Afghanistan and Iraq ground to a halt, as reports of torture prisons and civilian carnage – of failure – replaced the sense of a mission successfully accomplished, and as the American economy experienced an accelerated and profound depression, an introspective sense of pending doom became more and more dominant in the American imperial gothic.

This introspective and discordant gothic is more apocalyptic and potentially more critical of imperial practice. It manifests in the form of torture and invasion narratives that testify to discursive discord and ambiguity in ways that recall postcolonial scholar Homi K. Bhabha's observation that the 'English book' that informed the expansion of the British empire was inherently ambiguous and therefore ultimately failed to command imperial authority.[3] Certainly, any text that attempts to describe the encounter with the Other is bound to acknowledge a certain ambiguity or even the possibility of hybridity. The infectious nature of the gothic Other recognises that the borders upon which any imperial project relies, and which many imperial gothic texts seek to represent in various ways, are in fact permeable. Thus, the imperial gothic of the period describes how both ontological and epistemological borders must be defended against gothic onslaught.

From this perspective, there is a concurrent critique at work in the more introspective American imperial gothic. A set of discordant narratives produced in the post-9/11 era even imagines modernity and capitalist Anglo-America as an engine of horror. The ambiguity noted by Bhabha in relation to British

2 Brantlinger, *Rule of Darkness*, 230.

3 Bhabha, *The Location of Culture*, 161.

literature permeates narratives of torture and reverse colonisation in particular. These narratives do contain a concurrent ideological discord that sheds doubts on the stability of the borders that these same narratives insist must be erected and defended.

However, even the most discordant American imperial gothic does not succeed in dismantling the centrality of US empire. The narratives that position the West as infected by an economy of torture become a part of this very economy; the terrible acts of torture that these narratives position as endemic to capitalism are peddled to an audience interested primarily in a spectacle of gore. Similarly, the apocalyptic flood that has cleansed the world in the post-apocalyptic imperial gothic has not swept away the imperial paradigm as such. New colonies form and these battle the gothic native in new yet recognisable forms.

## The US and Britain: Continuities and Discontinuities

To focus on the contrastive element of this study, I have observed a number of parallels between the British and the American imperial gothic that signals a certain similarity between the ways in which empire and culture interact in these two contexts. It is important to note that American gothic culture did not simply model itself on British fiction. The American gothic had an imperial vein from the very start, and while it was inspired by the British imperial gothic during certain historical key phases, it is importantly different from the British imperial gothic in many ways.

During the early stages of American history, when the border was continually pushed westward, colonisation and colonial violence were everyday occurrences within the recognized borders of the nation-state itself. By contrast, Britain (or Anglo England) had colonised the territories of the British isles hundreds of years prior to the invention of the gothic genre so that colonial violence and development typically took place far from the centre.[4] Also, in recent years the American imperial gothic is much more intimately related to military, industrial and large entertainment production companies – to the military–industrial–entertainment complex – than the British form ever was. The American imperial gothic is furthermore narrated and even performed by media that had not even been invented by the time the British empire began to decline. These discontinuities are important to note. They are intimately related to the specific historical development of the United States and of the advance of Western modernity. It is crucial to heed this historical situation to understand the pervasiveness of the American imperial gothic at the present time.

4 Of course, colonial violence was performed also within the British isles during this period, in particular in Ireland and this was also recorded by the British imperial gothic.

However, it is also important to observe a crucial continuity between the imperial gothic of these two empires. While the British and American forms of the imperial gothic respond to different historical events and are produced by very different institutions and individuals, they seem to operate in very similar ways. Both are obsessed by the notion of violence as a masculine, regenerative practice, and both see this violence as part of a Darwinian context. Both forms of imperial gothic seem to grow almost spontaneously out of the conventional gothic in response to moments of imperial crisis, and both forms lend metaphorical support to colonial practice. In short, the British and the American imperial gothic perform very similar ideological work within their specific historical contexts and with the aid of related but different narratives.

## Captivity, the Military Solution and Agency

Two tropes that this study has traced from their inception in the imperial gothic of the late eighteenth century into the present are captivity and the military solution. These two concepts can be usefully discussed in relation to the notion of agency. To recapitulate, captivity here means the removal of a defenceless person by the gothic Other from a modern context to a primitive one. As discussed, there are variants of this. Gothic transformation of the captive into a native and primitive state through magic, forced genetic mutation, viral infection or simply through ideological conditioning is also a form of captivity narrative. The loved one who is transformed into a werewolf, a vampire, a zombie or one of the possessed must also be rescued. The rescue may take the form of reverse transformation through magic or medical treatment, but it can also, paradoxically, consist of euthanasia. As in many non-gothic captivity narratives, it is better to die than to remain the captive of the Other or trapped in the subjectivity of the Other.

Captivity, of course, most directly signals a loss of agency. At the same time, in a related transformation, captivity feminises the captive. In other words, the captive is deprived of agency because the captor now controls this person but also and importantly because captivity is imagined as a peculiarly feminine state. It is important here that the gothic Other as captor is almost invariably also a sexual predator. In this way, the masculine subject who has been deprived of the captured female becomes stripped of the possibility of sexual agency. Without the female, all enterprise grinds to a halt; territories cannot be colonised, empires cannot be built, utopias cannot be established.

The captivity trope – even the threat of possible captivity – is one of the most important notions that legitimise the military solution. Thus, the military solution can be seen as the retrieval of lost agency. This is, in some imperial gothic narratives, perceived as a difficult plight. In *Edgar Huntly*, the violence with which the ideological, territorial and sexual borders of the new American empire are policed and expanded is perceived as a necessary yet terrible practice. In many ways, the euthanasia dispensed to those who have irrevocably crossed over into the ontological and epistemological territory of the gothic Other is also a tragic form of the military solution. Shooting your wife after she has turned into a zombie is not pleasant, but neither is it a duty that can be shirked. In most cases, however, the military solution fulfils the function of regenerative ritual. This is true regardless of whether the violence takes the form of a large military campaign or manifests as a displaced lynching ceremony. To perform violence is to retrieve a lost manhood and, simultaneously, to re-establish the imperial status quo. The masculine and imperial subject acquires power (agency) over those he slaughters, whether he guns them down with his M16A assault rifle or hangs them from a dogwood tree.

The moment when the path towards the military solution opens before the protagonist has become increasingly fetishised in recent imperial gothic. In the gothic/military first-person shooter as well as in much imperial gothic film and literature, the moment when the gun is located, when it is grabbed from a rack of similar rifles, is also the moment when the avatars and protagonists of these narratives achieve agency. In a future where war has become constant, violence – the military solution – is the only true form of agency.

This is a crucial observation in relation to the American imperial gothic and perhaps also in relation to the United States as a nation that has become increasingly obsessed with guns. Only the human with the gun has political, social, and sexual agency. Only the human with the gun can affect change. In a future of constant warfare, the soldier is the only true citizen.

## Borders

As I have argued, the gothic is a form of culture that reveals the various ideological, material and economic borders that structure Western society to be permeable. It is a culture that allows for, sometimes even encourages, a certain hybridity. The gothic subject crosses, sometimes repeatedly, the border that separates Self from Other, light from darkness and good from evil. The bite of the zombie or the vampire is transformative. The alien can house its offspring in the bodies or the minds of the West. The invader becomes the invaded and the torturer becomes the tortured. These constant crossings between different states are disturbing and encourage consideration both of the act of transgression and of the nature of the border itself. When the gothic is at its most effective, it directs its audience's attention to such issues.

The imperial gothic is similarly obsessed by the porous nature of various borders. The same vampires, zombies and aliens infect the human species.

However, the imperial gothic typically notes the ease with which borders can be crossed only to stress the importance that these borders must be reinforced. In Christopher Farnsworth's novel *Blood Oath*, discussed in Chapter 9, White House employee and secret agent 'Griff', the veteran in the War on Horror fought in the novel's pages, tells the newly recruited Zack that 'Whatever it takes, we have to keep that border between light and dark. Or we lose. Everything. Every one of us will die.'[5] These are the stakes and the focus of the imperial gothic. Hybridity may be a distinct possibility, but it is very rarely tolerated.

Just like the fear the Other manifests in the form of an actual monster in the imperial gothic, the borders that must be reinforced at all costs, lest we all perish, also take physical shape. The barriers behind which the military shelters with their machine guns and armoured vehicles, waiting for the onslaught of the gothic horde, are perhaps the most common visual representation of this border. The film adaption of *World War Z* (2013) illustrates this in a number of vivid sequences, the most striking being a scene set in Israel during the global zombie pandemic that forms the rationale of this narrative. Unlike the zombies of Max Brooks's original novel, the undead in this movie are supernaturally fast and aggressive, modelled not only on the similarly fast zombies of *28 Days Later* or Zack Snyder's *Dawn of the Dead* but also on tigers, frenzied by sensing their prey, or on salmon jumping waterfalls driven by the imperative of procreation.[6] In *World War Z*, the frantic zombies gather at a gigantic wall, frantically climbing onto and over each other in pursuit of the people who live inside the confines of the wall and who stand guard on top of it. The stakes are as clear as Griff makes them out to be: the border must be kept at all costs or we will all die.

## Memory and the Post-Trauma of History

To turn from the tropes of captivity and the military solution to the gothic as a mode of communication, it can be observed that the gothic is often described as a form of remembering. According to much scholarship on the gothic, the gothic is the literature of the repressed. This is a nominally Freudian model, of course, where the horrors of an individual's past cannot be completely forgotten. They keep asserting themselves through distorted memories and through various psychological disorders. Much gothic criticism has transposed this model onto the history of (imperial) Western nations and argued that repressed memories of the practices of empire, of slavery, of genocide, of torture, murder and abuse will not remain hidden and repressed; they take form in gothic culture. The gothic thus haunts the modern subject by remembering the many horrors

5 Farnsworth, *Blood Oath*, 22.

6 Max Brooks, *World War Z* (New York: Crown, 2006).

that have accompanied, and still accompany, capitalist modernity. Empire is a trauma that the gothic cannot stop rehearsing and so this very genre can be seen as a manifestation of a collective, guilt-informed, post-traumatic stress disorder.

This may be a useful way of understanding the anti-Enlightenment gothic and also some of the more recent gothic. As David Skal has argued, horror films during the 1960s and 1970s manifest many of the symptoms of post-traumatic stress disorder.[7] If the anti-Enlightenment gothic effectively remembers that which the Enlightenment society wants to forget but has to remember, it bootlegs 'past the guardians of Reason' not just the 'irrationality of experience and life itself',[8] but also – and more importantly – the many atrocities upon which Western modernity relies.

However, and as this study has argued, the American imperial gothic often functions differently in relation to memory and trauma. The American imperial gothic is not the post-traumatic disorder manifesting in culture, it is an attempt to manage such manifestations. Thus, the American imperial gothic initiates a project of remembering but then turns it into a comforting ritual of forgetting. When the violence against the Native American, the transported slave, the freedman, the Filipino rebel, the Korean or Vietnamese soldier, the Afghan or Iraqi insurrectionist is remembered in the gothic, this memory is also modified. When the Middle Eastern terrorist spouts fangs and scales, when he shambles down the street as the undead, feeding on women and children, infecting them with his own abject physiology and ideology, the violence required to put him down becomes unproblematic. Thus, the memory of the actual violence performed is radically altered by the American imperial gothic. This suggests that the imperial gothic is not, in fact, a culture of remembering but one of forgetting. It brings the horrors of the past to our attention but only so that they can be altered, managed and forgotten.

## Modernity, Postmodernity and Late Modernity

A crucial concept in this book has been modernity. As discussed above, modernity and the Enlightenment principle have been frequent targets of the gothic. However, as argued in this book, the imperial gothic typically pits modernity against the primitive in ways that may suggest that modernity is problematic, but still positions it as the best, indeed the only, bulwark there is if the powers of darkness should be kept at bay. In this way, the imperial gothic does not seem to envision or long for a societal and historical development that deviates from the current trajectory of modernity.

7 Skal, *The Monster Show*, 311.

8 Fiedler, *Love and Death*, 140.

Of course, such a development has been hotly debated in sociological, cultural and historical writing. During the late twentieth century, a number of writers proposed that the world had left modernity behind and entered what became termed the postmodern phase of history. This assumption was based partly on a series of geopolitical events and partly on the emergence and digital transformation of global news and entertainment media. The geopolitical events that were believed to signal the end of modernity consist, importantly, of the decolonisation that took place as the European empires crumbled in the aftermath of World War I but also of the fall of the Soviet Union and the end of the Cold War in the late 1980s. At the time these geopolitical transformations occurred, Western society was also changed by the arrival of new forms of media and by the advent of jet travel. During the initial stage, global journalism, radio, television, and the emergence of new, popular and often revolutionary cultural forms enabled new ways of understanding space and time. The perception of space and time and the subject's role and position in society became increasingly complex in the wake of the information revolution enabled by digital technologies during the final years of the twentieth century. In particular, Jean Baudrillard, building on ideas from Jacques Derrida and Michel Foucault, famously argued that media in general and digital media in particular are able to simulate the world to such an extent that it has become pointless to discuss any relationship between the simulated and the real; the postmodern subject inhabits a simulated universe, what Baudrillard terms 'simulacra'.[9] In *Empire* (2000) Michael Hardt and Antonio Negri even refigured empire in relation to this postmodern society into a ubiquitous but essentially stateless formation of capitalist power that is seen to preclude traditional state-driven imperialism and colonialism.[10]

The idea that citizens of the West now inhabit a postmodern world gained popularity partly because it quickly became not just a view of history but also an aesthetics and a mode of cultural and social interrogation. Before long, art, fashion, architecture and literature began to explore the possibilities that Baudrillard's and other postmodern philosophers' notions seemed to offer. One such possibility was the freeing of the subject. If the world is essentially a (media) construct, subject positions can be endlessly reinvented so that the dislocation of the subject from the real is also a freeing of the subject. Similarly, the study of culture and history was transformed by the notion that the world we inhabit is essentially a construct, a representation. Indeed, this very study relies on the notion that the apocalyptic narratives partake in such representations. I

9 Jean Baudrillard, *Simulacra and Simulation* (Ann Arbor: University of Michigan Press, 1994), first published as *Simulacres et Simulation* (1981).

10 Michael Hardt and Antonio Negri, *Empire* (Cambridge, MA: Harvard University Press, 2000).

have argued that these narratives strive, for different reasons and in different ways, to cement the notion that empire is the essence of modernity and that the US citizen must be constantly vigilant against all that threaten it.

The modes of cultural interrogation that I employ in this study can be traced to postmodern theory in general and to the postmodern notion that culture constructs rather than reflects reality, often in order to support dominant power structures. However, the results of this study at the same time suggest that while digital communication and jet-fuelled travel may indeed have compressed time and space, Western society is characterised by an intensification rather than a transformation of modernity. Gothic culture still seeks to negotiate the pressures of modernity and empire rather than those of postmodernity.

This is not a very controversial idea. Many sociologists and historians have revised the notion that the geopolitical and cultural changes of the twentieth century should be understood as a departure from, or a move beyond, modernity. Craig Calhoun has argued that since capital accumulation is still the basic economic activity, there is little evidence that we have left modernity behind: 'Modernity, if this is what we wish to call our age, continues.'[11] Similarly, David Harvey has also contended that while there have been changes in how the world is perceived, 'these changes, when set against the basic rules of capitalist accumulation, appear more as shifts in the surface appearance rather than as signs of the emergence of some entirely new postcapitalist or even postindustrial society'.[12] Similarly, Zygmunt Bauman has recognised a shift from production to consumerism in his writing but prefers to think of this shift as marking the beginning of what he terms 'liquid' modernity.[13] Finally, Anthony Giddens has suggested that the transformations that took place during the past century do not signal postmodernity but instead mark the beginning of a 'radicalised modernity era' that he terms 'late modernity'.[14]

This study comes to the same conclusion, albeit by a different route. Modernity still informs economic, cultural and military practices on both the local and global levels. As much as we like to look back 100 years, or 200 years, and imagine that we now live in a different era, in an age that has left the atrocious practices of empire behind for a brave new world, the neocolonial ambitions of the United States, the borders established by 'fortress Europe', the cementation of global North–South and East–West relations, and the ways that this present is negotiated in culture, indicate that the world we inhabit is not postcolonial or postmodern in the temporal and historical sense.

---

11 Craig Calhoun, 'The Infrastructure of Modernity' in *Social Change and Modernity*, edited by Hans Haferkamp and Neil J. Smelser (Berkeley: University of California Press, 1992), 232.

12 Harvey, *The Condition of Postmodernity*, vii.

13 Zygmunt Bauman, *Liquid Modernity* (Cambridge: Cambridge University Press, 2000).

14 Anthony Giddens, *Modernity and Self-Identity: Self and Society in the Late Modern Age* (Stanford: Stanford University Press, 1991).

This is the concluding observation of this study: the present is strikingly similar to the past but not because history moves in circles. Rather, history moves much more slowly than we imagine, and culture, its constant companion, moves equally sluggishly. The American imperial gothic is ultimately saying the same thing today as it said at the beginning of the nineteenth century, which is the same thing the British imperial gothic was saying 100 years ago: 'Empire may not be forever. We must be armed and constantly vigilant, always prepared for the violence that is the only way to defend the ideological and territorial borders that separate our modernity from the sheer darkness and abject primitivism of the Other.' It is arguably not until we recognise the archaic nature of this statement, its implicit desire to cement old structures and practices of violence, that it becomes possible to transition into a state beyond modernity.

# Bibliography

## Books and Other Publications


Achebe, Chinua. 'An Image of Africa: Racism in Joseph Conrad's *Heart of Darkness*.' In *Reclaiming the Human Sciences and Humanities through African Perspectives*, Volume II, edited by Helen Lauer and Kofi Anyidoho, 929–40. Accra: Sub-Saharan Publishers, 2012.

Adams, John Quincy. *An Address, Delivered at the Request of the Committee of Arrangements for Celebrating the Anniversary of Independence at the City of Washington on the Fourth of July 1821*. Cambridge: Hilliard and Metcalf, 1821.

Ahmad, Aalya. 'Gray Is the New Black: Race, Class, and Zombies.' In *Generation Zombie: Essays on the Living Dead in Modern Culture*, edited by Stephanie Boluk and Wylie Lenz, 130–46. Jefferson: McFarland, 2011.

Aradau, Claudia, and Rens van Munster. *Politics of Catastrophe: Genealogies of the Unknown*. London: Routledge, 2010.

Arata, Stephen D. 'The Occidental Tourist: *Dracula* and the Anxiety of Reverse Colonisation.' *Victorian Studies* 33, no. 4 (1990): 621–45.

Ashcroft, Bill, Gareth Griffiths, and Helen Tiffin. *The Empire Writes Back*. London: Routledge, 1989.

Auerbach, Nina. *Our Vampires, Ourselves*. Chicago: University of Chicago Press, 1995.

Bacevich, Andrew J. *American Empire: The Realities and Consequences of U.S. Diplomacy*. Cambridge, MA: Harvard University Press, 2002.

Bacevich, Andrew J. *The Limits of Power: The End of American Exceptionalism*. New York: Metropolitan Books, 2009.

Balibar, Étienne. *Masses, Classes, Ideas: Studies on Politics and Philosophy before and after Marx*. New York: Routledge, 1994.

Baudrillard, Jean. *Simulacra and Simulation*. Ann Arbor: University of Michigan Press, 1994.

Bauman, Zygmunt. *Liquid Modernity*. Cambridge: Cambridge University Press, 2000.

Bell, Alden. *The Reapers Are the Angels*. New York: Henry Holt, 2010.

Berger, James. *After the End: Representations of Post-Apocalypse*. Minneapolis: University of Minnesota Press, 1999.

Beville, Maria. *Gothic-Postmodernism: Voicing the Terrors of Postmodernity*. Amsterdam: Rodopi, 2009.

Bhabha, Homi K. *The Location of Culture*. London: Routledge, 1994.

Bhambra, Gurminder K. *Rethinking Modernity: Postcolonialism and the Sociological Imagination*. London: Palgrave Macmillan, 2007.

Bishop, Kyle William. *American Zombie Gothic: The Rise and Fall (and Rise) of the Walking Dead in Popular Culture*. Jefferson: McFarland, 2010.

Blackmore, Tim. "'Is This Going to Be Another Bug-Hunt?": S-F Tradition versus Biology-as-Destiny in James Cameron's *Aliens*.' *Journal of Popular Culture* 29, no. 4 (1996): 211–26.

Blatty, William Peter. *The Exorcist*. New York: Harper & Row, 1971.

Boot, Max. 'Imperial Misadventure: What Went Wrong in Somalia.' *The Weekly Standard*. March 28, 1999. http://www.weeklystandard.com/Content/Protected/Articles/000/000/010/351llyyx.asp.

Boot, Max. 'The Case for American Empire: The Most Realistic Response to Terrorism Is for America to Embrace Its Imperial Role.' *The Weekly Standard*. October 14, 2001. http://www.weeklystandard.com/Content/Public/Articles/000/000/000/318qpvmc.asp.

Boot, Max. *The Savage Wars of Peace: Small Wars and the Rise of American Power*. New York: Basic Books, 2002.

Boot, Max. 'U.S. Imperialism: A Force for Good.' *National Post*, May 13, 2003. http://www.cfr.org/iraq/us-imperialism-force-good/p5959.

Botting, Fred. *Gothic*. London: Routledge, 1996.

Bould, Mark. 'Apocalypse Here and Now: Making Sense of *The Texas Chain Saw Massacre*.' In *Horror at the Drive-In: Essays in Popular Americana*, edited by Gary D. Rhodes, 97–112. Jefferson: McFarland, 2003.

Bourne, J.L. *Day by Day Armageddon*. Nashville: Permuted Press, 2007.

Bourne, J.L. *Day by Day Armageddon: Beyond Exile*. Nashville: Permuted Press, 2010.

Bourne, J.L. *Day by Day Armageddon: Shattered Hourglass*. Nashville: Permuted Press, 2012.

Brantlinger, Patrick. *Rule of Darkness: British Literature and Imperialism, 1830–1914*. Ithaca: Cornell University Press, 1988.

Briefel, Aviva, and Sam J. Miller. 'Introduction.' In *Horror after 9/11: World of Fear, Cinema of Terror*, edited by Aviva Briefel and Sam J. Miller, 1–10. Austin: University of Texas Press, 2011.

Brooks, Max. *World War Z: An Oral history of the Zombie War*. New York: Crown, 2006.

Brown, Charles Brockden. *Edgar Huntly; or, Memoirs of a Sleep-Walker*. Philadelphia: H. Maxwell, 1799.

Brundage, W. Fitzhugh. 'Conclusion: Reflections on Lynching Scholarship.' *American Nineteenth Century History* 6, no. 3 (2005): 401–14. doi: 10.1080/14664650500381116.

Burnham, Gilbert, Riyadh Lafta, Shannon Doocy, and Les Roberts. 'Mortality after the 2003 Invasion of Iraq: A Cross-Sectional Cluster Sample Survey.' *The Lancet* 368, no. 9545 (2006): 1421–8. doi: 10.1016/S0140–6736(06)69491–9.

Burroughs, Edgar Rice. *A Princess of Mars*. 1917. Reprint, Rockville: Phoenix Science Fiction Classics, 2010.

Burroughs, Edgar Rice. *The Land That Time Forgot*. Chicago: A.C. McClurg, 1918 and 1924.

Bush, Barbara. *Imperialism and Postcolonialism*. Harlow: Pearson, 2006.

Bush, George W. 'Commencement Address at the United States Naval Academy in Annapolis, Maryland, May 25 2001.' In *Public Papers of the Presidents of the United States: GEORGE W. BUSH (2001, Book I)*. Washington, DC: United States Government Printing Office, 2001a. http://www.gpo.gov/fdsys/pkg/PPP-2001-book1/pdf/PPP-2001-book1.pdf.

Bush, George W. 'Address to the Nation on the Terrorist Attacks September 11, 2001.' In *Public Papers of the Presidents of the United States: GEORGE W. BUSH (2001, Book II)*. Washington, DC: United States Government Printing Office, 2001b. http://www.gpo.gov/fdsys/pkg/PPP-2001-book2/pdf/PPP-2001-book2.pdf.

Bush, George W. 'The President's Radio Address September 15, 2001.' In *Public Papers of the Presidents of the United States: GEORGE W. BUSH (2001, Book II)*. Washington, DC: United States Government Printing Office, 2001c. http://www.gpo.gov/fdsys/pkg/PPP-2001-book2/pdf/PPP-2001-book2.pdf.

Bush, George W. 'Remarks in a Meeting with the National Security Team and an Exchange with Reporters at Camp David, Maryland September 15, 2001.' In *Public Papers of the Presidents of the United States: GEORGE W. BUSH (2001, Book II)*. Washington, DC: United States Government Printing Office, 2001d. http://www.gpo.gov/fdsys/pkg/PPP-2001-book2/pdf/PPP-2001-book2.pdf.

Bush, George W. 'Remarks on Arrival at the White House and an Exchange with Reporters September 16, 2001.' In *Public Papers of the Presidents of the United States: GEORGE W. BUSH (2001, Book II)*. Washington, DC: United States Government Printing Office, 2001e. http://www.gpo.gov/fdsys/pkg/PPP-2001-book2/pdf/PPP-2001-book2.pdf.

Bush, George W. 'Remarks to Employees in the Pentagon and an Exchange with Reporters in Arlington, Virginia September 17, 2001.' In *Public Papers of the Presidents of the United States: GEORGE W. BUSH (2001, Book II)*. Washington, DC: United States Government Printing Office, 2001f. http://www.gpo.gov/fdsys/pkg/PPP-2001-book2/pdf/PPP-2001-book2.pdf.

Bush, George W. 'Address before a Joint Session of the Congress on the United States Response to the Terrorist Attacks of September 11 September 20, 2001.' In *Public Papers of the Presidents of the United States: GEORGE W. BUSH (2001, Book II)*. Washington, DC: United States Government Printing Office, 2001g. http://www.gpo.gov/fdsys/pkg/PPP-2001-book2/pdf/PPP-2001-book2.pdf.

Bush, George W. 'Remarks Welcoming General Tommy R. Franks and an Exchange with Reporters in Crawford, Texas December 28, 2001.' In *Public Papers of the Presidents of the United States: GEORGE W. BUSH (2001, Book II)*. Washington, DC: United States Government Printing Office, 2001h. http://www.gpo.gov/fdsys/pkg/PPP-2001-book2/pdf/PPP-2001-book2.pdf.

Bush, George W. 'Remarks at the Argonne National Laboratory in Argonne July 22, 2002.' In *Public Papers of the Presidents of the United States: GEORGE W. BUSH (2002, Book II)*. Washington, DC: United States Government Printing Office, 2002a. http://www.gpo.gov/fdsys/pkg/PPP-2002-book2/pdf/PPP-2002-book2.pdf.

Bush, George W. 'Remarks to the Community in South Bend, Indiana September 5, 2002.' In *Public Papers of the Presidents of the United States: GEORGE W. BUSH (2002, Book II)*. Washington, DC: United States Government Printing Office, 2002b. http://www.gpo.gov/fdsys/pkg/PPP-2002-book2/pdf/PPP-2002-book2.pdf.

Bush, George W. 'Remarks at a White House Reception for Veterans November 11, 2002.' In *Public Papers of the Presidents of the United States: GEORGE W. BUSH (2002, Book II)*. Washington, DC: United States Government Printing Office, 2002c. http://www.gpo.gov/fdsys/pkg/PPP-2002-book2/pdf/PPP-2002-book2.pdf.

Byron, Glennis, and Aspasia Stephanou. 'Neo-Imperialism and the Apocalyptic Vampire Narrative: Justin Cronin's *The Passage*.' In *Transnational and Postcolonial Vampires: Dark Blood*, edited by Johan Höglund and Tabish Khair, 189–201. London: Palgrave Macmillan, 2012.

Calhoun, Craig. 'The Infrastructure of Modernity.' In *Social Change and Modernity*, edited by Hans Haferkamp and Neil J. Smelser, 205–237. Berkeley: University of California Press, 1992.

Calhoun, Craig, Frederick Cooper, and Kevin W. Moore. *Lessons of Empire: Imperial Histories and American Power*. New York: The New Press, 2006.

Carroll, Noël. 'King Kong: Ape and Essence.' In *Planks of Reason: Essays on the Horror Film*, edited by Barry Keith Grant, 212–39. Metuchen: The Scarecrow Press, 1984.

Chakrabarty, Dipesh. *Habitations of Modernity: Essays in the Wake of Subaltern Studies*. Chicago: University of Chicago Press, 2002.

Chase-Dunn, Christopher, Andrew K. Jorgenson, Thomas E. Reifer, and Shoon Lio. 'The Trajectory of the United States in the World-System: A Quantitative Reflection.' *Sociological Perspectives* 48, no. 2 (2005): 233–54. doi: 10.1525/sop.2005.48.2.233.

Chesney, G.T. *The Battle of Dorking: Reminiscences of a Volunteer*. 1871. In I.F. Clarke *The Tale of the Next Great War: Fictions of Future Warfare and of Battles Still-to-Come*. Liverpool: Liverpool University Press, 1995.

Chomsky, Noam. *Hegemony or Survival: America's Quest for Global Dominance.* New York: Metropolitan Books, 2003.

Clarke, I.F. *The Tale of the Next Great War: Fictions of Future Warfare and of Battles Still-to-Come.* Liverpool: Liverpool University Press, 1995.

Clarke, I.F. *Voices Prophesying War 1763–1984.* London: Oxford University Press, 1966.

Classen, Elvira. 'Media Transmitted Values Transfer: The US at "War Against Terrorism" and Its Implications for the Information Society.' In *Cultural Imperialism: Essays on the Political Economy of Cultural Domination*, edited by Bernd Hamm and Russell Smandych, 136–46. Ontario: Broadview Press, 2005.

Clover, Carol J. *Men, Women and Chain Saws: Gender in the Modern Horror Film.* Princeton: Princeton University Press, 1992.

Conrad, Joseph. *Heart of Darkness.* 1899. Reprint, London: Dover Thrift, 1990.

Cooper, Marc. 'Lights! Cameras! Attack! Hollywood Enlists.' *The Nation.* November 21, 2001. http://www.thenation.com/article/lights-cameras-attack-hollywood-enlists#.

Cronin, Justin. *The Passage.* 2010. Reprint, New York: Ballantine Books, 2012.

Cronin, Justin. *The Twelve.* New York: Ballantine Books, 2012.

Cross, Stephanie. 'Justin Cronin: "It's Not the End of the World, You Know...".' *The Independent.* October 28, 2012. http://www.independent.co.uk/arts-entertainment/books/features/justin-cronin-its-not-the-end-of-the-world-you-know-8229142.html.

Crow, Charles L. *American Gothic.* Cardiff: University of Wales Press, 2009.

Curtis, Claire P. *Postapocalyptic Fiction and the Social Contract: 'We'll Not Go Home Again'.* Lanham: Lexington Books, 2010.

Davis, Ronald L. *Celluloid Mirrors: Hollywood and American Society since 1945.* Forth Worth: Harcourt Brace College Publishers, 1997.

Davison, Carol Margaret. 'Blood Brothers: Dracula and Jack the Ripper.' In *Bram Stoker's Dracula: Sucking through the Century 1897–1997*, edited by Carol Margaret Davison, 147–72. Toronto: Dundurn Press, 1997.

Day, Julia. 'US Steps Up Global PR Drive.' *Guardian.* July 30, 2002. http://www.guardian.co.uk/media/2002/jul/30/marketingandpr.terrorismandthemedia.

Defoe, Daniel. *The Life and Strange Surprizing Adventures of Robinson Crusoe.* London: W. Taylor, 1719.

Der Derian, James. *Virtuous War: Mapping the Military–Industrial–Media–Entertainment Network.* Boulder: Westview Press, 2001.

Derry, Charles. *Dark Dreams 2.0: A Psychological History of the Modern Horror Film from the 1950s to the 21st Century.* Jefferson: McFarland, 2009.

Dery, Mark. *I Must Not Think Bad Thoughts: Drive-By Essays on American Dread, American Dreams.* Minneapolis: University of Minnesota Press, 2012.

Deterding, Sebastian. 'Living Room Wars: Remediation, Boardgames, and the Early History of Video Wargaming.' In *Joystick Soldiers: The Politics of Play in Military Video Games*, edited by Nina B. Huntemann and Matthew Thomas Payne, 21–38. London: Routledge, 2010.

Devetak, Richard, 'The Gothic Scene of International Relations: Ghosts, Monsters, Terror and the Sublime after September 11.' *Review of International Studies*. 31, no. 4 (2005): 621–43. doi:10.1017/S0260210505006662.

Dixit, Jay. 'The War on Terror.' *Wired Magazine*. August 2006. 96–100. http://www.wired.com/wired/archive/14.08/warterror.html.

Doyle, Arthur Conan. *The Lost World*. 1912 Reprint. London: Hodder & Stoughton, 2012.

Dunant, Sarah, and Roy Porter. *The Age of Anxiety*. London: Virago, 1996.

Eby, Cecil Degrotte. *The Road to Armageddon: The Martial Spirit in English Popular Literature, 1870–1914*. Durham: Duke University Press, 1987.

Edelstein, David. 'Now Playing at Your Local Multiplex: Torture Porn.' *New York Magazine*. February 6, 2006. http://nymag.com/movies/features/15622/index1.html.

Edwards, Justin D. *Gothic Passages: Racial Ambiguity and the American Gothic*. Iowa City: University of Iowa Press, 2003.

Edwards, Justin D. and Agnieszka Soltysik Monnet. 'Introduction: From Goth/ic to Pop Goth.' In *The Gothic in Contemporary Literature and Popular Culture: Pop Goth*, edited by Justin D. Edwards and Agnieszka Soltysik Monnet. 1–18. London: Routledge, 2012.

Elliott, Larry. 'Decline and Fall of the American Empire.' *The Guardian*. June 6, 2011. http://www.guardian.co.uk/business/2011/jun/06/us-economy-decline-recovery-challenges.

Faludi, Susan. *The Terror Dream*. New York: Picador, 2007.

Farnsworth, Christopher. *Blood Oath*. London: Hodder & Stoughton, 2010.

Farnsworth, Christopher. *The President's Vampire*. New York: Putnam, 2011.

Ferguson, Niall. *Colossus: The Price of America's Empire*. New York: Penguin, 2004.

Fiedler, Leslie. *Love and Death in the American Novel*. 1960. Reprint, Champaign: Dalkey Archive Press, 1996.

Finney, Jack. *The Body Snatchers*. 1954. Reprint, New York: Scribner, 1998.

Fox, William T.R. *The Super-Ppowers: The United States, Britain and the Soviet Union – Their Responsibility for Peace*. New York: Harcourt, Brace, 1944.

Fukuyama, Francis. 'The End of History?' *The National Interest* 16, no. 3 (1989): 3–18.

Fumento, Michael. 'Hollywood Goes to War.' *New York Sun*. October 25, 2007. http://www.nysun.com/opinion/hollywood-goes-to-war/65253/.

Gelder, Ken, ed. *The Horror Reader*. London: Routledge, 2000.

Gibbon, Edward. *The History of the Decline and Fall of the Roman Empire*. London: Strahan & Cadell, 1776–89.

Giddens, Anthony. *Modernity and Self-Identity: Self and Society in the Late Modern Age*. Stanford: Stanford University Press, 1991.

Go, Julian. *Patterns of Empire: The British and American Empires, 1688 to the Present*. New York: Cambridge University Press, 2011.

Goddu, Teresa A. *Gothic America: Narrative, History, and Nation*. New York: Columbia University Press, 1997.

González, Roberto J. *Militarizing Culture: Essays on the Warfare State*. Walnut Creek: Left Coast Press, 2010.

Goodrick-Clarke, Nicholas. *The Occult Roots of Nazism: Secret Aryan Cults and Their Influence on Nazi Ideology*. New York: New York University Press, 1985.

Gowan, Peter. 'Contemporary Intra-Core Relations and World Systems Theory.' *Journal of World-Systems Research* 10, no. 2 (2004): 471–500. http://www.jwsr.org/wp-content/uploads/2013/03/jwsr-v10n2gs-gowan.pdf.

Greenberg, Karen J., ed. *The Torture Debate in America*. Cambridge: Cambridge University Press, 2006.

Greenwald, Glenn. 'What Collapsing Empire Looks Like.' *Salon*. August 6, 2010. http://www.salon.com/2010/08/06/collapse/.

Haggard, H. Rider. *King Solomon's Mines*. London: Cassell, 1885.

Haggard, H. Rider. *She*. London: Longmans, Green, 1887.

Hardt, Michael, and Antonio Negri. *Empire*. Cambridge, MA: Harvard University Press, 2000.

Harvey, David. *The Condition of Postmodernity: An Enquiry into the Origins of Cultural Change*. Oxford: Blackwell, 1990.

Harvey, David. *The New Imperialism*. Oxford: Oxford University Press, 2003.

Heffernan, Teresa. *Post-Apocalyptic Culture: Modernism, Postmodernism, and the Twentieth-Century Novel*. Toronto: University of Toronto Press, 2008.

Hendershot, Cyndy. *Anti-Communism and Popular Culture in Mid-Century America*. Jefferson: McFarland, 2003.

Herbert, James. *The Spear*. London : New English Library, 1978.

Hersey, John. *Hiroshima*. New York: Alfred A. Knopf, 1946.

Hilfrich, Fabian. *Debating American Exceptionalism: Empire and Democracy in the Wake of the Spanish–American War*. Basingstoke: Palgrave Macmillan, 2012.

Hobson, J. A. *Imperialism: A Study*. London: James Nisbet, 1902.

Hogan, Chuck, and Guillermo del Toro. *The Strain*. New York: HarperCollins, 2009.

Hogan, Chuck, and Guillermo del Toro. *The Fall*. New York: HarperCollins, 2010.

Hogan, Chuck, and Guillermo del Toro. *The Night Eternal*. New York: HarperCollins, 2011.

Holland, Jack. '"When You Think of the Taliban, Think of the Nazis": Teaching Americans "9/11" in NBC's *The West Wing*.' *Millennium: Journal of International Studies* 40, no. 1 (2011): 85–106. doi: 10.1177/0305829811408680.

Huntington, Samuel P. *The Clash of Civilizations and the Remaking of World Order.* New York: Simon & Schuster, 1996.

Hustis, Harriet. 'Deliberate Unknowing and Strategic Retelling: The Ravages of Cultural Desire in Charles Brockden Brown's *Edgar Huntly.' Studies in American Fiction* 31, no. 1 (2003): 101–20.

Höglund, Johan. 'Mobilising the Novel: The Literature of Imperialism and the First World War.' PhD diss., Acta Universitatis Upsaliensis, Studia Anglistica Upsaliensia, Uppsala, 1997.

Höglund, Johan. 'Electronic Empire: Orientalism Revisited in the Military Shooter.' *Game Studies* 8, no. 1 (2008). http://gamestudies.org/0801/articles/hoeglund.

Höglund, Johan. 'Militarizing the Vampire: Underworld and the Desire of the Military Entertainment Complex.' In *Transnational and Postcolonial Vampires,* edited by Johan Höglund and Tabish Khair, 173–88. London: Palgrave Macmillan, 2012.

Ignatieff, Michael. 'The Burden.' *New York Times Magazine.* January 5, 2003. http://www.nytimes.com/2003/01/05/magazine/05EMPIRE.html?pagewanted=all.

Jacobs, Harriet Ann. *Incidents in the Life of a Slave Girl.* Boston: Thayer & Eldridge, 1861.

Jean, Susan. '"Warranted" Lynchings: Narratives of Mob Violence in White Southern Newspapers, 1880–1940.' *American Nineteenth Century History* 6, no. 3 (2005): 351–72. doi: 10.1080/14664650500381058.

Johnson, Chalmers. *Blowback: The Costs and Consequences of American Empire.* New York: Metropolitan Books, 2000.

Johnson, Chalmers. *The Sorrows of Empire: Militarism, Secrecy, and the End of the Republic.* New York: Metropolitan Books, 2004.

Johnson, Chalmers. *Nemesis: The Last Days of the American Republic.* New York: Metropolitan Books, 2006.

Johnson, Paul. 'From the Evil Empire to the Empire for Liberty.' *The New Criterion,* 21 (June 2003): 20. http://www.newcriterion.com/articles.cfm/From--ldquo-the-Evil-Empire-rdquo--to--ldquo-the-Empire-for-Liberty-rdquo-1714.

Kaplan, Amy. 'Romancing the Empire: The Embodiment of American Masculinity in the Popular Historical Novel of the 1890s.' *American Literary History* 2, no. 4 (1990): 659–90.

Kaplan, Amy. *The Anarchy of Empire in the Making of U.S. Culture.* Cambridge, MA: Harvard University Press, 2002.

Kaplan, Amy, and Donald E. Pease, eds. *Cultures of United States Imperialism.* Durham: Duke University Press, 1993.

Kaplan, Caren. 'Precision Targets: GPS and the Militarization of US Consumer Identity.' *American Quarterly* 58, no. 3 (2006): 693–713.

Kaplan, Robert D. 'Indian Country.' *Wall Street Journal.* September 21, 2004. http://online.wsj.com/article/0,,SB109572689960923141,00.html.

Kaye, Heidi. 'Fin-de-siècle Fears: *The X-Files* as Contemporary Gothic.' In *Fictions of Unease: The Gothic from Otranto to* The X-Files, edited by Andrew Smith, Diane Mason, and William Hughes, 202–10. Bath: Sulis Press, 2002.

Kermode, Frank. *The Sense of an Ending.* 1966. Reprint, Oxford: Oxford University Press, 2000.

Khair, Tabish. *The Gothic, Postcolonialism and Otherness: Ghosts from Elsewhere.* London: Palgrave MacMillan, 2009.

Kilday, Gregg. 'Eerie Links between "Harry Potter," Osama bin Laden: Why Movie May Benefit.' *Hollywood Reporter.* May 2, 2011. http://www.hollywoodreporter.com/news/eerie-links-between-harry-potter-184109.

King, C. Richard, and David J. Leonard. 'Wargames as a New Frontier: Securing American Empire in Virtual Space.' In *Joystick Soldiers: The Politics of Play in Military Video Games*, edited by Nina B. Huntemann and Matthew Thomas Payne, 91–105. London: Routledge, 2010.

King, Geoff. *New Hollywood Cinema: An Introduction.* New York: I.B. Tauris, 2002.

King, Stephen. *Cell.* New York: Scribner, 2006.

King, Stephen. *Salem's Lot.* 1975. Reprint, New York: Anchor Books, 2011.

Kipling, Rudyard. 'Mark of the Beast.' In *Life's Handicap.* 1899. Reprint. London: Macmillan, 1991.

Klavan, Andrew. 'What Bush and Batman Have in Common.' *The Wall Street Journal.* July 25, 2008. http://online.wsj.com/article/SB121694247343482821.html.

Klein, Naomi. *The Shock Doctrine: The Rise of Disaster Capitalism.* New York: Knopf Canada, 2007.

Kolko, Gabriel. *Main Currents in Modern American History.* New York: Pantheon Books, 1976.

Koontz, Dean. *City of Night.* New York: Bantam Books, 2005.

Koontz, Dean. *Dead and Alive.* New York: Bantam Books, 2009.

Koontz, Dean. *Lost Souls.* New York: Bantam Books, 2010.

Koontz, Dean (co-written with Kevin J. Anderson). *Prodigal Son.* New York: Bantam Books, 2005.

Koontz, Dean. *The Dead Town.* New York: Bantam Books, 2011.

Labott, Elise. 'U.S. Gives $43 Million to Afghanistan.' *CNN.* May 17, 2001. http://articles.cnn.com/2001–05–17/us/us.afghanistan.aid_1_ban-on-poppy-cultivation-afghanistan-afghan-refugees?_s=PM:US.

Lacy, Mark J. 'War, Cinema and Moral Anxiety.' *Alternatives: Global, Local, Political* 28, no. 5 (2003): 611–36. http://www.jstor.org/stable/40645126.

Lakoff, George. 'War on Terror, Rest in Peace.' *AlterNet.* July 31, 2005. http://www.alternet.org/story/23810/war_on_terror,_rest_in_peace.

Lakoff, George, and Mark Johnson. *Metaphors We Live By.* Chicago: The University of Chicago Press, 1980.

Lane, Anthony. 'This Is Not a Movie.' *The New Yorker*. September 24, 2001, 79–80. http://www.newyorker.com/archive/2001/09/24/010924crci_cinema?currentPage=all.

Lansing, Robert. *The Peace Negotiations: A Personal Narrative*. 1921. Reprint, Teddington: The Echo Library, 2007.

Lenoir, Timothy, and Henry Lowood. 'Theatres of War: The Military–Entertainment Complex.' http://www.stanford.edu/class/sts145/Library/Lenoir-Lowood_TheatersOfWar.pdf.

Little, Douglas. *American Orientalism: The United States and the Middle East since 1945*. London: I.B. Taurus, 2003.

Litwack, Leon F. 'Hellhounds.' In *Without Sanctuary: Lynching Photography in America*, edited by James Allen, 8–37. Santa Fey: Twin Palms Publishers, 2000.

London, Jack. 'The Unparalleled Invasion.' In *The Complete Short Stories of Jack London*, vol. 2, edited by Earle Labor, Robert C. Leitz III, and Milo Shepard, 1234–46. Stanford: Stanford University Press, 1993.

Loomba, Ania, Suvir Kaul, Matti Bunzl, Antoinette Burton, and Jed Esty. 'Beyond What? An Introduction.' In *Postcolonial Studies and Beyond*, edited by Ania Loomba, Suvir Kaul, Matti Bunzl, Antoinette Burton and Jed Esty, 1–38. Durham: Duke University Press, 2005.

Lowenstein, Adam. 'Spectacle Horror and *Hostel*: Why Torture Porn Does Not Exist.' *Critical Quarterly* 53, no. 1 (2011): 42–60. doi: 10.1111/j.1467–8705.2011.01976.x.

Luckhurst, Roger. *Science Fiction*. Cambridge: Polity, 2005.

Lye, Colleen. *America's Asia: Racial Form and American Literature, 1893–1945*. Princeton: Princeton University Press, 2005.

Maberry, Jonathan. *Patient Zero*. New York: St Martin's Griffin, 2009.

Markovitz, Jonathan. *Legacies of Lynching: Racial Violence and Memory*. Minneapolis: University of Minnesota Press, 2004.

Marsh, Richard. *The Beetle: A Mystery*. London: Skeffington and Son, 1897.

Marsh, Richard. *The Joss: A Reversion*. London: White, 1901.

Mason, A.E.W. *The Four Feathers*. London: Macmillan, 1902.

Matheson, Richard. *I Am Legend*. 1954. Reprint, New York: Tor, 2007.

McAlister, Melani. *Epic Encounters: Culture, Media, and U.S. Interests in the Middle East since 1945*. Berkeley: University of California Press, 2001.

McCarthy, Cormac. *The Road*. New York: Alfred A. Knopf, 2006.

McLellan, Heather. 'Devs Announce *Medal of Honor: Warfighter* Charity Project.' *The Escapist*. Last modified June 13, 2012. http://www.escapistmagazine.com/news/view/117891-Devs-Announce-Medal-of-Honor-Warfighter-Charity-Project.

McSweeney, Terence. 'The Land of the Dead and the Home of the Brave: Romero's Vision of a Post-9/11 America.' In *Reframing 9/11: Film, Popular Culture and the 'War on Terror'*, edited by Jeff Birkenstein, Anna Froula, and Karen Randell, 107–16. New York: Continuum, 2010.

Merritt, Abraham. *The Face in the Abyss*. New York: Horace Liveright, 1931.

Mignolo, Walter. *The Darker Side of Western Modernity: Global Futures, Decolonial Options*. Durham: Duke University Press, 2011.

Miller, Frank. *Holy Terror*. Burbank, CA: Legendary Comics, 2011.

Mogen, David, Scott P. Sanders, and Joanne B. Karpinski. 'Introduction.' In *Frontier Gothic: Terror and Wonder at the Frontier in American Literature*, edited by David Mogen, Scott P. Sanders, and Joanne B. Karpinsky, 13–27. London: Associated University Presses, 1993.

Monnet, Agnieszka Soltysik. *The Poetics and Politics of the American Gothic: Gender and Slavery in Nineteenth-Century American Literature*. Farnham: Ashgate, 2010.

Morrison, Toni. *Playing in the Dark: Whiteness and the Literary Imagination*. New York: Vintage, 1992.

Morton, Ray. *King Kong: The History of a Movie Icon from Fay Wray to Peter Jackson*. New York: Applause Theatre & Cinema Books, 2005.

Murphy, Cullen. *Are We Rome? The Fall of an Empire and the Fate of America*. Boston: Houghton Mifflin, 2007.

Naisbitt, John. *High Tech/High Touch: Technology and Our Accelerated Search for Meaning*. London: Nicholas Brealey, 1999.

Nakamura, David, and Tom Hamburger. 'Put Armed Police in Every School, NRA Urges.' *The Washington Post*. December 12, 2012. http://articles.washingtonpost.com/2012-12-21/politics/35950179_1_gun-regulation-national-school-shield-program-gun-violence.

Newell, Diane, and Victoria Lamont. 'Savagery on Mars: Representations of the Primitive in Brackett and Burroughs.' In *Visions of Mars: Essays on the Red Planet in Fiction and Science*, edited by George Slusser and Eric S. Rabkin, 73–9. Jefferson: McFarland, 2011.

*New York Magazine*. 'Blue: What Everyone Would Remember First.' August 27, 2011. http://nymag.com/news/9–11/10th-anniversary/blue-sky/.

Nossal, Kim Richard. 'Lonely Superpower or Unapologetic Hyperpower? Analyzing American Power in the Post-Cold War Era.' Paper for presentation at the biennial meeting of the South African Political Studies Association Saldanha, Western Cape, June 29–July 2, 1999. http://post.queensu.ca/~nossalk/papers/hyperpower.htm.

Pagden, Anthony. 'Imperialism, Liberalism, & the Quest for Perpetual Peace.' *Daedalus* 134, no. 2 (2005): 46–57. http://www.jstor.org/stable/20027977.

Pick, Daniel. *Faces of Degeneration: A European Disorder, c.1848–c.1918*. Cambridge: Cambridge University Press, 1989.

Poe, Edgar Allan. *The Narrative of Arthur Gordon Pym*. New York: Harper and Brothers, 1838.

Poole, W. Scott. *Monsters in America: Our Historical Obsession with the Hideous and the Haunting*. Waco: Baylor University Press, 2011.

Porter, Lynnette R. *Unsung Heroes from the* Lord of the Rings*: From the Page to the Screen*. Westport: Greenwood Publishing, 2005.

Pratt, Mary Louise. *Imperial Eyes: Travel Narrative and Transculturation*. London: Routledge, 1992.

Punter, David. *The Literature of Terror: A History of Gothic Fictions from 1765 to the Present Day*. 2 vols. London: Longman, 1996.

Rardin, Jennifer. *Once Bitten, Twice Shy*. London: Orbit Books, 2007.

Ravenscroft, Trevor. *The Spear of Destiny: The Occult Power behind the Spear Which Pierced the Side of Christ*. London: Neville Spearman, 1973.

Roberts, Les, Riyadh Lafta, Richard Garfield, Jamal Khudhairi, and Gilbert Burnham. 'Mortality before and after the 2003 Invasion of Iraq: Cluster Sample Survey.' *The Lancet* 364, no. 9448 (2004): 1857–64. doi: 10.1016/S0140–6736(04)17441–2.

Robb, David L. *Operation Hollywood: How the Pentagon Shapes and Censors the Movies*. New York: Prometheus Books, 2004.

Rommel-Ruiz, W. Bryan. *American History Goes to the Movies: Hollywood and the American Experience*. London: Routledge, 2011.

Rony, Fatimah Tobing. *The Third Eye: Race, Cinema, and Ethnographic Spectacle*. Durham: Duke University Press, 1996.

Rowe, John Carlos. 'Poe, Antebellum Slavery, and Modern Criticism.' In *Poe's Pym: Critical Explorations*, edited by Richard Kopley, 117–39. Durham: Duke University Press, 1992.

Rowlandson, Mary. *The Sovereignty and Goodness of God: Being a Narrative of the Captivity and Restoration of Mrs. Mary Rowlandson*. Cambridge: Samuel Green, 1682.

Said, Edward. *Orientalism*. New York: Vintage, 1978.

Sampson, Robert. *Yesterday's Faces: A Study of Series Characters in the Early Pulp Magazines. Volume 3: From the Dark Side*. Bowling Green: Bowling Green University Popular Press, 1987.

Seeley, John Robert. *The Expansion of England: Two Courses of Lectures*. 1883. Reprint, New York: Cosimo, 2005.

Sharp, Patrick B. *Savage Perils: Racial Frontiers and Nuclear Apocalypse in American Culture*. Norman: University of Oklahoma Press, 2007.

Sharrett, Christopher. 'The Horror Film in Neoconservative Culture.' In *The Dread of Difference: Gender and the Horror Film*, edited by Barry Keith Grant, 253–76. Austin: Texas University Press, 1996.

Shelley, Mary. *Frankenstein*. London: Lackington, Hughes, Harding, Mavor & Jones, 1818.

Sherman, Fraser A. *Screen Enemies of the American Way: Political Paranoia about Nazis, Communists, Saboteurs, Terrorists and Body Snatching Aliens in Film and Television*. Jefferson: McFarland, 2011.

Shiel, M.P. *The Yellow Danger*. London: Grant Richards, 1898.

Showalter, Elaine. *Sexual Anarchy: Gender and Culture at the Fin de Siècle.* New York: Viking, 1990.
Sigler, Scott. *Infected.* New York: Crown Publishing, 2008.
Sigler, Scott. *Contagious.* New York: Crown Publishing, 2008.
Singer, Peter. *The President of Good and Evil: The Ethics of George W. Bush.* New York: Dutton, 2004.
Singh, Amritjit, and Peter Schmidt, eds. *Postcolonial Theory and the United States: Race, Ethnicity, and Literature.* Jackson: University Press of Mississippi, 2000.
Skal, David J. *The Monster Show: A Cultural History of Horror.* London: Plexus, 1993.
Slotkin, Richard. *Regeneration through Violence: The Mythology of the American Frontier 1600–1860.* 1973. Reprint, Norman: University of Oklahoma Press, 2000.
Smicker, Josh. 'Future Combat: Combating Futures.' In *Joystick Soldiers: The Politics of Play in Military Video Games*, edited by Nina B. Huntemann and Matthew Thomas Payne, 106–21. London: Routledge, 2010.
Smith, Andrew, and William Hughes. *Empire and the Gothic: The Politics of Genre.* London: Palgrave Macmillan, 2003.
Smith-Rosenberg, Carroll. *This Violent Empire: The Birth of an American National Identity.* Chapel Hill: University of North Carolina Press, 2010.
Spivak, Gayatri. 'Can the Subaltern Speak?' In *Marxism and the Interpretation of Culture*, edited by Cary Nelson and Lawrence Grossberg, 271–313. Urbana: University of Illinois Press, 1988.
Spooner, Catherine. *Contemporary Gothic.* London: Reaktion Books, 2006.
Stevenson, Robert Louis. *The Strange Case of Dr. Jekyll and Mr. Hyde.* London: Longmans, Green, 1886.
Stoker, Bram. *Dracula.* London: Archibald Constable, 1897.
Streeby, Shelley. *American Sensations: Class, Empire, and the Production of Popular Culture.* Berkeley: University of California Press, 2002.
Toh, Justine. 'The Tools and Toys of (the) War (on Terror): Consumer Desire, Military Fetish, and Regime Change in *Batman Begins*.' In *Reframing 9/11: Film, Popular Culture and the 'War on Terror'*, edited by Jeff Birkenstein, Anna Froula, and Karen Randell, 127–40. New York: Continuum, 2010.
Turner, Fredrick Jackson. *The Frontier in American History.* New York, Henry Holt, 1920.
Turse, Nick. *The Complex: How the Military Invades Our Everyday Lives.* New York: Metropolitan Books, 2008.
Tziallas, Evangelos. 'Torture Porn and Surveillance Culture.' *Jump Cut: A Review of Contemporary Media* no. 52 (2010). http://www.ejumpcut.org/archive/jc52.2010/evangelosTorturePorn/index.html.
Valantin, Jean-Michel. *Hollywood, the Pentagon and Washington: The Movies and National Security from World War II to the Present Day.* London: Anthem Press, 2003.

Wald, Priscilla. *Contagious: Cultures, Carriers, and the Outbreak Narrative*. Durham: Duke University Press, 2008.

Waller, Gregory A. 'Introduction to *American Horrors*.' In *The Horror Reader*, edited by Ken Gelder, 256–64. London: Routledge, 2000.

Weinstock, Jeffrey. *Charles Brockden Brown*. Cardiff: University of Wales Press, 2011.

Wells, H.G. *The War of the Worlds*. London: Heinemann, 1898.

Wheatley, Dennis. *They Used Dark Forces*. London: Hutchinson, 1964.

Wheeler, Mark. *Hollywood: Politics and Society*. London: BFI Publishing, 2006.

Williams, William Appleman. 'The Frontier Thesis and American Foreign Policy.' *Pacific Historical Review* 24, no. 4 (1955): 379–95.

Wood, Amy Louise. *Lynching and Spectacle: Witnessing Racial Violence in America, 1890–1940*. Chapel Hill: University of North Carolina Press, 2009.

Wood, Robin. 'An Introduction to the American Horror Film.' In *Planks of Reason: Essays on the Horror Film*, edited by Barry Keith Grant, 107–41. 1984. Reprint, Oxford: The Scarecrow Press, 2004.

Worland, Rick. 'OWI Meets the Monsters: Hollywood Horror Films and War Propaganda, 1942 to 1945.' *Cinema Journal* 37, no. 1 (1997): 47–65.

Yerxa, Donald A., ed. *Recent Themes in Military History: Historians in Conversation*. Columbia: University of South Carolina Press, 2008.

Young, Elizabeth. *Black Frankenstein: The Making of an American Metaphor*. New York: New York University Press, 2008.

Zimmer, Catherine. 'Caught on Tape? The Politics of Video in the New Torture Film.' In *Horror after 9/11: World of Fear, Cinema of Terror*, edited by Aviva Briefel and Sam J. Miller, 83–106. Austin: University of Texas Press, 2011.

## Films and Other Media

*24*. Created by Joel Surnow and Robert Cochran. 2001–10. Los Angeles, CA: Fox Broadcast Television Network.

*28 Days Later*. Directed by Danny Boyle. 2002. London: DNA Films. 2003. DVD Widescreen Special Edition.

*300*. Directed by Zack Snyder. 2007. Burbank, CA: Warner Bros.

*2001 Maniacs*. Directed by Tim Sullivan. 2005. Santa Monica, CA: Lionsgate.

*A Nightmare on Elm Street*. Directed by Samuel Bayer. 2010. Los Angeles, CA: New Line Cinema.

*Alien*. Directed by Ridley Scott. 1979. Los Angeles, CA: 20th Century Fox, 1999. DVD.

*Aliens*. Directed by James Cameron. 1986. Los Angeles, CA: 20th Century Fox, 2004. DVD.

*Aliens vs. Predator: Requiem*. Directed by Greg and Colin Strause. 2007. Los Angeles, CA: 20th Century Fox, 2008. DVD.

*America's Army*. 2002. United States Army.

*Apocalypse Now*. Directed by Francis Ford Coppola. 1979. Beverly Hills, CA: United Artists.

*Avatar*. Directed by James Cameron. 2009. Los Angeles, CA: 20th Century Fox, 2010. Blu Ray.

*Batman*. Directed by Tim Burton. 1989. Burbank, CA: Warner Bros.

*Batman Begins*. Directed by Christopher Nolan. 2005. Burbank, CA: Warner Bros., 2005. DVD.

*Battlefield 3*. 2011. Stockholm: EA Digital Illusions CE.

*Battle: Los Angeles*. Directed by Jonathan Liebesman. 2011. Culver City, CA: Columbia Pictures, 2011. DVD.

*Battleship*. Directed by Peter Berg. 2012. Universal City, CA: Universal Studios, 2012. DVD.

*Beginning of the End*. Directed by Bert I. Gordon. 1957. Studio City, CA: Republic Pictures.

*Black Christmas*. Directed by Bob Clark. 1974. Film Funding Limited of Canada.

*Black Hawk Down*. Directed by Ridley Scott. 2001. Culver City, CA: Columbia Pictures.

*Blade*. Directed by Stephen Norrington. 1998. Los Angeles, CA: New Line Cinema.

*Blade II*. Directed by Guillermo del Toro. 2002. Los Angeles, CA: New Line Cinema, 2002. DVD.

*Blood Feast*. Directed by Herschell Gordon Lewis. 1963. Box Office Spectaculars, 2000. DVD.

*Blood Feast 2*. Directed by Herschell Gordon Lewis. 2002. New York: Shriek Show, 2003. DVD.

*Body Snatchers*. Directed by Abel Ferrara. 1993. Burbank, CA: Warner Bros.

*Bram Stoker's Dracula*. Directed by Francis Ford Coppola. 1992. Culver City, CA: Columbia Pictures.

*Cabin Fever*. Directed by Eli Roth. 2002. Santa Monica, CA: Lions Gate Films.

*Call of Duty: Modern Warfare*. 2007. Santa Monica, CA: Activision.

*Captivity*. Directed by Roland Joffé. 2007. Santa Monica, CA: Lionsgate, 2007. DVD.

*Cloverfield*. Directed by Matt Reeves. 2008. Hollywood, CA: Paramount Pictures.

*Color Me Blood Red*. Directed by Herschell Gordon Lewis. 1965. Box Office Spectaculars.

*Confessions of a Nazi Spy*. Directed by Anatole Litvak. 1939. Burbank, CA: Warner Bros.

*Creature from the Black Lagoon*. Directed by Jack Arnold. 1954. Universal City, CA: Universal Studios, 2007. DVD.

*Crysis*. 2007. Frankfurt: Crytek.

*Crysis 2*. 2011. Frankfurt: Crytek.

*Crysis 3*. 2013. Frankfurt: Crytek.

*Dawn of the Dead.* Directed by George Romero. 1978. Laurel Group Inc.

*Dawn of the Dead.* Directed by Zack Snyder. 2004. Universal City, CA: Universal Studios, 2004. Full Screen Edition DVD.

*Dominion: Prequel to the Exorcist.* Directed by Paul Schrader. 2005. Burbank, CA: Warner Bros.

*Doom*. 1993. Richardson, Texas: id Software.

*Doom 3*. 2004. Richardson, Texas: id Software.

*Dr Jekyll and Mr Hyde*. Directed by Lucius Henderson. 1912. New Rochelle, NY: Thanhouser Company. http://vimeo.com/20026199.

*Dr Jekyll and Mr Hyde*. Directed by Herbert Brenon. 1913. Universal City, CA: Universal Studios. http://archive.org/details/DrJekyllAndMrHyde1913.

*Eight Legged Freaks*. Directed by Ellory Elkayem. 2002. Burbank, CA: Warner Bros.

*Exorcist: The Beginning*. Directed by Renny Harlin. 2004. Burbank, CA: Warner Bros., 2005. Widescreen Edition DVD.

*Falling Skies*. Created by Robert Rodat. 2011–present. Atlanta: TNT.

*Far Cry*. 2004. Frankfurt: Crytek.

*Frankenstein*. Directed by J. Searle Dawley. 1910. New York: Edison Studios. http://archive.org/details/FrankensteinfullMovie.

*Frankenstein*. Directed by James Whale. 1931. Universal City, CA: Universal Studios, 2006. 75th Anniversary Edition Universal Legacy Series DVD.

*Freddy vs. Jason*. Directed by Ronny Yu. 2003. Los Angeles, CA: New Line Cinema.

*Friday the 13th*. Directed by Sean S. Cunningham. 1980. Georgetown Productions.

*Full Spectrum Warrior*. 2004. Los Angeles, CA: Pandemic Studios.

*Ghost Ship*. Directed by Steve Beck. 2002. Burbank, CA: Warner Bros.

*G.I. Joe: Retaliation*. Directed by Jon M. Chu. 2013. Hollywood, CA: Paramount Pictures.

*G.I. Joe: The Rise of Cobra*. Directed by Stephen Sommers. 2009. Hollywood, CA: Paramount Pictures.

*Green Zone*. Directed by Paul Greengrass. 2010. Universal City, CA: Universal Studios.

*Halloween*. Directed by John Carpenter. 1978. Falcon International Pictures.

*Halloween Resurrection*. Directed by Rick Rosenthal. 2002. Burbank, CA: Dimension Films.

*Harry Potter and the Sorcerer's Stone*. Directed by Chris Columbus. 2001. Burbank, CA: Warner Bros.

*Hellboy*. Directed by Guillermo del Toro. 2004. Culver City, CA: Columbia Pictures, 2004. DVD.

*Homefront*. 2011. New York: Kaos Studios.

*Hostel.* Directed by Eli Roth. 2005. Culver City, CA: Screen Gems, 2006. Director's Cut DVD.

*Hostel: Part II.* Directed by Eli Roth. 2007. Culver City, CA: Screen Gems, 2007. DVD.

*I Am Legend.* Directed by Francis Lawrence. 2007. Burbank, CA: Warner Bros.

*I Am Omega.* Directed by Griff Furst. 2007. Burbank, CA: The Asylum.

*I Know What You Did Last Summer.* Directed by Jim Gillespie. 1997. Culver City, CA: Columbia Pictures.

*In the Valley of Elah.* Directed by Paul Haggis. 2007. Universal City, CA: Summit Entertainment.

*Invasion of the Body Snatchers.* Directed by Don Siegel. 1956. Los Angeles, CA: Allied Artists Pictures Corporation.

*Invasion of the Body Snatchers.* Directed by Philip Kaufman. 1978. Beverly Hills, CA: United Artists, 2007. DVD.

*Jason X.* Directed by James Isaac. 2002. Los Angeles, CA: New Line Cinema.

*John Carter.* Directed by Andrew Stanton. 2012. Burbank, CA: Walt Disney Studios, 2012. DVD.

*King of the Zombies.* Directed by Jean Yarbrough. 1941. Los Angeles, CA: Monogram Pictures.

*King Kong.* Directed by Merian C. Cooper and Ernest B. Schoedsack. 1933. New York: RKO Pictures, 2006. DVD.

*King Kong.* Directed by John Guillermin. 1976. Hollywood, CA: Paramount Pictures, 2005. DVD.

*King Kong.* Directed by Peter Jackson. 2005. Universal City, CA: Universal Studios, 2006. DVD.

*Kuma War.* 2004. New York: Kuma Reality Games.

*Legion.* Directed by Scott Stewart. 2010. Culver City, CA: Screen Gems, 2010. DVD.

*Medal of Honor: Warfighter.* 2012. Los Angeles, CA: Danger Close Games.

*Mimic.* Directed by Guillermo del Toro. 1997. Burbank, CA: Dimension Films.

*Monster from the Ocean Floor.* Directed by Wyott Ordung. 1954. Lippert Pictures, 2001. DVD.

*Monsters.* Directed by Gareth Edwards. 2010. London: Vertigo films.

*Night of the Living Dead.* Directed by George A. Romero. 1968. The Walter Reade Organization, 2001. DVD.

*Predator.* Directed by John McTiernan. 1987. Los Angeles, CA: 20th Century Fox.

*Predator 2.* Directed by Stephen Hopkins. 1990. Los Angeles, CA: 20th Century Fox.

*Princess of Mars.* Directed by Mark Atkins. 2009. Burbank, CA: The Asylum, 2009. DVD.

*Psycho.* Directed by Alfred Hitchcock. 1960. Hollywood, CA: Paramount Pictures.

*Quake 2*. 1997. Richardson, Texas: id Software.

*Quake 3 Arena*. 1999. Richardson, Texas: id Software.

*Quake 4*. 2005. Madison, WI: Raven Software and Richardson, Texas: id Software.

*Raiders of the Lost Ark*. Directed by Steven Spielberg. 1981. Hollywood, CA: Paramount Pictures, 2005. DVD.

*Red Dawn*. Directed by Dan Bradley. 2012. Santa Monica, CA: Film District.

*Rendition*. Directed by Gavin Hood. 2007. Los Angeles, CA: New Line Cinema.

*Resident Evil*. Directed by Paul W. S. Anderson. 2002. Frankfurt: Constantin Films, 2002. DVD.

*Resident Evil: Apocalypse*. Directed by Alexander Witt. 2004. Frankfurt: Constantin Films, 2004. DVD.

*Resistance: Fall of Man*. 2006. Tokyo: Sony Computer Entertainment.

*Resistance 3*. 2011. Tokyo: Sony Computer Entertainment.

*Return of the Vampire*. Directed by Lew Landers. 1944. Culver City, CA: Columbia Pictures.

*Return to Castle Wolfenstein*. 2001. Los Angeles, CA: Gray Matter Interactive.

*Revenge of the Zombies*. Directed by Steve Sekely. 1943. Los Angeles, CA: Monogram Pictures, 2009. Monogram Pictures, V-4 Sky Patrol, Murder by Invitation, Law of the Jungle, *Revenge of the Zombies*. DVD.

*Ringu*. Directed by Hideo Nakata. 1998. Tokyo: Toho Company.

*Saw*. Directed by James Wan. 2004. Santa Monica, CA: Lionsgate, 2005. DVD.

*Skyline*. Directed by Colin and Greg Strause. 2010. Universal City, CA: Universal Studios.

*Spec Ops: The Line*. 2012. Novato, CA: 2K Games.

*Super 8*. Directed by J. J. Abrams. 2011. Hollywood, CA: Paramount Pictures.

*Tarantula*. Directed by Jack Arnold. 1955. Universal City, CA: Universal Studios.

*The Avengers*. Directed by Joss Whedon. 2012. Burbank, CA: Walt Disney Studios.

*The Beast from 20,000 Fathoms*. Directed by Eugéne Louiré. 1953. Burbank, CA: Warner Bros., 2003. DVD.

*The Birds*. Directed by Alfred Hitchcock. 1963. Universal City, CA: Universal Studios.

*The Birth of a Nation*. Directed by D.W. Griffith. 1915. Hollywood, CA; David W. Griffith Corp. 1998. DVD.

*The Crazies*. Directed by George A. Romero. 1973. Cambist Films.

*The Crazies*. Directed by Breck Eisner. 2010. Beverly Hills, CA: Overture Films.

*The Darkest Hour*. Directed by Chris Gorak. 2011. Universal City, CA: Summit Entertainment.

*The Dark Knight*. Directed by Christopher Nolan. 2008. Burbank, CA: Warner Bros., 2008. DVD.

*The Dark Knight Rises*. Directed by Christopher Nolan. 2012. Burbank, CA: Warner Bros., 2012. DVD.

*The Exorcist.* Directed by William Friedkin. 1973. Burbank, CA: Warner Bros.

*The Four Feathers.* Directed by Shekhar Kapur. 2002. Hollywood, CA: Paramount Pictures.

*The Frighteners.* Directed by Peter Jackson. 1996. Universal City, CA: Universal Studios.

*The Hurt Locker.* Directed by Katheryn Bigelow. 2009. Burbank, CA: Warner Bros., 2007.

*The Invasion.* Directed by Oliver Hirschbiegel and James McTeigue. 2007. Burbank, CA: Warner Bros., 2007. DVD.

*The Invisible Man.* Directed by James Whale. 1933. Universal City, CA: Universal Studios, 2000. DVD.

*The Last House on the Left.* Directed by Wes Craven. 1972. Hallmark Releasing.

*The Last Man on Earth.* Directed by Ubaldo Ragona and Sidney Salkow. 1964. Los Angeles, CA: American International Pictures.

*The League of Extraordinary Gentlemen.* Directed by Stephen Norrington. 2003. Los Angeles, CA: 20th Century Fox, 2003. Widescreen Edition DVD.

*The Lord of the Rings: The Fellowship of the Ring.* Directed by Peter Jackson. 2001. Los Angeles, CA: New Line Cinema.

*The Lord of the Rings: The Two Towers.* Directed by Peter Jackson. 2002. Los Angeles, CA: New Line Cinema.

*The Lord of the Rings: The Return of the Ring.* Directed by Peter Jackson. 2003. Los Angeles, CA: New Line Cinema.

*Them!* Directed by Gordon Douglas. 1954. Burbank, CA: Warner Bros.

*The Men Who Stare at Goats.* Directed by Grant Heslov. 2009. Smokehouse Pictures.

*The Monster That Challenged the World.* Directed by Arnold Laven. 1957. Beverly Hills, CA: United Artists.

*The Mortal Storm.* Directed by Frank Borzage. 1940. Beverly Hills, CA: Metro-Goldwyn-Mayer.

*The Mummy.* Directed by Karl Freund. 1932. Universal City, CA: Universal Studios, 1999. DVD.

*The Mummy.* Directed by Stephen Sommers. 1999. Universal City, CA: Universal Studios.

*The Mummy Returns.* Directed by Stephen Sommers. 2001. Universal City, CA: Universal Studios.

*The Omega Man.* Directed by Boris Sagal. 1971. Burbank, CA: Warner Bros.

*The Ring.* Directed by Gore Verbinsky. 2002. Universal City, CA: Dreamworks.

*The Searchers.* Directed by John Ford. 1956. Burbank, CA: Warner Bros., 1997. DVD.

*The Silence of the Lambs.* Directed by Jonathan Demme. 1991. Los Angeles, CA: Orion Pictures.

*The Texas Chain Saw Massacre*. Directed by Tobe Hooper. 1974. Bryanstone Pictures, 2006. 2-Disc Ultimate Edition DVD.

*The Texas Chainsaw Massacre*. Directed by Marcus Nispel. 2003. Los Angeles, CA: New Line Cinema, 2004. DVD.

*The Walking Dead*. Episode no. 1, first broadcast October 31, 2010 by AMC. Directed by Frank Darbont and written by Frank Darabont, 2011. *The Walking Dead*: The Complete First Season DVD.

*The West Wing*. Episode no. 0, season 3, first broadcast October 3, 2001 by NBC. Directed by Christopher Misiano and written by Aaron Sorkin, 2004. *The West Wing*: The Complete Third Season DVD.

*The X-Files*. Created by Chris Carter. 1993–2002. Los Angeles, CA: Fox Broadcast Television Network.

*Top Gun*. Directed by Tony Scott. 1986. Hollywood, CA: Paramount Pictures, 2008. DVD.

*Transformers: Dark of the Moon*. Directed by Michael Bay. 2011. Hollywood, CA: Paramount Pictures, 2011. Blu Ray.

*Two Thousand Maniacs*. Directed by Herschell Gordon Lewis. 1964. Box Office Spectaculars.

*Underworld*. Directed by Len Wiseman. 2003. Culver City, CA: Screen Gems, 2004. Widescreen Special Edition DVD.

*United 93*. Directed by Paul Greengrass. 2006. Universal City, CA: Universal Studios.

*V*. Created by Kenneth Johnson. 2009–11. New York: ABC.

*Van Helsing*. Directed by Stephen Sommers. 2004. Universal City, CA: Universal Studios, 2004. Widescreen Edition DVD.

*War of the Worlds*. Directed by Steven Spielberg. 2005. Hollywood, CA: Paramount Pictures.

*Winchester '73*. Directed by Anthony Mann. 1950. Universal City, CA: Universal Studios.

*White Zombie*. Directed by Victor Halperin. 1932. Beverly Hills, CA: United Artists, 1999. DVD.

*Wolfenstein 3D*. 1992. Richardson, Texas: id Software, 1994. Mac OS.

*World Trade Center*. Directed by Oliver Stone. 2006. Hollywood, CA: Paramount Pictures.

*World War Z*. Directed by Marc Forster. 2013. Hollywood, CA: Paramount Pictures.

*Zero Dark Thirty*. Directed by Kathryn Bigelow. 2012. Culver City, CA: Columbia Pictures.

# Index

Note: numbers in brackets preceded by *n* are footnote numbers.

For Product Safety Concerns and Information please contact our EU representative GPSR@taylorandfrancis.com
Taylor & Francis Verlag GmbH, Kaufingerstraße 24, 80331 München, Germany

www.ingramcontent.com/pod-product-compliance
Lightning Source LLC
Chambersburg PA
CBHW071357100726
47908CB00004B/1027
*9781138249103*